FALLING ANGELS

A MAXX KING THRILLER
BOOK 3

JOHN H. THOMAS

ISBN Paperback - 979-8-9906720-7-9

ISBN Hardcover - 979-8-9906720-8-6

Cover Design by Nick Castle @ Nick Castle Design

Editing and formatting by Jason Letts @ Imbue Editing

DEDICATION

For five wonderful grandchildren.
Dreamers and doers,
Creative explorers,
And my inspiration for the future.

PREFACE

Before diving into this trilogy's third and final book, I want to express my deep gratitude to the readers who have joined me on this adventure. *The Maxx King Thrillers* have been both challenging and richly rewarding. If you enjoyed *Thunderbird Rising* and *Masters of War*, I hope you find this chapter equally captivating and as rewarding as the journey that brought us here.

Although this book concludes the trilogy, Maxx may appear in additional standalone storylines. Please visit my website at www.realjohnthomas.com if you are interested in Maxx or other characters and would like to learn more. I always enjoy hearing from readers!

EPIGRAPH

Are we fallen angels who didn't want to believe that nothing is nothing and so were born to lose our loved ones and dear friends one by one and finally our own life, to see it proved?

—Jack Kerouac

There are no angels in war.

—Elon Musk

PROLOGUE

JUNE 1979

Maxx felt a sharp blow to the back of the head.

Grabbing his head with a tight grip, Maxx swiveled around, his eyes scanning for the cause of the impact. Beneath his fingers, he felt the warm trickle of blood seeping through his hair, not a gusher but enough to confirm his suspicion—he'd been hit with a rock. *Rocks don't just fall from the sky*, he thought with a wave of confusion. Someone had deliberately thrown it at him, but no one was visible.

The sun lowered toward the horizon, casting short, sharp shadows along the dusty road back to Maxx's farm. The air was warm with the smell of summer, and the leaves on the trees were still green but hinting at the coming change. Maxx was awkward at thirteen. His height and size made him stand out. His shoulders were hunched, his steps heavy, as if he carried an unseen burden. His oversized backpack added to his clumsy appearance.

He was almost home. The familiar sight of the farm's leaning barn and the farmhouse silhouette against the dropping sun were usually a source of comfort. Today, the walk was fraught with the echoes of the school day, the laughter and taunts that had followed him out of the school gates still ringing in his ears. It hadn't helped when he'd had to stay after classes to clean up a mess someone else had made. He hadn't complained. He simply smiled and got it done.

"Hey, look, it's *Extra Large*!" The voice came from behind, sharp and mocking him with a nickname he'd come to hate. Maxx turned to see Jake, a skinny boy from the next grade, flanked by a couple of his friends. They'd been hiding in the tall ryegrass. They were a common sight. Wherever Jake went, jeering followed.

Maxx's heart sank, his cheeks warming with a flush of embarrassment. He tried to ignore them, quickening his pace. The gravel crunched louder under his oversized, hand-me-down boots, betraying his escape attempt.

Jake jogged beside him, his laughter like the caw of obnoxious crows. "What's the rush, big guy? Afraid you'll have to talk to a girl?" His friends snickered, their laughter mingling with the wind in the trees.

Maxx's fists clenched inside his pockets, his emotions a tangled mess of hurt and anger. He wanted to disappear, to blend into the landscape like the shadows lengthening around him.

"Leave me alone," he muttered, his voice not as strong as he wished.

"Oh, come on, don't be such a pussy!" another boy chimed in, condescending. "Can't the big boy handle a little friendly teasing?"

Maxx felt the sting of tears at the corner of his eyes, not from sadness but from frustration, from the unfairness of it all. He was big, yes, but he was also sensitive, a loner by nature, preferring the company of his thoughts and the farm animals to the uncertainty of interacting with others.

He turned his head away, focusing on the path ahead, the

farm coming into view, promising refuge. But the calls kept coming, like stones thrown at his back.

"Look at him. He's gonna cry!" Jake exclaimed, his voice rising with the thrill of torment. "What's wrong, Maxx? You need your mom to protect you?"

Maxx's pace quickened, his heavy boots kicking up dust, his breath coming in short, angry huffs. He could feel the heat of embarrassment turning into something else, a fire of defiance slowly kindling. But his natural inclination was to retreat, avoid confrontation, his size making him feel even more out of place and vulnerable.

"Bet he doesn't even know how to fight," one of the boys taunted, their laughter now a chorus echoing through the trees. "My dad said your old man is a coward, too. Like the Kenny Rogers song on the radio."

Maxx stopped suddenly, his shadow long and daunting in the fading light. He turned to face them, his eyes narrowing, the farm behind him like a fortress he was defending. "I know how to fight," he said, his voice low, surprising even himself.

The threat was hollow. He knew how to wrestle well enough, but that was not fighting, and the thought of violence made his stomach churn. He'd seen what happened when his father got angry, which frightened him.

Jake took a step back, perhaps sensing the sincerity in Maxx's tone or maybe seeing his sheer size. "Whatever, man. We were joking," he said, his voice losing some of its edge, but the smirk remained.

The group moved on, their laughter fading into the distance, leaving behind a silence filled with the sounds of the farm—a distant cow's moo, the rustle of corn stalks. Maxx watched them go, his heart pounding not with fear but with a new, confusing mix of anger and resolve. He turned toward home, the farm now not only a place to escape to but one where he could be himself, where his size was not a subject of ridicule but a part of who he was.

As he walked, the gravel under his feet felt less like an adversary and more like a path leading him back to where he belonged. Maxx, with each step, felt the weight of his loneliness but also the strength of his solitude, knowing that here at least he was understood, even if only by his mom and grandma rather than his peers.

Maxx grew up under the infinite, often moody skies of Eastern Washington, where the farm was an integral part of his identity. The air was always thick with the rich, earthy scent of soil, the sweet tang of ripe fruit, and the sharp, sometimes overwhelming odor of manure.

The experience of farm life was both physically demanding and character-building. Maxx would wake before dawn, the chill air biting at his cheeks as he walked barefoot across the dew-damp grass to the barn, the blades cool and slightly slick under his feet. Feeding the chickens and milking the cows always made him smile, no matter how tired. The sound and feel of it all grounded him in the farm's rhythm.

When he was home from his duty stations, his father's presence was as much a part of the farm's landscape as the tools he used. His handshake was firm, a silent testament to the strength he expected from his son, the texture of his work-worn hands a map of his life's labor.

"Life's hard, Maxx. Toughen up, boy," he'd say, the coarseness of his voice matching the ruggedness of the tools they wielded, the metal cold and hard against their skin as they worked.

His mother was the gentle touch in this rugged world. In the garden, her hands would guide him, showing him how to feel for the correct ripeness of tomatoes, the velvety leaves of basil, and the prickly leaves of cucumbers.

"Don't let him make you think strength is only physical,"

she'd murmur, referring to his father. "Real toughness lies in here." She placed her small, weathered hand over his heart.

His grandmother was the heart of the farm. She would take his hand, hers small but strong, as they walked through the orchard or canned jams and vegetables in her kitchen. Despite her small size, the sensation of her carrying him as a child was a memory of warmth and safety.

The afternoon sun was beginning its descent, casting long, golden rays across the farm, painting the world in hues of amber and shadow. As he approached his grandmother's cabin, a small outbuilding his dad had built for her, his heart sank. The door was open wide, which was never the case. With his mother in town and his father on the road for a few days, he felt his stomach clench in fear.

He pushed the door open slowly, the creak of the hinges slicing through the silence. The kitchen, usually a refuge of joy with its yellow wallpaper and the comforting aroma of baking, was now a scene of chaos. The air smelled of spilled coffee mingling with something more sinister. The wood floor, smooth and welcoming from years of use, felt rough and foreign under his boots as he stepped inside.

In the heart of the home, his grandmother trembled in the corner. Two men loomed over her, menacing. One had a scar on his cheek, jagged and angry, his eyes wild, his breath reeking of alcohol. The other, taller and thinner, looked at Maxx with an unfocused, predatory gaze, his movements sluggish yet threatening.

"Grandma!" Maxx's voice wavered unsteadily, his heart pounding against his chest like a drum. His grandmother's wide eyes met his, filled with fear but also a silent plea for help.

"Run home and lock the door, Maxx. They want money," she said in a soft voice.

"You heard your grandma, kid. Run along before we hurt you too," the tall man slurred.

Maxx's mind raced as his emotions spun into a whirlwind of fear, anger, and the urgent need to protect his grandma. He reached for the buck knife his father had given him, hidden in his back pocket, its wood handle familiar in his hand. The knife was a tool for chores, and it startled him to see it in his hand.

The scarred man sneered, "Look who's here to play hero!" His voice was a menacing drawl.

"Leave her alone!" Maxx cried, his voice steadier now, the knife feeling like a dangerous weapon, not a tool of the farm but of survival.

The taller man lunged, his movements a blur. Maxx's instincts, honed by wrestling and his father's hard lessons in the barn, kicked in. He dodged, the coarse fabric of the intruder's shirt brushing against him, the sensation of it rough and unsettling. His hand, slick with sweat, gripped the knife handle tightly.

A struggle ensued, bodies colliding with the force of desperation. Maxx felt the jarring impact of hitting the floor, the thick planks unforgiving against his back. The scarred man was on him, his breath hot and reeking, the smell of alcohol overpowering. Recalling a move from wrestling practice, Maxx managed to use his legs, kicking out and feeling the jarring impact as his feet connected and sent the man staggering into the counter.

"You little shit!" the man growled, but Maxx was already moving, rolling to his feet, his heart in his throat, every sense heightened. He could feel the heft of the intruder's leather jacket under his fingers as he grappled for control, the slickness of sweat from their struggles, and the slippery, hard floor beneath them.

With a surge of adrenaline, Maxx managed to push the scarred man back, the knife now held in front of him, moving shakily but with intent. "Get out!" he bellowed, fueled by fear, not for himself but for his grandmother. "Leave or I'll kill you!"

Seeing the shift, the other man moved to grab his companion, but in the chaos, Maxx's foot caught him, sending him sprawling. The sound of his head hitting the wall was a hollow thud in the kitchen.

His grandmother, finding her voice, shouted, "Maxx, be careful! Get my shotgun!"

Now on the defensive, the intruders exchanged a look, realizing the tables had turned. With a curse, the scarred man pulled his companion up, and they stumbled out, the door slamming as they ran in a fit of panic.

Maxx sagged against the counter, the knife now a heavy reminder of what had transpired. His hands shook, not from the adrenaline, but from the terror of what could have happened. With its scattered dishes and the lingering scent of fear, the kitchen felt alien and profoundly important— place where his bravery had been tested and proven.

"Grandma, are you okay?" he asked as he moved to her, his arms wrapping around her small, trembling form. The warmth of her embrace was a stark contrast to the cold terror he'd first felt. Her heartbeat was a reminder of what he'd fought for.

She nodded, tears in her eyes. "Thanks to you, my giant angel."

The farm outside continued its silent vigil as the sun set, casting long shadows through the windows. The air slowly returned to the familiar scents of home. But inside Maxx, a struggle was brewing—a new understanding of his strength, not in muscle or weaponry, but in heart and determination.

But the air also felt heavy with fragments of regret. Should he have been more decisive, more ruthless? This question haunted him, a thorn in his heart. His nature, shaped by love and resistance to his father's threatening violence, had resulted in hesitancy that felt like a betrayal.

Over the next few days, he replayed the scene. Could he have disarmed them faster, been more aggressive? The weight of his choices loomed like a storm. "What if I'd failed?" he repeated, digging for truth or absolution, the farm's silence echoing his doubts.

In these moments of darkness, Maxx sought solace in the farm's embrace, yet found only the hard lessons of what could have been, the silent judgment of the land he loved, and the heavy burden of his reflections. The old barn became his shelter from the world. A place that had witnessed the passage of seasons, its wooden beams sagging with age, the air heavy with the scent of hay and the musk of livestock.

One afternoon, a few days after the intrusion, Maxx sat alone in the old barn. Light streamed through gaps in the roof, casting long shadows across the dirt floor, where the tools of his daily life were scattered—the rough handles of shovels and the cool, smooth metal of baling wire. The barn was a place of labor and contemplation, where the quiet was only broken by the occasional rustle of cats chasing a mouse or the distant cluck of chickens.

His father, a silhouette against the afternoon sun, stood in the open door. Upon his return home, his figure appeared as solid as the barn itself. The man's hands, hard and calloused from years of military service and farm work, held out a black pistol to Maxx. The gun shone with a dull luster, its metal cold to the touch, a foreign object among the familiar farm tools. The grip was textured, demanding a firm hold, and its balanced weight was a stark contrast to the tool handles Maxx was accustomed to.

"Here," his father said, his voice a low rumble, like the distant thunder over the fields. "This is yours now."

Maxx gripped the pistol, sensing the heavy burden of the formidable .45 caliber firearm as it nestled into his palm. Renowned for its ability to neutralize threats swiftly because of its substantial size, the gun was more than an instrument of defense; it was a symbol, a rite of passage.

"I've carried this old Springfield for many years. It's saved my life more than once. I think it's yours now. You've earned it. The world is changing, and your mom and grandma will need a man around here when I'm gone."

"Is this what you wanted for me, Dad?" Maxx asked, his voice barely above a whisper, the question hanging between them, mingling with the dust dancing in the sunbeams. His emotions were a tumult of pride, confusion, and a longing for his father's approval. The gun felt like a bridge between them, but also a barrier. It represented his father's world in the Marines, one of discipline and duty, so different from the simplicity and comforting familiarity of farm life and family.

His father's eyes met his, weathered by sun and too much whiskey. "It's not about what I want, Maxx. It's about what you need. To protect those you love. To be a man. Gentle and kind, but dangerous and violent when you need to be."

Maxx looked down at the gun, running his thumb over the checkered grip, feeling the texture under his skin, the harshness a metaphor for the path he was being set upon. "To protect," he echoed, thinking of his grandmother, the incident that had haunted him with guilt and resolve. The gun was not merely metal and mechanics; it was a lesson, a burden, a promise.

"I know it's not easy," his father continued, stepping closer, filling the space between them with the thick tang of old leather and gun oil. "Life out there isn't like our life here." He gestured vaguely toward the barn door, where beyond was the world, vast and unpredictable. "I wish it weren't so, but this won't be the last time you'll face bad men. And they won't always run so easily."

Maxx nodded. The gun's weight now added to the weight of his father's expectations, of the legacy he was being handed.

"I'll use it right," Maxx promised, his voice steadier now, his resolve hardening like the gunmetal in his hand. He felt the gun's cold surface against his skin, a reminder of the hard lessons learned from his father, the love of his family, and the unyielding life on the farm.

His father clapped him on the shoulder, the touch firm but warm, a rare gesture of affection. "I know you will. You've got a good heart, Maxx. Remember, strength isn't just in this." He tapped the gun. "But here." He pointed to his own heart, echoing what Mom had said.

As his father walked away, leaving Maxx alone with the gun and his thoughts, the barn seemed to settle back into its usual calm. Still, within Maxx, a storm of emotions raged—the pride of acceptance, the fear of responsibility, and the fierce love for the land and family that had shaped him. He looked at the gun again, feeling its texture and weight, and now understood that it was not only a weapon but a part of his identity—a new chapter in the story of his life.

His grandmother's reassurance, her hand in his, was like the first signs of deep understanding. The warmth of her skin was a testament to resilience, and her grip was a reminder of the strength that had shaped him. "You're a good boy, Maxx. Make yourself a home where your heart can find peace," she had said.

One evening, over a bowl of homemade ice cream, he said quietly to no one in particular, "Maybe being a giant isn't about size." A flash of determination crossed his face. "It's about having a heart big enough to do whatever it takes to protect Grandma, Mom, and everyone I love."

After another spoonful, Maxx gazed into the distance. In a hushed tone, as if speaking to a future unseen, he murmured, "I'm going to grow up to be the biggest, meanest giant ever."

DAY ONE

1

I WANT YOU BACK (OR ONE MORE CHANCE)

MARCH 2002

The night air in the Hindu Kush was thin and cold, slicing through Maxx King's consciousness as he awoke wedged in a crevice on the edge of a cliff.

His head throbbed with a dull, insistent ache, and his body felt like it had been used as a battering ram. He was on the rocky ground, his tactical gear torn, the scent of his blood mingling with the dust of the Afghan earth. Playing hide-and-seek behind wispy clouds, the moon offered fleeting glimpses of light, casting eerie shadows over the rugged landscape below.

Above, a meteor shower painted the sky with streaks of fire, each meteor a silent omen, starkly contrasting with the flashing lights of gunfire and the explosive bursts that briefly lit up the distant hills. The heavenly lights seemed to mimic the war below. The sounds of distant skirmishes, the staccato of automatic weapons, and the deep, earth-shaking thumps of rocket-propelled grenades and mortar fire melded into a symphony of destruction.

Maxx tried to piece together the blur of memories among this strange dance of light and sound. His last clear image was of Anderson. His face twisted in betrayal or desperation, the muzzle flash of his gun. Then, stumbling backward, the fall—an endless drop into darkness. His condition was dire. His left arm hung at an awkward angle, likely broken, and his ribs screamed in protest with each shallow breath. The bitter cold was seeping into his bones, the chill of shock setting in.

His chest ached intensely where Anderson's bullet had struck. Despite the protection of the ballistic plates in his body armor, the force of the bullet had slammed into him with the crushing power of a sledgehammer, leaving a deep, throbbing pain that radiated through his ribcage with every breath.

The sound of hurried footsteps scrambling over the broken shale and the murmur of voices broke through his haze. English, so at least he knew it wasn't the Taliban—or worse—coming for him. Sargent Zeller's Green Beret team, shadows in the night, had located him. The medic knelt beside him, his hands moving with a calm efficiency that belied the situation's urgency.

"King, you with us?" Zeller's voice was a lifeline in the dark.

"Yeah," Maxx groaned, his voice rough. Even uttering the one word was a challenge.

The medic worked quickly under the dim light of a tactical flashlight, stabilizing Maxx's arm and applying bandages to his wounds. "You've been out for about an hour. It's one in the morning. We've been looking all over this mountainside for you. I don't know how you survived that fall."

"Oh, you know, I figured gravity was optional today," Maxx slurred through his swollen lips. "Looks like I was right."

As the medic continued, Zeller briefed Maxx, his voice low but clear even over the sound of the distant battle. "The Taliban pulled back into the tunnel. They disappeared like smoke shortly after midnight."

"Did you see Anderson and Grey?" Maxx asked gruffly when his head stopped spinning for a moment.

"We're not sure, but a couple of the guys saw a man and woman wearing US uniforms go into the tunnel shortly after the Taliban skedaddled. There aren't any other Americans in this sector that I know of."

Maxx's mind raced. Anderson, one of their own, had turned. But why? Grey had never trusted him, and he'd always gotten a bad gut feeling about the guy, but he'd never sensed that he was dangerous enough to shoot anyone on his team.

Zeller gave him a rundown on Operation Anaconda. "They're in the thick of it in Shah-i-Kot. The enemy's dug in deep. Every ridge and every cave seems to have them, like here. They took heavy fire coming in—RPGs, machine-gun nests from the high ground. Air support's been spotty, but it's a beautiful sight when it hits.

"We've pushed them back some, but they know this terrain like the back of their hands, popping out from nowhere. We're holding the line, but it's tough going. We need more birds in the sky or we'll be in for a long night, although we're giving as good as we're getting."

Despite the pain, Maxx's attention sharpened. The tunnels were a labyrinth, a known Taliban stronghold and the likely location of Smith's device. It didn't matter, though. If Anderson and Miss Grey were in there, they would have to be pursued, regardless of the risk.

"We can't wait for support if they're that tied up," Maxx said, his voice gaining strength. "They're in that cave, and if Anderson's gone rogue, Smith could be behind this."

Zeller nodded, his face grim in the intermittent moonlight. "Agreed. We go after them now."

Memories flashed before Maxx's eyes—Anderson's betrayal, the gunshot, the fall. Was Anderson working for Doctor Smith? The thought gnawed at him. Smith, the rogue scientist whose trail had led them here, could have turned Anderson with promises of power, money, or perhaps harm.

With each breath sharper than the last, Maxx pushed himself up, pain shooting through his body but overridden by determination. "Let's move. We can't let them get away."

Zeller and the medic helped Maxx to his feet, their collective determination a silent force in the night. As they prepared to climb the mountain and enter the dark, unknown depths of the tunnels, Maxx felt the stress of his mission on his shoulders. Every step was a gamble, every shadow a potential enemy, but the truth about Anderson and Smith was ahead in the heart of the Afghan mountains under the watch of a meteor-streaked sky.

***

The late-afternoon sun cast long shadows across the Capitol, seeping through the windows of Senator Jane Traficant's office. She sat behind her polished mahogany desk, immersed in the dim light and the weight of her secrets.

Jane tapped her manicured fingernails on the desk as she considered her next move. Wearing a dark, high-neck sweater underneath a gray, tailored blazer, she mirrored her public image of a long-term conservative politician. Her hair, a striking silver color styled in soft waves, framed her head, giving her a distinguished and well-groomed look. Confident on the outside, her roiling emotions remained buried beneath her public facade. She had decades of experience hiding her inner demons.

Her door opened abruptly, and Colonel Hanssen walked in, uninvited, his entrance marked by the sharp click of his black, spit-shined dress shoes against the marble floor. They hadn't spoken since a covert meeting in the park a few hours ago, where they discussed their clandestine operations under the guise of a casual stroll.

Senator Traficant's eyes narrowed, surprise mingling with

irritation. "Hanssen, what are you doing here? This isn't the place."

"I understand, Senator," Hanssen replied, his voice low and urgent, "but time is running out. I've got people looking everywhere for Mr. Green. So far, no sign, but I'll turn over every rock as discreetly as possible. He can't have gotten far without leaving a video or electronic trail."

"Damn the discretion. Colonel, you do not seem to understand how precarious our position is," she said harshly. "We now have less than twenty-two hours."

Hanssen took a step back and cocked his head to one side. "Why didn't you tell me the time constraints when we met earlier?" he asked with barely masked annoyance.

Traficant glared back at him. "Because I just found out myself. Two hours ago, Thunderbird made it clear we had only twenty-four hours to deliver the encryption key or the location of the missing virus to them. If we don't deliver, we'll suffer the consequences. You, me, everyone."

"What a mess," he murmured. "I've made no progress locating the virus in Afghanistan, either. It's missing. With Operation Anaconda underway, it's like finding a needle in a haystack that's on fire."

Traficant leaned back, her fingers drumming on the desk. "And the code? Have you had any luck undoing Mr. Green's encryption since we can't find him?"

Hanssen shook his head. "The NSA's cybersecurity team says it'll take weeks to decode."

The air felt heavy with the gravity of their predicament. They had not one but two critical issues to resolve: determining the location of a potentially catastrophic virus that had been lost somewhere in Afghanistan and the disappearance of Mr. Green, whose insider knowledge could bring everything crashing down around them.

"Who can we trust?" Traficant murmured, more to herself than to Hanssen.

"Our options are thin," Hanssen replied, scanning the room as if expecting eavesdroppers. "We might need someone outside our usual channels. Someone with no political ties or moral uncertainties."

Traficant's eyes flickered with a dawning realization. "The assassin from Japan that the Defense Department uses for arm's-length work. Last I heard, he was in Seattle working on a family business, so he might be available at the right price. What is his name?"

"You must mean Kage. He's extremely risky," Hanssen acknowledged, "but with the deadline looming, we need someone who can act fast and decisively. He's definitely capable."

The decision was fraught with danger, but desperation called for unconventional measures. Kage, known for his efficiency and discretion, had been a whispered name in the inner circles of intelligence agencies for years. As a freelance contractor, he took on assignments from the highest bidder, whether from within Japan or abroad. He had navigated through life with a moral compass that pointed only toward himself and to some extent his family's legacy. The Japanese criminal world and the US government were his frequent customers.

His skills made him a legend in the underworld. He was known as both a protector and an enforcer of secrets. His name was occasionally mentioned in Washington as a solution of last resort. He always delivered.

"Get his number," Traficant ordered her, voice firm despite the storm of doubt and fear swirling inside her. "He's our best shot at getting the answers we need before Thunderbird decides we're out of time."

Hanssen nodded, pulling out his secure phone. "I'll do it now. But, Jane, if this goes south—"

"I know," she cut him off, her face set in a mask of determination. "We're playing with fire, but what choice do we have?"

As Hanssen dialed a number he rarely used, the beeping of his phone seemed to echo the ticking of an unseen clock, each second bringing them closer to either salvation or doom. They were about to involve a wildcard, a move that could save their plan or unravel everything.

***

Torashi glided quietly down the empty sidewalk, scanning for an inconspicuous place to grab a bite while waiting for the likely phone call.

On the edge of the International District, where the city's action barely touched, was a small, unassuming sushi restaurant named Kage no Sake. Its exterior was modest with wooden slats and a noren curtain at the entrance bearing the restaurant's name in elegant kanji, suggesting a place to find peace amidst the American city's disorder.

He'd eaten there before, and they carried a wide variety of sake. He'd always interpreted the restaurant's name to be a favorable omen, so he'd tried to relocate it. The atmosphere was warm with low lighting casting a soft glow over the dark wood and tatami mats. The air was rich with the aroma of fresh seafood, rice vinegar, and the delicate aroma of green tea. The lunch crowd hadn't arrived, so there was plenty of open seating.

Torashi sat at the near-empty counter, choosing a spot that allowed him to keep his back to the wall while facing the entrance. He was a figure whose presence seemed to blend into and command the space around him. He was tall for a Japanese man, standing at 5'11", with a lean yet muscular physique, the result of years dedicated to the art of intense physical training. His jet-black hair was slicked back, offering a no-nonsense look practical for his unique line of work. His attire was a dark, tailored suit that concealed various tools of his trade while maintaining an understated elegance.

Torashi's face was a map of his life's trials, with a prominent scar that ran from his cheek to his jaw—a memento from a betrayal at seventeen that had nearly ended his life. His dark and intense eyes seemed to absorb the light, giving little away but taking in everything. When it appeared, his smile was shark-like—a facade that held charm and threat, with visible gaps between his teeth, adding to his predatory allure.

He came from a lineage of spies, the Kage family, known for their mastery over silence and shadow. Raised in a secluded part of Tokyo, his childhood was more about discipline than play. His father taught him the virtues of silence and patience, while his mother taught him the fine arts of manipulation, turning human psychology into a weapon. Their home was a fortress of secrets, with hidden rooms and training areas where young Torashi learned to navigate the world of espionage.

Now in his thirties, Torashi was a freelance operative, his reputation a whisper among those who knew where to listen. He was infamous for his close-combat skills, particularly with a knife, a preference born from the necessity of silent kills. His smirk, often the last sight for those who crossed his path, was as much a psychological weapon as his physical ones.

As he savored a piece of salmon nigiri, his hand, thick with calluses and scars from handling sharp weapons, moved with a grace that belied its strength. Before him, the sushi chef, an artist with his blade, worked with a focus that mirrored Torashi's intensity. He grinned openly while watching the razor-sharp blade flash.

Kenji, a busboy barely out of his teens, disrupted the peace. His uniform was slightly askew, indicating his newness to the job. He approached Torashi's plate prematurely, a mistake that could have had dire consequences in another setting.

"Excuse me, I'm not done." Torashi's voice was low, the calm before the storm. His scar seemed to throb with repressed anger.

"I... I'm sorry, sir. I thought you were finished," Kenji stammered, his face paling under Torashi's penetrating gaze.

The quick spike of tension was palpable, like the charged air before a thunderstorm. In a blur, Torashi reached beneath his jacket, resting his hand on the knife handle. Instinctively assessing the unlikely threat from the disheveled busboy, he chose not to let this minor incident escalate. He left the knife in its sheath and grinned. His expression was wildly incongruent with the tension in his body. Recognizing Torashi from previous visits, the manager intervened flamboyantly.

"Ah, Kage-san! What an honor to see you here again," he greeted, his tone smooth, aware of the delicate balance of power in the room. He gently corrected Kenji, sending him off with a pat on the shoulder, then turned back to Torashi, offering a warm towel as a gesture of peace.

"Forgive the interruption, Kage-san. Please, enjoy your meal at your leisure," the manager said, his eyes conveying respect for the man whose presence was both a privilege and a potential threat.

Torashi nodded, his smirk softening into something that could almost be mistaken for gratitude. As he returned to his meal, the sushi before him offered a moment of respite in a life woven with shadows, where every action, even in an obscure sushi restaurant, could be a prelude to death.

2

EPIPHANY

In the brackish chill of early morning on March 2nd, the Shah-i-Kot Valley was shrouded in darkness, pierced only by the occasional burst of gunfire and the sharp, echoing blasts of conflict. Lieutenant John Weih, his face smeared with dirt and sweat, moved through the rocky ridges, his boots crunching over the uneven ground. His unit was part of Operation Anaconda, but the night had taken an unexpected turn.

The lieutenant was in a uniform that had barely been dirtied. He looked like he'd stepped out of a parade except for a few sweat stains. Buzz cut, light stubble on the chin, Texas accent, and not a day over twenty-one. He'd seen the most intense action of his short military career only a few hours ago. He was still trying to calm down.

At 0130, under the cover of a shadowed moon, Lieutenant Weih and his squad navigated the treacherous terrain of the Shah-i-Kot Valley, their night vision goggles casting everything in an eerie green glow. They were moving quietly, almost invisibly, when the unexpected sound of metal against metal and hushed, frantic voices caught their attention.

Beyond a curve in the rutted road, they stumbled upon an

operation that wasn't in their intel. A Taliban group, their silhouettes sharp against the smoldering remnants of what once was an unmarked supply convoy, was moving. The trucks, now nothing more than twisted metal and scorched frames, were silent, victims of an earlier ambush. The air was still thick with smoke, and the smell of burnt rubber and diesel was overwhelming.

The Taliban fighters, clad in a mix of traditional garb and modern military gear, moved with frantic urgency. They were unloading canisters from the destroyed convoy's wreckage, each clanging as it was tossed or dragged onto the ground. These weren't the typical munitions; they were cylindrical, slightly larger than a man could easily carry alone, and bore no visible markings of standard military supplies.

The insurgents, their faces masked by scarves to shield them from the dust and to obscure their identities, worked in pairs. One would unhook the canisters while another would drag or roll them toward the dark maws of the caves that pockmarked the mountainside. These caves, natural fortresses, were ideally suited for hiding supplies or setting up ambush points.

Weih, observing from behind a boulder, noted the methodical yet hurried pace. The Taliban seemed to understand the value of what they were salvaging, moving with an intensity that suggested these weren't ordinary goods. The clatter of metal, the occasional whispered command in Pashto, and the scuffling of boots against stone painted a picture of a well-orchestrated theft under the cloak of night.

He signaled his unit to fan out, securing positions that would give them a tactical advantage. His mind raced. The mission had escalated from a reconnaissance operation to an engagement with an unknown element. The canisters could be anything from munitions to something more hazardous. The decision to engage was made in seconds, driven by the need to reclaim what was a possible strategic asset.

As Weih prepared to order the attack, he couldn't shake off the unease. The urgency of the Taliban, the mystery of the convoy's contents, and the implications of what might happen if these canisters ended up in the wrong hands—it all hung in the balance of the next few moments in this hidden valley under the Afghan stars.

Lieutenant Weih, originally from Texas, had joined the Army in the wake of September 11, driven by a mix of patriotism and a desire to take action. Now, as the new officer in charge of a unit engaged in a chaotic, hostile environment, the responsibility weighed heavily upon him. Their small convoy, attacked several hours ago, had miraculously suffered no deaths, but two of his men were wounded. Ammunition was green, their gear fully operational, but the encounter had left them on edge.

Weih's heart pounded against his chest as he signaled his men to take positions. The night was silent, save for the distant howl of a jackal. His hand gestures were precise but shaky. His squad, a mix of veterans and recruits, moved with disciplined haste, understanding the gravity of their situation. The distant thunder of explosions added a sense of urgency to their movement.

Suddenly, the sharp crack of automatic weapons erupted. Bullets ricocheted off the rocks, sending shards of stone flying. The air filled with the acrid smell of cordite, and the night was alive with the sounds of war. Not the distant kind of combat, the kind that gave a person the feeling that every breath could be the last.

"Take cover!" Weih bellowed, diving behind a boulder.

Sergeant Kerro, a seasoned non-commissioned officer with a thick New Jersey accent, was beside him, his M4 ready. "They're all over the hill, LT!" he shouted over the din, his face grim under the green glow of his night vision goggles.

"We're outnumbered," Weih grunted, scanning the landscape for movement. "But we're not outgunned. Keep your asses down and return fire on my command!"

The Taliban fighters, scattered among the rocks and crags, had anticipated this route, expecting reinforcements for the convoy they'd recently ambushed. Their resistance was relentless. The valley echoed with the staccato of small arms fire and an occasional grenade blast. Every shot from the enemy seemed to seek out the American soldiers, the bullets buzzing like a swarm of invisible, angry bees.

"We need to push forward to the high ground," Weih instructed, his voice level despite the adrenaline coursing through him. "Kerro, take a few of the veterans and flank left. I'll cover from here with the rest of the squad."

Kerro nodded, his expression one of grim determination. "Got it, LT. We'll give 'em hell." He signaled to several men, and they moved out behind him, shadows against the night, using every bit of cover the terrain offered as they leapfrogged to the enemy's flank.

As the firefight intensified, Weih's mind was on the canisters they'd glimpsed earlier. The implications were ominous, but survival was the immediate concern. His radio crackled with static. "Command, we need air support ASAP. We're bogged down and taking heavy fire!"

The calm reply was a welcome sound amidst the chaos. "A-10s inbound. ETA five minutes."

Five minutes felt like an eternity under fire, but it was the lifeline they needed. Weih kept his team engaged, conserving ammo where possible and precisely picking off targets.

The low growl of the A-10 Thunderbolts cut through the night. The Warthogs approached, their engines roaring like beasts of the sky. The subsequent strafing runs were a symphony of destruction, the 30mm Avenger cannons spitting fire and lead, scattering the Taliban like leaves before a hurricane.

The engagement ended almost as quickly as it had begun. The section of the valley, once a cacophony of battle, now settled into an eerie calm, punctuated by the groans of the wounded and the metallic smell of blood mingling with dust.

Weih stood, surveying the aftermath. "Status report!" he called out, his voice echoing off the rocks.

Kerro, emerging from the shadows, his uniform dusted with earth, reported, "We took out a good number of 'em, LT. No casualties on our side, but we've got a couple more wounded."

Weih nodded, checking for canisters littered among the debris. "Secure the perimeter, Kerro. I need to know what those canisters are. And get the wounded men back to the Humvees."

Once the smoke cleared, Lieutenant Weih approached the remains of the convoy, his boots crunching over the scorched earth. The twisted metal of the vehicles bore the unmistakable signs of a recent violent encounter. Scattered amidst the debris were the metal canisters, their surfaces marred with strange, ominous markings—symbols that were distinctly not of standard military issue but carried an air of something more sinister.

Weih's mind raced as he examined the symbols, which seemed almost like a foreign language or coded warnings. Chemical weapons? Here in Afghanistan? The implications were chilling. His gaze caught the subtle insignia on one of the truck fragments, now barely visible under the ash and soot—indications that this had indeed been a US convoy, likely a covert operation, possibly involving the CIA.

The presence of unusual munitions in this volatile region raised questions that were as terrifying as they were perplexing. Why would the CIA be transporting something so dangerous through such a volatile territory? Was this part of a covert operation gone wrong or something even more clandestine?

Weih felt the stress of the situation pressing down on him. These canisters, if they contained what he feared, could change the entire dynamic of his mission. With the immediate threat neutralized, Weih's unit began gathering the supplies they could. But the canisters were too numerous to transport back in their Humvees. He pondered the risk of leaving them behind, a potential boon for the Taliban, if they were indeed chemical agents.

Weih's radio crackled with static as he tried to reach command for guidance on a secure channel. "Command, this is Lieutenant Weih. We've encountered unmarked canisters with suspicious symbols. Possible chemical agents. Request immediate instructions." The response was garbled, lost to the limitations of the mountainous terrain.

Desperate for guidance, Weih pulled out his cell phone, the screen's light an eerie glow in the dark. He dialed Maxx King, his fingers trembling slightly from the battle adrenaline still coursing through him.

Even though he'd only met Maxx recently, he knew he was a person he could trust. It had been clear that Maxx and the Green Beret team were engaged in a highly secretive operation. His instincts told him there might be a connection between Maxx's operation and these odd canisters. The phone buzzed with an unnatural sound amidst the quiet that had fallen over the valley after the battle.

As he waited for Maxx to answer, Weih scanned the area, his eyes catching the reflection of starlight on the canisters. His mind was a tumult of strategy and concern. Should he secure the area, risk moving the canisters, or await further instructions from Command? Each choice weighed heavily on him, the silence of the night amplifying his indecision.

Finally, the phone connected, but before he could speak, the line was filled with static and a faint yet urgent voice. "Weih, I'm up to my neck right now. I'll call you back in five mikes!"

***

In the heart of Washington, D.C., the Eisenhower Executive Office Building stood as a testament to the grandeur of American architecture. Its ornate French Second Empire style, with its reddish sandstone facade and intricate window designs, dominated the landscape. Colonel James "Jim" Hanssen, a US Army officer, navigated through the echoing marble corridors, his polished leather shoes clicking with each purposeful step.

Colonel Hanssen's office was on the second floor, a room that seemed almost too opulent for the military attitude he embodied. The walls were lined with dark wood paneling, contrasting sharply with the lighter exterior hues. His desk, a massive piece of furniture, was littered with papers, maps, and a solitary picture frame angled toward him, showing a younger version of himself in uniform alongside his old platoon. A large window offered a view of the White House, a constant reminder of the power and politics that swirled around him.

Dressed in an impeccably tailored gray suit, Hanssen cut an authoritative and enigmatic figure. His presence was like that of a hawk, his eyes scanning with military precision and underlying suspicion. The creases on his face, etched from years under the sun and amidst the dust of conflict, spoke of a life lived on the edge of danger. His posture, straight as an arrow, was a relic of his military upbringing, but there was something in his gaze, a glint that suggested layers of thought, perhaps even deceit.

The door shut with a thud as he entered his office, mirroring the frustration brewing within him. He was furious about being drawn further into a situation spiraling out of control. The meeting with the senator had left a bitter taste in his mouth. He was now entangled in a web where one wrong move could spell disaster. He couldn't back out now; to do so would ruin his reputation and make him as dirty as the senator. Hanssen was no quitter.

He sat heavily in his leather chair, the springs creaking under his weight. His mind drifted back to Vietnam, specifically to the Lam Son 719 operation in 1971. As a young lieutenant, he had led his men into what was supposed to be a decisive strike against North Vietnamese supply lines. Instead, it had turned into a debacle, resulting in significant casualties. The operation was widely regarded as a failure.

The jungle had swallowed up his men, the enemy had outmaneuvered them at every turn, and hope had seemed lost. But Hanssen had rallied his troops, adapting strategies on the fly and using guerrilla tactics he had learned from the enemy. Against all odds, his platoon extracted valuable intelligence and disrupted supply lines enough to make a difference. Although initially a catastrophe, that operation had shaped him into the leader he was today.

With this new political quagmire, he felt that same sense of being outflanked and outgunned. But as in Lam Son 719, he knew he needed to keep his wits about him to find a way through the mess. He couldn't afford to have his name associated with another debacle. The stakes were higher, the enemies less visible, but past victories in the face of defeat strengthened his resolve.

Looking at the White House, Hanssen knew this was not merely another battle. It was a high-stakes, clandestine action that he intended to win, no matter how dirty the fight would become.

His alliance with the senator had been calculated, one fueled not by loyalty or shared ideology but by his raw hunger for power. He had joined her not out of respect but from a deep-seated need to prove himself, to erase the lingering shadow of his past failures, notably the debacle of Lam Son 719, which had haunted his career like a specter.

In his mind, aligning with the senator was his ticket to redemption and elevation. If the Thunderbird virus were to succeed, it would catapult the senator to unprecedented heights of power. And in that new world order, Hanssen envisioned himself as indispensable, no longer the overlooked colonel but a key architect of America's future military strategy.

Making certain this virus was successfully deployed was also his chance to exact revenge on those who had passed him over for promotion, to outshine those officers now established in the Pentagon's upper echelons. He was more intelligent and more cunning, and this was his opportunity to demonstrate it. With the senator's success, his days as a low-level officer would end, and he would finally wash away the stench of past failures with the intoxicating scent of power.

Hanssen was absorbed in the latest intelligence reports, looking for clues about the whereabouts of the elusive Mr. Green, when the phone on his desk rang. He glanced at the caller ID, his face softening slightly as he recognized the name; it was Lieutenant Colonel Tom Williams, his old Vietnam platoon mate and a man he trusted with his life.

"Jim, it's Tom." The familiar, gravelly voice came through the line, tinged with urgency.

"Tom, good to hear from you. What's happening in the sandbox?" Hanssen leaned back, his chair creaking under him.

"Something strange has come up," Williams stated, his tone low, secretive. "We received a call from a Lieutenant Weih out in the field about some canisters they stumbled upon. Command is in a stir because we can't get through to him for clarification. We lost contact after the initial connection, and with Anaconda in full chaos, he's in the wind. The message was...odd."

Hanssen's eyes narrowed. "Canisters? Describe them."

"That's the thing. We don't have much intel. But it crossed my desk, and I thought about that convoy you mentioned before, the one you were looking for. We don't have any official records of munitions like that on the ground. There's speculation it might be chemical stuff moving out of Iraq."

Hanssen's mind raced back to the missing convoy, supposedly carrying something highly sensitive—perhaps it was the missing virus. No official records existed, only whispers and his deductions. "Could be," he said cautiously, "but I'd have to see the markings on the containers."

Williams sighed, the sound heavy with a shared history and the weight of their current predicament. "Exactly. But here's the kicker, Jim. There's no way I can leave command, but I could justify sending out a search squad for a status check since we can't establish contact. I'd send a flyover, but that won't give you the information you need in time."

Hanssen nodded to himself, already plotting the next moves. "Tom, if those canisters are what I think they are, this could be big. I need someone out there. Do you know anyone who can do this discreetly?"

"I can arrange something, but it'll need to look routine. What exactly are we looking for?"

"The markings on those canisters. I need photos, Tom. I can make it worthwhile for you. People are strongly motivated here to find those missing canisters. I'm talking private money, probably enough to retire comfortably on."

Williams paused, considering the implications. "You think these are the canisters you're looking for?"

"More than think, Tom. I'm virtually certain. I need to know for sure, and those markings will tell me. If you can get me that picture as soon as possible, I'll ensure your involvement won't be forgotten when the dust settles."

There was a moment of silence, the line crackling with the weight of their shared past and the unsaid agreements that had kept them alive in Vietnam. "All right, Jim. I'll have a search team out there in a couple of hours under the guise of checking communications, but you owe me one hell of a favor."

Hanssen broached a rare, genuine smile. "You always did keep the score, Tom. Get me those photos and consider it done. You can buy a drink with an umbrella to thank me later."

"Stay sharp, Jim. I'll be in touch," Williams said before the line went dead.

Hanssen hung up, his fingers drumming on the desk as he stared at the White House through his window. The game was afoot, and if his hunch was correct, the odds had shifted dramatically in his favor. He'd need to play this one close to the chest, but with Williams in Afghanistan, he had an ally where it counted. Now, he needed to prepare for whatever came next, knowing the truth about the Thunderbird virus might soon come to light.

3

RUNAWAY TRAIN

Mr. Green's breath was labored as he and Dr. Xi hurried through the busy industrial outskirts of South Seattle, their footsteps echoing on the sidewalk and abandoned parking lots. Every car slowing down was a potential threat, causing them to move with unaccustomed haste. The city's skyline was a silhouette against the cloudy sky, the vast Puget Sound an inky, reflective expanse in the distance.

Mr. Green, a portly man in his fifties, wore a cream Hawaiian shirt with vibrant pink flowers and green leaves, which fluttered with each heavy step. His khaki pants and Birkenstocks were not ideal for running, but they were what he'd been wearing in the office. He hadn't considered dressing more appropriately for the weather and his planned escape. Despite the cold, his face, tanned from years under the Californian sun and frequent trips to the tanning salon, was set with determination and a light sheen of sweat.

Beside him, Dr. Xi matched his pace, though with more grace. His dark jacket over a gray turtleneck gave him an academic look, his thick, unruly hair slightly askew from the run. His bushy gray eyebrows furrowed in concentration, his glasses reflecting the dim light. His calm demeanor belied the urgency of their flight.

Several hours ago, they had covertly exited the Tacoma facility in Pioneer Square. The Tacoma building and underground complex were the heart of the Thunderbird project, where vital information about the Thunderbird virus was encrypted. This virus, meant to be a weapon against the invading race known as the Others, was something neither Green nor Xi could overlook. Their moral compasses rebelled against the genocide of another species, even if it meant Earth's survival, even if it meant their survival.

As they slowed to a brisk walk, trying to catch their breath, they reached a bus stop, the only shelter in sight. The glass enclosure provided some relief from the breeze blowing off Puget Sound. The bench was empty, and the streets were quiet except for the traffic and hum of the surrounding city. Green used an old newspaper to brush off the bench and then lowered himself unceremoniously onto the carved and graffiti-covered seat.

"Let's take a moment and rest," Green said, motioning for Xi to sit. "They probably know we've left the facility and are looking for us. But we've walked several miles, and a few minutes of rest won't make any difference."

Xi took off his glasses and wiped the steamed lenses. "We can't go to the airport, nor the ferry or train," he said after a moment to catch his breath. "They'll be watching all exits."

Mr. Green nodded, searching their surroundings for any sign of pursuit. "We need somewhere off the grid. Somewhere they won't think to look immediately."

"This is your hometown," Xi said. "What do you suggest?"

"Mt. Rainier," Green suggested, a plan forming. "There are cabins up there near the ski resort, secluded. We stay in the area, but they'll never think of looking for us up there. We can blend in with the tourists coming to ski and buy us some time."

Mr. Xi looked at Green's outfit. "I hope they have some suitable clothing in these cabins. You are dressed for the beach, not skiing."

Given the limited options, the decision was made quickly. With its forested slopes and isolated cabins, Mount Rainier offered the seclusion they desperately needed. The environment was harsh, with the mountain's imposing air and the ever-present risk of sudden weather changes, but it was their best shot.

They hitched a ride with a local trucker who asked no questions but didn't hesitate to comment on Green's clothing and seemingly recent relocation from Southern California. The landscape shifted from urban to rural, the road winding into the foothills, where pine trees began to dominate the scenery.

The cabins they chose were small and rustic, with no modern amenities like internet or phone signals—perfect for hiding. The air was crisp, and the silence was broken only by the rustling of leaves and occasional wildlife.

With barely a glance in the rearview mirror, the truck driver dropped them off at the cabins closest to the entrance of Mount Rainier National Park. It was a rustic retreat known as Three Bears Cabins, proudly proclaiming itself "the best cabins in the Pacific Northwest." Although the cabins were exactly the out-of-the-way place Green had imagined, he couldn't help but think the word "best" was doing a lot of work in their marketing.

After Green checked them in using all the cash he had in his wallet, he paused and looked at Xi skeptically. "Can I trust you, Xi? Your government, they're in this deep. As deep as my government."

Xi met his gaze, the afternoon light catching in his glasses. "I am not with them on this, Mr. Green. You will have to trust me."

The trust between them was fragile, built on the common

ground of their current crisis rather than any longstanding alliance. Green had been betrayed before, especially by those around Senator Traficant, and even Xi had been his adversary less than a week ago. Now, their only allies were Miss Grey, a sharp federal agent with Homeland Security and a heart for truth, and Maxx, the towering ex-soldier who Green had misled at the project's onset.

Inside the cabin, the atmosphere was tense. They knew their time was limited, but how limited? The walls creaked with the mountain's breath, the environment both their defense and potential prison.

"We need to figure out our next move," Green said, pacing the small space. "We can't stay here very long."

Sitting by the window, Xi observed the sun glistening on the snow outside. "We need allies. Can someone help us distribute the truth about Thunderbird's intentions?"

Outside, the forest whispered secrets, but their decisions hung heavy within the cabin. They had escaped for now, but freedom was fragile, surrounded by betrayal and the looming threat of capture. Their only hope was to expose the truth, but trust was their scarcest resource in a world where even allies could turn.

In the looming shadow of Mount Rainier, the late-afternoon light bled through the windows, casting long, ominous shadows that danced with the flicker of the fireplace. Mr. Green, who was wrapped head to toe in a blanket, his teeth chattering from the chill that seemed to penetrate his very bones, sat as close to the fire as he could.

"Why did I have to wear shorts today?" he muttered.

Xi returned with crinkling plastic, carrying some candy and sodas. The Skittles and Cokes were the only items in the vending machines outside the cabin office. It was the only food they could buy, because they were down to their last spare change and didn't want to risk using a credit card. They couldn't draw any attention.

"Thought this might keep us going," Xi said as he placed the items on the table. "The Diet Coke is for you." He smirked.

Mr. Green's eyes, cautious and cold, stared at Xi. "Thanks," he muttered, his breath visible in the cool air of the cabin. "I'm practically a popsicle at this point. And I'm not on a diet either."

The cabin was silent except for the fire's crackle and the distant howl of the wind, which seemed to echo the tension between them. "Tell me more about the Others," Green pressed, his voice a whisper of curiosity.

Xi's face was half-lit by the firelight, giving him an almost haunted appearance. "The device... We've had it for decades in China, as you know. We played with fire, thinking we were in control despite the accident at Tangshan. However, it was only recently that we realized the true stakes. It never occurred to us, to me, that two civilizations, not only one, would have similar communication devices. I was shocked and embarrassed by this revelation when we met in Hawaii. It's been a race against time since September to decode their language, to prevent them from using our technology against us."

Green's mind raced with the implications. "And your real purpose? Is it to prevent an invasion or something else?"

Xi's fingers drummed a nervous rhythm on the table. "To avoid the disasters they could trigger. If we can intercept or block their commands ..."

They continued to feed logs into the fire as they discussed their options. "Maybe we should speak to them directly," Green suggested with hope and dread. "Bypass Traficant, bypass Thunderbird."

"How?" Xi's voice was sharp. "The devices are in China and Afghanistan. We're stuck here with no car and no way to leave without being seen."

Green wrapped the blanket tighter around him, feeling the burden of their situation. "By going to China... But can I trust you, Xi? Is this your way to lead me into a trap?"

The fire popped, sending sparks flying, mirroring the tension in the room. Xi's eyes were dark, unreadable. "We're beyond trust at this point, Mr. Green. The invasion has started. Waiting here is not only our death sentence but possibly the end for humanity."

Doubt crept into Green's mind, a sensation foreign to him. What if he had misjudged everything? What if Traficant was the ally, not the adversary? Yet the clock was ticking, and every second felt like a step closer to an unseen precipice.

"We can't sit here eating candy," Green finally said, his voice a mix of resignation and resolve. "This is madness."

Xi leaned forward, his face now in shadow. "Then we must go to China. My lab, the device. It's our only chance to communicate, to make them understand, or at least to try. But we must move soon under the cover of night."

The cabin seemed to close around them, the walls whispering the dangers ahead. Outside, the last light of day vanished, leaving them in darkness punctuated only by the fire's dying glow. Green felt the uncertainty of their decision like a noose around his neck. Was this their salvation or their doom?

Mr. Green and Dr. Xi sat in silence for a time, listening to the crackling of the dying fire in the hearth. The glow from the embers cast long shadows across the room, flickering over the worry etched on their faces. Green eventually broke the heavy silence, his voice low with concern. "Can we even make it to China? With Chairman Zemin branding you a traitor, Xi, isn't it suicide to even try?"

His glasses reflecting the firelight, Dr. Xi sighed, his Chinese accent growing thick with fatigue. "I am indeed marked as a traitor in Zemin's eyes, believing I've sided with the Americans.

However, my lab in Beijing holds the key to our research. We must find a way."

Their conversation was interrupted by the incessant ringing of the pay phone outside the cabin's office. It rang with urgency, making both men tense.

After several minutes of the loud, annoying ringing, Xi peeked through the curtains. After a few minutes of the constant ringing, he watched the manager, a robust woman with curly, untamed hair wearing a flannel shirt over a stained apron, stomp out of the office to answer the phone. Her raspy voice carried through the thin walls as she yelled at the caller and then slammed the receiver down.

She glanced angrily toward Xi, peeking through a gap in the heavy curtains. "I'm not y'all's damn secretary," she yelled loudly so that anyone listening would get the message.

"I wonder if that comment was meant for me," Xi muttered as he stepped back from the window.

Green, feeling the hunger gnaw at him, having survived only on Skittles and Diet Cokes since they left, turned to Xi. "What do you think that was about?"

Before the manager reached the office door, the pay phone rang again. She swiveled on her heel, stomping back to the phone, glaring the entire time. Picking up the receiver, she immediately started yelling again. After several minutes, the yelling diminished, and her anger dissipated. She began to laugh raucously moments later. Taking a pen stuck in her messy hair, she wrote on her hand and returned to the office. She had left the phone dangling by its cord.

Green nervously stood from his chair. "What is going on out there?" he asked.

Before Xi could respond, the cabin manager treaded heavily to their door, her boots thudding on the wooden porch. "You two have a private call. Some guy says he'll pay me a hundred bucks to get you on the phone. He has already run his credit card. Go answer it so he doesn't call again." She gestured to the swaying phone receiver.

Green and Xi exchanged wary glances. "How do we know it's not a trap?" Xi whispered, suspicious.

The manager pounded on their door. "I know ya'll are in there. I saw you looking out from the curtains. Let's go."

Xi and Green, still wrapped in his blanket, awkwardly followed her to the pay phone. They were nervous but unable to shake the feeling that ignoring the manager now would only raise more problems. If the manager got irritated enough to call the police, it would be over.

"Hello," Mr. Green squeaked as he held the phone near his ear, allowing Xi to listen too.

The man on the phone identified himself as Gene Heckman, Green's security lead at the Tacoma facility.

Gene's voice was tense yet familiar, but Green was not in a trusting mood. "How do I know it's you, Gene?" he asked.

"Green, you made me remove all the Skittles from the vending machines in the break room because you hate them so much, remember? Who else would know that?"

Xi looked surprised, turning to Green. "Why didn't you say anything?"

"I didn't want to complain after your comment about my diet," Green sighed. "It wasn't very nice."

Convinced that Gene Heckman had managed to call him on a pay phone in the middle of nowhere, Green asked, "How did you track us down so quickly?"

Gene explained that he had been using a tracker he'd placed in Green's Birkenstocks. He'd been tracking him for days under orders from Senator Traficant but had now turned against her due to Miss Grey's intervention.

"I've arranged for Billie to take you to get more suitable

clothes and replace the shoes. Grab something to eat and then head over to Riffe Lake. Trust me, we need to move fast. Traficant is hot on my tail. I told her you were making a beeline for the Canadian border, so I bought you a little time."

"Who's Billie?" Green asked.

"That'd be me, genius," the office manager said as she grabbed the cabin blanket off his shoulders. "That's my property, not your new jacket."

Billie climbed into her Subaru, which was parked near the office entrance. The car, covered in bumper stickers advocating for whales and green energy and with a bike rack on the roof, was ready to leave.

"Going night fishing, huh?" she asked with a knowing smirk as they climbed into her car.

The hour-long drive was tense, the evening dark, the road winding through dense forest until they reached the deserted boat launch at Riffe Lake. Green's suspicions crested. There were no boats, no signs of life. *Did she bring us out to this remote place to die?* he wondered.

Suddenly, the silence was broken by the roar of an engine, and a seaplane descended, its floats gently kissing the water. The plane pulled up to the dock, and the engine died. Despite his size, the pilot climbed onto a pontoon and stepped expertly onto the boat dock.

He was a rugged man with a beard streaked with white, wearing a leather jacket that had seen better days. "Harry Cull, friend of a friend. I owe him one or three," he said, introducing himself. His voice carried a hint of the wild.

As Xi and Green buckled themselves into the plane seats, Cull explained, "Gene told me to tell you to watch out for Torashi Kage." He grimaced. "Senator Traficant hired him to hunt you down. He's bad news."

"Who is Kage, and how will I recognize him?" Green asked,

his nervousness showing. He popped the last few Skittles into his mouth and puckered.

"A very, very bad man," Cull grumbled as he closed the cabin door with a thud, sealing them in.

4

EVERY BREATH YOU TAKE

Faraj counted the bullets in his rifle magazine. *Only seven left*. He was running low on ammunition and needed to replenish his supplies before the next attack. The Americans were relentless in pressing forward, and another attack could happen at any moment.

In the deep, echoing chambers of the Hindu Kush, where sunlight had long ceased to intrude, Faraj and his colleagues had fortified their position late last night. It had held, but not without sacrifice.

With his wiry black hair and beard that had begun to gray under the stress, Faraj sat hunched over a desk littered with schematics and tools. His attire, Iranian military pants and boots with a threadbare rock concert t-shirt beneath a lab jacket, was as much a display of his identity as the device they guarded.

With uncharacteristic urgency, Dr. Smith paced the damp, narrow tunnel of their makeshift lab, continuously cleaning his thick glasses. The tunnel walls glistened with condensation, the moisture seeping from the snow-capped peaks above, creating a constant drip that echoed throughout the cavern system.

The main lab area was a modest space with wobbly tables cluttered with scientific equipment, bare wiring hanging from makeshift supports, and screens flickering with data gathered while monitoring the device. Thick electrical cables snaked along the floor and fastened down to prevent falls, leading to the power generators tucked away in a side tunnel. The hum was a constant backdrop to the lab activities.

The floor was uneven with loose pebbles and small puddles from the dripping water, making every step a cautious one. The acoustics were such that sounds from one part of the cavern could carry far, a double-edged sword in their defensive strategy. The natural echo could mask movements while amplifying the slightest sound, making stealth nearly impossible.

His shadow flickered across the walls as Dr. Smith moved, merging with the shadows cast by the minimal lighting they dared to use, preserving their hidden status. Each step he took was on ground, where history, both geological and human, had left its mark in a place where the secrets of the universe were now being fiercely guarded against those who sought to usurp them.

The night had been long, filled with gunfire and the occasional tremor of explosions too close for comfort. The Taliban, along with a handful of Iranian Quds protectors, had retreated into the cave system at midnight, setting up defenses to shield the alien communication device from American forces. The tunnels were a labyrinth of traps, each turn and dogleg designed to disorient and delay. The American soldiers, cautious or perhaps hesitant with their use of explosives, had made little headway into the cavern despite constant assaults.

"Faraj, how are we holding up?" Dr. Smith's voice echoed through the tunnel, his tone betraying a mix of fatigue and determination.

"Stable for now, Doctor," Faraj replied, his voice steady. "The traps are working as expected. The Americans are slow, probably trying to avoid triggering the device."

Outside the cave system, the paths were treacherous, barely visible in the early-morning light. The trails were narrow, hugging the mountainsides where one misstep could plunge a man into an abyss. The wounded were being evacuated hurriedly through these routes, their retreat a testament to the harshness of the terrain as much as the ferocity of the conflict.

"The tear gas was a mistake on both sides," Faraj continued, adjusting his gas mask hanging loosely around his neck. "It did nothing more than irritate our eyes and throats for those without masks initially, but we're prepared now."

Dr. Smith nodded, his eyes scanning the latest reports. "The Americans want this device intact. It's clear. But they'll push harder soon or overwhelm us. We have no reinforcements coming. Until we get directions from the device, we will fight to the last person."

Faraj's eyes flickered with a fierce resolve. "We must not let that happen. This device... It's not technology; it's our future, our link to a better world. Allah Akbar."

The conversation paused as they listened to the muffled sounds of movement. The American forces were probing, testing their defenses again, perhaps waiting for the right moment to escalate. The air was thick with tension and the faint chemical tang of tear gas that had seeped through cracks in their defenses.

"We need to reinforce the choke points," Faraj suggested, pointing at a map spread out before them. "If they get through here, we're compromised."

Dr. Smith agreed, his mind racing through scenarios. "Do it. I'll check on the status and power levels of the device. If they get too close, we might need to consider the unthinkable."

The thought of destroying the cavern and burying the

device under the mountain before communication was complete was a bitter pill to swallow. They both knew the device was likely indestructible, but success would be uncertain without the ability to communicate with the Others. But both men knew it was a contingency they might have to face.

Faraj's life, marked by loss and survival from his village in Kush to this secretive enclave, had taught him the value of sacrifice for a greater cause. His dedication to the project was not only professional but deeply personal—a way to honor those he'd lost and to fight for a future he believed in. He would not falter when facing this test of his devotion.

As they prepared for another day of defense, the rising sun outside cast long shadows into the cave, a reminder of the world beyond their subterranean struggle, a world they hoped to change with the secrets held within the alien machine.

Dr. Smith moved to stand in front of the communication device. This apparatus, a technological enigma and mystery, was unlike anything human hands had ever crafted. The alien device, often called the "cube," was a large, black metallic object with a smooth, sinister surface. It was roughly the size of an oversized refrigerator and had a pitch-black hue that seemed to absorb any light around it. The device's presence carried the promise of interstellar connection.

Next to Smith, Li Jing monitored the device's status with her sharp intellect and even sharper gaze. Her features were delicate, yet her expression was one of intense concentration. Her lengthy black hair in a bun revealed a face that could shift from serene to stormy in moments. Her hands, usually steady, now tapped impatiently on the console as they waited for the device to emerge from its standby mode, where it had been since the night before.

Suddenly, as if promoted by Li Jing's agitation, the device began to emit complex light patterns and pulse waves. A soft hum filled the cavern, signaling the device's activation. Data streamed across the monitoring screens. Lights flickered in a sequence that seemed to represent an indecipherable language, and then there was stillness. The connection was established. The device's demonstration was both awe-inspiring and menacing.

"The Others," Dr. Smith whispered in awe.

A voice, not human but understood, echoed through the chamber. "Your situation has been assessed. Our forces are encountering significant resistance from the Americans. They will not reach you in time."

Li Jing's eyes widened, her mind racing with the implications. "What do we do?" she asked, betraying her usual composure.

"You must abandon the device as quickly as possible and escape," the voice instructed. "We will communicate further details later. Not all ears are trustworthy."

"What will happen to the device?" Smith queried, his concern evident.

"It cannot be harmed. Leave it. We will trigger an earthquake after your evacuation to seal the tunnels, trapping the Americans. We will direct you to another device and recover this device at a later time."

Smith nodded, absorbing the gravity of the situation. "And how do we communicate in the meantime?"

"Use your personal device. Go to a discreet location for privacy."

Li Jing's face contorted in shock at the disclosure that Smith held a personal device. Doctor Smith had kept its existence a secret from her, and it was evident from the look on her face that she felt betrayed by the sudden, public revelation.

Smith turned to Li Jing, apologetic but firm. "I'll need to handle this alone." He walked away toward his sleeping quarters, a tiny, rustic room hewn from the tunnel wall. The room was stark and utilitarian, with a rickety door that provided a semblance of privacy. It was an atmosphere of bare necessity rather than comfort.

Li Jing watched him leave. Even in the dim light of the tunnels, her face was a dark mirror of hurt and burgeoning anger.

Smith activated his personal device inside his room, a compact version of the cavern's centerpiece. The connection with the small metallic cube was intense and disorienting. With the immediate connection, it felt as if the device was alive and communicating directly with him in a low, thunderous rumble that gradually formed into a language only he could understand.

"We want you to come to us, Dr. Smith," the subconscious voice said, clear and direct. "But Li Jing is a liability, a distraction, and unstable. Bring your assistant, Faraj, in her place."

Smith felt a pang of concern, not for Li Jing but for the situation he now found himself in. The Others' trust in him was evident, but at what cost? Li Jing would not go quietly into the night. His silence stretched.

"I understand. Faraj and I will prepare to leave."

As he returned to the main cavern, the tension was palpable. Li Jing's eyes met his, searching for answers he couldn't give. The device, now silent, stood as a monument to their achievements and the harsh realities of their secrets.

With his instructions clear, Dr. Smith moved deliberately through the makeshift lab in preparation for departure. His glasses, perpetually smudged from the damp air, were a constant companion, and he cleaned them with absent-minded precision. His hair, now more white than gray, mirrored the gravity of his current plans.

Li Jing stood near him, her eyes fixed on the flickering screens that displayed the device's status. Her long black hair was pulled back in a tight bun, her face illuminated by the soft glow of the monitors, revealing lines of stress and determination.

Smith saw her steal a glance at him, her silhouette outlined by the glow of the control panels, her attention only partially fixed on the alien device they had built their lives around. He believed she would do anything for him, but now doubt began to cloud his certainty. The walls seemed to close around him, the air thick with the scent of earth and the stench of cordite. Danger suddenly felt much closer than the sound of gunfire in the tunnel.

"Doctor Smith," Li Jing spoke up, sounding hurt as she confronted him, "is there something you're not telling me?"

Smith looked up, his expression a mask of surprise and a tinge of guilt. "What do you mean?" He rubbed his temples, feeling the strain of their situation. "We do not have time for this conversation right now."

She took a step closer, her voice rising slightly. "Don't you care for me?" The question was more of a plea, her vulnerability bare in the echoing silence of the cave.

"Of course I do," Smith responded, his voice softening. "You're the most important person in my life, as a colleague, as a friend." His words were sincere, yet they made her flinch like he'd struck her.

"Then why make this difficult?" Her tone was sharp, her eyes flicking toward Faraj, who was adjusting some equipment a few feet away, seemingly oblivious to the tension. "Why share secrets with him and not me?"

Smith sighed, running a hand through his thinning hair. "It's not about secrets or favoritism. It's about the project, about keeping us all safe. Faraj has his role, and you have yours."

The sounds of American soldiers outside grew louder, the reality of their perilous situation bleeding into their conversation. Yet the personal tension between Li Jing and Doctor Smith felt as pressing, if not more so.

"Why does it feel like I'm losing my place?" Her voice trembled with the effort to keep her emotions in check, her gaze never leaving Smith. "I've given everything to this project, to you."

Smith stepped closer, his eyes searching hers. "You haven't lost your place. You're irreplaceable. But we're under siege and need to trust each other more than ever. We'll establish ourselves in a new location and move forward from there. Trust me."

"I need to know everything," she insisted, her voice a desperate whisper. "Or do you not trust me?"

Smith reached out, placing a reassuring hand on her shoulder. "I trust you with my life, but some truths might endanger us more than help. We must be strategic."

The cave seemed to shrink, the weight of their predicament pressing down on them. Smith's feelings for Li Jing were tangled—admiration, fear, and a desperate need to escape this situation. The project was his lifeline, his future, but now it was also his battleground for trust with a killer.

As the sounds of conflict grew nearer, Doctor Smith knew trust might be a luxury he couldn't afford. Yet with the threat of discovery so close, he needed to believe Li Jing would remain steady, even as the seeds of distrust threatened to sprout. He took a deep breath, steadying himself.

***

In the dim, flickering light of the cavern, Li Jing's heart hammered against her chest.

The cave walls seemed to close around her, the air was heavy with the smell of earth and the electric buzz of the machinery and arc lamps. She glanced at Doctor Smith, his outline highlighted by the panel lights, his attention focused on the alien device they had poured their lives into. She would do anything for him.

What is he not telling me? Li Jing wondered, her mind racing. She had always believed she was his primary confidant, the one he trusted above all others. But lately, doubts had begun to gnaw at her. The way he spoke to Faraj with a tone hinting at shared secrets made her skin prickle with jealousy and suspicion. And the sudden revelation of a personal device was too much for her to ignore.

With his wild, wiry hair and a Synchronicity Tour T-shirt, Faraj stood beside Smith, his presence a constant reminder of her insecurities. *He's favoring him, isn't he?* she thought, her gaze sharpening as she watched them. Faraj's intelligence was undeniable, his dedication palpable, but to Li Jing, he was nothing more than a threat, a potential usurper in her carefully constructed world.

The sounds of the American soldiers outside grew louder, the threat of intrusion looming like a dark cloud. The claustrophobia intensified, each breath feeling like a struggle against the weight of the earth above them.

Li Jing's thoughts spiraled back to her father, Dr. Xi, a man whose abandonment had left a scar that never healed. His betrayal as a child had evolved into his betrayal of their homeland. In her mind, he was a traitor for helping the Americans. She vowed silently, "Smith won't do this to me." She wouldn't be abandoned and disrespected again.

Her eyes flicked back to Faraj, her mind painting him as an obstacle, an enemy. The jealousy was visceral, fueled by a life of feeling second best, of being left behind. Her hands itched to pull out her dagger and plunge it into his dirty neck.

She imagined scenarios in which she could remove him, where his absence would secure her place by Smith's side. "If I have the chance," she mused darkly, her hand subtly tightening around the screwdriver she had been using, the potential for violence flickering in her thoughts.

As the tension in the cave escalated, the sounds of conflict drew nearer, and Li Jing's internal turmoil mirrored the external chaos. She was caught between her need for trust and the overwhelming desire to ensure her survival and dominance in this underground world. Her feelings for Smith were complex: admiration, fear, and now a desperate need to cling to him to prove her indispensability.

The project, their shared secret, was more than science; it was her lifeline, her proof of worth. But as the soldiers' shouts echoed closer, she realized the fragility of their situation. Trust was a luxury she might not be able to afford now. Her doubts about Smith, Faraj, and her place in this intricate dance of power and knowledge were becoming all-consuming. She had become a creature of violence, and controlling the beast was becoming increasingly impossible in these tight quarters.

Li Jing took a deep breath, steadying herself. She needed to focus to survive, but the seeds of distrust, jealousy, and revenge were planted deep, ready to burst at any moment.

5

READ BETWEEN THE LINES

Barth angrily kicked the stone wall.

The tunnel was a jagged wound carved into the Hindu Kush mountainside. Its walls were slick with dampness and streaked with veins of quartz that glinted faintly in the dim light filtering through gaps in the rock. The air hung heavy with the stink of sweat and the acrid tang of gunpowder drifting in from the chaos of Operation Anaconda outside.

Barth Anderson, CIA Director and clandestine operative extraordinaire, leaned against a rough outcropping, his sharp hazel eyes narrowing as he surveyed the shadowy passage. His once-pristine uniform was now a tattered mess—jacket torn at the shoulder, tactical vest askew, and boots smeared with dust and blood that wasn't his own. His silver-streaked hair, usually slicked back with meticulous care, fell in disarray across his forehead, giving him the look of a disheveled predator.

Beside him, Miss Grey slumped against the wall, her petite frame swallowed by a bulky tactical vest she'd scavenged from the Rangers who had escorted her here. Her dark hair was matted with sweat and grime, clinging to her tired, olive-toned face. Dark circles underscored her closed eyes as the first rays of dawn crept through a fissure overhead, casting a soft, golden glow over her. She looked almost tranquil, as if exhaustion had finally dragged her under after a night spent pinned between the American forces hammering the mountainside and the Taliban blocking every passage leading deeper into the tunnel complex.

Anderson snorted softly, the sound dripping with disdain. "Sleeping beauty, huh? Guess the end of the world's not enough to keep you on your toes." His voice was a low rasp, edged with the sarcasm that had long been one of his proudest personality traits.

He shifted, wincing as a shard of rock dug into his back, and glanced toward the tunnel's rear. There was a narrow route out —an escape hatch of sorts—snaking through the labyrinth to the backside of the mountain. They'd tried to crawl out last night, only to find it thick with Iranian Quds Force operatives. Anderson had taken one look at their cold, disciplined stares and muttered, "Yeah, those bastards would shoot me just for breathing their air." Not that he'd blame them, because he'd like to shoot them too.

He'd been lucky to find this hidden entrance to the tunnel complex, unguarded and tucked behind a jagged overhang. That was before Miss Grey and Maxx King had stumbled into his path before the fighting turned the main entrance of the tunnel complex into a meat grinder. He'd planned to use this overlooked access to slip deeper into the complex, maybe to track down Doctor Smith and that damned device—wherever it was—or maybe to meet him. Who could say? Anderson's motives were a tangle of ambition and deceit, knotted tighter by his allegiance to Senator Traficant. He wasn't sure where the truth ended and the lies began.

His mind drifted back to the night before when he'd put a bullet into Maxx King's chest, that big ape. The memory flickered like a grainy film reel. Maxx, broad-shouldered and earnest, stepping between Anderson and Grey with that infuriating hero complex of his. When Maxx had turned his back on him, Anderson couldn't restrain himself any longer and pulled the trigger out of spite. The suppressor had muffled the sound of the gunshot, and Grey's muted screams had been a jagged counterpoint as he'd dragged her into the tunnel, her wrists bruised under his grip.

"Why'd you do it?" Grey's voice broke through his reverie, faint and hoarse from hours of shouting over the gunfire outside. She wasn't asleep after all—playing possum. Her eyes were open now, glinting defiantly as she stared him down.

Anderson shrugged nonchalantly. "Maxx was an overgrown Boy Scout in a world that eats them for breakfast. He'd have turned me in without a second thought. You, on the other hand..." His gaze sharpened. "You've got something I need, sweetheart. That code Green used to lock up the Thunderbird file—gimme."

"I've told you a hundred times," she snapped, voice rising despite her exhaustion, "I don't know anything about it. Green never shared the encryption key with me."

"Bullshit," he spat, leaning closer until his breath brushed her cheek. "You're a terrible liar, Grey. Always have been." Last night, he'd pressed her for hours, pacing the tunnel like a caged panther, his questions relentless. "Give me the damn code, and maybe you'll walk out of here," he growled, slapping his palm against the wall.

She'd held firm, jaw set, and he'd wanted to throttle her then and there—Senator Traficant's orders be damned. "Do whatever it takes," the senator had said over a crackling line before they had descended into this pit. Although he would love to follow through on that statement, that was before he'd realized he might need a bargaining chip to get out of the situation. Anderson's phone was useless here, with no bars and no lifeline to Traficant. He was on his own.

He rubbed his temples, fatigue gnawing at the edges of his composure. The tunnel's chill seeped into his bones, and his eyelids grew heavy. One moment's rest, he told himself, letting his head tip back against the stone. The world blurred then faded.

A sudden weight slammed into his chest, jolting him awake. Grey was on him, her tied hands unsuccessfully clawing for the Glock holstered at his hip. "You hijo de puta!" she hissed, her nails raking his forearm as she fought to twist the gun free. Anderson snarled, adrenaline surging, and shoved her back. She was scrappy, athletic strength fueled by training and desperation, but he was stronger, meaner. He caught her wrists, twisting until she gasped, and pinned her beneath him, knees bracketing her hips.

"Big mistake, darling," he growled, his usual cool unraveling into something feral. His free hand hovered over her throat, fingers twitching. Grey might be a "get out of jail free" card if she were alive, but he was past thinking clearly about consequences. She'd pushed him too far, and the consequences were distant now. "You think you stand a chance against me?"

Her eyes blazed, unyielding even as her breath came in ragged bursts. "Go ahead, Barth. Prove you're the monster everyone knows you are."

Before he could decide whether to snap her neck or let her up, a deafening roar shook the tunnel. Dust rained from the ceiling, and the thunder of boots and gunfire swelled louder, closer. The Americans were storming the main entrance to the caves, their assault collapsing the Taliban's defenses like a tidal wave. Shouts in English and Pashto tangled with the crack of rifles, the sounds of grenades reverberating through the stone. It sounded like hell set free.

Anderson froze, his grip on Grey loosening as his mind raced. Stay here and the Americans might find him, might ID him as a traitor, thanks to Miss Grey. Or he could bolt for the back exit and take his chances with the Iranians. They'd kill him on sight, sure, but maybe he could talk his way out, spin a story about defecting with secrets to sell. Or there was that hidden entrance—partially blocked now, but if he could squeeze through, maybe he'd reach Smith before the Americans caught him.

He hauled Grey to her feet, keeping the Glock trained on her chest. "Move," he barked, shoving her toward the tunnel's depths. "We're not done yet."

"Where are we going?" she demanded, stumbling but keeping her glare fixed on him.

"Somewhere that's not here," he shot back, a smirk tugging at his lips despite the chaos. "Unless you'd rather I put a bullet into that thick skull of yours. Your call, princess."

The narrow tunnel stretched ahead, dark and uncertain, as the sounds of war closed in. Anderson's heart pounded with a mix of dread and exhilaration. Whatever came next—Smith, the device, or a bullet with his name on it—he'd play the game his way, like always.

***

"Who do I have to kill around here to get more Twizzlers?" Maxx grumbled to himself.

The Hindu Kush mountains loomed like silent titans over the jagged battlefield, their peaks clawing at the gray March sky of 2002. Inside a rough-hewn tunnel, Maxx crouched behind a crumbling boulder, his breath ragged, his chest throbbing where Anderson's bullet had smashed into the ceramic plate only hours before.

The fall over the cliff hadn't helped either—his ribs ached with every movement—but he shoved the pain aside. Miss Grey was still out there, a prisoner to that CIA traitor, Anderson, and Maxx wasn't about to let her die. Worse still, Doctor

Smith and his lunatic sidekick, Li Jing, were dug deep in this hellhole with something far more dangerous than guns or bombs.

Maxx flexed his dirt-streaked hands, his fingers raw from seven hours of clawing through Taliban defenses. He jammed the last Twizzler he'd been saving into his mouth and took a swig of water from Zeller's canteen. He couldn't lose focus now, not with Gabby's worried voice echoing from their last call. "I need you, Maxx. I love you."

Beside him, Sergeant Zeller spat into the dust. His Green Beret team fanned out along the tunnel's uneven walls. The air stank of wet stone and tear gas, the latter still stinging their eyes from an earlier volley. The troops were a mess—yellow on ammo, battered but not broken. A Ranger named Hicks nursed a shallow shrapnel wound on his leg while Corporal Diaz coughed through the lingering haze, his rifle still steady. They were exhausted, their faces gaunt, but Maxx's grim determination and Zeller's steady growl of leadership kept them moving. As Zeller liked to say, "The only easy day was yesterday."

"Seven hours of this bullshit," Zeller muttered, wiping sweat from his brow. "Feels like we're digging to China."

Maxx snorted, peering around the pile of rubble from a grenade blast. "That might be truer than you realize. Smith's in there. I can feel it. We're close."

"Yeah, well, we're outta time," Zeller replied, his voice low. "Reinforcements ain't coming. Taliban's dug in like ticks, and we're bleeding dry. We go all-in now or we're done."

A murmur rippled through the team. Hicks nodded, tightening the bandage on his leg. "I'm in. Let's finish this."

Diaz cracked a dry smile. "Rather die fighting than sit here counting how many bullets we have left."

Maxx met Zeller's gaze, the unspoken agreement passing between them. "Overwhelming assault," Maxx said. "No holding back."

Zeller barked orders, and the team snapped into motion. Maxx took point, his M4 carbine pressed to his shoulder as they surged forward. The tunnel narrowed, its jagged walls glowing faintly with bioluminescent fungi, casting eerie shadows. Taliban fighters popped from crevices, their AKs chattering. Maxx dropped one with a burst to the chest, ducking as return fire chipped the rock above his head.

Behind him, Zeller roared, "Push, damn it! Push!" A grenade sailed past, detonating in a flash of dust and screams. Hicks charged a machine gun nest, silencing it with a bayonet before a bullet grazed his arm. Diaz laid down covering fire, his rounds pinging off stalactites.

It was brutal, inch-by-inch chaos, but they were finally breaking the back of the defensive positions.

Maxx's vision blurred from exhaustion, but he kept moving, driven by the thought of Smith's smug face and Li Jing's cackling madness. The vision of her glee in killing Hovis was etched into his memories. After what felt like an eternity, the gunfire dwindled. The last Taliban defender fell, and the tunnel opened into a cavernous chamber.

The sight stopped everyone, except Maxx, cold.

A massive black metal cube dominated the large cavern, its surface smooth and alien, humming with a low, unnatural vibration. Wires snaked from its base to a makeshift power plant, droning in the cave's rear. The Green Berets and Rangers froze, weapons half-raised, staring at the thing.

"What in God's name..." Zeller breathed.

Maxx stepped forward, his jaw tight. "That's why I've been after Smith. It's an ultrasecret alien communications device—some technology we can't even wrap our heads around. He's trying to turn it on and use it against us. Not my first rodeo, unfortunately."

Diaz blinked, tearing his gaze from the cube. "Alien? You're serious?"

"Dead serious," Maxx said. "Smith's obsessed with it. He thinks it'll make him a god. Li Jing's along for the carnage. But if they activate it, it's not only messages—it's earthquakes, volcanoes, and who knows what else. Wicked stuff. We're all dead or trapped if that happens."

Hicks shifted uneasily. "So what's the plan? Blow it up?"

Maxx shook his head. "Can't. These things are indestructible. Even trying might trigger it, anyway. We either stop Smith or cut its power."

Zeller snorted, slinging his rifle over his shoulder. "Great. Let's call tech support and get them to unplug it."

Maxx paused, then smirked despite himself. "Sarge, you're a genius."

"Finally, someone agrees with me," Zeller said as he patted himself on the back.

The Americans fanned out, searching the chamber. The power plant whirred louder as they approached—a tangle of cables and turbines fed by an underground stream rushing through a sliding gate to channel the water flow.

Maxx knelt by the setup, frowning. "No obvious disconnect. I can't even see how these cables are attached. They seem like part of the device."

Zeller cursed. "So we're screwed?"

"Wait," Diaz said, peering over the water channel's edge, "there's probably a way to close off the valve down there. If we stop the flow, the turbines stop. No power."

Maxx leaned over, squinting into the dark, murky water. His stomach twisted. He hated water—hated it even more after that ferry incident last year when he'd nearly drowned.

Sergeant Zeller looked into the water, eying his reflection. "Why is that water so dark, anyway? I thought underground water was supposed to be pure in the mountains."

"Good question," Maxx said with a hint of anxiety. "Can't you close the valve from up here?"

"Nah," Diaz said. "Let me jump in and feel around." Diaz set down his rifle and stripped off his vest and boots. "Besides, I want to freshen up in case we run into any good-looking women."

"Go for it," Maxx said as Diaz dove into the dark water. "I'll stay up here and make sure we don't get ambushed while you're taking a bath."

Diaz grinned at Maxx when he bobbed on the surface. "Come on in, man. See, there are no sharks in here!" He dove below the inky water's surface and disappeared.

6

DARK WATERS

The command center at Bagram Airfield hummed with restless energy.

Lt. Colonel Tom Williams of the 101st Airborne leaned against a cluttered desk, nursing a lukewarm coffee that tasted more like motor oil than usual. In his fifties and starting to develop a bit of a gut, he'd drunk a lifetime's worth of lousy coffee.

The cavernous room hummed with the sounds of radios, clacking keyboards, and the low murmur of officers and staff as they juggled the chaos of Operation Anaconda. Maps of the Shah-i-Kot Valley plastered the walls, dotted with red and blue pins marking friendlies and foes—or what they *thought* were friendlies and foes—the air stank of sweat, stale cigarettes, and stress.

Williams wasn't part of the inner circle here. That privilege belonged to Major General Hagenbeck, the Commanding General of the 10th Mountain Division, who was the senior commander responsible for planning and executing the operation. He and his 10th Mountain Division cronies darted in and out of a soundproofed briefing room like bees guarding a hive.

Something was up—something beyond the messy slugfest in the valley. The coffee chatter among the staff hinted at it. Whispered rumors of "special cargo" and "off-book ops." Williams caught snippets as he passed a knot of lieutenants refilling their mugs.

"Heard they lost a whole unit out there," one muttered.

"Yeah, and Command's acting like it's no big deal," another replied, glancing over his shoulder.

Williams frowned, swirling his coffee. He'd been awake all night but working on a side project for his old squad mate, Colonel Jim Hanssen, who had called from God knew where, voice crackling over a secure line, asking him to locate a missing unit with some unmarked canisters—suspicious ones. He'd told Tom there was a big payday if they were what he was looking for. Hanssen wouldn't say more but dangled that carrot of "private money" and hung up. Williams had dispatched a search and rescue team within the hour, but eight hours later, the situation was a mess—and he still hadn't called Hanssen back.

"Colonel Williams!" Captain Reese, a wiry logistics officer, jogged over, his brow slick with sweat despite the chill. "Got an update on that S&R team you sent out."

Williams straightened, setting his cup down. "Let's hear it."

Reese hesitated, glancing at the bustling room. "They're gone, sir. Ambushed near Weih's last-known position. No survivors, no bodies. Gone."

Williams's voice sharpened. "What about the drone feed?"

"Confiscated, sir. Hagenbeck's team swooped in and locked it down. I only saw a few frames before they yanked it—it looked like Weih's unit was in a defensive posture. But there was something else. Shadows moving. Not Taliban. Too fast, too...weird."

Williams's gut tightened. Shadows? He'd seen enough in

Vietnam with Hanssen to know "weird" could mean trouble. "Explain, Captain."

Reese shifted uncomfortably. "Not Taliban, sir. It sounds nuts, but the drone caught *something* before it cut out. Command's dodging questions, and my request for a second team got shot down flat."

"Shot down by whom?"

"Major Pearson, sir," Reese said, nodding toward a stern-faced officer barking orders across the room. "Said we're stretched too thin already."

Williams rubbed his jaw, the stubble rasping under his fingers. He didn't like this. Hanssen's cryptic call, the missing unit, the confiscated footage—it smelled like a side operation, and not the kind CENTCOM had been planning. He grabbed his headset and waved Reese along. "Come on. We're getting answers."

They crossed the command center to a bank of monitors where Staff Sergeant Lopez, a thin tech with dark circles under her eyes, was hunched over a console. "Lopez, pull up the latest sitrep on the valley," Williams ordered.

She glanced up, bleary-eyed. "Sir, it's a mess out there. Taliban's dug in deeper than we thought—maybe a thousand strong now. But the chatter's odd. Some units are reporting 'unknown contacts.' Not ours, not theirs. Hagenbeck's got the 10th Mountain pushing east, but the special ops guys are acting cagey."

"Cagey?" Reese pressed.

Lopez tapped a key, bringing up a grainy feed of the battlefield. "Task Force 11's been redirecting air support away from known targets. It's like they're chasing something else. And this." She pointed to a blinking dot on the map. "That's where Weih's unit went dark, right in the middle of it."

Williams stared at the screen, his mind racing. Hanssen's canisters weren't some lost munitions stash—this felt bigger, darker. He'd scoff if Reese hadn't seen that footage. "Lopez, any chance you can dig up that drone video?"

She shook her head. "Locked tight, sir. Hagenbeck's inner circle has it under wraps. I'd need a direct order from Command to even try."

"Damn it," Williams muttered and turned to Reese. "What's your take?"

Reese frowned, crossing his arms. "I'd guess foreign special ops. Chinese? No mass casualties, no big moves. Just...probing. But if Weih's team stumbled onto them *and* those unidentified canisters, that's why Command's clamming up."

"Or why Hanssen's so hot to find them," Williams added quietly. He stepped away, pacing toward a quieter corner of the room. Hanssen had promised a payday, but if this was Chinese tech—or worse, Iranian weapons—maybe the reward was more significant than a fat check. Perhaps it was power. He needed to know more before he dialed that number.

"Sir!" Lopez called, waving him back. "Got something on the horn—fragmented SOS from a Ranger squad near Weih's last ping. They're pinned down, screaming about 'things in the rocks.'"

Williams strode over, snatching a headset. "Patch me in."

Static crackled, and then a panicked voice broke through. "Command, this is Delta Two! We're under attack—unknown hostiles! Not Taliban, not even human! They've got—oh God, they're everywhere—"

The line cut to dead air. Williams ripped off the headset, slamming it on the desk. "Reese, Lopez, with me. We're talking to Pearson."

They found Major Pearson near the briefing room, his face a mask of exhaustion and irritation. "Colonel Williams," he said curtly, "what now?"

"I need a second search and rescue team out there," Williams said, voice low but firm. "Weih's unit's gone, my first

S&R's gone, and now I've got Rangers screaming about 'things' attacking them. What the hell's happening, Major?"

Pearson's eyes narrowed. "You're not cleared for that, Tom. Stick to logistics. Hagenbeck's handling it."

"Handling what?" Williams snapped. "I've got men dying out there, and you're confiscating footage like the CIA is running a special. If this is a side op, I deserve to know. I'm losing teams."

Pearson hesitated, then leaned in, voice barely a whisper. "Drop it, Colonel. You don't want this. Orders came from above Hagenbeck—way above. Those canisters Weih recovered? Not ours. Not anyone we know. The spooks deny any knowledge."

Williams stared at him, pulse pounding. "Then whose?"

Pearson straightened, his expression hardening. "Get back to your post. That's an order."

As Pearson walked away, Williams turned to Reese and Lopez. "He's scared," he muttered. "They all are."

"What now, sir?" Reese asked.

Williams didn't answer right away. He thought of Hanssen—his old friend, always one step ahead, always chasing the next big score. Hanssen knew more than he'd let on. And if Command was covering it up, the payday might be less about money and more about leverage...or survival.

"Get me a secure line," he said finally. "I need to make a call. But first, Lopez, find me anything you can on that drone feed. Backchannels, whatever it takes."

Lopez nodded grimly. "Yes, sir."

Williams stepped outside into the frigid Bagram air, lighting a cigarette with shaking hands. The Hindu Kush stretched out above, a fortress of war and secrets. Whatever Weih had found, it was Pandora's box, and Hanssen wanted it. Williams exhaled a plume of smoke, his mind made up. He'd get the truth, one way or another.

***

"Go for it," Maxx had said to Diaz as he descended into the dark water.

Maxx felt a little guilty about not jumping into the water to help, but his PTSD was in control for the moment. Every second Diaz stayed below the inky water, his anxiety only increased. Better to stay up top, ready to shoot anything other than Diaz that popped out of the water.

After a minute or two, Diaz resurfaced and shook his head, coughing. "Couldn't move it. The handwheel to open the sluice gate is stuck. Something's jammed in the gearbox. Need another pair of hands."

"Go," Zeller ordered a nearby soldier, Corporal Terry. "Help him."

Terry nodded, stripping off his gear and plunging into the icy water with a splash. He surfaced a moment later, teeth chattering. "It's stuck bad, Sarge. I can feel the wheel, but it won't budge without more muscle."

Maxx stared at the water, his heart hammering. Every instinct screamed at him to stay put, to wait for another solution. But there wasn't enough time. Smith could trigger the device any second, burying them all. He thought of that ferry, the cold grip of being trapped in the car as it went under. This couldn't be worse than that. Could it?

"Damn it," he muttered, shrugging off his gear and untying his boots. "I'm going in."

Zeller grabbed his arm. "You sure, King? You look like you're about to puke."

"No choice," Maxx said, forcing a grim smile. "Watch my gear, Sarge."

Maxx took a deep breath and jumped. The water hit him like a slap, icy and black, swallowing him whole. His chest tightened, panic clawing at him, but he kicked downward, following Terry's faint silhouette. The current tugged at his injured arm, and he gritted his teeth against the pain. His boots brushed the slimy bottom, and he groped blindly until his hands found the handwheel. Terry and Diaz were there, straining against it.

Holding up his fingers, Maxx counted down from three. When he signaled, they heaved, muscles burning, but the wheel barely twitched. Something hard—debris, maybe—jammed the gears. Maxx clawed at it, his lungs screaming for air.

Something bumped into him.

It was heavy, alive, brushing his leg in the dark. A shudder ran through Maxx as he pictured cave creatures, that grotesque monster in *The Hobbit*, or something even worse. Before he could react, it wrapped around his ankle and yanked. He thrashed, losing his grip on the wheel as the thing—whatever it was—dragged him deeper into the murk. His hand grazed something sharp—a stalagmite?—and he grabbed it, anchoring himself. The creature tightened its grip, pulling harder.

"Get off me!" Maxx's muffled yell, a desperate gurgle, fought the pressure of the water.

Maxx kicked wildly, his foot connecting with something soft. The pressure eased, and he lunged back to the wheel, Diaz at his side. Together, they wrenched it free of the debris—a rusted chunk of metal—and turned. The wheel groaned, then spun, and the sluice gate slammed shut. Above, the turbines slowly began to whine to a stop.

Everyone above water had been increasingly concerned with the device and the power generator. They remained motionless, struck by disbelief, as the device's lights changed rapidly from yellow to green, then to a flashing red. The cube began to hum precisely when the generators ceased functioning. With an audible sigh of relief from the soldiers, the lights on the device went dark, leaving the cavern in an ominous silence.

Maxx broke the surface, gasping, Terry hauling him onto the bank. Zeller was there, pulling him up. "You okay, you crazy bastard? What happened?"

Maxx coughed, shivering, water dripping from his hair. "Yeah...something's down there, Sarge. Didn't like me much. Do they have sharks in these caves?"

Hicks laughed, clapping his shoulder. "No, man. But you're a damn hero, King."

Zeller pointed at the blood running down Maxx's leg. "Better get that taken care of. Looks like you got snagged on something sharp."

Maxx managed a weak grin, glancing at the now-silent cube. They'd stopped it, for now. But Smith and Li Jing were still out there, and Miss Grey was still in danger. He pushed to his feet, ignoring the ache in his bones. "Let's move. We're not done yet."

Zeller nodded, signaling the team. "You heard the man. The only easy day was yesterday."

Everyone groaned but began checking their ammo. The unit organized to press deeper into the tunnels, chasing the shadows of Smith and Li Jing.

The tunnel stretched endlessly in front of Maxx, sweat-streaked grime painting his weathered face. He'd already gotten filthy after his brief swim shutting off the water to the generators. His muscles ached, his left leg throbbed from the jagged gash earned in the underwater encounter, and his ears still rang from the night-long firefight.

Beside him, Sergeant Zeller led the Green Berets—six men remaining, all hollow-eyed and battered, their breaths shallow as they pushed deeper into the damp, claustrophobic dark. Their mission hadn't changed: capture or kill Doctor Smith, the rogue DARPA scientist turned traitor hiding somewhere in this labyrinth. At least they didn't have to worry about Smith's device anymore. And somewhere in these tunnels, Miss Grey had disappeared with Anderson.

The air grew thick, tinged with the coppery scent of blood. Zeller raised a fist, halting the team. Ahead, sprawled across the tunnel floor, was a heap of Taliban fighters—still and likely dead. Maxx crouched, his flashlight beam sweeping over the bodies. Their skin was blistered and blackened as if scorched from within. One man's eyes bulged, frozen in a scream, while another's hands clutched at his chest, fingers twisted into claws. A third had blood oozing from his ears, staining the dirt beneath him: no bullet wounds, no shrapnel—grotesque, inexplicable ruin.

"Ah shit," Maxx muttered to himself. *How am I going to explain this?*

"What the hell happened here?" Zeller's voice cracked. He turned to Maxx, eyes narrowing. "King, you've been tight-lipped since we started this op. I'm tired of running in the dark. What do you know about this shit? What's Smith got that does *this*?"

Maxx straightened, wiping sweat from his brow. The team's gaze bore into him, a mix of exhaustion and suspicion.

He exhaled sharply and looked away. "I don't know what killed them, Zeller. But I'll tell you what I *do* know. That device Smith was running back there wasn't to get interstellar weather updates and start the occasional earthquake. It's a two-way coordinator. For an invasion."

"Why the hell would a bunch of aliens want to invade Afghanistan?" Diaz asked incredulously.

Maxx looked at Diaz as if he'd grown a third arm. "Not Afghanistan, you ass. Earth."

Zeller's jaw tightened. "Invasion of Earth? What are you talking about? Who's invading?"

Maxx shook his head. "I know this sounds nuts, but it's a

fact, and we don't have time to stand around jawing about it. Operation Anaconda? Yeah, it's about kicking Taliban ass post-9/11, but that's the cover. The real mission is to stop Smith, secure that thing, and block whatever's coming. Starting an earthquake is only their opening salvo."

"Anything else you can enlighten us on? Like right now," Zeller barked.

Maxx plunged ahead. "There's more. Back in that flooded chamber, something hit me underwater. Dragged me down fast—claws or tentacles, I don't know. I barely got free. I think it was one of *them*—the aliens—trying to cut the power or take me out."

A ripple of unease swept through the team. Private Hicks, a wiry kid with a bloody, bandaged arm, muttered, "Aliens? You serious, man?"

Corporal Ruiz, clutching his rifle tightly, spat into the dirt. "This is nuts. We're chasing a freaky scientist, not little green men."

"They're not green," Maxx said grimly. "At least, I don't think they are. And they're not little. I think this is an advance force—the Others. Smith's device was calling the rest."

Zeller stepped closer, his voice low and taut. "Why are they fighting us now? If they're prepping a major invasion, why tip their hand?"

"Maybe they're desperate," Maxx replied, his mind racing. "Maybe Smith's losing control of the situation—or them. He's a scientist, not a soldier. If he's cornered down here, he might be cracking. That device could be his bargaining chip or his death sentence."

"Are Anderson and Grey mixed up in this madness?" Zeller pressed, nodding toward the tunnel ahead. "They disappeared into the tunnels ahead of us. Where the hell are they?"

Maxx's gut twisted. Anderson and Grey had vanished into the tunnels after Maxx had fallen off the cliff. "I don't know if

Anderson is trying to hook up with or capture Smith. Either way, it's not good for Grey. But we need to find her. She saved my ass. I owe her."

"Or maybe the aliens got to them first," Ruiz muttered. The team exchanged glances, the stress of it sinking in.

The tunnel trembled faintly, a low rumble vibrating through the stone. Dust sifted from the ceiling, and Hicks flinched. "Seismic activity?" he whispered.

"Or them," Ruiz growled.

Zeller squared his shoulders, his voice regaining its edge. "We move. If we stay here, we're going to end up like them," he said as he pointed at the Taliban bodies.

Maxx nodded, adrenaline surging past the pain, and stepped past the pile of dead soldiers. "Smith's close. I can feel it. If he's desperate, he'll make a mistake. If Anderson is alive, we find him. Then I'm going to kill both of them." He gritted his teeth. "Let's end this."

The team advanced, weapons raised, the tunnel narrowing around them like a noose. Ahead, a faint glow flickered—artificial, unnatural. Smith was near, and with him were answers...or doom. The rumble grew louder, the air electric with menace, and Maxx knew the climax was rising, unstoppable, pulling them all into its gaping jaws.

7

EVERY MILE A MEMORY

Gabby Fisher sat alone in her room at the Salish Lodge, the distant rumble of Snoqualmie Falls filtering through the window.

The room was warm and rustic, with heavy wooden beams and a plush bed she couldn't wait to sink into—especially after the stress of the last few days. She'd ordered room service earlier: a plate of alder wood roasted salmon with herb butter and a side of garlic mashed potatoes, paired with two glasses of crisp Yakima Valley chardonnay. The food was comforting, but it couldn't fill the hollow ache in her chest.

Maxx King, her boyfriend, was in Afghanistan "saving humanity," and she'd vanished from Seattle to spare him the worry. God, she missed him—his steady voice, his quiet strength. The wine dulled the edges, but loneliness clung to her like damp air.

Less than twelve hours earlier, Gabby had walked out of TechCom for the last time. Her footsteps had echoed through the empty office, each one a hammer blow of resolve. Once a beacon of innovation, the Thunderbird project had morphed into something sinister, its unknowns clawing at her peace of mind.

She'd paused at her desk, sliding the photo of her and Maxx on the Bainbridge ferry into her backpack, the frame glinting in the window's light. She'd left her badge, keys, and computer behind, scrawling a message on the whiteboard, "Embrace today. Tomorrow is only a promise, not a given. Hugs, Gabby."

Then her phone buzzed to life with Andres's text. "Maxx sent us back to make sure you're safe. OMW."

Panic surged. She'd trashed her SIM card, spotted Andres and Glen in the parking lot, and fled down the stairwell as the elevator dinged. Although she regarded them as friends, they had been Maxx's long-time companions and had been together in the military. She was sure Maxx had sent them here to keep an eye on her while he stayed in Afghanistan. But she wanted to disappear without involving them. Snow had greeted her in the alley, a fleeting goodbye from Seattle as she disappeared.

The morning found her drifting between coffee shops, her jeans and North Face jacket blending into the crowd, her glasses shielding her face. When she'd had enough of hopping from coffee shop to coffee shop, she went to a location where no one would ever consider looking for her. She'd spent the early evening in a grimy motel off Highway 99—ironically named The Thunderbird Motel—dozing off upright in an ancient chair, her body now stiff and protesting. No one would ask any questions or expect to find her there.

When it was sufficiently dark, she'd taken a series of cab rides to make her trail impossible to follow if someone persistent tracked her to the motel. She didn't know if anyone was looking for her, but she was confident that Andres and Glen wouldn't give up easily.

"Downtown, please," she'd told the first cab driver, her

voice wobbling into a fake Dallas drawl to hide her British accent.

The driver, a stocky man with a beat-up Sonics cap, glanced back. "You sound like you're auditioning for something. Where are you really from?"

"Uh, Dallas," she said, tugging her hood tighter. "Long day, you know?"

"You got that look like you're dodgin' somebody." He chuckled. "I've seen it before. Ex? Cops?"

Gabby forced a smile. "I'm taking a mini vacation from the grind."

He shrugged, dropping her near the waterfront. She switched through two more cabs, each ride a blur of lights and lies until she landed at Salish Lodge. At the desk, she'd faced a clerk with tired eyes and a clipboard.

"Name?" he asked, pen poised.

"Betty Lou Smith," she said, the fake twang faltering. "Payin' cash."

He raised an eyebrow. "Dallas, huh? You don't sound like the prior guests we've had from Texas. The room is $250. No funny business, ma'am."

"Promise," she said nervously, sliding the bills over. She wasn't sure he bought it, but he handed her a key, anyway.

Now, in her room, Gabby's mind churned. *I walked away from everything—TechCom, Maxx, my life.* The photo in her bag felt like a lifeline to a past she couldn't reclaim. She'd cut ties to protect Maxx, to let him focus on his mission, but the weight of it crushed her. *Will he even know I'm gone?* She felt raw, unmoored, equal parts determined and terrified.

Her resolve flickered. *I wanted to be strong for you, Maxx, but I'm breaking.* The past six months at TechCom replayed—breakthroughs shadowed by breakdowns, the Thunderbird project's unknowns clawing at her stability. *Did I really think I could vanish?* She imagined Maxx's voice, steady and warm.

"You're safe, Gabby. I've got you." But he wasn't here, and the fantasy crumbled. *I need you home, Maxx. I can't go through this alone.*

Exhausted, she turned off the lights and stood by the window. The falls glowed in the mist, a silver ribbon slicing through the night—beautiful, almost otherworldly. The hotel reminded her of the television show *Twin Peaks*, which had been on about ten years ago. It was groundbreaking for its eerie, surreal vibe and cult following, which wasn't helping improve her mood.

She pressed her forehead to the glass, letting the coolness steady her. Movement snapped her focus, a man sprinting along the path below, his coat flapping. Two figures chased him, their shapes unmistakable—Andres's quick gait, Glen's massive frame. Her stomach dropped. *Coincidence? Or did they follow me? And who was that man?*

Gabby's hand found the Glock in her bag. She couldn't hide, not now. She was already beginning to wonder if she was cut out for a life of running.

She slipped the gun into her pocket, pulled on her jacket, and cinched the hood tight, shadowing her face. She stepped into the hallway with a deep breath, locking the door behind her. It was the second time she'd stepped onto "the ice" in twenty-four hours—that thin, treacherous line between safety and the unknown.

***

The air outside the Salish Lodge was thick with tension, the faint roar of Snoqualmie Falls echoing in the distance. The mist enveloped them, and the falls' roar was a steady pulse. Andres Sandoval and Glen Piper stood shoulder to shoulder, their breaths visible in the chilly March evening.

Ahead of them, an Asian man darted through the parking

lot, his dark suit blending into the shadows as he pursued a figure Andres recognized instantly—Gabby, Maxx's girlfriend. She stumbled, her long, dark hair catching the moonlight before disappearing around a corner. The man chasing her was no stranger either. Torashi Kage. They'd been tracking him all day, constantly one step behind.

Kage cut a menacing silhouette, his lean, muscled frame forged in years of ruthless discipline. Hair slicked back tight, framing a jagged scar slashing from cheek to jaw. He was draped in a tailored black suit and white shirt, his dark eyes burning with a predator's gleam. Turning, his grin flashed gapped teeth, a sinister blend of charm and threat.

At 5'9", Andres carried himself with the quiet strength of a former Special Forces operative. His short, dark hair framed sharp, angular features, and his soulful brown eyes burned with focus. A neatly trimmed mustache and slight stubble roughened his otherwise polished look, and his casual jacket clung to his athletic build.

Beside him, Glen was a towering presence at 6'2", his linebacker frame radiating power. His black skin gleamed under the parking lot lights, his cropped hair nearly shaved, and a full beard softening his otherwise intimidating demeanor. His southern drawl cut through the silence as he called out.

"What's this all about, huh?" Glen's voice boomed, steady and accusing. "You chasing that woman like there's a race and you're in second place."

Kage slowed, turning with a feigned look of confusion. "I'm never in second place," he said, his voice smooth, accented faintly with something unplaceable. "I'm enjoying the scenery. Beautiful falls, yes? You two should relax and enjoy the view."

"Bullshit," Andres snapped, stepping forward. "We know who you are, Kage. You've been tailing Gabby all day. What the hell do you want with her?"

Kage's smile widened, though his eyes remained cold.

"You've got me all wrong. I don't know this...Gabby, you say? I'm on a brief business trip from Tokyo."

Glen crossed his massive arms, his stare unyielding. "Don't play dumb with us. We've been one step behind you since we landed this morning. You're messing with the wrong folks."

Andres and Glen had flown in from Bagram that morning, a grueling 12.5-hour haul on a C-5 Galaxy. They had been lucky the flight refueled midair, avoiding a layover in Germany. The jet stream had shaved off an additional hour, landing them at McChord Air Force Base midmorning.

They hadn't showered and only raced through a McDonald's drive-thru to get from the airbase to TechCom as quickly as possible. Their former squadmate Maxx had asked them to protect Gabby at all costs. He couldn't return to Seattle and asked Andres and Glen to find her. Maxx wasn't the type to ask for favors lightly—he'd saved their lives more times than they could count. In the past week, Gabby had been almost killed twice, and Maxx didn't think any of it was a coincidence. He didn't believe in coincidences.

When Andres rushed into Gabby's office this morning, she had vanished earlier, leaving a cryptic message on the whiteboard. Now, here they were, facing down this scar-faced pendejo who didn't know what he'd stumbled into. Or maybe he did and didn't care.

Andres jabbed a finger toward Kage. "You don't want to get crossways with her boyfriend, trust me. He'll shoot first and sort out the mess later. And Glen and I aren't much nicer. Walk away, Kage."

Kage's politeness thinned, his voice dropping to a hiss. "You should stay out of my business, little man." He nodded at Glen. "And you don't scare me. Back off, or you'll regret it."

He drew a knife from his sleeve, the blade glinting wickedly. Andres and Glen froze. Kage's movements were lightning fast. Their hands hovered near their concealed weapons, but neither drew—a standoff. Kage's eyes flicked between them, calculating.

"Hey!" a gruff voice interrupted. A groundskeeper, bundled in a heavy jacket, shuffled toward them from the lodge entrance. "What's going on here? Take it somewhere else!"

Kage seized the distraction, bolting toward the shadows. Andres cursed under his breath. "Glen, we can't let him—"

"Gabby!" Glen pointed. She'd reappeared, darting toward the steep stairs leading down to the bottom of the falls. They hesitated, torn between the fleeing Kage and the person they were supposed to protect. If Kage got away, he'd be even more dangerous now that he knew they were on to him. They wouldn't see him coming next time.

The area around Snoqualmie Falls was a postcard of Pacific Northwest beauty, even in the dim light of early March. The falls thundered 268 feet into the river below, mist rising into the crisp air and clinging to the evergreens—Douglas firs and cedars—that framed the scene. Beautiful, but a sense of menace hung heavy in the mist.

The stairs Gabby raced toward descended sharply from the lodge's overlook, a winding path into the dark, damp trail below. Andres and Glen stood at the edge, their boots crunching on gravel, torn between their quarry and mission.

"She's heading down there," Glen said, his voice tight. "We have to get her before she's gone."

Andres's gaze flicked to Kage, who'd slipped through the parking lot and reached the valet stand at the front of the hotel. The slim man shoved the attendant aside, snatching keys from the board and leaping onto a sleek black motorcycle. "Hey!" the valet shouted, stumbling back as Kage revved the engine, the roar cutting through the night. He pointed a finger at the kid like a gun, silencing him, then peeled out.

"Damn it!" Andres growled. "I'll follow Kage. You get Gabby."

Glen nodded. His massive frame was already moving. "Be careful, man. That snake's slippery and has some nasty moves." He vanished down the trail after Gabby, swallowed quickly by the shadows and mist.

Andres sprinted to the valet, who was still reeling. "Car—now!" he barked. The kid fumbled, pointing to a silver Toyota minivan idling nearby. Andres slid behind the wheel, the engine humming as he floored it after Kage. The road from the lodge to the Snoqualmie Depot was a short, scenic stretch along Railroad Avenue—barely over a mile—but at night, with speeds climbing, it felt like a gauntlet.

The minivan's tires squealed as he pushed it past sixty mph, far beyond the thirty-five-mph speed limit. The Cascade foothills loomed on either side, dark and dense, the Snoqualmie River a shadowy ribbon to his left. Mist from the falls hung in the air, slicking the pavement. He passed the park entrance then the small bridge over the river, the water's rush a dull roar beneath him. Ahead, Kage's motorcycle wove dangerously, its taillight a red, unblinking eye in the night.

Focus, Andres, he told himself, hands gripping the wheel. *This guy's fast, but you've got the edge. You know these roads. Don't let him get away*. His mind raced. Maxx trusted him with Gabby. Now she was out there with Glen while Kage slipped through his fingers. What was he after? Why her? The uncertainty gnawed at him, but he shoved it down. He was missing some significant puzzle pieces, but this was the time for action, not questions.

The train depot came into view, its steep-roofed silhouette stark against the sky. Kage was heading straight for it. Andres gritted his teeth. *Not tonight, you spooky son of a bitch.*

The Northwest Railway Depot loomed ahead, a relic of 1890 with its wooden facade and steep roof. Beyond it stretched the railroad, its historic coaches silent in the off-season night. Andres closed the gap when Kage slipped on the wet road, the

Toyota's engine screaming as he bore down on Kage. The motorcycle swerved, but Andres didn't hesitate. He jerked the wheel, slamming the car's front end into Kage's rear tire.

The bike spun out, skidding across the pavement in a shower of sparks before crashing into a cluster of outdoor train exhibits near the depot. Andres slammed on the brakes, the minivan fishtailing to a stop. He leaped out, heart pounding, and approached the wreckage. Kage sprawled beside the twisted motorcycle, motionless. *He's hurt*, Andres thought, adrenaline spiking. *Maybe dead.*

He edged closer, wary. "Kage? You done, or do you want me to call the police?"

Kage moved fast. He sprang up, grinning that shark-like grin, and lunged. Andres barely registered the knife before it plunged into his side, a searing jolt of pain that buckled his knees. He hit the ground hard, blood pooling beneath him, warm and sticky on the cold, wet ground.

Kage loomed over him, laughing—a low, guttural sound. "Live long enough to die slow, little man. I warned you I would never come in second place." He jumped into the open door of the minivan, put it in drive, and spun around back toward the falls, leaving Andres gasping on the pavement.

Pain radiated through him, sharp and relentless. *I've failed*, he thought, staring at the clouds. *Gabby's out there, and Maxx... I let him down.* His vision blurred, the lights fading as blood soaked his jacket. *Everyone I love...I couldn't protect them.* He swallowed the lump in his throat. The sound of the minivan's engine faded, masked by the mist, replaced by the distant rush of the falls. Andres's world slipped into darkness.

8

(IN)DECISIONS

The increasingly frigid air bit at Maxx's lungs as he pressed forward through the labyrinthine tunnels beneath the Afghan mountains.

For hours, Maxx, Sergeant Zeller, and their Green Beret team had pursued Taliban fighters deeper into the cavern system after breaching their outer defenses. Dust clung to their sweat-streaked faces, and the weight of exhaustion dragged at their limbs.

The tunnel widened abruptly, and a sliver of sunlight pierced the gloom ahead. Maxx squinted as the team emerged into a small, jagged chamber where the ceiling had collapsed, exposing a patch of open sky. The sudden brightness felt like another world after hours underground. His cell phone, silent and useless in the tunnels, erupted in a cacophony of beeps and vibrations, startling the team. A dozen messages and texts flooded in, the device shaking in his gloved hand.

He scrolled quickly. Nothing from Gabby. His heart sank at the emptiness. A terse text from Andres caught his eye. "We're in Seattle, trying to locate Gabby. Don't worry. We'll find her." What the hell did that mean? Was she missing? Hurt? Before he could process it, a slew of missed calls from Weih popped up. As he began to dial him back, the phone rang. Weih's name flashing on the screen.

"Maxx, thank God," Weih's voice crackled through, tight with urgency. "Where have you been?"

"Up to my neck fighting in these damn tunnels," Maxx answered, wiping sweat from his brow. "It's been a real picnic. What's your sitrep? You still got those canisters?"

"Yeah, still got them," Weih said. "We hauled them into a cave like you told me to, defensive perimeter and all. We contacted an S&R team eight hours ago—they were on their way cross-country. But they never showed up. No word, nothing. Ghosted us."

Maxx frowned, glancing at Zeller, who stood nearby, cradling his weapon and listening intently. "What happened?"

"No clue," Weih admitted. "Since then, it's been chaos out here. It feels like we're in the eye of a hurricane with action all around us, but we're in some kind of pocket. F-14s and F-18s have been pounding the entire valley. I don't know who they're providing close air support to, but it isn't us. My scouts have been spotting movement in the hillsides all morning. Shadows, figures, but they don't get close. Weird as hell, Maxx. Can't tell if they're ours, Taliban, or...something else."

Maxx's gut tightened. "What are you saying?"

"I don't know, man," Weih said, frustrated. "The lookouts are telling me they don't move right, but they can't get a bead on them. I've tried calling you, Command, or anyone a dozen times, but no connection. Why's it working now?"

Maxx stared up at the open sky, the signal finally free of the tunnel's chokehold. "We hit a break in the rock. It's the first light we've seen in hours. What do you need, John? Lay it out."

Weih hesitated. "We're sitting ducks with these canisters. Do we wait longer? Take them and run? Make a break for it? I need a call, Maxx. I'm in way over my head."

Maxx's mind raced. Those canisters—he didn't know their contents, but Miss Grey's cryptic warnings echoed in his head. A virus, she'd said, meant for the Others. A failsafe designed to stop the invasion of the Others if Operation Anaconda failed. Had Weih's team stumbled onto it? Were they exposed? His judgment screamed to double back and secure the canisters, but Smith, the mad scientist they'd chased for hours, was still ahead, and Grey's life hung in the balance. The longer he delayed, the slimmer her chances.

"Maxx?" Weih pressed. "You still there?"

"Yeah," Maxx said, voice low. "Hide the canisters, John. Bury them deep in a cave, somewhere no one'll stumble onto them. Don't tell a soul but me where they are. No one but me and a priest if you're getting last rites."

"You're scaring me, Maxx," Weih said. "What did I get caught up in?"

"I'll tell you when this is over and we can laugh about it over a beer. Going or staying is your call. Hold the line or get to Command. Either way, you're in deep shit. I can't get to you fast enough. Sorry, brother."

A long pause. "You're leaving us out here?"

"I don't have a choice," Maxx snapped, guilt clawing at him. "I'm sorry, man. I hate this situation as much as you do. There's no good play. Keep your ass down and stay frosty."

The line went dead. Maxx shoved the phone into his vest, cursing under his breath. Zeller stepped closer, his weathered face creased with concern. "What's your plan, King?"

Maxx exhaled sharply, staring at the tunnel ahead. "Lieutenant Weih's pinned down with some weird munitions that I might or might not know something about. If it's what I think it is, he's in a mess of epic proportions. But Smith's still in the wind, and Grey's running out of time. This is way past the usual snafu, Zeller."

He spat into the dirt. "These mysterious munitions might be

a significant part of this mess. Do you think they're worth Weih dying over?"

"Rationally, yeah," Maxx said, rubbing his jaw. "Biggest immediate risk or reward if they're what I think. But my gut's pulling me after Smith. Finish this, save Grey. I can't save everybody, and it's pissing me off."

Zeller nodded slowly. "Gut's rarely wrong. What'd you tell Weih?"

"Hide them and hold or run. He's screwed either way." Maxx's voice broke. "I'm struggling here, man. My girl's disappeared in Seattle, Grey's dead or being dragged around by a psycho, and now this fiasco with Weih. I've got no one I can work out the angles with."

Zeller's eyes narrowed. "You got me, Cowboy. Spill it. What's going on?"

Maxx hesitated then let it pour out. "Those things that killed the Talibs back there? They're real. Aliens, Zeller. That's what we're up against. I sound crazy for saying this, but I mean to settle it. We might not walk out of here."

Zeller didn't flinch. He adjusted his grip on his rifle. "Aliens, huh? Figures it'd be something batshit. So we're up the creek, no paddle?"

"Pretty much," Maxx said, a thin smile tugging at his lips. "Except if I'm going down, I'm going out with a bang. No matter what it costs. But I don't expect you and your guys to go Leroy Jenkins with me. No one will hold it against you if you walk, especially now that you know the score."

"We're not leaving the party without you," Zeller replied, clapping Maxx's shoulder. "Smith's ahead. Let's get the SOB."

Maxx nodded, shoving his doubts aside. The sunlight above felt like a cruel tease—a fleeting glimpse of a world he might never see again. He took a deep breath of the cold mountain air and turned back into the tunnel's gloom, chasing the enemy, Grey, and a fate he couldn't seem to escape.

The team pressed on, the echo of their boots an unsteady drumbeat in the dark. Maxx's mind churned. Gabby's silence gnawed at him, Andres's vague text a splinter he couldn't get out of his head. Seattle was a world away, yet it tethered him, breaking his focus. He pictured her face, smiling and fearless, and wondered if she'd slipped beyond his reach. And Grey was somewhere in these mountains, and every second lost brought her closer to death.

"King," Zeller's voice broke through. "You good?"

"No," Maxx admitted, eyes fixed ahead, "but I'll be better when Smith's dead."

Zeller chuckled darkly. "That's the spirit."

Minutes bled into one another as they continued to track their quarry. The tunnel twisted, narrowed, and then widened again, the air growing colder. Maxx's phone stayed silent now, its brief lifeline severed by stone. Weih's fate weighed on him. Had he hidden the canisters? Held the line? Or was he already gone, swallowed by the chaos?

"Zeller," Maxx said suddenly, slowing his pace, "if those canisters are the virus, and the Others get 'em..."

"We're toast," Zeller finished. "Humanity's toast."

"Yeah." Maxx's jaw tightened. "But if we stop Smith and get Grey, maybe we buy time." Command can send another team for Weih."

"Big if," Zeller said. "You sure about this?"

"No, but it's what we've got."

Zeller grunted in agreement, and they pushed deeper. The tunnel grew tighter, forcing them to crouch, their rifles scraping against the rock. Maxx's thoughts drifted to what Weih had said. *Weird sightings, movement that didn't feel human.* The Others were close. He could sense it in the prickling at his neck. Were they attacking?

Distant shouts snapped him alert—Farsi voices, Anderson's mixed in among them. Maxx signaled the team, adrenaline surging. This was it. Weih or not, he'd finish what he started. For Gabby. For Grey. For whatever shred of humanity still clung to this war-torn hell.

"Ready?" he whispered to Zeller.

"We're locked and loaded," Zeller shot back.

Maxx took a deep breath, then charged toward the sound, deeper into the mountain.

***

The cold March air nipped at Andres's exposed skin as he sprawled on the damp ground near the Snoqualmie train depot, the twisted wreckage of a sleek, black motorcycle a few yards away. Blood seeped from a deep wound in his side, staining the pavement beneath him. His breaths came in shallow, ragged gasps, his vision alternating between darkness and a gauzy haze. He didn't hear the soft footsteps approaching until a shadow loomed over him.

"Oh my goodness," a woman gasped. Marge Beckman knelt beside him, middle-aged with graying hair framing a friendly face, her nurse's instincts kicking in. She worked at the emergency room at the nearby Swedish Hospital and had seen her share of trauma, but finding a man bleeding out by the depot wasn't how she'd expected her evening walk to end. "Hold on, honey. You're hurt bad."

Andres groaned, his mind sluggish. Pain throbbed through his body, sharp and relentless. "What...happened?" he mumbled, blinking up at her.

"You tell me," Marge said, digging through her purse for anything useful. She pulled out some gauze pads she kept for emergencies with the grandchildren and pressed them tightly against the wound. "Looks like you crashed your motorcycle on the wet roads, but this puncture... It's deep, almost like a stab wound. You're lucky it missed an artery by a hair, but you've still lost a lot of blood. Too much." She frowned, her hands steady despite the urgency. "I don't have my phone. We need to get you to a hospital fast."

Memories flickered back to Andres in jagged pieces. He'd been chasing Torashi Kage, the Japanese assassin, through the winding roads near Snoqualmie. Torashi had stolen the motorcycle back at the Salish Lodge, weaving recklessly until he lost control and crashed. Andres had stopped, thinking the man was dead. But Torashi wasn't dead, faking it. He'd sprung up lightning fast, blade flashing in the dim light. As fast as Andres was, he hadn't reacted in time. The knife plunged into his side, and Torashi had left him there to die, a smirk on his angular face.

"I want you to die slowly, little one," Torashi had said, his voice cold and clipped. But he'd severely misjudged Andres.

Andres clenched his teeth against the pain, gritting out, "Gabby... He's after Gabby."

Marge's brow furrowed. "Who is Gabby?" She looked around in horror, thinking she'd missed another rider in the accident.

"Oh, she's not here," Andres murmured when he saw the look on her face.

Before she could respond, headlights cut through the night. A rusty pickup screeched to a halt, and Glen leaped out, his massive frame filling the space. He'd grabbed his truck from the parking lot at Salish Lodge, his face flushed with panic.

"Andres! Man, you're alive!" Glen rushed over, glancing at Marge. "I'm his friend. I'll take him to the hospital."

Marge hesitated, her eyes narrowing. "An ambulance would be better. He's in terrible shape and lost a lot of blood."

"No time," Glen rasped, gripping Andres's arm and pulling him into his arms despite the moans. "We've got to move. He's alright. I've seen him hurt much worse. Faster this way."

Andres barely nodded. "Yeah, he can get me there quicker. Please, lady, trust us. I'm feeling much better. Gracias."

Marge's gaze darted between them, catching the glint of a gun under Glen's jacket. Her lips pressed into a thin line. "You boys mixed up in something illegal, aren't you? I don't like this."

"Please," Andres said, his voice weak but insistent, "we'll be fine. Let him take me."

Reluctantly, Marge stepped back. Glen easily hoisted Andres into the pickup, though he accidentally bumped his friend's head against the passenger door. Andres winced but didn't complain as Glen laid him across the bench seat.

The truck peeled out, spraying gravel, speeding not toward the hospital but in the opposite direction. Marge stood on the corner, shaking her head as they disappeared into the night.

Inside the pickup, Glen's knuckles whitened on the steering wheel. "I lost Gabby, man. She took off through the woods below the falls. She's like greased lightning, and I ain't built for cross-country. I chased her as far as possible, but she hit the hills, and the woods swallowed her up."

Andres shifted, pain shooting through him. "Torashi...did you see him?"

"Nah," Glen said darkly, "or I'd have wrung his skinny neck. Everyone's skinny to me, though." He forced a half grin, but it faded fast. "After I lost Gabby's trail, I went back to the hotel and grabbed my ride. I tried calling you, but there was no answer. I guess you were busy. Valet said you'd headed this way, so I followed."

"We've got to find her," Andres said, his voice tight. "There's no use trying to track her in these woods while it's dark. Let's check the hotel. Maybe she left something in her room."

"No hospitals, though," Glen added. "I'll take you to someone who can patch you up after. Off the books."

They reached Salish Lodge, and the old pickup skidded into the lot and avoided the valet. The lobby was eerily quiet as they staggered inside, Andres leaning heavily on Glen. The desk manager was nowhere to be seen. Glen frowned, peering behind the counter, then cursed under his breath. The manager was tied up in the back room, a purple bruise blooming on his forehead.

"Asian guy jumped me," the man stammered when Glen cut off his gag. "Knocked me out and took some room keys."

"Gabby's room," Andres said, his stomach sinking.

"Help me," the manager pleaded, struggling against the ropes.

"Certainly," Andres said with a groan. "Was he looking for anyone in particular?"

"He was looking for a British woman, probably here by herself."

"Did you tell him where she was?" Glen growled.

The hotel manager gulped. "No, because we don't have any British women staying here. I told him there were several women, but none of them were British. That's why he took all four keys.

Andres raised his eyebrows. "What about a Chinese woman who speaks with a British accent? Is anyone with that description staying here?"

"Oh, you mean Betty Lou." The man shrugged. "She had a British accent but was pretending to be from Texas. Worst accent I've ever heard."

"That's her," Andres said with a lopsided grin. "What room is she in? We need to get to her before he does."

"She's in 214," the manager said. "Now, will you please untie me?"

"No can do," Glen replied, grabbing a spare key for room 214 from the desk.

"Sorry, buddy. We'll let you go soon, but we're on the clock." Ignoring the manager's protests, they turned toward Gabby's room as quickly as Andres could walk.

When they arrived, the door hung ajar. Glen went in first, clearing the space, then waved Andres inside. The room was trashed, Gabby's backpack gutted, clothes and papers strewn across the floor. Amid the chaos, a note was on the bed. "Call me if you want this to end nicely. If you run, they'll find you in pieces."

"Torashi," Andres muttered, clutching his side as he sat heavily on the bed.

They grabbed what was left of Gabby's stuff and headed out. As they hurried past the valet, Glen barked, "Check on your boss back there!" He jumped into the driver's seat. Andres slid carefully into the passenger side, reading off the phone number from the note. He dialed, his hands trembling.

The line clicked, and a familiar voice answered. "Well, well. You're doing the right thing by calling me now, Miss Fisher. Where are you?"

"Torashi," Andres growled. "What do you want with Gabby?"

The assassin chuckled, low and sharp. "Disappointing that it's you on the line. Next time, I won't be so charitable. As for Gabby, she's Maxx's girl, isn't she? I want Maxx. Tell him to meet me—man to man—and I'll leave her be. Otherwise, he'll get her back one part at a time."

Andres exchanged a glance with Glen. "Whatever you're involved with, Kage, I'm warning you, you are in over your head by threatening Maxx."

"Oh, I understand he's a dangerous man," Torashi said, sounding pleased. "That's exactly why I want to meet him. He killed a former colleague of mine. A man I've been trying to kill for many years. I don't like that Mr. King robbed me of that pleasure."

Andres shook his head. "That's insane."

"No, it is a matter of honor. Maxx killed Haoyu, ruining my

chance for revenge. Now, I must exact my revenge on Maxx to complete the circle. It's an elegant ending."

"Enough of this madness," Andres snarled. "Where and when?"

"Fremont Bridge Troll. Ten hours from now," Torashi said. "Tell Mr. King to come alone, or someone dies in his place."

The call ended. Glen's brow creased. "Maxx can't get here by noon. Torashi is going to notice."

"Won't matter," Andres said, his voice hard. "He'll be dead. I'll go in close after I get patched up. It's personal now. You stay on overwatch."

Glen nodded grimly, turning the car toward Seattle and the shadow of the troll.

9

HUSH

Jiang slammed a fist on the desk, the thud echoing like a gunshot. "Enough!" His voice sliced through the stillness, loud and sharp.

The air in General Secretary Jiang Zemin's office crackled with unspoken fury on that biting March evening. Tucked within Zhongnanhai's fortified embrace, the room was a cold testament to power. A hulking desk squatted at its center, strewn with crumpled reports and a single, silent telephone. Bare walls loomed, except for a faded map of China pinned askew behind him—a silent witness to the nation he'd sworn to elevate.

Jiang sat bolt upright, his broad, oval face a mask of weathered resolve framed by thick, black-rimmed glasses that sharpened the glint in his dark, almond-shaped eyes. At seventy-five, his smooth skin bore faint creases—battle scars of decades spent wielding authority—while his high cheekbones and prominent jawline cast a shadow of stern dignity. His thin lips pressed into a hard line, but the fire in his eyes roared with the weight of a decision he could no longer delay.

He slammed a fist on the desk a second time for emphasis.

"I've watched the Americans flail against these damned aliens —Thunderbird, the Others—while we sit here like cowards, waiting for scraps!"

Mr. Fu, his assistant and most trusted bodyguard, stood rigid in the corner, a stiff silhouette with a face pinched tight by years of obedience. He stepped forward, hands clasped behind his back, his voice a cautious murmur. "General Secretary, the XINXI program was meant to—"

"Meant to?" Jiang snapped, cutting him off. He leaned forward, glasses glinting under the harsh light. "It was meant to make us gods among nations, Fu! Advanced weapons, unchallenged power—China leading the world while the Americans bleed out against those invaders. And what do I have instead? Liu's corpse and Xi's treason!"

Fu flinched, though his tone remained steady. "Liu miscalculated, sir. The lies about the earthquake—he thought it would pressure Xi to sway Thunderbird. It backfired."

"Backfired?" Jiang's laugh was a bitter bark. "Thunderbird saw through us—called us liars to our faces! And Xi? Vanished, probably spilling every secret to the Americans as we speak. I should've gutted him myself before he had the chance."

He rose abruptly, scraping the chair against the floor, and paced to the window. Beyond the glass, the red walls of the Zhongnanhai compound, the political heart of the Communist Party of China, stood sentinel under a darkening gray sky, the serene shimmer of its two calm lakes a mockery of the chaos churning within him.

He'd orchestrated this gambit for six months: leverage the alien war, secure their technology, and crown China the preeminent military force. The XINXI program had been his sharp, precise blade aimed at Thunderbird's trust. But mistrust had dulled it, Liu's deceit had snapped it, and Xi's disappearance had buried it. Jiang's patience, once a steel thread, had frayed to a silk strand.

He whirled back to Fu, eyes blazing. "I am done lurking in shadows. I want the Others—their weapons, their alliance. If my staff can't deliver victory, I'll deal with our enemies myself."

Fu's brow creased, a rare crack in his composure. "The Others, sir? After Xi's failure, the team was in disarray. Shu's barely settled in as the new lab leader. He might not—"

"Might not?" Jiang's voice dropped to a dangerous growl. "I don't reward for 'might not,' Fu. I want results, not whining. Make the arrangements. We're going to the XINXI lab. Now."

Fu straightened, nodding briskly. "At once, General Secretary. I'll ensure the route's clear."

Jiang grabbed his jacket, his movements sharp with purpose. "And Fu," he added, pausing at the door, "if anyone dares to stall me down there, you know what to do. I'm through with these childish games."

Fu's lips quivered—a ghost of a grimace—before he replied, "Understood, Chairman. They'll answer, or they'll bleed."

Jiang stormed out, Fu trailing like a shadow, the weight of his ambition a storm brewing in his wake. Zhongnanhai's corridors swallowed them, leading toward a reckoning no one could escape.

The Zhongnanhai compound, a sprawling fortress of red walls and barbed wire west of the Forbidden City, was a labyrinth of history and secrecy. Its two lakes, Zhonghai and Nanhai, darkened under the March sunset, their peaceful beauty a vivid contrast to the guarded tension within. Huairen Hall loomed in the distance, its traditional pavilion roof a reminder of imperial legacies, while Xinhua Gate stood as the ceremonial threshold to China's political heart.

Beneath it all, rumors whispered of tunnels and bunkers, a subterranean network born of Cold War paranoia and modern necessity. No one outside the inner circle knew the truth, but Jiang moved with the confidence of a man who held its secrets.

The journey to the XINXI lab took them deep underground

through reinforced corridors lit by harsh fluorescent lights. The air grew cooler and heavier as they descended.

Jiang's mind churned. Liu's execution had been a necessity. Failure could not be tolerated, but Xi's disappearance gnawed at him. Had he misjudged the scientist? No matter. The Others, the rival alien faction, might yet be the key. If his underlings couldn't deliver Thunderbird's trust, perhaps direct communication with their enemies would yield results. He needed someone competent, someone who wouldn't cower or deceive him.

The lab was a sterile chamber of gleaming metal and blinking consoles, dominated by the alien communication device—a hulking, metallic-looking cube. Its surface shimmered faintly with a greenish tint as if it were alive. It had a smooth, sinister appearance, seeming to absorb all light, giving it an eerie, otherworldly presence.

Standing beside the apparatus was Dr. Shu, the new project leader. He was a thin man with sharp features and an air of quiet arrogance. He turned as Jiang and Fu entered, offering a curt bow.

"General Secretary," Dr. Shu said, his tone clipped. "I wasn't informed of your visit."

"I don't require your permission to inspect my program," Jiang replied, his eyes narrowing. "Liu failed me. Xi betrayed me. I want results, not excuses. I must speak to the Others directly."

Dr. Shu's lips twitched, a flicker of condescension crossing his face. "That's not how it works, General Secretary. The device isn't a telephone. We're still deciphering its functions. Xi's notes were incomplete, and the risks—"

"Silence!" Jiang's voice cracked like a whip, silencing the room. The handful of technicians at their stations froze, eyes darting nervously. "I don't care for your lectures. I want it done."

Shu straightened, his tone growing colder. "With respect, General Secretary, you don't understand the complexities. Forcing it could destabilize the entire system. We could lose everything."

Jiang's gaze darkened. He turned his head slightly toward Mr. Fu, a silent signal. Before Shu could react, Fu lunged forward with startling speed, seizing the scientist by the throat.

A choked gasp escaped Shu as Fu drove a concealed blade into his chest, twisting it with brutal precision. Blood splattered across the tile floor, and Shu crumpled, lifeless, his arrogance extinguished in an instant. The technicians recoiled, stifling cries of horror.

Jiang stepped over the body, his expression unchanged. "Who here can tell me what's possible, not what I cannot do? Think carefully before you answer."

A woman stepped out from the darkness of the lab—a woman, middle-aged, with a calm demeanor that belied the chaos around her. Dr. Fang Lizhi adjusted her glasses and met Jiang's stare without flinching. "I can, General Secretary. I've studied Xi's work. The device can be activated, but it will take time to calibrate. There's a risk—an earthquake, potentially catastrophic. Xi warned of it."

Jiang tilted his head, considering her. "Is this lab earthquake-proof?"

"Yes," Dr. Fang replied. "Reinforced to withstand cataclysmic seismic activity."

"Then do it," Jiang said, his voice low and steady. "Damn the consequences."

Dr. Fang hesitated only a moment before nodding. She moved to the console, her fingers flying across the controls as she initiated the emergency contact override Dr. Xi had designed before his departure—a desperate measure meant as a last resort to initiate contact. Without the override, communication could only occur at a time designated in advance by the Others.

However, the override had never been tested. It was theoretically impossible to initiate contact, and therefore it violated the operating procedures provided to the XINXI team by the Others. The team was well aware that the one time the protocols had been disregarded was in Tangshan. That neglect had resulted in a massive earthquake.

The device hummed to life. Technicians exchanged panicked glances, but Fang remained focused, her voice steady as she barked orders.

Dr. Fang's fingers danced across the console, and with a decisive flick, the alien communication device shuddered awake. A ripple of light erupted from its flat surfaces, ceiling lights igniting in a cascade of pulsing colors. Deep blue bleeding into fiery red then fading to an unearthly violet. The patterns swirled and shifted, not mere decoration but a visual code, signaling the device's link to the alien network. A chill seeped from its metal shell, the surface cooling so sharply that condensation beaded on its edges, stark against the lab's sterile warmth. Jiang stepped closer, his breath visible in the sudden drop, his eyes narrowing as he tracked every flicker.

"Move faster!" he barked, his voice penetrating through the hum that now trembled from the device—a low, resonant vibration that thrummed through the floor and up the spines of everyone present. The air thickened, charged with a prickling energy, like the prelude to a thunderstorm. A faint trace of ozone curled into the room, sharp and electric, conjuring memories of rain-soaked summers laced with something otherworldly.

Technicians flinched, their panicked glances darting between the device and Jiang, whose presence loomed larger than the machine itself.

"Power levels rising," Fang reported, her voice taut but

steady as she wrestled with the controls. "Power stabilizers holding—for now." Her focus never wavered, though her knuckles whitened against the console's edge.

The device's hum deepened into a rhythmic rumble, a sound felt in the chest as much as heard, its cadence pulsing like a heartbeat—or a language. Jiang tilted his head, straining to decipher it, his fists clenching as time seemed to stretch. Seconds dragged into eternity, the lab suspended in a surreal haze where every breath felt borrowed.

A technician stumbled back, clutching his head, his whisper barely audible. "It's... It's too much." Another froze, wide-eyed, caught between awe and dread as the lights bathed his face in shifting hues.

Jiang whirled on Fang, his glasses glinting with the device's glow. "Is it working? Tell me now!" His tone was a whip, snapping through the charged air.

"Yes," Fang shot back, her voice rising to meet his. "It seems to be connecting, but it's unstable. Xi's override is pushing it too hard!"

The vibrations sharpened, rattling tools off tables and sending a glass beaker crashing to the floor. The ozone stench grew pungent, stinging the nostrils, while the light patterns accelerated into a frenetic dance. Jiang's pulse quickened, his mind racing with the stakes—China's dominance, his legacy, teetering on this alien brink. He slammed a hand on the console beside Fang, leaning in close. "Make it obey me, Fang! I want to speak to the Others—now!"

Her eyes flicked to him, a flicker of fear hidden beneath her determination, but the rumble spiked into a guttural roar before she could answer. The floor lurched, a crack splitting the concrete as the device's power surged beyond containment. Technicians screamed, scrambling for cover, while Fang gripped the console, her voice a desperate shout over the chaos. "It's overloading! Hold on!"

Jiang stood unshaken, his gaze locked on the device, its light searing into his vision as the lab trembled on the edge of collapse.

***

The lab steadied, its reinforced walls groaning faintly as the tremors subsided.

Once a shrieking tempest of light and sound, the alien communication device fell eerily quiet—yet it wasn't dormant. Its surface dimmed to a soft glow, green and yellow lights flickering along what might have been a control band, and a steady hum betrayed its persistent draw of power. Dust hung in the air, mingling with the sharp ozone stench, while shattered glass crunched underfoot. The technicians huddled near the walls, their faces pale, but Jiang stood unbowed, his gaze fixed on the machine.

"What's happening?" he demanded, his voice a blade slicing through the silence. He rounded on Dr. Fang, who leaned against the console, wiping sweat from her brow. "It's stopped. Why isn't it dead?"

Fang straightened, her glasses catching the device's faint light as she studied the readouts. "I don't know," she admitted, her tone clipped but unshaken. "It's still active, drawing power, stable for now. The indicators are green and yellow, meaning it's on standby, waiting for something, but I can't say what."

Jiang's eyes narrowed, his thin lips curling into a snarl. "Can't say? I don't have time for your ignorance, Fang." He stepped closer, looming over her. "You have one hour to make contact—or Fu will slit your throat. I'm done with failures."

Fang met his stare, her calm unshaken by the threat. "Go ahead and kill me," she said, her voice steady, almost mocking. "Then who will run it for you? Mr. Fu? One of these trembling wrecks?" She gestured at the technicians, who shrank further into the shadows. "You've lost Xi. Liu's dead. Can you afford to lose me, too? Kill me after it works, if you must. But I will know I died honorably."

Jiang's jaw tightened, his fists clenching, but before he could retort, the device jolted. Jiang watched, arms crossed, his composure unshaken even as the floor trembled faintly beneath his feet. Mr. Fu stood nearby, still wiping Shu's blood from his hands with a cloth, his face impassive.

"Contact established," Fang said suddenly, her eyes widening as she studied the readouts. "It's the Others. They're responding."

A distorted voice crackled through the device, guttural and alien yet somehow intelligible. "Who dares summon us?"

Jiang stepped forward, his voice cutting through the tension. "I am Jiang Zemin, leader of China. We wish to be your allies."

The voice paused, then laughed—a harsh, grating sound. "You think us fools? Your kind betrays at every turn. We see your ambition, human. It will be your ruin."

The fluorescent lights flared anew, a pulse of deep green washing over the lab as the hum surged into a rhythmic growl. The air crackled, time stretching once more, and a guttural voice erupted from the machine, cold and alien. "Where is Xi?"

Jiang shoved past Fang, planting himself next to the device. "I am the leader of China. Xi is my underling."

The voice rasped, "We will speak with you temporarily until he returns. Do not contact us again without Xi present, or we will end this."

Jiang's pulse quickened, but he pressed on. "Will you honor my request for an alliance?"

"We have lost our coordinator in the desert mountains," the Others replied, their tone shifting to a grudging edge. "For this, we bargain. Normally, your impudence would earn immediate destruction."

"What do you want to bargain?" Jiang asked, his voice firm, sensing an opening.

"Intervene," the voice commanded. "Stop the Americans and Thunderbird from their assault in the desert war. Do this, and we grant you the weapons and power we intended for Doctor Smith—their strength, your gain. Refuse, and we will initiate an earthquake to bury you and your people. A deal you cannot refuse."

Jiang's mind raced, ambition flaring at the promise of power, but caution tempered his reply. "I'll consider it...if you give me assurances."

"None," the Others snapped. "You have twenty of our solar cycles to decide. Answer then or face ruin."

Fang interjected, her voice low as she glanced at the console. "That's roughly thirty-six hours, General Secretary."

The device's light winked out, the hum fading to a whisper as the connection severed. Silence crashed over the lab, broken only by Jiang's sharp intake of breath. He turned, his face a storm of anger and exhilaration—fury at their insolence, excitement at the prize within reach. His glasses glinted as he paced, muttering, "A day and a half to bend the world to my will. Or break it."

Fang watched Jiang, her expression unreadable, arms crossed. Doubt flickered in her eyes, a subtle tightening of her lips betraying her skepticism. He spied the reluctance, pausing mid-step. Could she be trusted? Xi had fled, and Liu had faltered. Fang was his last thread to this alien power, but her calm defiance gnawed at him. He needed her, for now. But after?

His gaze hardened, a decision simmering as the lab's shadows deepened around them. *The game is far from over.*

10

HERE TO REMIND YOU

"I need to rest for a moment," Li Jing snapped at the guide as she crawled forward.

The air in the cave was thick with dust and the sour tang of sweat. Li Jing's boots scraped against the jagged stone as she crawled through the narrow tunnel, her knees raw after so many hours of navigating this labyrinth. Behind her, Doctor Smith grunted, his breath uneven. Faraj, his other assistant, moved with infuriating ease ahead of them, his wiry frame slipping through the tight passages like a shadow.

The Taliban guide muttered curses in Pashto, his voice echoing off the damp walls. They'd been lost for hours, circling back on their tracks after the Others attacked. No one knew why the aliens had turned on them. Smith's personal communication device, a small metallic cube of tech meant to connect him to the Others, had gone silent. He had communicated his suspicions about the Americans sabotaging the main relay, imagining that it was likely only a temporary setback.

Li Jing's chest tightened as she glanced back at Smith. His face, illuminated by the flickering glow of their headlamps, was etched with exhaustion. She wanted to ask him what he was hiding—why he'd been so distant since the firefight with the American forces—but the words stuck in her throat. Instead, she pressed on, her distrust throbbing like an open wound.

Faraj's presence didn't help. She could feel his eyes on her, judging her, mocking her silently. She imagined driving her knife into his smug throat and watching the light leave his eyes. The thought steadied her, if only momentarily.

They'd stopped long ago to rest, huddled against the cold stone, eating scraps of stale bread and sipping from dwindling canteens. Now, hours later, the guide promised they were close to an exit. But he reminded them that the path outside the tunnels involved treacherous cliffside trails. Days more, he'd said. And their food and ammo were already dangerously low.

Li Jing's stomach growled, but her hunger was nothing compared to the ache in her heart. She needed Smith to see her, really see her—not as his assassin, his collaborator, but as something more. Her father, Dr. Xi, had abandoned her years ago, leaving her with nothing but a void she'd spent her life trying to fill. Smith was her anchor now, her purpose. She'd kill for him, die for him. But did he feel the same? She knew she was exhausted, and this was not the time or place for this conversation, but she couldn't stop.

"Smith," she said, her voice sharp in the confined space, "how much longer are we going to trust this guide? He's leading us in circles."

Smith wiped the sweat from his brow, his gray eyes meeting hers briefly before darting away. "He knows these caves better than we do, Li Jing. We don't have a choice."

"Don't we?" She stopped crawling, forcing him to halt behind her. "You've been quiet all day. What aren't you telling me?"

Faraj turned back, his dark eyes glinting with something she couldn't place. "Maybe he's tired of your nagging, Li Jing. Not everything's a conspiracy."

"Shut your mouth," she snapped, her hand twitching toward the knife at her hip. "I wasn't talking to you."

Smith sighed, his voice low and measured. "Quiet, both of you. We're all on edge. Let's keep moving."

But she didn't budge. "No, I need to know where we stand, Smith. After everything I've done for you—for us—are you still with me? Or are you planning to leave me behind like everyone else?"

The words hung heavily in the air. Smith's jaw tightened, but he didn't answer right away. Faraj snorted, and from somewhere behind them, the Taliban soldiers laughed, their raspy voices bouncing off the walls.

"Listen to her," one of them said in broken English. "Weak woman, whining like a child."

Li Jing's face burned, her fingers curling into fists. She wanted to scream, to lunge at them, but Smith's hand on her leg stopped her.

"Ignore them," he said quietly. "We've got bigger problems."

She shook him off, her voice trembling. "I need to hear it from you, Smith. Are you with me or not?"

He looked at her then, really looked at her, and for a fleeting moment she thought she saw something soften in his gaze. But then he turned away. "We'll talk later. Keep moving."

The rebuke stung more than she'd expected. She crawled on, her mind racing. He was pulling away—she could feel it. And Faraj, that snake, was weaseling closer to Smith's side. She'd seen how they whispered when they thought she wasn't listening. Her jealousy flared hot and bitter.

Hours later, they reached a wider chamber with a high enough ceiling to stand. Li Jing stretched her aching limbs, her eyes never leaving Faraj as he set down his pack. He caught her staring and smirked.

"What's the matter, Li Jing? You look like you want to say something."

She stepped nearer, her voice low and venomous. "I see you, Faraj. Playing the loyal dog, thinking you can take my place. You're nothing."

He laughed loudly enough to draw Smith's attention. "Your place? You're delusional. Smith keeps you around because you're useful, not because he wants you."

The words hit like a slap. Before she could think, she lunged, tackling him to the ground. Her fists flew, slamming into his chest, his face. He grunted, trying to shove her off, but she was relentless—until Smith's voice cut through the haze.

"Li Jing, stop it!"

Strong hands yanked her back. She stumbled, panting, as Smith stepped between them. Faraj wiped blood from his lip, glaring at her.

"What the hell is wrong with you?" Smith demanded. He grabbed her pistol from its holster and her knife from her sheath. He handed them to one of the soldiers. "You're out of control. I can't trust you with these right now."

Her chest heaved, tears prickling at the corners of her eyes. "You're taking Faraj's side? After everything I've done for you?"

"I'm not taking sides," he said, his tone cold. "I'm trying to keep us alive. You're making that harder."

The soldiers snickered again, and Faraj's smug look was unbearable. She turned away, her hands shaking. Smith didn't trust her. He was favoring Faraj, as she'd feared. The betrayal cut deep, reopening old wounds left by her father's departure.

Later, as they rested again, Smith pulled her aside. The others were out of earshot. Their headlamps dimmed as the batteries ran low. He looked weary, older than she'd ever seen him.

"Jing," he said softly, "I need to tell you something. Once we're out of these caves, I'll have to go away for a while. Alone. But I'll come back for you."

She searched his face, her heart sinking. He was lying—she

could hear it in the faint tremor of his voice, see it in the way his eyes wouldn't meet hers.

"Don't lie to me, Smith. I can tell you're not coming back."

He hesitated then shook his head. "It's not like that. I need you to trust me."

"Trust you?" Her laugh was bitter. "You're abandoning me, like he did."

"Who?"

"My father," she spat. "Dr. Xi. He left me, and now you're doing the same. I've given you everything—my loyalty, my love —and it's still not enough."

Smith's expression hardened. "This isn't about you, Li Jing. It's about the mission. The Others, the Americans—they're closing in. I have to move quickly, or I will be replaced. It may already be too late."

"Then take me with you," she pleaded, stepping closer. "I can't stay behind. I won't."

"I can't," he said, and the finality in his voice shattered something inside her.

She stumbled back, her mind spiraling. He was leaving her. After all she'd done—killing for him, following him into this pit—he was casting her aside. The void yawned wider, swallowing her whole. She couldn't live without him. She wouldn't.

At the next stop, as the others slept, she cornered him again. Her voice was steady, but her eyes were wild. "Smith, listen to me. You take me with you, or I end it here. Right now, in these caves, I'll put a bullet in my head, and you'll have to carry that."

He stared at her, disbelief flickering across his face. "Jing, you don't mean that."

"I do," she said, her hand hovering near the knife strapped inside her shirt—the one they hadn't taken. "Choose. Me or nothing."

For a long moment, he said nothing. Then he turned away, his silence louder than any words. She watched him go, her heart breaking, her resolve hardening. The caves stretched endlessly before her, but all she saw was the edge of a cliff—and the choice she needed to make.

***

The Bigfoot Java coffee shop glowed faintly in the pre-dawn gloom, its neon sign flickering at 5:30 a.m.

Torashi sat at a corner table, his sharp eyes scanning the near-empty room. The quirky name grated on him, a petty irritation atop a mountain of frustrations. He'd been up all night, tracking leads that went nowhere, and now he nursed a cup of tea that tasted like seawater. His fingers tapped the table, a rare sign of the agitation simmering beneath his calm exterior. A seasoned assassin, Torashi prided himself on his discipline—years of espionage and close combat had honed him into a weapon of precision, but that calm was fraying this morning.

The barista, an awkward kid with a patchy beard and Carhartt beanie, shuffled over, wiping his hands on a stained apron. "You want a refill or what?"

Torashi's gaze flicked up, cold and cutting. "If you could make it right the first time, I wouldn't need another. This isn't tea. It's an insult."

The kid blinked, taken aback. "Uh, sorry, man. We don't get many orders for tea. I can try again—"

"Forget it," Torashi snapped, waving him off. "Stay away from me."

The barista muttered something under his breath and retreated. Torashi exhaled slowly, refocusing his attention on the mission.

Senator Jane Traficant and Colonel Hanssen had tasked him with hunting down Mr. Green, the rogue scientist who'd fled the Tacoma facility with encrypted data. They hadn't told him what the data included, but it must have been worth a fortune if Traficant had been personally involved. The decryption key was his target, along with Green's silence. But the pursuit had yielded nothing but dead ends, and the dishonor of failure gnawed at him. Worse, Traficant had lowballed his fee. For a job this vital, he deserved more. Much more.

His phone buzzed, and he answered without looking. "Hiroshi."

"Torashi," his handler said tersely. "Status?"

"Still nothing on Green," Torashi said, his tone flat. "But I've been thinking. Traficant only mentioned Green. I researched Dr. Xi's involvement independently. The Chinese might pay better for him. A double payday."

Hiroshi paused. "You're playing a dangerous game. With Xi involved, this must be a high-stakes affair. Something this risky would have to be cleared by Zhongnanhai. The Chinese don't mess around."

"And neither do I," Torashi replied. "I don't come in second, which means a bigger payday for both of us."

"Fine. Don't lose sight of the primary target. And what about Maxx King? Are you sure you should be mixing business with pleasure?"

Torashi's grip tightened on the phone. Maxx King. The name burned in his mind, a personal vendetta that had become an obsession. King had humiliated him last September, a debt Torashi intended to settle with blood. He'd tracked King's girlfriend, Gabby Fisher, to Snoqualmie Falls, but she'd slipped through his fingers. "I'll find him," he said. "Through her."

"You told me it was only Maxx," Hiroshi said, suspicion creeping into his voice. "What's with Gabby?"

"She's part of it now," Torashi admitted, his voice low and venomous. "I went through her hotel room. Her journals, her photos. She's mocking me, Hiroshi. She'll pay too."

"You're taking too many risks," Hiroshi warned. "Focus on

Green. The senator won't tolerate distractions. I'll ask around about Dr. Xi and see what I can find out."

Torashi ended the call without replying, his jaw tight. Hiroshi didn't understand. This wasn't about the mission anymore. It was about honor—his family name tarnished more every day Maxx King lived. He'd spent too long chasing King's girlfriend, rifling through her belongings, feeding his fixation. Green and Xi had slipped farther away because of it, but he couldn't stop. He wouldn't go home until they were all dead.

The barista returned, setting a fresh cup down with a clumsy thud that sloshed tea onto the table. "Here. On the house. Sorry about earlier."

Torashi stared at the mess then at the kid's sheepish grin. Something snapped. "You think this fixes it?" he said, his voice dangerously soft. "You think I'm some fool you can disrespect?"

"Man, chill," the barista said, stepping back. "It's just tea."

"Chill?" Torashi stood. His movements were fluid and deliberate. "You don't get to tell me anything."

The kid's eyes widened. "Look, I don't want trouble—"

"Too late." Torashi grabbed his arm, twisting it behind his back in one swift motion. The barista yelped, but Torashi dragged him outside, ignoring the early-morning chill. The parking lot was empty, lit only by a flickering streetlight. Perfect.

"Let me go!" the kid pleaded, struggling. "I'm sorry, okay?"

Torashi shoved him against the wall, his calm mask replaced by a twisted grin. "Sorry doesn't cut it. You're nothing. A worm who thinks he can look down on me."

"I didn't—I swear!" The barista's voice cracked, tears welling up.

Torashi drew his sleek blade, which glinted in the dim light. "I told you to stay away from me." He drove the knife into the kid's stomach, twisting it with a sickening crunch. The barista gasped, clutching at Torashi's coat, but he yanked the blade free and stabbed again then again, each strike precise yet frenzied. Blood pooled on the asphalt, dark and slick. The kid slumped, lifeless, his eyes staring blankly at the sky.

Torashi stepped back, wiping the blade on the barista's apron. His pulse steadied, the black mood lifting slightly. Killing was familiar, grounding. However, it didn't resolve the more significant issue. Green and Xi were still out there, and Gabby's trail had gone cold. He needed a new lead.

Back inside, he grabbed his coat and left a few bills on the table. The tea sat untouched, cold now. He stepped into the gray dawn, his mind racing. Gabby's disappearance at Snoqualmie Falls gnawed at him. She was clever, resourceful, and beautiful—qualities that only fueled his obsession. He'd underestimated her once. Not again.

A memory surfaced: her journal, found in the hotel room at the Salish Lodge. Scribbled notes about Maxx, about hiding from someone. Him. She'd known he was coming. The thought thrilled him, a predator savoring the chase. But it also pricked his ego. She'd outsmarted him, and that was unacceptable.

He climbed into the car he'd stolen after ditching the minivan, the engine purring to life. Green and Xi could wait a couple more hours. He'd head back to the falls to see if he could find her trail, or maybe she'd returned to her room. Thinking about either situation excited him.

As he drove, his thoughts drifted to the Chinese. If Traficant wouldn't pay what he deserved, maybe they would. Dr. Xi was their problem too—a traitor with secrets they'd kill to protect. A double payday was tempting, even if he despised working for the Chinese. He'd weigh it later. For now, Gabby was crowding his mind.

The road stretched ahead, winding back toward the falls. Torashi's calm returned, his focus sharpening. He was the best, a shadow no one could escape. Green, Xi, Maxx, Gabby—

they'd all lose, and he'd win. He always did. His family name demanded it. And he'd savor every moment of their end.

11

CLOSING WALLS, TICKING CLOCKS

Senator Jane Traficant stood in the grand entryway of her Georgetown townhome, her disheveled, silver hair catching the light from the crystal chandelier overhead.

The soft waves framed her head like an out-of-control halo, starkly contrasting the storm brewing beneath her polished exterior. She wore her usual dark, high-neck sweater beneath a wrinkled gray blazer, a uniform that typically projected authority and composure. But this morning, that facade was cracking, stressed by the wine stain on the front of her sweater. Her eyes, bloodshot from a hangover, darted to the antique mirror on the wall, reflecting a woman who had fallen asleep in her clothes after too much bourbon the night before. She barely recognized the frazzled figure staring back.

"What happened to me?" she whispered to her reflection.

The call from Hanssen had come shortly before 9:00 a.m., waking her out of a stupor. His voice was tight with urgency. "I think I found the virus canisters, Senator. However, Williams in Afghanistan, he's botched it. I don't see how we can make the deadline without a miracle."

She'd hung up, her stomach churning, and stumbled to her

home office, a sanctuary of opulence and oddity. The living room beyond the entry shifted from grandeur to something more eclectic—a plush velvet sofa faced a coffee table that doubled as art. At the same time, wingback chairs in exotic animal prints seemed to shimmer with movement. A massive white marble fireplace stood at the room's heart. Carvings of alien creatures and obscure folklore were a silent testament to her taste for intimidation and oddity over mere wealth. No one but her recognized the significance of the strange clock.

Above the fireplace, the clock ticked relentlessly. Its face was an ornate brass design, hieroglyphs stark against a black background, each second a hammer blow to her fraying nerves. It was 9:42 a.m., but the time displayed was an alternate one, indicating less than five hours—the deadline had arrived.

Time was slipping away, and with it everything she'd built over decades—power, influence, the carefully curated image of a Midwest conservative titan. If she failed now, the consequences wouldn't just be political ruin but apocalyptic. Hanssen's words echoed, "Likely found but inaccessible." A misstep in Afghanistan and a deadline she couldn't outrun. She needed more time.

Her gaze fell to the small, metallic cube on her desk—her personal communication device, a relic of secrets she'd guarded for years. She wrapped her hands around it, feeling the familiar chill as the fluorescent bulbs flared a deep blue, casting an eerie glow over the silk wallpaper. The temperature dropped, not uncomfortably but enough to prickle her skin. Time slowed, and she floated in a weightless void until she sensed another presence, alien and unyielding. Thunderbird.

"Please," she said, her voice steady despite the tremor in her chest. She fell to her knees, overcome with emotion. "I need more time. We have located the weapon, but it has been compromised in Afghanistan. Give us a few more days to use the virus. I guarantee it."

A response came instantly, an internal message measured yet laced with menace. "You have had time and wasted it. You assured us before that containment was under control and would be used against our enemies. Our last gift...an extra twelve Earth hours. That's all you have, servant. Fail, and we destroy Earth to stop the Others ourselves."

An extra twelve hours. The words sank into her like a stone, the air growing colder as the device hummed faintly, powering down. The silence that followed was suffocating. Less than a day to avert annihilation—or lose everything—her career, legacy, the world itself. She could feel its weight pressing down, her breath shallow as she paced the room, the clock now reading 9:43 a.m.

She had options, but they were dwindling—Williams securing the canisters to fix his mess, capturing Green and Xi, or begging Thunderbird again and risking their wrath. All the choices felt out of her grasp.

She grabbed the secure phone on her desk, slamming it to her ear in frustration as she dialed Hanssen. "What the hell is happening over there?" she snapped when he picked up.

"Williams underestimated the resistance," Hanssen replied, his tone clipped. "The Shah-i-Kot Valley... It's a disaster. We lost a search and rescue team attempting to secure the canisters, and there's a battle raging around the location. No one is allowed to enter or exit the area."

"And Green and Xi? Where are they? I thought Kage was supposed to be the best money could buy."

"He's working blind, Senator. We never told him the deadline. Perhaps we should consider giving Torashi a bonus to motivate him to meet our timeline."

She slammed the receiver down, her anger boiling over. Green and Xi—those sanctimonious scientists, disappearing while the world teetered. She pictured Mr. Green's smug face, endless lectures on ethics, and Dr. Xi's quiet arrogance. Traficant's hands shook as she poured another bourbon, the glass clinking against the crystal decanter. She took a mouthful, the burn doing little to dull her fear.

The clock ticked to 10:03 a.m. She needed a plan. Staggering back to the desk, she activated the cube again, the blue light flaring anew. "Twelve more hours isn't enough," she begged, her voice cracking. "Green failed, not me. They've all failed me. Give me another day. At least let me retrieve the canisters. I can do that."

"You test our patience, human," the voice replied, cold and deliberate. "Our gift of more time is generous. Earth's fate is your burden now. Do not contact us again until our enemies are infected with the virus—or not at all."

The connection severed, leaving her in that eerie silence once more. She hurled the cube across the room, watching it skid beneath the sofa. Failure meant annihilation—not her downfall but humanity's. Thunderbird would raze the planet to contain the Others. Her townhome, her power, her carefully crafted life—all ash.

She redialed Hanssen, her slurring voice a snarl. "Get me Williams on the line. Now."

Moments later, Williams's voice crackled through. "Good morning, Senator Traficant. What's this about?"

"You're too damn slow," she spat. "You have no idea what's at stake. I need those canisters, and we're out of time. Fix this, or I'll bury both you and Hanssen."

"Secure the canisters?" Williams cut in, his tone taking on a sudden edge. "You know I'm in the middle of a hot war zone, and I'm breaking the chain of command by simply talking with you. I'm doing all I can—"

"Don't lecture me!" Traficant shouted. "You've got hours, not days. Get me those canisters!"

She slammed the receiver down, her breath ragged. The clock read 10:19 a.m. Her anger at Williams and Hanssen burned hot, a convenient target for the terror clawing at her. Williams didn't know Thunderbird's ultimatum or feel the ticking seconds like she did. She'd made all of them scapegoats in her mind—if they failed, their incompetence, not her decades of maneuvering, had led to this brink.

Pacing the fireplace, she stared at the alien carvings, their strange eyes mocking her. The peculiar clock added an extra seven hours to reflect the updated deadline. Seeing Thunderbird's insulting concession of a few hours only infuriated her.

She'd built this life to inspire awe and fear, but now it felt like a gilded cage closing in. The bourbon bottle beckoned, but she resisted, her mind racing. Williams was a lost cause—Operation Anaconda's mess in Afghanistan was too chaotic to count on. Finding Green and Xi was her only chance. Not only were they missing, but they hated her. Torashi had to deliver them.

By 10:27 a.m., her nerves were raw. She called Hanssen again. "Update me on Torashi."

"I texted him but haven't reached him directly," he said. "He's asking questions, wants to know why the sudden rush."

"Tell them national security. He doesn't need to know," she growled. "Do what we're paying him for. Find or kill Green and Xi."

She dropped the phone, sinking into the velvet sofa. The clock's hands crept forward, each tick a dagger. Failure loomed—Earth reduced to rubble, her name wouldn't even be a footnote in its ruin. She clutched her throbbing head, silver hair tangled in her fingers, and muttered, "Kage, if you screw this up, I'll haunt you from whatever's left."

She'd gambled everything on people she despised, and now the world was in their hands. And they didn't even know it. Fear and fury struggled within her, but beneath it all was a hollow dread. Her time would end at 2:30 tomorrow morning. If they failed, Thunderbird wouldn't hesitate. And Jane Traficant, for all her power, would be nothing but dust in the wind.

***

As dawn broke near the churning beauty of Snoqualmie River, the woods stood drenched under a heavy gray sky. The air hung thick with mist, and a relentless drizzle soaked the towering pines and left the forest floor a sodden mess.

Gabby Fisher stirred inside an abandoned camping trailer, her body stiff from four hours of restless sleep. The sound that ripped her from sleep was sudden and jarring—a harsh, metallic clang that echoed through the trailer, followed by a deep, guttural grunt that seemed to vibrate in her chest. Her pulse surged, a frantic drumbeat against her ribs, as icy dread coiled in her gut.

Someone was out there, stalking closer, their intent unknown but undoubtedly dangerous. She scrambled upright, her breath catching in shallow gasps, and flattened herself against the trailer's cracked vinyl wall. The surface was cold and sticky with years of grime, pressing into her shoulder as she edged toward the window. Her trembling fingers brushed the pistol at her waist, drawing it free like a talisman, its familiar weight an anchor against the terror clawing at her mind.

"Who's there?" she whispered, a faint hiss swallowed by the damp air. Her voice quavered, betraying her fear, but she couldn't stop it. She leaned toward the window, its glass streaked with filth and spiderwebbed with cracks, distorting the world beyond into a murky haze. Shadows flickered in the gloom, twisting and shifting like phantoms in the mist. Her heart hammered louder, each beat a thunderclap in her ears, as she strained to make sense of the movement. Was it him—the man who'd hunted her through the woods? Had he found her already, his silent steps closing the distance while she slept?

Her grip tightened on the pistol, knuckles whitening, as she pressed her forehead to the window's edge, the chill seeping into her skin. Then, through the smeared glass, a shape resolved—a massive, hulking silhouette, broad and shambling. Her breath hitched, a silent scream lodging in her throat.

But as her eyes adjusted to the dimness, the tension ebbed enough for her to see. It wasn't a man. It was a bear, its matted fur glistening with rain, its snout buried in the rusted hulk of a garbage can. The beast pawed at the metal, sending a cascade of dented cans and soggy wrappers skittering across the muddy ground, its claws scraping with a sound like nails on slate. Gabby exhaled a shaky gust that fogged the glass, her body sagging slightly as the adrenaline drained. Just a bear. Not him.

Gabby slumped back, her breath misting in the chilly air. She was athletic and in her early thirties, her frame lean from exercise. Her black hair, usually neatly cared for, now fell in uneven tangles, streaked with mud from her flight through the woods. Her deep-brown eyes, sharp and wary, darted toward every sound. Her face was drawn tight with exhaustion and lack of sleep. Her North Face jacket kept her warm beneath the thin blanket, but her jeans were torn and muddy, and her boots scuffed—clothes that had seen better days but were still holding up despite the wet, cold weather.

Her mind rewound to the previous night, a jagged reel of fear and uncertainty. She'd been hiding in these woods since escaping a man who'd pursued her through the trails that descended from the falls.

It started near Salish Lodge, where she'd been staying. She'd glimpsed him through the trees—tall, angular, his movements deliberate—cornered by her friends, Andres and Glen. Their voices had carried on the wind, sharp with anger and threats, but the words blurred into a murmur when drowned out by the noise of the waterfall.

She couldn't tell who'd won that standoff, only that it ended with yelling and someone crashing through the underbrush after her. It sounded like Glen, his familiar baritone calling her name, but doubt gnawed at her. Was it a warning or a trap? She hadn't lingered to find out. She'd bolted, her legs pumping until the sounds faded, and she was alone with the river's murmur.

She'd trekked along muddy trails for hours, the Snoqualmie River her guide toward Fall City, nothing more than a wide spot on the road, but it had to be better than sleeping in the woods. Her lungs burned, her boots squelched, but she pressed on until she stumbled across a deserted campground. She looked through the few remaining trailers until she stumbled on one that was abandoned but hadn't been ransacked by people or animals.

The trailer squatted by the riverbank, a relic of forgotten summers, fishing trips, and river rafting. Its aluminum shell was dented and streaked with rust. One window was boarded up with splintered plywood. The door hung partially ajar, creaking on its hinges. Inside, it smelled of mildew and neglect, but it was dry. A threadbare blanket was crumpled on a sagging bench, and a dusty crate held a few bottles of Gatorade, their labels peeling. She'd curled under the blanket, sipped the stale lemon-lime drink, and dozed off into a fitful sleep.

Everything she owned—her backpack with cash, her passport, and her meticulously planned escape route—remained in her room in Salish Lodge. All she had now was her pistol, a compact 9mm tucked into her waistband, and her cell phone, powered off to avoid being tracked. The loss of that backpack gnawed at her. Without it, she was adrift, her plans unraveling. She couldn't stay here, exposed and vulnerable. She needed to try to reclaim what was hers. After a bout of indecision, she decided to hike back to the lodge.

The trek back was grueling but familiar, the woods a blur of dripping ferns and slick rocks. She crept, her boots sinking into the mud, the river's roar fading behind her. As she neared the lodge, its elegant silhouette loomed through the mist, all warm lights and steep gables. She crept closer, sticking to the shadows until she could see her room on the second floor.

The curtains were parted, and a faint beam danced inside—a flashlight. Her stomach tightened. Someone was there. She edged forward, catching a reflection in the glass door. It was him—the Japanese man tailing her, his angular frame hunched as he rifled through the room. His dark hair gleamed wetly, and his sharp features were set in concentration. What did he want? Andres and Glen had confronted him, but here he was, unscathed and searching.

She watched, motionless, as he slipped out the sliding door and leaped from the balcony, landing with a soft thud on the grass below. He vanished into the drizzle, leaving her room silent.

Gabby waited, counting the minutes, then climbed the exterior stairs, her pistol drawn. The door slid open easily, and she swept the room, her breath shallow. It was a wreck—drawers yanked out, the mattress flipped. Her backpack was gone. She hadn't seen him carrying anything when he jumped from the balcony, but someone had taken everything she needed to disappear.

She sank onto the mattress, the pistol resting in her lap. The weight of it all pressed down—running, hiding, losing. She had nothing left but the clothes on her back and the weapon in her hand. For a moment, she considered fleeing anyway, slipping into the night with no plan, no destination. But then her jaw tightened. She wasn't a quitter.

Why had she been running to begin with? It started nearly a week ago when she and Maxx were yanked back into the danger encompassing the Thunderbird project. Maxx's sudden departure to Afghanistan had left her unprepared to deal with the mounting threat. At first, she'd felt confident she could deal with the dangerous men with cold eyes and quick fists—until she'd watched her friend die.

Although she'd survived the attack, the violence brought the realization that she didn't understand their games. Maxx understood that world, but she didn't. This new man, this shadow chasing her, was another predator. If he wanted her, she knew now that he'd never stop. Better to face him on her terms.

A plan took shape, rough but resolute. She'd set a trap. He didn't seem that dangerous—not compared to the killer Haoyu she and Maxx had fought last fall, anyway. She'd seen worse, lived through worse. The woods were her advantage; after years of hiking in this area, she knew their twists, their hiding spots. She could lure him in and catch him off guard. Her fingers tightened around the pistol. She'd need bait, a way to draw him back. Maybe a call from her phone, a staged plea for help. Risky, but she was done being prey.

Gabby stood, the damp chill seeping through her jacket. The rain tapped against the window, a steady rhythm that matched her pulse. She didn't know who this man was or what he sought—her secrets, her life, something else entirely. But she'd find out. She'd make him regret chasing her. Then she could decide on her next step. *One day at a time*, she reminded herself.

With a final glance at the ruined room, she slipped out the door, disappearing into the misty woods once more, her mind already plotting the ambush that would turn the hunter into the hunted.

12

NO LOOKING BACK

The TSA jet shuddered as it touched down on the icy tarmac of Anchorage International Airport, its engines whining into silence.

Outside, the Alaskan darkness pressed against the small windows, a thick shroud unbroken by the sun, which wouldn't rise for another three hours. Mr. Green shifted uncomfortably in his seat, his portly frame straining against his brightly colored Hawaiian shirt. His tanned face glistened with a sheen of sweat despite the cold.

They had stopped at a used clothing store last night to buy him more suitable clothes for the cold weather, but the store didn't have shoes that fit his size-fourteen feet. Rather than cramming his toes into uncomfortable boots, he'd worn his Birkenstocks with thick socks. He looked silly, but he was past the point of caring.

Beside him, Dr. Xi sat calmly, his thick, unruly hair catching the dim cabin light. The older Chinese man, in his sixties, had bushy gray eyebrows that framed a thoughtful expression behind his glasses. His stubble-dusted chin hinted at days without a shave, but his demeanor remained unruffled. Across the narrow aisle, Harry Cull leaned forward, his rugged beard streaked with white and his leather jacket creaking as he moved. His restless eyes scanned the cabin, always searching for threats.

"All right, we're here," Harry said, his voice rough like gravel. "Refueling stop, then Beijing. You two still sure about this?"

Mr. Green rubbed his temples. "We don't have a choice, Harry. The CIA's been on me for months. I encrypted the virus data, but it's over if they can crack it before we get to Dr. Xi's lab."

Dr. Xi nodded slowly. "The lab in Beijing is our best shot. I have contacts who can break into the lab's communication system and help us. But we must move quickly."

Harry grunted, peering out the small window into the blackness. "Miss Grey pulled strings to get us this far. This plane's a nice touch, but I don't like sitting still too long."

The trio had started this leg of their journey in Portland, where Harry had expertly landed his seaplane on the Columbia River near Tomahawk Bay, a few miles from the Portland International Airport. A cab had whisked them to the private terminal, where Miss Grey's arrangements had a Department of Homeland Security jet waiting to get them far away from Seattle.

The original plan—to hide out at Harry's cabin in Hatcher Pass, a rugged retreat in the Talkeetna Mountains—had been scrapped mid-flight. Green and Xi had convinced Harry that Beijing was their only real option. Now, at 6 a.m. in Anchorage, they were at Signature Aviation's operations base, refueling for the long haul across the Pacific.

Green glanced at his watch. "How long is this going to take?"

"Hour, plus or minus," Harry replied, standing to stretch his legs. "Fuel's pumping now. Keep your head down and don't talk to strangers. Let me or the pilots handle the chatting."

The air felt heavy as they disembarked into the fixed-base operator's lounge—a practical, no-frills space with a few chairs and a coffee machine. The darkness outside was oppressive, and the fluorescent lights inside cast harsh shadows. Green plopped into a chair, his breathing labored. Xi stood near a window, hands clasped behind his back, while Harry paced like a calm, predatory animal. His eyes were not only looking but holding a primal awareness that missed nothing.

"You think they followed us?" Green asked, his voice low.

Harry stopped pacing. "Dunno. Shouldn't have been possible, but I don't trust clean breaks anymore."

Xi turned from the window. "If they know we're here, they'll assume China's next. We must assume Kage or his people will be waiting."

"Kage?" Green's eyes widened. "You think that lunatic will follow me to China?"

"He'll follow both of us," Xi corrected. "If Senator Traficant hired him, he won't stop." Before Green could respond, the lounge door swung open with a bang. A man in a black parka stormed in, his face obscured by a balaclava, wild eyes visible through the openings—a silenced pistol gleaming in his gloved hand. Time slowed as he raised the weapon, aiming straight for Green.

"Down!" Harry roared, tackling Green to the floor as the first shot whispered through the air, embedding itself in the padded chair where Green had been sitting. The heavy man yelped, his Birkenstocks slipping as he hit the floor hard, his breath knocked out of him.

Xi dropped behind a table. His calm shattered as he shouted, "Harry, the door!"

The assassin pivoted, firing again, but Harry was already moving. With a deep, savage growl, he lunged, slamming his broad shoulder into the man's chest. The gun clattered across the floor as they grappled, Harry's leather jacket ripping at the seams.

The attacker drove a knee into Harry's gut, but the rugged man didn't hesitate. He seized the assassin's arm, twisting it back until a sickening crack echoed through the room. The man screamed, and Harry finished him with a brutal headbutt, sending him crumpling to the floor in an unconscious heap.

Breathing heavily, Harry grinned widely. He retrieved the pistol and slipped the magazine into his pocket. "Amateur. But I'm still counting this as my cardio workout for today."

Green, still sprawled on the floor, clutched his chest. "I… I thought I was done. My heart's pounding like a drum."

"You're fine," Harry chuckled, hauling him up. "Get it together, man."

Xi emerged from behind the table, adjusting his glasses. "Who sent him?"

"Don't know, but it doesn't matter now," Harry said. "We're leaving. The plane's almost ready."

Green steadied himself against a chair, his tan face pale. "You saved my life, Harry. How'd you move that fast?"

Harry's steely gaze softened. "I'm not just some pilot, Green. I'm a friend of Maxx's. He sent me to protect you two after he talked to Grey. This Thunderbird thing… You two are in deep, and there are a lot of enemies out there. Kage's only one."

"Maxx?" Xi's bushy eyebrows rose. "I thought he was chasing Doctor Smith in Afghanistan."

"Yeah, he is," Harry said, holstering the pistol inside his jacket. "He's got my back, and now I've got yours. At all costs."

Green swallowed hard. "So you're going with us to China?"

"Damn right," Harry replied. "You're not shaking me now. I want one of those Hawaiian shirts as a souvenir of our world tour."

Minutes later, the refueling finished, and the trio boarded

the jet. The unconscious assassin was left for the passenger services staff to discover. As the plane taxied toward the runway, the first hints of dawn tinged the horizon, though the darkness still clung stubbornly. Green settled into his seat, sipping from a can of cola he'd grabbed from the vending machine, his nerves fraying.

"I told Miss Grey to ask Maxx about the 'doctor,'" he muttered. "The encryption key is tied to what I was drinking at his condo."

Xi tilted his head. "And what was that?"

"Dr. Pepper," Green said with a weak chuckle. "Stupid, right? But it was the best I could think of under pressure. And only Maxx would remember."

Xi's lips twitched into a rare smile. "Clever. We might need that key when we reach the XINXI lab."

In the co-pilot's seat, Harry called back, "Buckle up. Next stop's Beijing, and they won't be as easy on us as our little amateur friend."

The jet lifted off, piercing the Alaskan gloom, bound for China. Inside, the tension was palpable. Green fidgeted, Xi stared out the window, and Harry gripped the controls, his mind already planning for the threats ahead.

"So what's the plan in Beijing?" Green asked, breaking the silence.

Xi turned, his calm returning. "My lab at XINXI. My former colleagues there can assist us further in encrypting the virus data if necessary. I've got an ace up my sleeve—a backdoor into their communication system. They won't expect it."

Green glanced nervously over his shoulder. "And if Kage's waiting?"

"Then we fight," Harry said simply.

Green leaned back, closing his eyes. "I want this over. I never should've sent those plans to Thunderbird. I should have tried harder to find a way around Senator Traficant's directive."

"Too late for regrets," Harry said. "We're in it now, boys."

The jet climbed higher, crossing into international airspace. Below, the Bering Sea stretched endlessly, a dark mirror reflecting their uncertain fate. Green thought back to his call with Miss Grey, her voice steady as she'd promised to help. She'd delivered. Now, it was up to him to come through.

Xi spoke again, his tone restrained. "If they tracked us to Anchorage, they'll be waiting for us in Beijing."

"Let 'em come," Harry rumbled, cracking his knuckles. "I've dealt with worse."

They had enemies—Kage, the CIA, the Chinese, maybe others—but they also had each other. And in Xi's quiet confidence and Harry's determined intensity, Green saw a glimmer of hope. The XINXI lab was their goal, the Thunderbird virus the ticking time bomb. Whatever was ahead, they'd face it together. There was no looking back.

***

Torashi Kage stood under the garish yellow sign of Love's Travel Stop, a sprawling truck stop in Fife, south of Seattle. The clock on the pay phone read 7:52 a.m., and he couldn't help but smirk at the irony of the name. Love's. A place for diesel fumes and stale coffee, not sentiment. If there was anything Torashi enjoyed almost as much as money and killing, it was irony.

His black tailored jacket still carried faint streaks of the barista's blood from earlier that morning, a messy kill he hadn't bothered to clean up thoroughly. However, he'd taken the time to put on a clean white shirt and wipe off his custom-made John Lobb shoes—his preferred uniform of chaos.

He punched Senator Jane Traficant's secure line into the keypad, the cold, wet weather biting at his hands. His mood was sour. Gabby Fisher had vanished from the Salish Lodge. He'd broken into her room and seen her notes and maps but left them behind like a fool. When he went back, they were gone, snatched by someone more intelligent. Probably the giant clown who had been with Andres. Now he was empty-handed, and it annoyed him.

The phone rang twice before Traficant's voice cut through, sharp as a blade. "Kage? Tell me you've got something."

"Good morning to you too, Senator," he said dryly. "I'm working on it. Fisher's a ghost. She was at the lodge, but someone cleaned up after her. I've got no leads on her yet."

"Fisher? Why are you telling me about her? You're supposed to be focused on Green and Xi." Her voice spiked, incredulous.

"I think Fisher and Maxx King are the shortest route to finding Green," he lied easily.

"I was told you were the best. I paid you a fortune up front, and you're standing there with empty hands? This is unacceptable."

His jaw clenched. He leaned against the pay phone's metal frame, and the receiver pressed hard against his ear. "Watch your tone, Jane. I don't like being lectured. I've been chasing shadows all night because the intel you and Hanssen gave me was garbage. You want results? Give me something to work with."

"Don't threaten me," she snapped, but there was a hitch in her words, a crack he could hear even through the static. "I'm on a tight deadline here, Kage. If we don't handle this soon, it won't matter for either of us. Do you understand? We're both done."

He opened his mouth to bite back when a scrawny figure shuffled into view. A homeless girl, maybe sixteen, with matted hair and a ratty jacket, edged toward him. "Hey, mister, spare a dollar? I'm real hungry," she mumbled, holding out a shaky hand.

Torashi glared at her, his free hand twitching toward the

knife in his belt. "Get lost, whore," he growled, turning his back. She didn't budge, standing there and staring with sunken eyes. His temper flared. "I said beat it!"

"Please, one dollar," she pressed, stepping closer.

"Hold on," he barked into the phone then spun on her. He grabbed her by the collar and slammed her against the phone booth's side. She yelped, her thin frame folding under his grip. "Are you deaf? I told you to leave!" He cocked a fist, and she flinched, whimpering. He shoved her off with a grunt, watching her stumble into the gravel and scramble away. His pulse pounded as he returned to the call. "Sorry about that interruption."

Traficant's silence hung heavy for a moment. "Who was that?"

"No one. Local hooker." He rubbed his temple, refocusing. "You said deadline. How close are we talking? What's my priority here?"

"Green and Xi," she said, her voice tight. "Quit chasing second-bit players like Fisher. They're the key. Do you have any idea where they are?"

"Yeah, I tracked them. They're slippery. My contacts at the local airports marked them at Portland International. They caught a chartered flight to Anchorage. I sent a guy after them, but he's gone dark. A police scanner in the area reports that he was arrested at the airport. No word on Green or Xi, though."

She cursed under her breath, a low hiss through the line. "And your man? Can he be traced back to you?"

"No chance," he said, a flicker of arrogance in his tone. "He's a ghost. But here's the kicker. Green and Xi aren't in Anchorage anymore. They're on their way to Beijing."

"Beijing?" Her voice sharpened, tinged with something he couldn't quite place. "Why? Are they working with the Chinese?"

"Beats me," he said, shrugging. "Maybe they're selling your

information to a higher bidder. My point is that I'm arranging another hit. I have people in Beijing who owe me favors, but it's going to get messy. Bribes, officials, maybe an international incident. Are you okay with that, Senator?"

"Do it," she said, voice strained, almost brittle. "I'll cover the extra cost. Whatever it takes."

He caught the tremor in her voice, faint but there. She was angry, sure, but something else was eating at her. "More money's good. This contract is under the gun now, and Beijing won't be cheap. But you sound spooked, Senator. What am I missing?"

"Nothing," she said too fast. "Get it done, Kage. I don't care how. Green and Xi can't make it alive to wherever they're going in Beijing. Understood?"

"Crystal clear," he replied, but his eyes narrowed. She was hiding something, and he didn't like it. "I'll call you when it's arranged."

The line clicked dead, and he slammed the receiver down with a metallic clang. He stepped back, scanning the truck stop. The girl was gone, swallowed by the morning fog curling over the asphalt. His boots crunched on the gravel as he headed for his car, a sporty Honda Accord parked near the diesel pumps. His earlier kill still exhilarated him. However, the fact that Fisher was getting away was a nagging worry and he had to focus on Green and Xi. Beijing was a long shot, a mess of corruption and risk, but he'd make it work. He always did.

Sliding into the driver's seat, he lit a cigarette, the smoke coiling around his face as the engine growled to life. He stared at the lights on the freeway, the cigarette glowing red between his fingers. Traficant's panic stuck with him, a nagging itch he couldn't scratch. She'd flinched on the call, and not from his temper. What was she running from? He didn't trust her, but he didn't need to. Money was money, and blood was blood. He'd track Green and Xi, finish the job, and deal with her later if she tried to double-cross him.

The smoke stung his eyes as he exhaled, his mind already ticking through the contacts he'd need in Beijing. Bribes weren't cheap, and a high-profile hit like this could spark a diplomatic shitstorm. Messy didn't bother him—chaotic contracts were where he thrived.

As he pulled out of Love's Travel Stop onto I-5, the name lingered, a bitter joke in the back of his throat. Love had nothing to do with it. This was about survival—his. Traficant and the bodies he'd leave in his wake were a means to an end. He flicked the cigarette out the window, watching it spark against the pavement, and drove into the gray dawn, the shadow of Traficant's secrets following him like a ghost he couldn't shake.

13

IN THE SPOTLIGHT

Exhaustion was beginning to pull Barth to his knees, the endless darkness smothering any hope of seeing daylight again.

The Afghan cave system stretched like a labyrinth beneath the jagged mountains, a shadowed warren of stone and dust where secrets festered. Barth Anderson stumbled through its depths, his once-pristine uniform now torn and streaked with blood and grime. His silver-streaked hair hung limp, no longer slicked back with the meticulous care that defined him. His sharp hazel eyes darted, scanning the darkness as his boots scuffed against the uneven floor.

He was a man accustomed to control, a clandestine operative extraordinaire, now reduced to a hunted figure in a hostile land. He was drained after a full day of searching for Smith, evading American troops, and preventing Miss Grey from escaping. Behind him, the faint echoes of American Special Forces reverberated—pursuers he couldn't shake. Ahead, a new threat loomed.

Anderson rounded a corner and froze. Silhouetted against

the flickering light of a kerosene lamp stood a cluster of armed men, their faces obscured by keffiyehs, their weapons trained on him. Quds Force—Iran's elite operatives, not the Taliban security detail he had hoped to find. He'd stumbled into their camp. His mind raced, threading ambition and deceit into a plan. He raised his hands slowly, palms out, and forced a thin smile.

"Gentlemen," he said in broken Farsi, his voice steady despite the sweat beading on his brow. "I'm not your enemy. I have something you want, something very valuable."

The Quds leader, a wiry man with a hawkish gaze and a neatly trimmed beard, stepped forward. His English carried a clipped, precise edge. "You're American. CIA. I have seen too many of you lying dogs. Why should I listen when everything you say is untrue?"

Anderson's smile widened. "Because I can offer you, Miss Grey. She's with me—well, not willingly. But she's a bargaining chip. Take me in and she's yours. I'll even sweeten the deal. Call Senator Traficant in Washington. She'll confirm I'm working with Doctor Smith on a device—something your people would kill to have. Take me to Smith and I'll prove it."

The Quds leader tilted his head, eyes narrowing. "Smith? The one hiding in these caves? You expect us to believe you're his ally?"

"Believe what you want," Anderson replied, "but Grey's worth more alive than dead, for now. And I'm worth more to you as a partner than a corpse."

"You have a high opinion of yourself, Mr. CIA. I could kill you and take this woman you call Grey. Then I wouldn't have to deal with any more of your lies."

"Give me one phone call to speak with my boss. She will make it worth your time," Anderson said.

The leader studied him then barked an order. Two soldiers

stepped forward, frisking Anderson roughly before shoving him toward a tunnel. "Move," the leader said. "We'll see what you're worth."

Moments later, Anderson sat across from the Quds leader in a cramped chamber lit by a single flashlight. A satellite phone rested on an ammo crate between them. Anderson dialed, his fingers steady despite the ache in his bones. The line crackled then connected.

"Traficant," the senator said, sounding sharp and frayed.

"Anderson," he said with a creepy grin.

"Barth? Where the hell have you been? It's been almost twenty-four hours since you told me you found Smith's cave system. I've been losing my mind here."

Anderson leaned forward, straining to keep his tone relaxed. "I've been busy, Senator, lost in these damn caves, dodging American Special Forces. They're after Smith and me. But I've got a dicey situation. Quds forces grabbed me. They were sent to rescue Smith and get the Taliban out."

Traficant's breath hitched. "Quds? Barth, what are you—"

"Listen," he cut in. "They've got Grey. I told them she's leverage. They're willing to take her in exchange for weapons or cash. Cleaner than killing her, don't you think?"

A pause stretched across the line. When Traficant spoke again, her voice shook with tension. "Grey? Are you still going on about her? I told you before—do whatever it takes. Get the damn codes from her. I already approved this after you begged me to let you 'take care of her.' Have you gone soft on me?"

Anderson grimaced. "I've tried everything short of torture. Shooting her is one thing—quick, clean. Torture's a line I don't cross."

"Then don't," she snapped. "Tell the Quds to do it. I'll pay them from your share. The world's in my hands, Barth, and I'm not losing it because you've suddenly grown a conscience."

He shifted uncomfortably. "You sure about this? I've got doubts it'll work. She's stubborn as hell."

"Do it," Traficant said, her tone icy. "Don't call me again until you have the codes I need." The line went dead.

Anderson set the phone down, his stomach churning. He didn't like this—outsourcing the dirty work felt like a coward's move. But he was an amoral man driven by survival and ambition, not sentiment. He turned to the Quds leader, who'd been listening silently.

"Change of plans," Anderson said. "Hold off on Grey. Let me talk to her one last time. Let her know this is the end of the line if she doesn't give me the password."

The leader shrugged. "Your game, American. Don't waste my time."

They dragged Miss Grey into the chamber moments later, her wrists bound, her dark hair matted with dirt. She was a strong woman, her brown eyes blazing with defiance despite the bruises on her face. Anderson had underestimated her before—her loyalty to her family, her country, Andres, and Maxx ran deeper than he could imagine. She glared at him as the guards shoved her into a chair.

"You'll fail," she spat, her voice raw but unyielding. "I'd rather die than betray them. You think you're winning? The world's ending anyway if you screw this up. My death's only a matter of time."

Anderson leaned in, studying her. "You're tough, but everyone breaks eventually. Use your head, Grey."

"Not me," she said, her gaze locked on his. "Not for you. Not for your senator. My father taught me better. My family and friends are worth more than helping you."

Her resolve gnawed at him. He stood, pacing the small space. He could hand her over and let the Quds carve the code out of her. It'd be easy—clean hands, plausible deniability. But something in her certainty, her willingness to die, pricked at the edges of his amorality. He wasn't a good man, but he wasn't a butcher either. Still, Traficant's orders echoed in his skull. He turned back to the Quds leader.

"Start negotiations," he said, voice flat. "Grey and money. That's the deal."

The leader nodded, gesturing to his men. They were mid-discussion—bartering lives like livestock—when a shout echoed down the tunnel. Gunfire erupted, sharp and staccato, reverberating through the stone. Anderson dove for cover as American Special Forces breached the chamber, their red visible lasers cutting through the dark.

The narrow tunnels turned into a kill zone. Bullets ricocheted off walls, spitting sparks. Quds fighters scrambled, returning fire with disciplined precision, their AK-47s barking against the Americans' M4s. Anderson crouched behind a crate, his pistol drawn, heart pounding. A soldier lunged at him —a Quds man mistaking him for the enemy. Anderson fired, dropping him, then rolled as a burst of rounds chewed the ground where he'd been.

Grey, still bound, kicked out at a passing fighter, tripping him into the crossfire. She was a wild card, even now. The Americans pressed forward, their shouts drowned by the chaos, tight, coordinated movements clashing with the Quds' ferocity. Blood pooled on the stone, and bodies slumped in the shadows.

Then she heard gunfire and muffled explosions from the opposite tunnel. Anderson's head snapped toward it. Another force? Reinforcements for the Quds? Taliban maybe, or Smith's crew? The chamber became a meat grinder, caught between two fronts. A flash-bang grenade rolled in, exploding with a deafening roar, partially blinding him. Dust choked the air, and Anderson lost sight of Grey, the Quds leader, and everyone.

He crawled through the haze, his mind a tangle of survival and doubt. Traficant's plan was unraveling, and he was in the middle. The moral dilemma he'd brushed aside clawed back—Grey's defiance, her loyalty, her certainty. He wasn't sure who he was fighting for or if it mattered anymore. Surviving the next few moments was all he cared about now. The cave shook with another blast, and he pressed on, a shadow among shadows, crawling toward an exit he wasn't sure existed.

***

Maxx crouched low in the jagged shadows of the Afghan tunnel, the cold stone pressing against his knees.

Distant shouts had startled him, a chaotic blend of Farsi voices slicing through the thin air, with Anderson's familiar accent tangled among them. His pulse hammered in his ears, adrenaline flooding his veins. This was it. Whether or not they found Doctor Smith, he'd finish what he started—for Miss Grey, Gabby, and whatever shred of humanity still flickered in this cesspit. He glanced at Sergeant Zeller, the Green Beret's weathered face barely visible in the dim light filtering through the tunnel.

"Ready?" Maxx whispered, his breath a faint cloud in the chill.

Zeller's eyes glinted with resolve and exhaustion. "We're racked and stacked."

Maxx nodded, sucking in a sharp breath. Then he moved, sliding toward the sound, boots whispering against the rocky floor as he moved deeper into the mountain's belly. The Green Berets followed, a silent, lethal team of operators—six men, plus Sergeant Zeller, hollow-eyed and battered, their gear clinking softly in the damp, claustrophobic dark.

The shouting grew louder as they neared a bend in the tunnel. Maxx dropped to his stomach, signaling the team to do the same. They crawled forward, inching up to a ledge overlooking a small cavern.

Below, Anderson stood amid a knot of Quds Force soldiers, his posture relaxed, almost casual. Smiling. The Iranian elite unit moved with grim efficiency, and their rifles slung low but ready. Maxx's gut twisted as he spotted Miss Grey, her wrists bound, her dark hair tangled across her battered face. She slumped a few paces behind Anderson, flanked by two soldiers.

"What the hell is he doing?" Private Hicks muttered, his wiry frame tense beside Maxx. Blood seeped through the bandage on his arm, a souvenir from an earlier skirmish. "He's talking to them like they're old buddies."

"Looks like they're playing *Let's Make a Deal*," Corporal Diaz growled, his voice tight with anger. "Smirking like that? CIA bastard is selling something—or someone."

Sergeant Zeller's jaw clenched. "Quds don't negotiate with grins and giggles. Whatever Anderson's playing at, it's bad news for us—and especially her."

Maxx squinted, straining to catch the occasional word drifting up from below. Anderson gestured animatedly, his grin widening as the Quds soldiers nodded. Then they stepped aside, pulling Grey with them toward a narrower passage. She fought back, twisting against their grip, her boots scuffing the dirt. One of the soldiers yanked her arm hard, and she stumbled, a muffled cry escaping her lips.

"We've got to stop them," Maxx said, his voice low but urgent, "but we can't risk hitting her."

Zeller nodded, his gaze flicking between Grey and the Quds soldiers. "Agreed. We move carefully, catch them in the crossfire. Diaz, Hicks, you're on point. Terry, cover the rear."

Corporal Terry, a stocky man who'd wrestled open a sluice gate two days back to save them from a flooded tunnel, gave a curt nod. "On it, Sarge."

Maxx and the Green Berets slid into position, crouching behind a jagged outcrop as they watched the scene unfold below. Anderson paced in the cavern's dim light, one hand pressing a satellite phone to his ear, his voice a low murmur punctuated by sharp gestures. Two Quds soldiers hauled Miss Grey forward, her bound hands jerking as she resisted until they forced her into a rickety wooden chair near the center of the space.

She glared up at them, defiance etched into every line of her face, while Anderson ignored her, his conversation growing heated. The soldiers bickered in clipped Farsi, their voices rising and falling, occasionally casting wary glances at Anderson as if awaiting orders that never came.

The Green Berets settled into position, their breaths shallow in the oppressive dark, when Diaz stiffened, his rifle snapping upward as if yanked by an unseen force. "What the—something's up there!" His voice fractured, a raw, unsteady edge cutting through—unthinkable for a seasoned Special Forces soldier.

Maxx tracked his gaze to the cavern's ceiling, where an apparition slithered across the stone, not only fast but impossibly fluid, a writhing, ink-black shadow that defied form, coiling and dissolving in a heartbeat. It wasn't a trick of the light or a fleeting animal—nothing Maxx had ever witnessed in this world moved like that, a bizarre flicker, enough to rattle even Diaz's iron resolve.

"Diaz, what—" Zeller began, but a gunshot cut him off. Diaz's round ricocheted off the stone, the crack echoing through the tunnel. Below, the Quds soldiers spun toward the sound, weapons raised. Anderson's grin faltered, and Grey's head snapped up, eyes wide.

"Damn it, Diaz!" Hicks hissed. "Are you crazy?"

"I saw it move!" Diaz snapped, his hands trembling. "Like a shadow but alive. *Un demonio*!"

"No time!" Zeller barked. "They're onto us—go!"

The cavern erupted into madness. The Quds soldiers opened fire, bullets chewing into the ledge where Maxx and the team crouched. Diaz dropped low, laying down covering fire as Hicks tossed a concussion grenade. The explosion shook the tunnel, and dirt and rock rained down. Maxx glimpsed Grey tripping a Quds soldier, then using the confusion to shield herself.

Anderson crawled toward a narrow crack in the wall, abandoning her without a backward glance.

"We've got to get her out!" Maxx shouted over the gunfire, his eyes locked on Grey. "But don't hit her. Focus on the Quds!"

"Easier said than done!" Zeller yelled back. "Terry, flank left with me! Hicks, Diaz, hold this line!"

The team split, moving fast. Terry and Zeller darted along the ledge, aiming to cut off the Quds retreat. But a burst of automatic fire caught Terry mid-stride. He staggered, blood blooming across his chest, and crumpled against the wall. His rifle clattered to the ground, his body sliding onto the ground.

"Terry's down!" Hicks called, his voice raw. "Son of a—"

"Keep moving!" Zeller roared, dragging his focus back. "We're pinned here!"

Maxx fired at a Quds soldier closing on Grey, dropping him with a clean shot to the leg. The man screamed, clutching his thigh, and Grey broke free, scrambling toward a stack of crates. But more soldiers closed in, their shouts rising over the gunfire. The Green Berets were holding, but barely—attrition was bleeding them dry. Another soldier fell, a Quds bullet punching through his shoulder, and Hicks swore as he dragged the man back.

"We can't advance," Diaz said, reloading with shaking hands. "They've got the choke point. We're dying slowly here."

Maxx's mind raced. He couldn't lose Grey—not after everything. But the standoff was a meat grinder, and his team was unraveling.

From the opposite side of the tunnel, a new sound erupted—gunfire, sharp and rapid, followed by Farsi shouts of panic.

The Quds soldiers faltered, turning to face this unseen threat. One dropped, then another, their bodies jerking like marionettes on a tight string.

"What the hell's going on?" Hicks said, peering through the smoke. "What's happening to them?"

"No idea," Zeller replied, his tone grim. "But they're doing our job for us."

Maxx watched, heart pounding, as the Quds' line buckled. Shadows moved in the far tunnel—figures, fast and precise, cutting through the enemy with brutal efficiency. Friend or foe, he couldn't tell. Grey was still caught in the middle, crouched behind the crates, trying to press her bound hands to her ears.

"Should we move in?" Diaz asked, glancing at Zeller. "Get her while they're distracted?"

Zeller shook his head. "We don't know who's out there. Could be worse than Quds."

Maxx's fists clenched. Every instinct screamed at him to act, to rush down and pull Grey out of the crossfire. But doubt gnawed at him, cold and heavy. What if he led the team into a trap? What if this new force turned on them next? He'd lost Terry already—could he risk Hicks, Diaz, Zeller? His breath caught, a wave of despair crashing over him. This could be it—the moment he lost her, lost everything. His vision blurred, the cavern's edges fading as indecision locked his limbs.

"Maxx!" Zeller's voice cut through the haze. "Make the call—she's your friend!"

Maxx forced himself to focus, eyes finding Grey's silhouette amid the chaos. She was still fighting, still alive. The attackers—whatever they were—had the Quds reeling. It was a chance, slim and bloody, but a chance.

"All right," he said, voice steadying. "We go now. Diaz, Hicks, cover us. Zeller, with me. We grab Grey and pull back—fast."

Zeller nodded, a flicker of relief in his eyes. "Let's move."

The team surged forward, weaving through the gunfire and smoke. Maxx kept his sights on Grey, her struggling body a beacon in the madness. The tunnel shook with the clash of forces, the Quds caught between the Green Berets and their mysterious assailants. He didn't know who the newcomers were, but he didn't care. All that mattered was reaching Grey. A shred of hope he refused to let die.

14

COME ON, TRY A LITTLE

Maxx staggered forward, his boots crunching against the grit of the tunnel floor, a sharp pain flaring in his leg where something had bitten him in the murky, cavern water. Blood seeped through his fingers as he pressed his hand against the wound, but he forced himself to keep moving.

Ahead, the faint outline of Miss Grey lingered in his vision, a constant objective amid the carnage. The Green Berets surged with him, their breaths ragged, weapons tight in their grips. Sergeant Zeller stayed close, his jaw set, while Diaz and Hicks fanned out, laying down cover fire that echoed through the claustrophobic passage.

"Keep it tight!" Maxx barked, his voice hoarse but determined. "We're almost there!"

Zeller glanced at him, sweat streaking his dust-stained face. "You good, King? You're losing a lot of blood."

"I'll live," Maxx grunted, shoving the pain down. "Grey won't if we don't get in there and finish this."

The tunnel shuddered with the chaos of combat. Quds soldiers snarled and lunged, their movements desperate as the mysterious attackers, still unidentified, pressed them from the rear. Maxx drove his fist into the jaw of a Quds fighter, feeling the crack of bone under his knuckles. Zeller followed, slamming the butt of his rifle into another's temple. Diaz grappled with a third, his knife flashing before the soldier crumpled, lifeless.

"Hand-to-hand's all we've got left," Hicks called over the din, his voice tight as he wrestled a Quds operative to the ground. "Ammo's running thin, and we can't risk hitting Grey!"

"Then use your fists," Maxx barked, ducking a wild swing and driving his elbow into the attacker's throat. The man gagged, collapsing, but not before driving his knife into Maxx's side.

Maxx swore and pressed on, searching wildly for Grey. The last time he'd spotted her, she was slumped behind some crates, barely moving. His heart locked tight. Was she still breathing?

The Americans fought their way through, body by body, until the tunnel opened into the Quds' main camp. The air reeked of blood and charred flesh. Iranian soldiers were scattered across the ground, their bodies eerily still. But at the back edge of the small cavern, a pile of soldiers was half in the shadows.

Maxx paused, his flashlight cutting through the gloom. The scene mirrored the Taliban corpses they'd found hours earlier —blistered skin, twisted limbs, blood leaking from ears and eyes—no gunfire wounds. No shrapnel. It was a grotesque, unnatural death. Not that any death in this hellscape was natural.

"What the hell did this?" Diaz muttered, his voice trembling as he scanned the bodies. His rifle twitched in his hands.

"Doesn't matter," Zeller said, stepping over a corpse. "They're dead. We're not. Focus, soldier."

***

"King, we need to move!" Hicks shouted, his tone sharp. "We lost three already—Ramirez, Terry, Jenkins. The team's down to five. Let's not make it four."

Maxx's head snapped up. Three more men gone. The weight of the past day sank into his bones, heavier than the blood soaking his side. He forced himself to stand, wincing as the wound tore at him. "Right. We... We still find Grey. Regroup."

Diaz's eyes darted wildly, his grip on his rifle unsteady. "Regroup? With whom? We don't even know if we've got reinforcements behind us. And who killed these bastards? What if we're next?"

"Stow it, Diaz," Zeller growled, stepping closer. "We've got orders. Capture or kill Smith and rescue Grey. Nothing has changed."

"Orders?" Diaz laughed, a brittle, broken sound. "None of them know what's been going on down here. They've all vanished, and we're dying one by one!"

They reached a pile of bodies near the tunnel's mouth—Quds and Taliban tangled together in death. Maxx paused, catching his breath, when something shifted in the heap. A low groan rasped from the pile, and Diaz jerked his rifle up, finger hovering over the trigger.

"Something's alive!" Diaz hissed, voice pitching high. "We shoot it—now!"

"Stand down!" Maxx roared, shoving Diaz's barrel aside. "We don't know what it is."

"Are you crazy?" Diaz's eyes blazed. "It could be one of them—one of whatever did this! We can't take the chance!"

Zeller stepped between them, his tone stern. "King's right. We don't waste rounds on shadows. Could be a friendly."

"Friendly?" Diaz spat. "After all this? Nothing lived through that."

Maxx barely registered the distant shouts and gunfire

fading into silence. His world narrowed to the mass of lifeless bodies. If Grey was in there, he had failed her. After everything —Seattle, New York, dragging his friends into this mess—he'd let her down.

"King!" Zeller's voice cut through his haze. "We've got movement—retreating Quds. They're fighting something farther into the tunnel."

Maxx barely heard him. His gaze fixed on Grey—or what he feared was her body—buried under fallen Quds soldiers. He stumbled forward, dropping to his knees beside the corpses. His hands shook as he shoved the dead men aside, revealing an American uniform streaked with blood. Panic struck. Had he been too late? Had a stray bullet from their rush caught Grey? Or had the attackers—whatever they were—finished her first?

Maxx ignored the men surrounding him, crouching by the pile. His side throbbed, blood slicking his hand, but he reached out, pulling a corpse aside. Another groan, louder now.

"Help me," he said, glancing at Zeller.

Zeller nodded, joining him. Together, they heaved the bodies away, revealing a figure beneath—battered, bloodied, but alive—a man, his uniform torn, his face obscured by grime. Maxx's breath caught. Anderson?

The man coughed, a wet, pained sound, and lifted his head. His unfocused eyes met Maxx's, and recognition flickered—faint, uncertain. "King?"

Maxx froze. Behind him, Diaz muttered a curse, and Hicks tightened his grip on his weapon. Zeller leaned closer, squinting.

"Talk," Maxx said, his tone sharp. "Anderson, where's Grey?"

The man's lips parted, but before he could answer, a low rumble shook the tunnel. Dust rained from the ceiling, and a faint, unnatural hiss echoed from the darkness beyond. The team stiffened, weapons snapping up. Maxx's pulse pounded in his ears. Whatever had torn through the Quds and Taliban wasn't finished—and it was coming closer.

"King," Zeller said, his voice steady despite the tension, "what's the call?"

Anderson's eyes fluttered shut, whites rolling back as his head slumped. Maxx knelt swiftly, fingers pressing against the man's neck. A faint, erratic pulse flickered under his touch—alive but barely.

A hard knot tightened in Maxx's chest. Barth Anderson. The orchestrator, the one who'd dangled Smith as bait and sent him over the cliff. Was this all a calculated betrayal? Was Anderson the mastermind—or a piece on someone else's board, one Maxx hadn't yet spotted?

Zeller's voice broke the tension, sharp and practical. "We're dragging him along or leaving him? If he stays here, he's a dead man."

Maxx's gaze hardened, his voice a low rasp. "I don't know. But we're still in the fight. You said it—he's already got one foot in the grave."

Maxx couldn't bring himself to care about leaving him. Anderson had built this disaster, lured Miss Grey in, and now reaped the consequences. Maxx's focus was singular—Grey needed him, and he wasn't about to burden himself with Anderson's dead weight while she remained missing.

The tunnel fell silent, except for their ragged breathing. Hicks shifted uneasily, glancing at Zeller. "He's right, King. We've got no option but to move forward."

Maxx swallowed, forcing his mind to focus. "Then we leave him. We find Grey, figure out what's hunting us, and kill it."

They started moving toward the cavern exit, a limping, battered remnant of the team. Maxx's mind churned. The virus canisters... Had Anderson sold them out? Had Xi known? And Smith, the original target, what was his role in this nightmare?

Every step jolted his wounds, but the physical pain was

nothing compared to the doubt gnawing at him. Was he good enough? Had he lost his edge, chasing specters for men he couldn't trust?

***

The rain had fallen in sheets over Snoqualmie Falls last night, a relentless curtain that blurred the world's edges. Torashi Kage's blade had been quick and precise, a flash of steel under the street lights before Andres realized the fight had been lost. Kage had left him for dead by the side of the road, assuming the deep wound would finish what the knife had started.

Andres had woken up to find a nurse out for a late-evening stroll, helping him. She'd been a blur of motion in her yellow raincoat, kneeling beside him with a calm that belied the chaos. He'd been in shock when the familiar growl of Glen's old pickup cut through the downpour. The truck had screeched to a stop on the muddy shoulder, tires spinning before they caught traction.

Glen had tossed him onto the truck's bench seat. They'd driven to Salish Lodge, slipping into Gabby's hotel room under the cover of the storm. The place had been a mess, clothes strewn across the floor, a half-packed bag abandoned on the bed. They'd found a crumpled note that had led to a call with Torashi Kage before Andres had passed out from the pain and blood loss.

Now, hours later, Andres sat on a metal exam table in a veterinary clinic that smelled of antiseptic and wet dog. Glen's friend, Carla, a green-haired veterinary assistant, had stitched him up with steady hands, muttering about how she wasn't supposed to work on humans but making do, anyway.

The painkillers she'd given him from the emergency supply she kept locked in her desk drawer hit Andres hard. Despite his efforts to stay awake, they knocked him out cold. When he woke, the room spun briefly before settling, and Glen was there, pacing, holding a crumpled list of names and numbers they'd pulled from Gabby's backpack. After she vanished, they'd grabbed the information from her room at Salish Lodge, hoping it held some clue to where she'd gone.

"Anything?" Andres asked, his voice rough as he tested his side. The stitches pulled but held.

Glen shook his head, tossing the list onto a nearby counter. "Nada. I called everyone on there. Friends, coworkers, and some random taxi driver named Peter, who sounded like he was three beers deep. No one's seen her. They all kept asking, 'Is she okay?' Like I'd know. That's why I'm calling you!"

Andres grunted, sliding off the table. His legs wobbled but steadied. "We're wasting time. We need Maxx."

Glen nodded. "Yeah. If anyone knows where she might head, it's him. You sure you're up for this?"

"No, but I can't take any more of this dog smell," Andres said. However, the dog smell was much less frustrating than the pain in his side. "Call his cell. Hopefully, he can get a signal."

Glen fished his phone from his pocket and dialed. The line rang once, twice, then clicked over to Maxx King's familiar growl. "Yeah?"

"Hi, sweetheart, it's Glen," he said with a smirk. "I've got Andres with me. We're in Fremont. You still in the Stan?"

There was a pause, and then Maxx's voice came through, clipped and strained. "It's lovely this time of year. In some tunnels somewhere in the Kush. Been chasing shadows and getting shot at all day."

Andres leaned closer to the phone, wincing as he moved. "You hurt?"

Maxx snorted. "Shot, fell off a cliff, bitten by something, and stabbed," Maxx said flatly. "Overall, much better than the usual excursion. The team's patching me up now. What's going on there?"

Andres exchanged a look with Glen. "We've been trying to track down Gabby. She's taken off twice. It seems that she doesn't want to be found. Understandable considering someone is after her."

Maxx was silent for a moment or two. "Who is after her?" he growled.

"A hired gun named Torashi Kage. Do you know him? He seems to know you."

"He wants me," Maxx said, sounding exhausted. "Been hunting me since I took out that killer, Haoyu, last year. Gabby's bait. You sure she's still alive?"

"No," Andres admitted, "but if he's threatening her, he's got to keep her breathing until he's sure you're in play."

Maxx didn't respond right away. When he did, his voice was quieter, frayed at the edges. "Have you talked with Kage? The dude is crazy."

"Yeah," Andres said. "He's using her to get to you. He and I got into it when Glen and I caught him tracking Gabby. He stabbed me and took off. Then we intercepted the eerie message Torashi had left in Gabby's hotel room."

"What kind of message?" Maxx's tone sharpened.

Glen jumped in. "He said, 'Fremont Bridge Troll in ten hours.' That was almost eight hours ago. 'If Mr. King does not come alone, his woman will be collateral damage.' The call ended after that."

"In two hours," Maxx repeated. "Why'd you wait to tell me? You know I can't get there."

"Won't matter," Andres cut in, his voice hardening. "He'll be dead before he knows you're not there. I'm going in close once I'm patched up. Lean, mean fighting machine. It's personal now. Glen will be on overwatch."

"We're in a mess here. We turned off the comms device

earlier, but we're still lost. The Green Berets figured out we've been going in circles since this morning. Tunnels are a maze. Taliban and Quds are crawling around, guarding Smith. We found Anderson, but he was too far gone. Left him behind. Now we're after Grey, but Smith's still out there."

"Smith," Andres said. "Your white whale."

"Yeah," Maxx muttered. "And I'm starting to wonder if I'm breaking my promise chasing him."

"What promise?" Glen asked, frowning.

Maxx didn't answer directly. Instead, he said, "You know that old Springfield pistol I carry. That was my old man's. He gave it to me back in the day. He told me to use it right. 'Use it to protect the ones I love.' I swore I'd keep that balance. But here I am, halfway across the world, while Gabby's in Torashi's crosshairs. What's that say about me?"

Andres shifted, ignoring the stab of pain in his side. "Says you're human. Torn between two fights."

Glen jumped in. "That's heavy, Maxx. What's your move?"

"I don't know," Maxx admitted. "Team's pressing on. We've got to get out of these tunnels, but I'm running on fumes. If I abandon Gabby to get Smith, I'm not sure I can live with it. If I drop everything to save her, Smith slips away again, and Grey probably dies. Either way, I'm failing someone."

Glen leaned into the phone. "You're not failing yet. Andres has a plan. We take out Torashi at the bridge. We might get Gabby back before you even have to choose."

"Might," Maxx echoed. "That's a hell of a word to hang hope on."

"It's what we've got," Andres said. "You focus on getting out of there. We'll handle Fremont. You tell us what you need when you're stateside."

Maxx exhaled, a sound that carried the weight of too many decisions. "I need Gabby safe. I need Torashi gone. And I need to know if Smith's worth all this blood. Keep me posted. I'll call when we're topside."

The line went dead. Glen pocketed the phone, turning to Andres. "You sure about this? You're not one hundred percent. And I hate to say it, but Torashi already beat you once."

Andres smirked, though it didn't reach his eyes. "Torashi should've finished the job. I'm not giving him a second chance."

15

ONE SHOT, TWO TARGETS

Lieutenant Weih rubbed his hands together to warm them up. Another cold night stuck in this damn place, and he wasn't dressed for it.

The Shah-i-Kot Valley stretched before John Weih like a jagged wound in the earth, its rocky cliffs bathed in the pale light of a waning moon. The air was sharp with the odor of dust and cordite, a reminder of the chaos that had unfolded hours earlier.

Weih, a lean Texan, fresh out of training, with sun-bleached hair and a jaw set like steel, crouched beside a crumbling boulder. His M4 carbine rested comfortably across his knees. Around him, his squad hunkered down in the shadows of the valley, their breaths puffing faintly in the cold night air. Operation Anaconda roared in the distance, the din of gunfire and explosions echoing off the mountains.

Twenty-four hours ago, they'd stumbled into a firefight they hadn't expected. Weih's unit had been patrolling the treacherous terrain when they spotted a Taliban group scrambling around several destroyed transports, a clandestine CIA convoy.

The insurgents were hauling oversized canisters from vehicles, unlike any munitions Weih had ever seen, toward a network of caves carved into the cliffs. The containers were dull gray, larger than standard artillery or tank rounds. They bore no recognizable markings, only faint scratches that might have been serial numbers worn by time and weather.

"Somethin' ain't right about this," Sergeant Kerro had muttered beside him, his thick New Jersey accent cutting through the stillness. Kerro, a grizzled non-commissioned officer with a face like weathered leather, squinted at the abandoned canisters. "These ain't no munition that I've ever seen, Lieutenant. Look at them. Too damn big, and there's no base fuze."

Weih nodded, his gut twisting. They'd engaged the Taliban hard, trading bullets in a brutal skirmish. The enemy had fought like cornered wolves, desperate to protect their prize. Outnumbered and pinned down, Weih's squad held the line, eventually turning the tide. The surviving insurgents melted into the night, leaving the canisters behind.

"Command, this is Bravo Two-Three," Weih had barked into his radio, static crackling in response. "We've secured unknown munitions in the valley. Requesting instructions." The mountains swallowed his signal, leaving only garbled noise.

Frustrated, he'd used his cell phone, reaching out to Maxx King, whose voice was clipped and urgent, saying "Stay frosty, Weih. Hide the canisters and don't tell anyone about them."

His call with Maxx was eight hours ago. Since then, the valley had grown eerily quiet, the Taliban's absence unnerving. Weih's squad stayed low. Their nerves were frayed, watching the canisters like they might sprout legs and walk off.

Now, the faint whine of rotors broke the silence. Weih raised his binoculars, spotting a pair of Black Hawks from the 160th descending through the swirling dust. A combat search and rescue team had finally arrived to retrieve the canisters and pull them out. The choppers touched down one hundred yards away, kicking up a storm of grit that stung Weih's face. Figures in tactical gear spilled out, moving with purpose toward his position.

"Lieutenant Weih?" a voice called over the wind. A tall, broad-shouldered man approached, his face obscured by a balaclava until he pulled it down, revealing sharp features and a salt-and-pepper beard. "Captain Schumer, CSAR lead. We're here for those canisters."

Weih raised his eyebrows in surprise. *Command sent a captain out on a SAR run.* He stood, brushing dirt from his fatigues. "Good to see you, sir. Been a long damn wait."

Schumer surveyed the scene, lingering on the canisters scattered among the rocks. "Anaconda's been an epic disaster. We haven't been able to get through until now. What's the sitrep here?"

"Taliban hit us hard then pulled back after air support showed up," Weih said. "Left these behind. We were told to hold position, but we've had no contact since."

Schumer knelt beside a canister, running a gloved hand over its surface. "No markings. Heavy too. They look like ours, though. You didn't try to open them?"

"No, sir," Weih replied. "Didn't want to risk it without orders."

"Smart." Schumer stood, gesturing to his team. "Load what we can. Command wants these at Bagram ASAP."

Kerro shifted, his jaw tightening. "Hold up, sir. You're taking them and leaving us here?"

Schumer fixed him with a hard stare. "Orders are to secure as many canisters as we can carry and extract. You're to fall back on your own, Sergeant."

Weih shook his head, planting his boots firmly. "I'm not leaving till I know what's what."

"Lieutenant," Williams said, his tone sharpening as he

leaned in, "this isn't a debate. Command's calling the shots now. Load up your vehicles and move out."

"No, sir," Weih said, his voice steady but edged with defiance. "Something's off about this. Those canisters, the way the Taliban fought for them, I'm staying until we secure all of them."

Kerro stepped up beside him, crossing his arms. "We ain't leaving the LT, Captain. If you want to drag us out of here, you'll need more than harsh words."

Schumer's eyes narrowed. "That's mutiny, soldier. You're looking at a court-martial."

"Then court-martial us," Weih snapped. "I'm not abandoning my post till I get answers."

The rest of Weih's squad murmured agreement, boots shuffling nervously in the dirt. Tension crackled like static. Schumer exhaled sharply then turned to his comms. "Command, this is SAR One. Canisters located. Bravo Two-Three refusing extraction. Request confirmation on cargo."

There was a pause, and then a voice buzzed back, "SAR One, do those canisters match descriptions of viral munitions we've been tracking?"

"Yes, they do."

"Then secure what you can and return immediately. We'll deal with Bravo Two-Three later."

Schumer's expression darkened. He switched to a private channel, muttering, "Colonel Williams, you hearing this? Virus canisters confirmed." He listened, nodded once, and then cut the connection. "All right, load three and dust off. We don't have room for more."

The combat search and rescue team hauled three canisters toward the choppers, their movements hurried. Weih watched, unease gnawing at him. *Viral munitions?* What the hell had they stumbled into? The Black Hawks lifted off, engines roaring as they climbed above the valley, disappearing into the night.

Minutes later, a flash lit the horizon, followed by a dull boom. Weih grabbed his binoculars, his heart pounding. Through the lenses, he saw flaming wreckage spiraling down the mountainside. The SAR helicopters were gone, taken out by something fast and precise.

"What the hell," Kerro breathed, his accent thick with shock. "What kinda shitstorm are we in, LT?"

Weih lowered the binoculars, his mouth dry. "I don't know, Sergeant. But I'm damn glad we stayed."

"Think that was the Taliban?" Kerro asked, scanning the cliffs.

"Maybe. Or someone who doesn't want those canisters leaving this valley." Weih turned to the remaining containers, their dull surfaces glinting faintly. "King knew something, Command's scrambling, and now the second SAR team is dead. We're on our own."

Kerro spat into the dirt. "So what's the game plan? Sit tight and hope we don't get smoked?"

"For now," Weih said. "Keep eyes on the perimeter. If those were virus canisters, we're guarding a weapon nobody's supposed to have. Taliban, or whoever hit the SAR team, they'll be back."

The squad fanned out, retaking their defensive positions among the rocks. Weih crouched beside a canister, studying it. No markings, no clues, only cold metal under his fingers. Operation Anaconda thundered on, a distant storm, but a different war was brewing here in the valley. The promise of rescue had shattered with sudden chaos, and Weih couldn't shake the feeling they were expendable.

"LT," Kerro called softly, his voice low, "you think we're making it outta here alive?"

Weih met his gaze, the burden of command weighing him down. "We've got a job, Sergeant. Hold the line. Answers will come, one way or another."

Kerro grunted, settling back with his rifle. "Yeah, well, if I'm dying in this shithole, I'd sure appreciate one last cold beer."

Weih laughed. "You and me both." The night stretched on, heavy with the promise of more violence. The canisters sat silent, their secrets locked inside, while Weih, Kerro, and the squad waited, caught between duty and the unknown.

***

"Maxx," Zeller called, his stocky frame emerging from the tunnel's shadows. The Green Beret's hair was stringy with sweat, his rifle slung low. "Got something over here. You're going to want to see this."

Maxx followed, boots crunching on loose stone until they reached a shallow depression beside the tunnel's mouth. A pool of muddy water shimmered faintly, and beside it, sprawled next to a Qud corpse, was Miss Grey. Her dark-brown hair was plastered to her face, her skin smeared with mud she'd caked on like camouflage.

"She's half-dead," Zeller said, kneeling beside her. "Hypothermia's got her good. Anderson must've ditched her in the chaos."

Maxx's jaw tightened. "Diaz, get over here!"

Diaz, the team's medic, jogged up, his wiry frame moving with precision. His sleepy brown eyes assessed Grey as he dropped his pack. "She's bleeding too. Leg wound. Looks like shrapnel." He pulled out a thermal blanket and a med kit, his hands steady despite the urgency. "Maxx, back off. I've got this."

Maxx hovered, adrenaline still pumping. "She's my friend, Diaz. Tell me what to do."

"Stand there and don't crowd me," Diaz snapped, cutting away Grey's pant leg to reveal a gash oozing dark blood. "She's cold as hell and losing more. I need space." He pressed gauze to the wound and then injected a syringe of painkiller. "Come on, senorita, stay with me."

Maxx stepped back, fists clenched, watching as Diaz worked. The medic wrapped the blanket around her, rubbing her arms to coax warmth back into her body. Grey's eyelids fluttered, her lips blue but parting with a faint groan. "M-Maxx?" she rasped, her voice a thread.

"Yeah, it's me," Maxx said, crouching despite Diaz's glare. "Thought I lost you."

Her eyes focused, a weak smile tugging at her mouth. "Thought you were dead. Anderson shot you... Cliff..."

"Takes more than that to kill me," Maxx said, forcing a grin. "What happened to you?"

"Escaped... Hid," she murmured. "Quds ran. I followed... then this."

"You were taking a mud bath?" Maxx asked with raised eyebrows.

She tried to laugh despite the pain. "I kept motionless, trying to blend with the dead. I covered myself with mud. It worked in that alien film I'd watched as a kid.

Diaz snorted. "She's talking about *Predator*, man."

"Get to the chopper!" Maxx yelled.

Her chest rose faintly, her breaths shallow and ragged. She smiled weakly and nodded. "Yeah, that's the movie. It worked, didn't it?" She shivered, her gaze sharpening. "Update me."

Maxx hesitated, then said, "Anderson's gone. Quds scattered. We've been tracking Smith since last night, but we shut off the power to the alien communication device. I think we've got a bead on the virus canisters. But I haven't been able to get there. But Weih—"

Grey's brow furrowed, cutting him off. "Enough. Focus, Maxx. Smith's the priority. He's trying to organize the Others. And the virus, we can't let it slip. You know where Weih is?"

"Yeah," Maxx said, "he is holding his position. Weih's got

the canisters, which I think hold the virus, secured in Shah-i-Kot. They haven't been able to get a search and rescue team to help, so he and his squad are in danger of being overrun by the Taliban or whatever else is out there."

"Good." Grey's voice hardened, though her body trembled. "Don't trust Senator Traficant. She's playing us, Maxx. We've been pawns in a game we don't get. Smith and Traficant are two of a kind. They'll burn the world down if we don't stop them."

Maxx rocked back, the weight of her words sinking in. "Stop them both? Grey, that's impossible. I'm one man."

"You're not a quitter," she said, her tone fierce despite her frailty. "You and Gabby didn't quit last year, even with the odds against you. I know you won't stop until this is done."

He swallowed hard, echoes of Gabby's resolve stirring in his chest. She'd faced the abyss with him and kept going, and now Grey was shoving him toward the same edge again. "How the hell do I do this?"

"Go back to Weih," she said. "Secure the canisters then find Gabby. I'll handle Smith with Zeller and the team."

Maxx stared at her, incredulous. "You're barely alive, Grey. How are you going to chase Smith? Not to mention whatever is hunting the Quds. The Predators."

"I'll manage," she said, her eyes glinting defiantly. "When you talk to Andres, tell him I'm okay. Don't... Don't tell him how bad it is. He'll worry."

"Grey—" Maxx started, but Zeller cut in.

"She's right, brother," Zeller said, his deep voice steady. "Diaz will patch her up, keep her going. We'll carry her if we have to. You handle this virus stuff."

Diaz nodded, taping a fresh bandage over Grey's leg. "She's tough. I've got her vitals climbing. She'll hold, but I ain't carrying her."

Grey gripped Maxx's arm, her fingers icy but firm. "Go,

Maxx. Weih needs you. The virus can't get back into the hands of Traficant."

Maxx met her gaze, the fire in her eyes cutting through her agony. He nodded once, standing. "All right. Zeller, you're with Grey. Diaz, keep her breathing, or I'll find you. I have to find my way out of this maze to get to Weih before it's too late."

"We're on it," Zeller said, slinging his rifle. "We'll hunt Smith down. Don't get yourself killed out there."

"No promises," Maxx muttered, turning to the open air. The granite break framed a sky streaked with moonlight, the wind carrying the distant rumble of conflict. His team split here, Grey clinging to life, trusting him to hold the line elsewhere. The canisters, the virus, Smith, and Traficant all spiraled into a knot of impossibility. But quitting wasn't in him, and Grey knew it.

"Diaz," Grey called weakly as Maxx stepped away. "Tell me straight. How bad is it?"

Diaz glanced at her, his hands still busy with the med kit. "You're a mess, ma'am. Hypothermia's easing, but that leg's going to slow you down. Rest whenever you can. And don't be shy about asking for a lift."

She chuckled faintly, a dry sound. "No rest until Smith's done for good this time."

Maxx paused at the tunnel's edge, looking back. Grey was wrapped in the blanket, mud-streaked and pale, yet her resolve was etched on her face. The team stood guard, hulking silhouettes, while Diaz worked with quiet efficiency. They'd chase Smith through hell if she asked, and Maxx knew he'd do the same for Weih and the canisters.

The tunnel twisted back into the mountain, a grim path leading toward Shah-i-Kot. Maxx adjusted his gear, the weight of his pistol a familiar anchor—a reminder to keep his promises.

Senator Traficant's shadow loomed in his mind, a puppet

master he couldn't yet see. Smith and the Others, Thunderbird, and the virus were threads in a web threatening to strangle the world. Impossible or not, he'd cut through it to return to Gabby. His father's ghost whispered at his back, urging him on.

"Move out," he said to himself, voice lost to the echoes, and plunged into the tunnel, the granite swallowing him whole. Behind him, Grey's faint orders to Zeller drifted in the air, a promise to finish what they'd started.

The game was bigger than Maxx had ever imagined, but damn if he wasn't going to play it to the end. He owed that much to Gabby.

DAY TWO

16

AIN'T GOOD ENOUGH

Under Seattle's gray, drizzling sky, Andres Sandoval and Glen Piper parked on a side street near the Fremont Bridge.

The air carried a damp chill, and the faint roar of traffic overhead mingled with the soft patter of rain on the pavement. Below the bridge, the Fremont Troll loomed, a hulking concrete sculpture clutching an actual Volkswagen Beetle in its massive hand. Its single visible eye stared blankly into the distance, a quirky landmark that had fascinated Andres since he first heard of it.

Half man, half beast, the troll was an oddity born from a local art competition and unveiled on Halloween a decade ago, a strange guardian of this eclectic neighborhood. Andres was glad to be here in the middle of the day; the shadows cast by the bridge and the troll's jagged form would have felt far more menacing at night.

Andres adjusted the collar of his jacket, wincing slightly as the movement tugged at the fresh stitches in his side. The wound from the previous night throbbed, a stark reminder of Torashi Kage's blade slicing into him near the Salish Lodge. He had barely escaped with his life, left bleeding in the dark until a passerby found him.

Standing near the troll, he scanned the area with sharp, steady eyes. If Torashi had chosen this meeting spot and time, he would likely already be waiting, watching from some concealed hideout. Andres's strength had always been his stability and capacity to reason even when adrenaline surged. He clung to that now, forcing his mind to focus despite the pain, painkillers, and the stakes.

Beside him, Glen shifted his large frame, his huge hands resting on the door of his beat-up pickup truck. The old Ford was a patchwork of rust and faded blue paint, but it ran like a dream, and Glen trusted it as much as he trusted the sniper rifle hiding behind the truck's bench seat. The rifle, an M24 bolt-action Remington with a notched stock and a scope polished to perfection, was his lifeline in moments like this. He could hit a quarter ten times in a row at eight hundred meters.

Glen was a man of few words. His face was lined from years of hard living, but his eyes were sharp and calculating. "We stick to the plan," Glen said, his voice low. "You wait out of sight near the troll. I'll take the truck up the hill and find a good angle. If you give the signal, I'll take him out."

"The usual signal?" Andres asked.

"Steal home," Glen signed as he cycled through, touching his nose and ear in rapid sequence.

Andres nodded, though his jaw tightened. "I want him alive, Glen. I need to do this myself. He left me for dead. I deserve answers, and I deserve to end it."

His tone was firm, unyielding. He needed to know why Torashi had come for Maxx now after all this time. Glen's brow furrowed, skepticism flickering in his gaze, but he relented with a grunt. "Fine, but if it goes south, I'm not waiting for your permission, dude."

Glen climbed into the truck, the engine rumbling to life as

he drove off to find his overwatch position. Andres slipped into his hiding spot, a narrow nook between a graffiti-covered wall and a stack of old shipping crates across from the troll.

The damp concrete soaked into his boots, and the faint smell of rotting fish hung in the air. He crouched low, his eyes fixed on the troll's grotesque form, its concrete fingers curling around the Beetle like a predator with its prey.

The mist coated his face, but he barely noticed. His pulse was steady, his mind clear, yet a prickling sensation crawled up his spine. He was being watched. Before he could shift his position, a shadow moved in the alley behind him. Andres turned, his hand instinctively dropping to the knife sheathed at his belt.

Torashi stepped into view, his lean frame draped in a dark raincoat that glistened with moisture. His black hair was slicked back, and cold, unreadable eyes locked onto Andres. A faint smirk tugged at his lips as he twirled a blade in his hand, the same one that had nearly killed Andres the night before.

"Sandoval," Torashi purred, menace dripping from his smooth voice, "Maxx lacked the courage to face me, so he sent you instead. You won't be so lucky the next time we meet."

Andres straightened, ignoring the ache in his side. His heart thudded, but his voice remained even. "You're early. I figured you'd wait for me to show my face." He hoped Glen had found his perch, that the scope of that Remington was trained on Torashi right now. But he couldn't look, couldn't give away the plan. Instead, he tilted his head, studying the killer.

"Why now, Torashi? Maxx said you've been tracking him since last September."

Torashi's smirk widened, but his eyes narrowed. "You think you're clever, don't you? Always so calm, so rational. It's irritating, and we only met yesterday." He stepped closer, the knife catching the dim light filtering through the drizzle.

Andres tensed, his fingers tightening around his blade, but

he kept his tone casual, probing. "Irritating enough to tell me what's going on? You don't seem the type to waste time on personal grudges. Someone's pulling your strings."

The taunt struck a nerve. Torashi's grip on the knife faltered for a fraction of a second, and his voice dropped to a hiss. "You want to know before you die? Fine. I was hired by someone to find a rogue scientist. Since I was already in the area, I figured I'd take care of Maxx. Two birds, one stone." He sneered, taking another step. "The rest of you are just distractions until Maxx gets the courage to show up."

Andres's mind raced, piecing it together. Torashi's employer, likely someone in the government, wanted Maxx stopped before he could finish whatever he'd started overseas. Gabby was the key to finding Maxx, and Andres had walked into the crossfire while trying to protect her. It made sense now, a puzzle slotting into place. But there was no time to dwell on it. Torashi lunged.

The alley erupted into chaos. Rain-slicked pavement gleamed under their boots as Andres parried the first strike, metal clashing against metal. The air was thick with the smell of wet asphalt and the tang of adrenaline.

Torashi was fast, his movements fluid and precise, but Andres was grounded, his stability keeping him balanced on the slippery ground. He ducked a wild slash, countering with a thrust that grazed Torashi's arm—blood mixed with the rain, staining the dirty concrete. The killer grunted, his smirk replaced by a snarl, and came at Andres harder. Their knives locked, and for a moment they were face-to-face, breaths heaving, eyes burning with intent.

Andres's side screamed in protest as he twisted away from a brutal stab, the stitches straining. He stumbled, his boot slipping on a puddle, but he caught himself against the brick wall. Torashi pressed the advantage, aiming for his chest, but Andres rolled to the side, slashing at Torashi's leg. The blade bit flesh, and Torashi staggered, cursing. The fight was raw and messy, each man fueled by desperation and rage. Rain blurred Andres's vision, but he kept moving, kept thinking. He had to end this. He doubted Glen could find an angle to cover him in this alley.

A sudden shout broke through the haze. "Hey! Drop the weapons!" Two police officers on bicycles skidded to a stop at the mouth of the alley, their reflective vests bright against the gray. Andres froze, his chest heaving, while Torashi lowered his knife, his demeanor shifting instantly.

"Officers," Torashi called, his voice suddenly polished and pleading, "thank God you're here. This man tried to rob me. I'm a businessman from Tokyo."

Andres glared, wiping rain from his face. "He's lying! He's a killer. Arrest him!"

The officers hesitated, their hands hovering near their holsters. "Both of you, on the ground, now!" one barked, reaching for his radio to call for backup. Andres dropped his knife, raising his hands, but Torashi sank to his knees with a groan, clutching his leg.

"He stabbed me," Torashi whimpered, playing the victim with chilling ease.

One officer approached Torashi, bending to check his wound, while the other kept Andres in sight. In a flash, Torashi struck, plunging a hidden knife into the officer's inner thigh. The man cried out, collapsing, and Torashi bolted, disappearing around the corner as the second officer fumbled for his gun.

"Stop or I'll shoot!" the officer yelled, but Torashi was already gone, swallowed by a maze of dank alleys.

Andres started to rise, intending to pursue Torashi, but the remaining officer swung his weapon toward him. "Stay down! Hands where I can see them!"

Frustration boiled in Andres's chest, but he complied, sinking back onto the wet pavement.

The wounded officer groaned, clutching his leg as blood pooled beneath him. Sirens wailed in the distance, growing louder, and soon a squad car screeched to a halt nearby. Two more officers leaped out, barking orders.

Despite his protests that he was innocent, they cuffed Andres and hauled him to his feet. They shoved him into the back of the squad car, the door slamming shut with a thud. Through the drizzle, he saw Glen standing near the troll, his rifle missing, his expression unreadable.

Andres leaned back into the seat, his mind already working. Torashi had slipped away again.

***

The clock struck 12:30 p.m. as Torashi limped along a narrow street near the Fremont Bridge in Seattle. His dark eyes darted across the traffic, watching for the police.

The damp air clung to his skin, a bitter reminder of the mess he'd made. He had arranged through Andres Sandoval to meet Maxx King at the Fremont Troll at noon. The troll was a monstrous concrete sculpture lurking under the bridge like a predator—unpredictable and a little unhinged, like him. It was supposed to be a quick killing, a chance to tie up loose ends so he could focus on the attack on Green and Xi in Beijing. Their plane would land in only a few hours, and he had let the preparations slip. But since the attack had failed, his mind churned with Gabby and Maxx, an unsatisfied obsession coiling inside him. He wanted to make Maxx suffer, to drag his girlfriend Gabby into the chaos.

Torashi had staked out the troll, arriving well before noon. He'd watched Andres pull up with a large black guy in a beat-up truck that looked as if it was held together by rust. Andres had climbed out, heading to a watchpoint, while his friend drove off, the truck's exhaust coughing into the fog. "Amateurs," Torashi had muttered under his breath, smirking.

After the Salish Lodge altercation, he'd dug into the background for Andres—Maxx's friend, but the other man was a blank slate. Was Maxx bringing Andres as backup, or had he bolted? No one had seen him in Seattle for days. Torashi was beginning to think he'd skipped town and left Gabby behind.

The uncertainty stoked Torashi's anger. He slipped into a filthy alley with a view of the troll, the stench of garbage wrinkling his nose. "I hate this backwoods town," he snarled to himself, brushing dirt and blood off his jacket sleeve.

The fight had erupted quickly and sloppily. Torashi flexed his wounded arm, pain lancing through it. His leg was worse, a deep gash slowing him down, blood seeping through his ripped pants. "How did that bastard get the drop on me?" he hissed, replaying the clash. Andres had been fast, much faster than last night, somehow gaining the advantage on him. The wounds fueled his agitation. He needed to focus, but the mounting frustration begged for release.

Torashi slumped against the graffiti-smeared wall, his trembling fingers fumbling for his phone. He dialed, his jaw tight. "Hiroshi," he growled the moment the call picked up.

The line hissed before his coordinator's voice broke through, tentative. "Boss? What's up?"

"Green and Xi," Torashi said brusquely. "Beijing. Wipe them out. I don't care what it takes. Traficant's footing the bill."

A beat of silence stretched too long. "That's a powder keg," Hiroshi finally said cautiously. "Are you sure you can smooth things over with the Chinese afterward?"

"Yes," Torashi spat, his patience fraying. "Get it done." He jabbed the end call button and stuffed the phone back into his pocket, Hiroshi's hesitation scraping at his nerves. Other problems loomed larger, sharper.

He peered out, watching as the Seattle Police Department swarmed the alleyway by the troll. Andres sat in the back of a patrol car. "Got you now, my friend." Torashi yearned to walk over and finish Andres, but there were too many cops to act on that fantasy. The unknown black man crossed his mind. "Could I find him? Make him talk?" he mused aloud, then shook his head. "No, too risky." Gabby though—he had searched everywhere and found nothing. "Chasing is useless."

A jagged plan flickered to life in Torashi's churning mind, unformed and reckless. He'd dangle Maxx as bait—Gabby cared about him, that much he'd pieced together from scraps of intel. His fingers, still unsteady from the fight, dug into his pocket for a burner phone. He hunched over it, the alley's dim light casting harsh shadows on the screen.

With deliberate taps, he typed, "Maxx is hurt. Needs you. Meet at the old TechCom warehouse on Dexter at midnight." His thumb hovered over the send button then pulled back. He hadn't figured out the next step.

"How do I get this to her?" he muttered, his voice a low rasp. Gabby had become a ghost—no address, no habits he could pin down. A courier might work, some faceless runner she wouldn't suspect. Or maybe a note slipped somewhere she'd stumble across it—like a coffee shop she frequented, if he could guess one. He pictured her finding it, her face twisting with worry, rushing to save Maxx.

The thought sent a thrill through him, dark and electric. She'd come—he felt it in his bones. But the gap gnawed at him. How to reach her? His mind churned, options slipping through his grasp like wet sand. He needed a way, and soon.

First, he needed to vent. Hurting people steadied him. He climbed into the stolen Honda waiting for him at a pay parking lot and headed south toward Highway 99, the fog thickening.

He parked in the gravel lot outside a squat concrete building near the freeway. The Diesel Dog resembled a dive bar and strip club, crouching like a bunker in the dilapidated neighborhood. Neon signs flickered, casting red and blue reflections across rain-slicked streets. Inside, a jukebox hummed blues, cutting through smoke and stale beer. The bartender, grizzled and hollow-eyed, wiped the counter. "What'll it be?" he droned, barely glancing up.

"Japanese whiskey," Torashi said, sliding onto a wobbly stool. The tables were dirty, and customers in leather jackets were whispering in shadowy corners. Partially nude dancers swayed on a dim stage, sequins glinting.

Torashi's gaze locked on a truck driver at a corner table—broad-shouldered, flannel grease-stained, nursing a beer. Perfect. He limped over, blood streaking his leg. "You look like you've got nothing better to do," he said, voice low and sharp.

The driver glanced up, bleary-eyed but bold. "And you look more than half stupid, buddy. What's your problem?"

"You," Torashi grinned, feral. "Sitting there like you own this dump."

The driver stood, fists curling. "Say that again," he growled.

The bar hushed, eyes turning as Torashi squared up, pain forgotten, a smile revealing the gap between his teeth. He was ready to unleash.

17

WALKING ON A WIRE

The tunnel's air clung to Maxx like a shroud, heavy with dampness and the sour reek of unseen decay. Each breath was a struggle. His boots scraped the jagged stone floor, the feeble scuffing swallowed by the rock walls. Alone, he pressed on, every step a gamble against the unseen things that lurked beyond his flickering light, their presence a cold prickle on his sweat-slicked skin.

For twenty-four hours, he and the Green Beret team had wandered this labyrinth beneath the Afghan mountains, a maze of twists and dead ends that seemed to mock their every step. His knees were scraped raw from crawling, and he had several bumps on his head from hitting the low tunnel ceiling. His flashlight flickered, casting weak beams across jagged walls streaked with moisture. Exhaustion gnawed at him, but something sharper—a stubborn flicker of will—kept him moving.

He'd lost track of Grey and the team long ago, their voices swallowed by the tunnels' endless echoes. Alone, he pressed on, driven by a gut feeling that the way out had to be close. His fingers brushed the rough stone as he steadied himself, rounding a bend. The beam of his light swept across a familiar stretch of cavern, and his breath caught. This was the spot—the killing ground. Yesterday, it had been littered with Taliban bodies, crumpled forms of the enemy, their blood pooling in the crevices. Now, it was deserted. No corpses, no weapons, only smears of rust-colored stains on the floor, piles of spent brass casings, and a faint, metallic tang in the air.

Maxx crouched, running a hand over the ground. The evidence was there, but the bodies were gone. A prickling sensation crawled up his neck. He froze, scanning the shadows. Nothing moved, but the feeling of eyes on him was unshakable.

"Who's there?" he muttered. His voice bounced off the walls, unanswered. He straightened, gripping his flashlight tightly.

Farther along, he wandered into the main cavern, where the Others' device had sat—a hulking, alien cube of polished metal and pulsing light. That too was missing. His gaze shifted to the dark water lapping against the cavern's edge, its surface still and black as ink. He edged back, muscles tensing. The last time he'd gotten in the water, something had lunged at him in the murk, teeth sinking into his calf before he'd beaten it off. The scar still throbbed as a dull reminder. He wasn't taking chances.

The tunnel stretched ahead, and for the first time in a day, it felt...linear. Yesterday, they'd looped endlessly, trapped in some maddening circle. Had Smith or the Quds been coaxing them in loops on purpose? Or had something else—something in these depths—been toying with them? He shook his head. He would have plenty of time to consider the mystery of the last two days once this was over.

Step by step, the air became more alive and fresher. A faint glow winked in the distance—the exit. Relieved and in disbelief, he stumbled into the night, the March wind biting his sweat-soaked skin. The Afghan sky, a vast canvas of stars, meteors, and a bright crescent moon, sprawled above.

He fumbled for his cell phone, the battery icon blinking a feeble warning. Punching Lieutenant Weih's number, he pressed it to his ear.

"Maxx?" Weih's voice crackled through, strained but steady. "Where on earth have you been? It's been almost twelve hours. I was starting to think you were dead."

"Not dead but close to it. Lost in that damn tunnel," Maxx said, rubbing his jaw. "Did you stay with the canisters or bug out?"

"Still here with the mysterious canisters. The CSAR team grabbed three canisters, but their chopper was shot down shortly after taking off. We're pinned here, Maxx. The squad and I need to get out."

Maxx's jaw tightened. "Hold tight. I'm coming to you. I'll get you extracted. How many have you got left?"

"Six, including me. But it's dicey. Something's off about this place. I feel it."

"Yeah," Maxx said, glancing back at the tunnel mouth. "We'll figure it out when I get there. Protect the canisters and hang tight." The phone beeped, the cracked screen going dark. Dead. He cursed under his breath, shoving it into his pocket. It hadn't been dead before, but the tunnel had a way of draining everything—batteries, sanity, hope.

He needed a ride. The terrain ahead was a rugged sprawl of rock and dust, too far to cross on foot. His eyes caught movement—a pair of Humvees parked a quarter mile down the hill at the village they had cleared yesterday. The soldiers' silhouettes stood stark against the moonlight. Rangers. He recognized the squad. They'd escorted Grey to the tunnel last night before she'd vanished. Maxx jogged down the hill toward them, knees aching but determined.

Sergeant Lacey, a squat Arkansan with perpetual acne, leaned against one of the vehicles, barking orders to his men.

He straightened as Maxx approached. "King? Thought you were still inside."

"Got out," Maxx said, catching his breath. "Why are you guys still here?"

Lacey shook his head. "We were told to wait here for Grey since she's a VIP. She went up the hill with you and the Green Berets last night, then nothing. We saw some weird shit though. Shapes were moving out of that tunnel last night. Didn't look normal."

"She was kidnapped for a while, but she's back with the Green Beret team now," Maxx said.

"No shit," Lacey exclaimed. "Do we need to go in and help her?"

"Nah, they have the situation under control," Maxx lied. "I need to get to Weih's position. He's pinned down with his squad out in the valley. You boys up for a ride?"

Lacey's eyes narrowed. "We're supposed to hold here for Grey. Orders."

"Forget that. Grey's right as rain, and Weih's team is dying out there. I need your Humvees. We move now and pull them out. The kind of ranger danger you boys love."

Corporal Evans, a thin kid with a shotgun slung over his shoulder, piped up. "How are we doing this, Sarge? Are we sitting here or doing something?"

Lacey chewed his lip then nodded. "All right, King. You're lucky I'm tired of waiting while everyone else sees the action. Mount up, boys!" The Rangers scrambled, engines roaring to life. Maxx climbed into the lead Humvee beside Lacey, the vehicle rolling forward into the night.

"How are you planning to get through?" Lacey asked, voice jostling with the ride. "Word is something's letting people in that sector but not out. Like a damn trap your boy Weih is in."

Maxx stared ahead, the headlights carving a path through

the dark. "I'll deal with that when we get there. Whatever it is, it's not stopping me from reaching Weih."

Private Torres, operating the radio in the back, leaned forward. "You think it's the Talibs messing with us or something else?"

"Hell if I know," Maxx said. "Tunnel had us spinning all day, but it let me out. Maybe it's done playing games."

"Or maybe it's waiting," Lacey grunted. "You trust your gut on this, King?"

"Only thing I've got left," Maxx replied. "By the way, any of you have some Twizzlers?"

The Humvees rumbled on, dust swirling in their wake. The dark landscape blurred past—jagged hills, skeletal shrubs, and the occasional glint of metal from some abandoned wreck. Maxx's mind churned. Weih's platoon was holed up near a valley pass, surrounded by hostiles and whatever else lurked out here. The canisters—those strange, sealed containers they'd been guarding—were the key, but the search and rescue helicopter crash meant three were already lost. They might still turn this mess around if he could get Weih out with the rest.

The radio crackled, cutting through the engine's growl. Torres adjusted it, frowning. "Sarge, it's Colonel Williams from Command."

Lacey grabbed the handset. "Sergeant Lacey here, sir."

"Lacey, why are you out of position?" Williams' voice was clipped, hard-edged. "You were ordered to wait for the VIP. Is she with you?

"No, sir. She's with the Green Beret team. We took the initiative to extract Lt. Weih's team."

"Did you come up with this goat-rope plan on your own, Sergeant?"

"No, sir. We ran it by Maxx King when he came out of the tunnels. He assured me Grey is in no danger."

Maxx nodded his head affirmatively, averting his eyes.

"Listen close," Williams said. "King's not to be trusted. He has his own agenda and is not in the command structure. You keep him under watch. When you get to Weih's position, shoot first and ask questions later if he tries to move those canisters. That's an order."

Lacey's grip tightened on the radio, eyes flicking to Maxx. "Understood, sir. I'll handle it."

The line went dead. Maxx met Lacey's stare, the air in the Humvee thickening. "What'd he say?" Maxx asked, though he could guess.

Lacey didn't blink. "Says you're trouble and we should put you down if you step out of line."

Maxx leaned back, hands resting on his knees. "Williams doesn't know what's at stake. Weih's team and securing those canisters is all that matters right now."

"Maybe," Lacey said, voice low. "But I've got orders, King. You pull anything funny, my boys won't hesitate."

"Fair enough," Maxx said, keeping his tone even. "Get me to Weih. We'll sort the rest out after."

The convoy pressed on, tension coiling tighter with every mile. Maxx stared out the window, the night swallowing the dirt track ahead. Williams's warning gnawed at him, but he pushed it aside. Another name was added to his list of scores to settle another day.

The tunnel had let him go. The shadows had watched but not struck. He'd see it through whatever game was being played—to Weih, to the canisters, to the truth. The Humvees rolled toward the valley, and the faint sound of gunfire echoed in the distance, a beacon in the dark.

***

The night was a shroud of ink over the jagged hills of Eastern Afghanistan. The valley's silence was thick and deceptive, like the calm at the heart of a storm. Lieutenant Weih crouched behind a crumbling rock outcrop, his breath fogging in the cold air.

Operation Anaconda thundered in the distance, a jagged scar of gunfire and explosions. Still, in this forsaken pocket of the Shahi-Kot Valley, his platoon had been left alone since the search and rescue team left them four hours ago. The six remaining men, Weih included, had dug in around the hillside caves where they'd hidden the mysterious canisters, their mission cloaked in mystery even from themselves. Now, that silence was shattered.

The first Taliban rounds cracked through the darkness, spitting dirt and stone into the air. Weih ducked lower, his M4 carbine pressed tight against his shoulder as he squinted through the night vision goggles. Beside him, Sergeant Kerro barked orders to the four others, Brown, Dunn, Hicks, and Perez, their silhouettes darting between cover.

"Incoming! Northwest ridge! Lay it down, boys!" Kerro's voice was a gravelly lifeline in the chaos.

The Taliban assault was relentless, shadows shifting in the green haze of Weih's goggles, their numbers impossible to pin down. Bullets whined overhead, chipping away at their defenses. Hicks grunted as a round tore through his arm, blood black in the dim light, and Weih felt a cold dread settle in his gut. They were getting whittled down fast. Then pain erupted in his chest, a sledgehammer blow despite the ceramic plates of his body armor. He stumbled back, gasping, ribs screaming with every breath.

"I'm hit," he rasped, waving off Kerro's concerned glance. "Still in it. Keep firing!"

Kerro nodded grimly, slamming a fresh magazine into his rifle. "Command, this is Bravo Two-Three! We're under heavy fire, taking more casualties. Request immediate support, over!"

The radio crackled, the voice from Kabul distant and

strained. "Bravo Two-Three, no ground assets available for support. A-10s are inbound, ETA twenty mikes. Hold your position, over."

"Twenty minutes?" Brown spat, his SAW rattling as he sprayed bursts toward the encroaching enemy. "We'll be dust by then! I am red on ammo!"

Weih fumbled for the sat phone, dialing Maxx. The line clicked to voicemail, a flat tone mocking him. "Maxx, it's Weih. We're getting hammered out here. If you're still alive, get your ass back now!" He shoved the phone away, meeting Kerro's eyes in the flickering muzzle flashes.

The sergeant's jaw tightened, and he leaned closer. "John, if this is it...been an honor, sir."

"Stow that bullshit, Kerro," Weih snapped, forcing a grin despite the ache in his chest. "We're not done yet. Those Warthogs are coming, and I'm not dying in this shithole." He was green, under six months into leading this platoon, but he'd be damned if he let despair take them. "Dunn, Perez, check your nine! We hold until the cavalry arrives!"

A new sound cut through the din, a fierce, mechanical roar. Tracers streaked from the darkness beyond their perimeter, the high-pitched chatter of an M240 machine gun raking the tight gullies where the Taliban swarmed. Nine hundred and fifty rounds a minute chewed through the night, a relentless scythe. Farther off, the deep, thudding boom of an M2.50 caliber weapon echoed, its rounds punching through ridgelines nearly a mile away, shredding Taliban positions with surgical fury. Weih's heart leapt.

"Hell yeah!" he shouted, pumping a fist. "Someone's out there!"

The tide shifted fast. Shapes burst from the shadows, friendly silhouettes visible in the nightscopes, moving with lethal precision. Maxx and a squad of Rangers had arrived in a storm of gunfire and determination. The Taliban assault faltered, loosing a desperate volley of RPGs that streaked overhead, only to be answered by the M2's thunderous retort. Explosions bloomed along the ridges, and the enemy broke, scattering into the night like roaches when the lights flipped on.

Maxx ran up the hillside and climbed into the tunnel beside Weih, his face streaked with sweat and dust. "Miss me, Lieutenant?" He grinned, clapping Weih's shoulder.

"About damn time you decided to show up!" Weih shot back, relieved. "Thought you'd left us for dead."

"Never," Maxx said, peering over the rock. "Got held up by some Taliban technicals. But heads up, those A-10s are lining up. We need to call them off before they turn us into a puddle of goo."

A Ranger, Torres, scrambled up, radio in hand. "Thunder Hub, this is Reaper Two-One! Abort strike on our position, repeat, abort! We've got two Taliban technicals, half a click east, tearing ass out of here. Light them up instead, over!" The response crackled back, affirmative, and moments later the sky growled as the Warthogs banked away, their 30mm cannons roaring to life—the distinctive *BRRRRRRT*—in the distance. Twin fireballs erupted, illuminating the fleeing trucks' destruction.

The gunfire faded, leaving only the ringing in their ears and the pungent bite of cordite. Weih slumped against the rock, chest throbbing, as the A-10s circled overhead, securing the perimeter. Kerro, Lacey, and Maxx followed him into the back of the hillside tunnel, the air cool and damp against their sweat-soaked skin. Weih gestured to a shadowed corner where the canisters were, dull metal glinting faintly.

"There they are," he said, voice low. "My little friends."

Maxx crouched, inspecting them with a frown. "Yeah, these are virus canisters. Nasty shit. They're meant for covert use on some invading force. Whoever wants them is scared of these babies getting out into the wild. That's why they won't let anyone leave with them."

"So what's our next move?" Kerro asked, wiping blood from a cut on his cheek. "We can't haul these canisters back, or they'll take us out like they did the search and rescue choppers."

Maxx straightened, eyes hard. "We don't. We leave them here, make it clear we're walking away empty-handed. They might let us extract if they think we don't have them."

Weih nodded slowly, wincing as he shifted his weight. "I say we bury them in here. C-4 the cave entrance, so we don't open them up. Taliban won't dig through that mess."

Lacey, leaning against the wall, piped up. "Then we call the A-10s back for cover. Convoy to Bagram and get the hell outta Dodge."

"Agreed," Weih said, meeting their gazes. "Let's move."

They rigged the explosives, Dunn and Perez dragging the charges into place despite their wounds. Weih set the timer, and they stumbled into the night as the hillside shuddered, a muffled boom echoing as the tunnels caved in, burying the canisters in a tomb of rock and dust. The platoon gathered their fallen, Hicks and Brown limping but alive, the bodies of two others who were lost in the fight loaded gently into their only working vehicle and the two Humvees the Rangers had brought.

Torres waved from the lead vehicle. "A-10s are back on station. Mount up, ladies! We're rolling in two mikes!"

Weih climbed into the passenger seat of the second Humvee, Kerro at the wheel. The engines growled to life, and the convoy lurched forward, tires chewing over the rocky terrain. Above, the Warthogs prowled the night sky, their silhouettes dark against the stars.

"Bagram's waiting," Weih muttered, gripping his rifle as the pain in his chest flared. "Let's get the hell out of here."

Kerro glanced over, a faint smirk tugging at his lips. "You did good, LT. Not bad for a greenhorn from Texas."

Weih chuckled, the sound raw. "Yeah, well, you're stuck with me now." The convoy rumbled on, headlights cutting through the night, leaving the buried secrets of the hillside behind as they raced toward safety, the distant *BRRRRRT* of the A-10s their guardian angels in the dark.

18

PUT BACK TOGETHER

Mr. Green slumped into a hard plastic chair, rubbing his temples. "Fourteen hours crammed in that tin can, and now they've got us waiting like stray dogs. You'd think diplomatic passports would mean something."

Under the flicker of fluorescent lights, Dr. Xi, standing nearby with a Styrofoam cup of lukewarm coffee, gave him a sidelong glance. "They do, Green. They don't make the bureaucracy vanish. Relax. Our papers are coming."

The sky above Beijing International Airport glowed faintly with the first light of a cold dawn as Mr. Green, Dr. Xi, and Harry Cull sat in the lounge of the aging private terminal. The wind howled outside, rattling the windows and kicking up dust that swirled across the tarmac.

Harry Cull, pacing by the window, turned sharply. "Relax? Xi, you're texting your 'friend' about the lab like it's a casual brunch. What if she's compromised? We're not exactly here to sightsee."

Dr. Xi's fingers paused over his phone, his voice steady. "She's not. She'll get us in. Trust me, Harry. It's going badly at the lab. We can't afford to hesitate."

The air was dry and sharp, carrying a faint metallic tang from the city beyond. The terminal, built for VIPs and charter flights, was far from luxury: scuffed linoleum floors, rows of bolted-down seats, and a lingering smell of stale cigarette smoke. Their diplomatic passports were still en route from the US Embassy, a modest outpost opened in 1979, leaving them temporarily stranded after the long haul across the Pacific.

Harry frowned. "If the lab's as bad as you say, anyone could be a loose end."

"She won't help us directly, but she'll listen," Dr. Xi replied. "She knows what's at stake. Things at XINXI are...deteriorating. We're running out of time."

The trio had been on edge since leaving Anchorage, their mission cloaked in secrecy and assumed names. They were bound for the XINXI lab, a facility rumored to be spiraling into chaos, though the details XI had gotten from the secretive texts remained murky. After an hour of waiting, a harried embassy attaché finally arrived with their passports, and they were waved through customs with curt nods from the officials. Outside, the wind howled louder, tugging at their coats as they scanned the terminal's perimeter.

"They'll be watching us," Mr. Green said, his voice low. "MSS agents. We're not invisible."

Dr. Xi nodded. "The Ministry of State Security agents will be watching us, so we're not going straight to the lab. Look." He gestured toward a cluster of black sedans pulling to the curb, their tinted windows glinting in the morning light. "Our decoys."

Harry frowned. "Decoys? You're betting our lives on a shell game?"

"It's worked for me before," Dr. Xi replied. "We make a show of leaving for the embassy. They follow. We'll slip away later."

The plan unfolded with practiced precision. The three

appeared to climb into one of the black sedans, doors slamming shut as the convoy peeled away toward the embassy district.

An hour later, they emerged from a plain and unassuming garage at the airport in an unmarked Volkswagen Jetta, its tinted windows concealing them from prying eyes. Behind the wheel was Noah Smith, an Australian "businessman" with a weathered face and a sly grin. His accent was thick, his demeanor casual, but the trio suspected he was more than he seemed, likely a contractor for one of the US intelligence agencies.

"Bit of a tight fit, eh?" Noah chuckled as Harry squeezed into the front passenger seat, his knees brushing the dashboard. Mr. Green and Dr. Xi wedged themselves into the back, the compact sedan creaking under their weight.

"Bulletproof windows?" Harry asked, tapping the glass.

Noah winked. "Modified her myself. Never know when you'll need a bit of extra insurance."

The Jetta rolled into Beijing's morning rush hour, a snarl of honking horns and exhaust fumes. Traffic crawled along, the city waking up in a haze of dust and noise. Mr. Green leaned forward, peering through the windshield. "We're sitting ducks out here. If they figure out the decoy—"

He didn't finish. A sharp crack split the air, and the Jetta shuddered as bullets slammed into the driver's side window. Glass held firm, spiderwebbing but not shattering. Three Chinese men in dark jackets emerged from a van ahead, automatic rifles blazing.

"Down!" Noah barked, flooring the accelerator. The Jetta lurched forward, weaving through traffic as more rounds pinged off its reinforced shell.

Harry twisted in his seat. "They're not letting up! Who are these bastards?"

Noah tossed him a pistol, a sleek Beretta, its weight cold and solid in Harry's hand. "Take a shot if you get a clear one. Xi, Green, stay low!"

Harry rolled down his side window a crack, the wind roaring in his ears, and squeezed off a few rounds. One of the attackers stumbled, clutching his leg, but the others kept firing. Bullets sparked off the pavement, narrowly missing a cyclist who dove for cover. Noah swerved hard, clipping a parked scooter, and the Jetta fishtailed before regaining traction.

"They're not good enough for the MSS," Mr. Green shouted over the chaos, his voice tight. "Too sloppy. This has to be Torashi's crew."

Dr. Xi nodded grimly. "He's desperate to stop us. He's lost his mind organizing a hit on US embassy vehicles in the center of Beijing."

The gunfire tapered off as Noah gunned the engine, putting distance between them and their attackers. The Jetta's tires squealed as he cut into an alley, leaving the main road behind. Breathing hard, Harry lowered the pistol.

"That was too close. Why didn't they hit us harder?"

"They didn't expect the armor," Noah said, his grin returning. "Caught 'em off guard. But we're not out of it yet." His phone buzzed, and he glanced at the screen, his expression darkening. "Decoy convoy's been hit too. Overwhelmed. They know you're not there now."

Dr. Xi cursed under his breath. "Beijing will be on lockdown soon. We need another way to the lab."

Noah jerked the wheel, guiding the Jetta onto a narrow street lined with shuttered shops and crumbling concrete walls. "Got a back route in mind. Hang on."

The car jostled over uneven pavement, dodging stray dogs and piles of trash. Minutes later, they slowed at a police checkpoint, a pair of officers in crisp uniforms waving them down.

Noah rolled down his window, flashing a disarming smile as he handed over their diplomatic passports.

"Morning, mates," he chirped. "Taking these gents to a meeting."

The officer squinted at the documents then at Dr. Xi. "Purpose of visit?"

Dr. Xi leaned forward, his voice smooth and authoritative. "We're traveling to a classified discussion with the general secretary. Official business. I'm sure you understand the need for discretion."

The officer hesitated then grunted and waved them through. Noah tipped an imaginary hat and eased the Jetta forward, the checkpoint fading in the rearview mirror.

"Nice one, Xi," Harry said, exhaling. "Thought we were cooked."

"We're not there yet," Dr. Xi replied, his gaze fixed on the road ahead.

By noon, the Jetta pulled up to a forlorn building on the outskirts of a sprawling industrial compound. Dust coated its faded gray exterior, and the windows were boarded up, giving it the look of abandonment. The trio stepped out, the wind tugging at their clothes, as a figure emerged from the shadows of the doorway. Dr. Fang, a middle-aged woman with a calm demeanor, stood waiting. Her glasses glinted in the morning light, and her dark hair was pulled into a tight bun.

"Hurry in, Dr. Xi," she said, her voice steady but urgent. "We don't have much time."

Mr. Green shot Dr. Xi a wary look. "Is this your friend? She's not going to turn us over, is she?"

Dr. Fang's lips twitched, a hint of a smile. "I'm here to listen, not to betray. But you'd better move. The men from the MSS will be everywhere soon. And the lab's on the brink."

Dr. Xi nodded, stepping toward the door. "Let's go. Whatever's waiting inside, we'll face it together."

Harry slipped the pistol into his jacket pocket, his jaw set. "After that ride, I'm ready for anything."

The wind howled louder as they slipped inside. The door clicked shut behind them, sealing them off from the dusty chaos of Beijing's waking streets. Ahead loomed access to the XINXI lab, a Pandora's box of secrets they were about to crack open.

***

The convoy of three Humvees growled over the rocky terrain, headlights slicing through the pre-dawn gray as the convoy rumbled away from the valley. Maxx King gripped the edge of his seat, the jolting ride jarring his bruised spine.

A couple of hours earlier, they'd left the caves behind, collapsing them with C-4 explosives to bury the mysterious canisters and deny the Taliban their prize. It had been a brutal night. Two of Lieutenant Weih's platoon were lost, others wounded, but the A-10s had shepherded them out, their *BRRRRRRT* echoing in the distant hills. Now, Sergeant Lacey, the Ranger squad, and Weih's Two-Three raced toward Bagram, exhaustion heavy in the air, the wounded hanging on in the vehicles.

Weih, riding shotgun in the second Humvee, glanced at Kerro behind the wheel. "Bagram's close," he muttered, in pain from shrapnel in his side. "We made it."

Kerro smirked, eyes on the road. "Yeah, LT. Thanks to you and that guy Maxx."

Weih snorted as he glanced at the lead vehicle carrying Maxx. "Don't tell him. That's guys a pain in the ass already."

As the convoy crested a rise, Bagram Airfield sprawled into view, a hive of activity even at 0600. Relief washed over Maxx, the knot in his chest loosening. Planes taxied across the tarmac, their engines a low roar. Floodlights bathed the base in harsh white, soldiers and airmen moving with purpose—unloading crates, refueling birds, shouting orders. The tents of Viper City and makeshift buildings dotted the landscape, alive with the pulse of war. The frigid air was sharp with light sprinkles that tapped against the Humvees' windshields.

Maxx leaned forward, peering out. "Hell of a sight after that valley."

Torres, in the lead vehicle, twisted around, grinning. "Welcome back to civilization, boys! Hot chow and a cot calling my name."

Lacey, arm in a makeshift sling, laughed dryly. "If you call MREs and a leaky-tent civilization."

The convoy rolled to a stop near the edge of the airfield, engines ticking as they cooled. Maxx climbed out, stretching stiff limbs, his breath fogging in the chill. The Rangers and men of the Two-Three spilled from the vehicles, some limping, others hauling gear. Dunn and Perez, bandaged but upright, helped Hicks and Brown toward the medical tents. Weih slid from his seat, wincing as he landed.

"Let's report in and get patched up," he said, scanning the team. "Good work out there."

Maxx nodded, eyeing Viper City's tents in the distance. "Thought I'd charge my phone, check in with some old contacts. You good without me?"

"Yeah," Weih said. "Go. We'll catch up."

Before they could scatter, a first sergeant jogged up, his face taut. "Lieutenant Weih, Sergeant Lacey, Command wants you now. No talking to anyone."

Lacey frowned, slinging his rifle. "What's this? Are we in trouble?"

"Move," the sergeant snapped. "Orders."

Maxx paused his plan to hit Viper City, which was fading. The team's wary glances—Lacey, Kerro, Weih—pulled him back. "I'm with you," he said, falling in. "Might be a goat rodeo."

Weih shot him a look. "You sure, Maxx? You're a civilian. You're not officially part of the rodeo anymore."

"Positive," Maxx replied, voice low. "I want to ask about those tunnels. Something's not right."

Lacey snorted, limping along. "Not right? That whole place was a nightmare. Good luck getting Command to care with the shitstorm that's going on."

"They better care," Maxx said, "or we'll be burying a lot more people than we think."

They trudged toward the command post, boots crunching gravel, the air thick with jet fuel and damp earth. Sprinkles dotted their jackets, wind tugging at collars. They were still twenty yards away when Colonel Williams intercepted them, his face hard, eyes locking on Weih.

"Are you Lieutenant Weih from the Two-Three?"

"Yes, sir," Weih said nervously, glancing sideways at Maxx.

Williams took another drag on his cigarette as he strode up. "Did you bring me those canisters?"

Weih straightened, pain flickering. "Sir, the canisters were unstable. We collapsed the tunnels with C-4 to keep them out of enemy hands."

Williams turned to Maxx, voice like a dagger. "And you must be the infamous Mr. King. What's your business in all this, son?"

"Consulting," Maxx said, steady. "Helping Two-Three. We did what was needed."

"Did you?" Williams stepped closer. "I hear rumors of unauthorized activity in the mountains. You might be stuck here until we sort it out."

Maxx's jaw tightened. "I'm not here on vacation, Colonel. DHS sent me. I can call Director Vaughn—Miss Grey's boss—if you need proof. Maybe he'll provide more detail, but I won't."

Williams bristled, but a full colonel, older and authoritative, stuck his head out the door. "Williams, stand down. They're reporting to General Hagenbeck directly. Anaconda's his call."

Williams relented, glaring as he stepped back. The second colonel eyed Maxx. "Who's the civilian?"

"Maxx King, sir," Maxx said. "Department of Homeland Security Consultant."

"Military personnel only for this," the colonel said with a chuckle. "You're out."

Maxx nodded, frustration simmering. He turned to the team. "Stay safe. Lacey, if you can, get someone to those tunnels for Grey."

Lacey clapped his shoulder, wincing. "I'll push it, brother. Safe travels."

Maxx reached out and shook Weih's hand. "You did good, John. Stop by Seattle sometime. I'll buy you a beer and tell you how well you did. Going to find me some Twizzlers," Maxx said, forcing a smile. He peeled off, the team vanishing into the command post as wind scattered sprinkles across his face.

Alone, Maxx felt the night's weight settle in. Seattle beckoned—Gabby's voice, her smile. But Grey lingered in his mind, maybe still trapped in the tunnels, and Doctor Smith was still free. Was he abandoning them? He shook it off for the moment, heading for the airfield.

Maxx trudged across the bustling tarmac, the acrid scent of jet fuel stinging his nose as he wove between stacks of crates and scurrying ground crew. Ahead, a hulking C-17 Globemaster squatted near a loading ramp, its rear hatch yawning open as airmen wrestled pallets of gear aboard. Its destination was listed on a copy of the crate's manifest, visible under the floodlights: McChord Air Force Base, south of Seattle.

Maxx's pulse quickened—home turf, a straight shot back to the States, to Seattle and Gabby. He scanned the chaos and spotted a familiar figure barking orders near the plane's nose:

Sergeant Rawls, the grizzled flight master with whom he'd shared a smoky poker game in Kuwait years back, a man who would never shut up about losing twenty bucks over a bad hand.

Maxx jogged over, dodging a forklift, and called, "Sarge! You got room for one more?"

Rawls turned, his weathered face creasing into a scowl under his cap. He squinted, recognition dawning as he scratched at the gray stubble on his jaw.

"King? What the hell are you doing here? I thought you were out." His voice was a gravelly rasp, barely audible over the whine of the C-17's idling engines. He glanced at the clipboard in his hand, then back at Maxx. "No manifest, no dice. You know the rules."

Maxx stepped closer, lowering his voice, his breath fogging in the cold. "Come on, Rawls. I'm beat to hell and need to get stateside yesterday. You still owe me twenty for that flush I laid down."

Rawls groaned, rolling his eyes as he shifted his weight, his flight suit creaking. He glanced toward the load crew then back at Maxx, his frown deepening. "You're getting on my nerves, you know that? This bird's full of troops, gear, medevacs. I stick you on, and I'm explaining it to some brass with a stick up his—"

"Please," Maxx cut in, his voice steady but edged with desperation. He met Rawls's gaze, unflinching, the sprinkles beading on his helmet. "I've been in the shit out here. I need to get home. Call it even for that poker night."

Rawls hesitated, chewing the inside of his cheek. He muttered a curse then jerked his head toward the ramp. "Fine. Get in and keep your head down. I didn't see you, and you didn't see me. Move before I change my mind."

Maxx flashed a tired grin, clapping Rawls on the shoulder. "Always knew you were a softie, Sarge."

"Get outta here," Rawls growled, returning to his clipboard as Maxx slipped past, blending into the shadows of the C-17's cargo bay.

Maxx settled into a vacant seat as the plane roared to life. The C-17 lifted off, Bagram fading, but he knew in his bones that the fight was far from finished.

19

WITH FRIENDS LIKE THESE

Doctor Smith stood at the cracked window of the abandoned Buddhist monastery, staring out into the snow flurries that danced across the Hindu Kush. His thick glasses fogged slightly in the frigid air, and he wiped them with a shaky hand. His mind was not on the cold but on the unraveling threads of his escape plan.

The monastery clung to the jagged cliffs like a forgotten relic. Its once-sacred halls now hollowed out by time, looting, and neglect. The mid-morning air bit with a vicious chill, snow flurries swirling in chaotic spirals as a massive storm brewed on the horizon.

The monastery's crumbling stone walls, pockmarked by centuries of wind and war, offered scant shelter from the elements. Statues of serene Buddhas, their faces eroded or shattered by vandals, stared blankly into the dimness. Faded frescoes peeled from the ceilings, curling like dead leaves, while the wooden beams overhead groaned under the weight of neglect.

It was a ruin, but better than the suffocating tunnels below or the exposed, treacherous peaks above. One of many abandoned sanctuaries in the region, it remained unexplored, its isolation a shield against the ongoing conflict and the inaccessibility of the terrain.

Inside, Smith stood near a window covered with plastic, his breath fogging in the frigid air as he fumbled with his personal communication device. The small, alien-crafted cube felt heavier in his hands than ever. He absentmindedly wiped his glasses again with a trembling hand, his hair more white than gray, catching the diffused light streaming through the snow-laden clouds.

He tapped the device again, his fingers stiff from the cold, but the power it once emitted was silent. Dead. His jaw tightened as he glanced toward the tunnel's entrance, a shadowed gateway carved into the rock below the monastery. For the last day, he had been sending Taliban soldiers into that labyrinth, leading the Americans in circles and keeping them from tracking his small group. But now, the silence from the alien communication device told him the game had dangerously shifted.

"They've secured the tunnels," he muttered, his voice a mix of fatigue and concern. "The Americans must have found it and cut the power. The Quds forces are gone. No signal, no backup."

Li Jing, bundled in a tattered coat, looked up from where she crouched near a small fire she had coaxed to life with scavenged wood. Her dark eyes narrowed, sharp and perceptive. "Gone? You said they'd hold the line. You said we had time."

Doctor Smith turned, his gaze cold. "I said what I knew then. Things change. The device is offline, and the Quds haven't responded in hours. We're on our own."

Faraj stepped closer, his breath puffing in the icy air as he adjusted the rifle slung over his shoulder. The past week's stress had caused the gray hair in his beard to spread to his wiry black hair. "The Taliban soldiers are still with us, Doctor. Eight of them. They'll fight if the Americans come. But we can't stay here forever. That storm's closing in fast, and we must make our way to Tehran."

Doctor Smith rubbed his temples, his mind racing. Before the device had gone silent, the Others, those enigmatic voices from beyond, had spoken through it. Their message had been cryptic. "We want you to come to us..." What did it mean? Were they offering escape, power, or knowledge? The instructions were maddeningly vague, but one thing was clear. They had secretly forbidden him from bringing Li Jing. The implication gnawed at him. She was a danger now, a loose end. He had kept the true nature of their treachery from her, feeding her half-truths about their mission, using her skills as his assistant and assassin while keeping her in the dark. She had trusted him, followed him across the world, and now the Others had drawn a line.

He straightened, his decision hardening. "Faraj, get the men ready. We're moving out toward Iran. The storm will cover our tracks."

Li Jing stood, her fists clenched. "Iran? What are you talking about? We're supposed to stay here and hold the position until the Quds regroup. You can't abandon the plan!"

Doctor Smith avoided her gaze, his voice flat. "The plan's dead, Li Jing. You've been a good assistant, but we part ways here. I have to go. Alone."

Her face twisted, disbelief transforming into rage. "A good assistant? That's all I am to you? After everything? You dragged me into this and promised me we were in it together, but now you're abandoning me? You lying bastard!"

She lunged at him, her hands clawing for his throat, but two of the Taliban soldiers quickly grabbed her arms, yanking her back. She thrashed against them, her screams echoing off the stone walls. "You used me! You coward! You think you can toss me aside like my father?"

Smith stepped back, his eyes flickering with something like guilt. He pushed it down, his hubris swelling over the tiny fractures in his conscience. She had been useful, yes, but nothing more. He told himself she had always known her place, though the lie tasted bitter even in his mind. He had misled her, exploited her loyalty, and now he would sever the tie. Power beckoned, and he would not let sentiment drag him back.

"Faraj," he said, turning to his other assistant, "stay here with two of the men. End this quickly. Mercifully. I'm not a monster. I don't want her to suffer, and I don't want to hear her screams. Wait until I'm gone then catch up to me when it's done."

Faraj hesitated, his dark eyes flicking between Smith and the struggling Li Jing. "Are you certain about this, Doctor? She may still be useful to us when we reach Tehran."

Doctor Smith's voice hardened. "She's a liability now. The Others were clear. She can't come. Do it, Faraj. That's an order."

Li Jing's screams turned to sobs as she sank to her knees, still held by the soldiers. "You're the devil! You think you're some savior, but you're nothing! They'll see through you, Smith! I was a fool to believe that you loved me!"

He didn't look at her. "We're leaving now," he said to the remaining Taliban fighters. "Pack up. We head west. The storm will hide us." With that, he strode toward the monastery's entrance, his boots crunching on the frost-covered stone. The wind howled outside, snow whipping through the doorway as he stepped into the swirling white, his small contingent of soldiers trailing behind.

Faraj watched him go then turned to Li Jing. Her face was streaked with tears, her body trembling from cold and fury. The two Taliban men tightened their grip, awaiting his command. He pulled a knife from his belt, its blade glinting dully in the firelight. "It's about time," he said quietly. "Finally, he's made his choice."

Li Jing's eyes burned with hatred as she spat at Faraj, the saliva striking his boot with a wet slap, her voice raw and ragged from screaming. "You're all the same—spineless dogs groveling at his feet. You've been worming your way in, stealing my place, pushing him away from me. You'll regret this, Faraj. He'll turn on you next, and I'll laugh from the other side."

Faraj's jaw locked tight, his dark gaze sharpening with a loathing that matched hers in intensity. With a flick of his knife, he scraped the spit from his boot, his silence a cold rebuttal louder than any words. He gave a curt nod to the Taliban soldiers, who jerked her arms and hauled her toward a darkened corner of the monastery, her furious cries fraying into the howl of the rising wind.

Faraj followed, the knife dangling from his hand, each step slow and filled with anger. Doctor Smith had called it mercy, a swift and clean death, but to Faraj, it felt like betrayal mixed with a grim triumph. He ran his finger along the cold blade's edge while licking his dry, cracked lips.

Smith distanced himself from the tragedy inside by stepping out into the deepening snow, his mind already racing ahead to Iran, to the promise of the Others. The monastery's gray walls blended into the storm behind him, a crumbling tomb for the trust he had destroyed.

He cleaned his glasses absently, the gesture mechanical, as if wiping away the last traces of doubt. He had chosen power over loyalty, and though Li Jing's screams lingered in his ears, he convinced himself it was necessary. It was not personal. She had been a helpful tool until she became a liability. The Americans might have control of the tunnels, and the Quds might be lost, but he still had a personal communication device, even if it was temporarily unresponsive. The Others would guide him, elevate him. He was no monster, he told himself again, instead an emissary, a fallen angel chasing a better world.

The wind roared around Smith, snow sticking to his

glasses, but he pressed on, head down. The small band of Taliban fighters struggled to match his pace. In the distance, the Hindu Kush loomed, silent and unforgiving. The flurries thickened into a wall of white, burying the past beneath its icy cloak.

"Faraj will catch up soon," he murmured as his voice faded into the storm.

***

The wind howled as they slipped inside the decrepit building. The heavy door clanged shut behind them, muffling the chaos of Beijing's waking streets.

Inside, the building revealed itself as a cavernous warehouse, its vast emptiness stretching into gloom. Rust streaked the metal beams overhead, and the concrete floor was littered with broken crates and scraps of tarpaper. The air smelled of stale oil and decay, a testament to years of neglect. Dr. Fang led them across the open space, her footsteps echoing, until they reached a narrow metal staircase tucked against the far wall.

Dr. Xi paused at the top, his voice low. "This was my private route. In and out, there are no security checks. No cameras cover this section of the lab."

Mr. Green raised an eyebrow, his sharp blue eyes scanning the shadows. "Clever. Kept you off the grid."

"Had to," Xi muttered, starting down the stairs. "Too many eyes otherwise."

The metal stairs groaned under their weight as they descended three floors, the air growing cooler and heavier with each step. Mr. Green's wrinkled shirt clung to his thick frame, damp with sweat despite the chill, while Harry's boots clomped heavily behind. At the bottom, Dr. Fang swiped her security badge against a panel, and a thick steel door hissed open, revealing a space that jolted Mr. Green's senses awake.

The lab's interior was a stark departure from the decrepit shell above: a maze of gleaming consoles and tangled wires orbiting the alien communication device at its core. Beyond a wall of thick observation glass, the hulking cube shimmered faintly, its greenish surface swallowing the dim light like a void. It stood as a silent sentinel, radiating an eerie presence that seemed to pulse with secrets they'd come to unravel. The sterile air buzzed with the faint hum of machinery, and the polished metal walls reflected the glow of blinking lights, casting jagged shadows across the floor.

They'd barely crossed the threshold when Dr. Fang turned to them, her calm demeanor unshaken despite the urgency in her voice. "I'm glad you are here, Dr. Xi. Things have spiraled since last night." Her glasses caught the faint glow of a nearby console, and her tight bun seemed almost too perfect for the chaos she described.

Dr. Xi narrowed his eyes, his voice low and edged with suspicion. "Spiraled how?"

Dr. Fang's lips twitched, not quite forming a smile. "Yesterday evening, Chairman Jiang stormed into the lab with Fu in tow. He was insisting on contacting the Others directly despite the risks. Dr. Shu tried to reason with him and received a knife to the heart for his efforts. Jiang's patience snapped. I'm barely holding back the device's potential to destroy the lab and Beijing."

Dr. Xi's jaw tightened, and his voice clipped. "He's insane. That override was never tested. It could trigger another Tangshan. Or worse."

Mr. Green grunted, shifting his weight. "Sounds like a man who's lost the plot. What's his reasoning for taking the risk?"

"Power, it's always power with him," Dr. Fang replied, her tone flat. "He's furious that Xi slipped away. He thinks you're feeding secrets to the Americans. He wants the Others' weapons, their alliance, anything to outpace Thunderbird and the Americans."

Mr. Green's stomach twisted, anxiety coiling like a snake in his gut. He'd trusted Xi and brought him across borders and backroads to keep Thunderbird's secrets safe. Now, Jiang's paranoia painted them all as traitors. "So he's gambling China's future on a device he can't control. And us—what's he planning if we're caught?"

Dr. Fang met his gaze, unflinching. "If the MSS finds you here or anywhere, you're dead—the chairman's orders. There won't even be a show trial. He's past reasoning."

A sharp voice sliced through the tension from deeper within the lab. "Dr. Fang! I'm afraid the power is spiking again. We may have only minutes, not hours as we thought." The young technician, staring at the monitors with wide, anxious eyes, became even more alarmed when he recognized Dr. Xi.

Dr. Xi strode toward him, Mr. Green and Harry trailing close. The lab's sterile air grew colder as they neared the device, its low rumble vibrating through the floor. "What's the situation?" Xi asked, troubled.

Dr. Fang glanced up, her frown deepening. "Your communication override is live. The device is connecting, but it's unstable. The power is spiking and could tear this place apart. The Others have given Jiang thirty hours to respond."

"Respond to what?" Xi asked with raised eyebrows.

"To respond to their offer. If he stops the Americans in the desert war, they will give him the weapons and power he wants. If he refuses, they will cause an earthquake to bury us."

"That's insanity," Dr. Xi said. "If China attacks the Americans, there will be a global war. Both of those choices lead to destruction. We must stop the Others and Jiang."

The technician fidgeted, his voice trembling. "We tried to warn him, Dr. Xi. Last night, Dr. Shu said it was too risky to contact the Others, and Chairman Jiang... He—"

"Had him gutted," Dr. Fang finished bitterly. "Fu didn't even blink. Jiang's lost it, thinks he can bully the Others into bowing to him."

Mr. Green scratched his head. "And you're still running the connection? Why not shut it down since it's so unstable?"

Dr. Fang barked a bitter laugh. "Shut it down? Jiang's got men posted outside. If we stop, they'll storm in and finish us. Luck is the only thing keeping it from melting down."

Dr. Fang's eyes darted to Dr. Xi. "You designed this, Doctor. Can't you stop it? Jiang's wrong. You didn't betray us. We know that."

Xi's face darkened, a flicker of guilt crossing his features. "I built it to communicate, not to force contact. The override was a failsafe, not a weapon. Jiang's twisting it into something I never intended."

Fang shook her head, her voice low. "Intended or not, it's on us now. Jiang's betting we'll crack before the machine does."

Mr. Green's gaze swept the group, the weight of their words sinking in. Jiang's brutality wasn't only aimed at Xi—it was against them all, a mad grab for power that could bury Beijing in rubble. "So we're trapped," he said, his voice cold. "Either the device blows or Jiang's goons do us in."

Harry nodded grimly. "Unless we outmaneuver him. Fang's calibrating it—might buy us time to slip out and figure out another plan."

Dr. Xi's voice rose, determined. "Slip out? No! This is what we came here to do. Stop the Others. Jiang has only forced a confrontation before we were prepared."

"Then we fight," Harry growled, patting the weapon in his jacket. "I didn't train to die like a cornered rat in a lab."

Dr. Xi crossed his arms, his tone firm. "Fighting's a last resort. If Fang stabilizes the device, we could use the connection to our advantage."

Mr. Green's mind raced, the sting of betrayal fueling his

resolve. The senator had sold them out, forcing them to run. Jiang had turned their work into a death trap, but they weren't helpless.

"Dr. Fang," he called, turning to her, "can you pull the calibration off to buy Xi and me some time?"

She didn't look up from the monitor, her voice steady over the growing rumble. "I can try, but if the power spikes again, we're done."

Green muttered, "Better than waiting for Jiang to bury us."

The technician wrung his hands. "What if he's watching? He'll know we're against him."

"He already does," Fang said, her eyes hard. "That's why we're here, pawns in his game until we flip the board."

The device's hum sharpened, the floor trembling beneath them. Mr. Green felt the cold certainty of their predicament settle in his bones. Betrayal had brought them here—Jiang's, Senator Traficant's—but survival meant turning it back on them.

"Then we flip it," he said, his voice carving through the chaos. "Dr. Fang, do your best. We're not dying for his madness."

As the lab shuddered, the group braced themselves, caught between a tyrant's ambition and an alien unknown. Their fates hinged on a thread of trust.

20

THE THORN TWISTS

"Dr. Fang, recalibrate the backdoor protocol," Xi said, his voice clipped. "We need to stabilize it without tipping them off. The Others must think they're still in control."

Beside him, Dr. Fang adjusted a dial, her brow furrowed. Fang's hands paused mid-motion. "You're sure this won't trigger another spike? Last time, we nearly lost containment."

"I'm certain," Xi replied, glancing at the device. "Keep it passive. We're buying time, not starting hostilities."

The air in the XINXI lab vibrated with the low thrum of machinery, a heartbeat for the device at the room's center—a sleek, obsidian artifact that seemed to drink in the light. Its surface, unmarred by seams or buttons, pulsed faintly.

The technician, a young man hunched over a laptop, piped up, his voice trembling slightly. "Dr. Xi, the subatomic readings are fluctuating again. Should I adjust the dampeners?"

"No," Xi snapped. "Monitor only. We can't risk interference until we know what we're dealing with."

Green shifted, crossing his arms. "You're playing a dangerous game, Xi. If this backfires, we're not underground—we're buried."

Xi motioned Green toward a corner of the lab, away from Fang's ever-watchful gaze. The lab's walls were lined with blinking monitors and coiled cables that snaked like veins across the floor. The air grew colder there, the device's hum fading to a whisper.

Xi's eyes gleamed with urgency as he lowered his voice. "Listen, Green. Six months ago, we were blind. For forty years, we poked at this thing, learning nothing. Then the AI breakthroughs came, and that American spy we had placed at TechCom filled the gaps. The real key? Direct communication with the extraterrestrials."

Green's jaw tightened. "You're saying you've been talking to them?"

"Not talking like we did with Thunderbird," Xi corrected. "Decoding. Their signals woke this device up. I've watched the instruments—subatomic changes, invisible to the old metrics. No heat, no vibration, but activity. It's a receiver and a generator, Green. It takes in small signals then sends out something massive. We couldn't measure it before because our tools weren't precise enough."

Green's eyes narrowed. "And now?"

"Now we know the responses are almost entirely preprogrammed," Xi said, his voice dropping. "A signal triggers routines baked into its core, but we can't trace the endpoints. Up there in New York City, I saw firsthand how it ignored our shielding. Hundreds of feet of rock, sealed labs—none of it matters. The signals go through."

The technician's voice broke their huddle. "Dr. Xi, power levels are steady, but I'm seeing a new frequency. Should I log it?"

"Yes," Xi called back then turned to Green. "We thought the device was dormant without a power source, but it's always waiting in standby mode. However, a direct power connection is needed to generate a seismic response. Geothermal, solar, seismic—the cleaner the energy, the more powerful the reaction."

Green rubbed his chin, glancing at Dr. Fang, who whispered to the technician. "Why not bring Fang into this? She's your friend, isn't she?"

Xi's face tensed. "She is, but I'm not blind. She's ambitious. Jiang's watching her, and she knows it. If she smells weakness, she'll use it to climb over me. I must solve this question first, then we'll see how loyal she is."

Green's voice hardened. "And me? Do you trust me, or am I another pawn you keep in the dark?"

Xi met his gaze, unflinching. "I trust you, but there are things I can't tell you yet. When the time's right, you'll know everything."

Green's stomach twisted. He wanted to believe Xi, but the man's evasiveness gnawed at him. "Fine," he said, forcing calm, "but don't make me regret this, Xi."

"Dr. Xi!" the technician shouted, his screen flashing red. "The backdoor... It's working! Data's coming through!"

Xi and Green rushed to the console, Fang stepping aside with a wary glance. The screen displayed a cascade of numbers, a river of ones and zeros that seemed alive. The device's faint green pulse quickened, casting eerie reflections across the lab's steel surfaces. The technician's fingers flew over the keyboard, sweat beading on his forehead.

"Try to slow it down," Xi ordered. "Visualize the data flow. We need to see what's happening—transmissions in and out."

The screen flickered, resolving into a graph of jagged peaks and valleys. Green leaned closer, his breath catching. "That's it, isn't it? The transmission."

"Yes," Xi said with excitement. "We're intercepting their signal. Look, there's the inbound trigger, small and sharp. Now watch the outbound."

A massive spike dwarfed the graph, its edges fraying into

static. Fang gasped softly. "That's what destabilized it. The Others rejected our controls, and the device responded."

"Can we pause the incoming transmissions?" Green asked, his heart pounding.

Xi nodded. "Technician, isolate the inbound signal. Insert our instructions. Protocol seven, now."

The young man hesitated, then typed furiously. The device's pulse slowed, its glow dimming to a faint shimmer. The screen froze, and the data flow suspended like a held breath. Silence gripped the lab, broken only by the technician's ragged breathing.

"We did it," Xi whispered. "We're in."

Green stared at the screen, adrenaline surging. The implications hit him like a wave. They could see the device's inner workings—its triggers, its responses. More than that, they could introduce their instructions. The Others' commands, meant to unleash chaos, were now theirs to redirect. He imagined the device as a loaded gun, its trigger blocked by his finger.

"What now?" Fang asked, her voice edged with suspicion. "We've stopped them, but for how long?"

Xi's eyes gleamed. "We make it useless to them. No event, no threat. We can't cut a wire, but we can choke their signals, make the device ignore them."

Green's pulse hammered in his ears as he stared at the screen, the data flow twisting like a living thing. His voice came out sharp, almost a shout. "Hold on, there's a workaround! The secondary frequency is still alive. It's rerouting the damn signal!"

Xi's head snapped up, his face paling under the lab's harsh lights. "What? That shouldn't be possible." He leaned over the console, eyes darting across the flickering graph. A low curse escaped him. "You're right. It's climbing fast. Technician, amplify that band! We have to choke it before it locks us out!"

The technician's hands shook, fumbling over the keys. "I'm

trying, but it's... It's resisting!" Sweat glistened on his forehead as the screen pulsed red, the secondary spike clawing upward. The device's hum grew louder, a menacing drone that seemed to press against Green's skull.

"Do it faster!" Green snapped, his fists clenching. He could feel the seconds slipping away, the Others clawing back control. If they lost this, the whole lab—maybe more—could pay the price.

The technician hit a final command, and the spike shuddered then collapsed into a flatline. The hum faltered, retreating to a faint buzz. Green's breath caught. He locked eyes with Xi. "That was too damn close. What about the rest? Smith's device, others we don't know about... Can we stop them, or are we delaying the inevitable?"

Xi's face tightened. "That's the next problem to solve. We've cracked this one, but every device might have a unique electronic signature. We're not out of danger yet. And more danger if the Others discover we can disable this device before we have disabled all of them."

The technician leaned back, exhausted. "It's stable for now. No new signals."

Fang crossed her arms, her gaze darting between Xi and Green. "Am I missing something? Would you like to update me on what you've been working on?"

Green forced a smile. "Testing a theory, Doctor. It's nothing to be concerned about."

Her eyes lingered, sharp and unyielding, before she turned back to her console. Green caught the look, a prickle of unease settling in his gut. Fang wasn't buying it, and that spelled trouble. The lab's hum seemed louder now, a reminder of the forces they'd barely contained. They'd won a battle, but the war was far from over.

As Xi adjusted the monitors, Green stared at the device, its surface still and silent. He could imagine the machine was watching them, waiting for their next move. He wondered what Xi wasn't telling him and whether Fang's suspicions would unravel everything before they could find out.

***

The night shadows clung to Senator Jane Traficant's Georgetown brownstone like a hazy shroud.

Inside, the air was thick with the sour tang of red wine and desperation. Jane slumped in her office chair, her silk blouse untucked, stained with crimson splotches from the two empty bottles on her desk. Her gray hair, usually carefully arranged, hung in limp strands over her face, mascara smudged beneath her eyes. Papers, folders, and half-eaten takeout containers littered the room, a chaotic testament to her unraveling. The clock on the bookshelf ticked mercilessly, each second a hammer against her skull.

A sharp knock at the front door jolted her upright. She froze, her hand clutching the stem of a wineglass. Who would dare come at this hour? Her first thoughts were of the FBI as she pictured herself being led out in handcuffs under the bright lights of the media.

Stumbling to her feet, she shuffled to the door, her bare feet catching on a stray manila folder. Peering through the peephole, she saw the blurry silhouette of Colonel Hanssen, his jaw set like granite under the porch light.

She flung the door open. "What the hell do you want, James?" Her voice was a slurred growl.

Hanssen stepped inside without invitation, his uniform crisply pressed despite the hour. His gray eyes scanned her messy blouse, a flicker of disgust crossing his face. "You're giving up, Jane, throwing it all away when we can still win. Do you even have the spine to see this through?"

She laughed, a bitter, jagged sound, and swayed toward

him. "Me? Am I giving up? You're the one who screwed this to hell and back!" Her finger jabbed at his chest. "You were supposed to manage the dispersal of the Thunderbird virus in Afghanistan. You promised me that there would be combat troops ready to clean up the mess. And what do I get? Nothing! You've ruined everything, you incompetent fool!"

Hanssen's lip curled. "Careful, Senator. You're not exactly the picture of control tonight."

Her hand lashed out, cracking across his cheek. The sound echoed in the foyer. He didn't flinch. Instead, he chuckled, a low, derisive rumble that made her blood boil.

"Pathetic," he said. "Even your tantrums lack conviction."

She turned away, staggering back to her office, where she collapsed into her chair. Hanssen followed, his polished shoes heavy on the hardwood. The clock read 1:35 a.m. Her eyes darted to it, panic tightening her chest. "Thunderbird's deadline is almost here," she muttered. "An hour. We've got one damn hour."

Hanssen leaned against the doorframe, arms crossed. "Williams called me an hour ago. I thought telling you the good news in person would be best. He knows where the canisters are. They're in some caves in the Shah-i-Kot valley, buried but secure. We need to dig them out and deploy them."

She stared at him incredulously. "That's all? Dig them out? In an hour? Are you out of your mind?"

"Williams is working on it," Hanssen said coolly, "but he wants more money. He says it's too risky now. Command's now hip deep in this, paying close attention."

Jane slammed her fist on the desk, sending a pen skittering to the floor. "More money? Everyone's bleeding me dry!" Her voice cracked, the irony not lost on her. She, who had orchestrated this plan over the past forty years, was now cornered and manipulated by her pawns. She rubbed her temples, the wine dulling her thoughts. "Fine," she spat. "Call him."

Hanssen pulled a secure phone from his pocket and dialed. After a moment, he handed it to her. The line crackled, and Lieutenant Colonel Williams answered. "Senator, no offense, but I don't trust you. Do we have an agreement on my fee?"

She glared at the phone as if it were Williams himself. "I'm wiring it now. Check your damn account."

A pause, then the sound of typing. "All right," Williams said. "It's there, but you have bigger problems than me. The general knows those canisters are dangerous after he debriefed the soldiers who discovered the canisters. He's talked to his superiors, and they've decided to retrieve them now, no matter what else is happening in the valley."

Jane's stomach lurched. "They're pulling them out?"

"There's a task force moving in," Williams continued. "Heavy equipment, tanks for support. They're heading to the caves to dig out the canisters and bring them to Bagram. You've got three hours before they get there. After that, I'm done. Don't contact me again. Tell James that goes for him too." The line went dead.

Jane's hand trembled as she set the phone down. Three hours. Not even enough time to breathe, let alone salvage her plan. Hanssen watched her. "What now, Jane? Are you going to sit there and drown in wine or do something?"

She ignored him, fumbling in her desk drawer for her personal device, a sleek black cube reserved for one purpose. Her fingers shook as she attempted to contact them: Thunderbird. Hanssen's eyes widened, a rare crack in his composure.

"You're contacting them? Now? Are you insane?"

"Shut up, James," she hissed, concentrating on a message. "We need more time. I have a solution. This can still work." She hit send, her breath catching as she waited. The cube remained inactive. Silence stretched, heavy and suffocating. "Come on," she whispered. "You promised me until 2:30. Answer me."

Hanssen paced, his polished shoes scuffing the rug.

"They're done with you, Jane. Do you think Thunderbird cares about your excuses? They'll burn us both if we fail."

She shot him a venomous look. "You'd love that, wouldn't you? To see me fall? You've hated me from the start."

He stopped, looming over her desk. "I don't hate you. I pity you. You thought you could control this, but you're a drunk playing with matches, and now the fire's coming."

"They're not responding," she said, her voice barely above a whisper.

"Then we move," Hanssen said. "We get to Williams, push him to intercept that task force. Delay them, sabotage the equipment, anything until we can arrange for someone else to recover the canisters."

She shook her head, sinking back into her chair. "It's over, James. The general knows. Command's watching. We can't touch those canisters now."

He slammed his hand on the desk, making her jump. "So that's it? You're rolling over? After everything we've done, you're going to quit?"

Her eyes burned, but she refused to cry. "What else is there? You failed me. Williams failed me. Thunderbird's done with me. I'm not the one who lost this. You all did."

Hanssen straightened, his face hardening. "Keep telling yourself that, Jane, but don't expect me to save you when they come for you, and they will." He turned and strode toward the door.

"Where are you going?" she called, her voice breaking.

"To clean up your mess," he said without looking back. The door slammed behind him, leaving her with the ticking clock and the weight of her choices.

Jane stared at the cube, its metallic surface dormant. Outside, the night pressed against the windows, indifferent to her collapse. She reached for the wine bottle, forgetting it was empty, and let her hand fall. The plan had been perfect:

unleash the virus, let it spread chaos among the Others, then she'd step in with Thunderbird, savior to a terrified world. Her power would be absolute and unassailable. But perfection had crumbled under incompetence and greed.

She rose unsteadily and shuffled to the window. The street was empty, but she felt eyes watching, waiting. Thunderbird's silence was a death sentence, and she knew it. Tanks rumbled toward the caves somewhere in Afghanistan, carrying her dreams to ruin. She pressed her forehead against the cool glass, her breath fogging the pane.

"Damn you all," she whispered. The clock struck 1:45 a.m., and the world felt smaller, closing in like a trap.

21

HELL HATH NO FURY

"You're shivering, Li Jing," Faraj said, his voice smug over the howl of the blizzard. "Cold feet already? Or scared to die?" His dimming flashlight beam danced across the snow, cutting through the dark corridors as they trudged through the abandoned monastery.

Li Jing's teeth chattered, but her eyes burned with defiance. "Scared? Of you?" she spat, her breath clouding in the icy air. "Smith's the coward, sending you to do his dirty work." Her words were sharp, but her heart twisted. Doctor Smith, the man she'd loved, had ordered her death. Betrayal stung worse than the bitter wind clawing at her face.

The Afghan mountains loomed like silent giants, their peaks lost in the swirling snow. The blizzard roared, a relentless beast, piling drifts against the crumbling walls of the monastery. Li Jing's boots sank deep in the drifts of snow, each step a battle against the cold that numbed her fingers and seeped into her thin jacket. Faraj led the way, his heavy coat barely shielding his wiry frame. Behind them, two Taliban soldiers followed, their scarves fluttering, rifles slung low. Their eyes, scarcely visible, flicked between Faraj and Li Jing, heavy with distrust.

"Keep moving," the taller soldier growled, his voice muffled by the storm. A jagged scar ran across his cheek, catching the flashlight's glow. "No tricks, Faraj. Smith said you are to finish this."

Faraj laughed, too loudly and too forcefully. "Oh, I will. It's an honor I've been dreaming of." But his sideways glance at the soldiers betrayed his unease. He didn't want her blood on his hands and wanted them to do it.

The monastery's sanctuary emerged from the snow like a forgotten graveyard, its arches and spires broken, devoured by time. Wind screamed through gaping windows, scattering flakes across the path. Li Jing's hands clenched in her pockets, her mind racing despite the fog of despair. Smith's betrayal was an open wound, joining the scars left by her father. The soldiers' cold stares confirmed her thoughts: Faraj was the same kind of man.

Inside the monastery's shrine hall, the air was no warmer. Snow dusted the stone floor, piling in corners where the roof had collapsed. The walls, etched with faded carvings, stood as mute witnesses to their grim errand. Faraj stopped, his flashlight casting shadows.

"This is far enough," he said, his voice echoing faintly. The soldiers leaned against a cracked pillar, watching, their breath steaming in the chill.

Li Jing faced him, her voice low, venomous. "So Smith told you to kill me because he's done with me. And you're happy to play his dog?" Her dark hair clung to her face, wet with snow, but her gaze was unflinching. Fury was overtaking her grief, a consuming fire banked against the cold.

Faraj paced, his boots scuffing the icy stone. "You're better off here, Li Jing. Dying with dignity." His words tumbled out too fast, too many. "Out there with Smith? You'd be a burden.

This is mercy. I won't even kill you, not really. I'll knock you out, leave you in the snow. It'll be like going to sleep. Peaceful."

The wind moaned outside, rattling loose stones in the walls. Li Jing's laugh was sharp, a blade in the dark. "Sleep? You think I want peace?" She stepped closer, her voice a hiss. "No, Faraj. If you're going to kill me, do it like a man. Come close. Use your hands. Look into my eyes when you take my life. I want you to feel it, to remember what love does to a woman like me." Her challenge hung in the air, daring him to act. She was done with the cowardice of men like Faraj and Smith.

The soldiers snickered, their low chuckles bouncing off the stone. The scarred one muttered, "Coward." Faraj's face flushed, his jaw tightening. The hall's shadows seemed to close in, stones cast in gloom. His face flushed, Faraj averted his gaze. Each nervous gesture indicated his concern that Smith might hear he had faltered.

"Fine," Faraj snapped, his voice trembling and loud with forced bravado. "You want to die? I'll do it. I'm no coward." He paced faster. "You deserve this, Li Jing. You betrayed Smith first, whispering to his enemies. You brought this on yourself." He steeled his nerves as the snowstorm raged beyond the walls.

Li Jing sank to the ground, turning her back to him, her shoulders shaking. "Go on then. Prove you're a man." Her voice dripped with contempt, goading him. She sat cross-legged, head bowed, as if offering herself. The soldiers' amusement faded into curiosity, their eyes glinting in the dim light. Snow swirled through a broken window, dusting Faraj's coat as he approached, his breathing heavy, ragged.

"I'm no coward," he whispered.

The air in the hall was thick, the cold a living thing. As Faraj bent to grab her arm, she moved like a viper. She drew a thin blade from her boot, its edge catching the flashlight's faded beam. In one motion, she drove it into his chest, piercing his heart. Faraj gasped, eyes wide, and collapsed onto her, his weight heavy. Li Jing screamed, a raw, guttural cry, as if she were the one dying. The sound echoed in the stone chamber, primal, shaking the hall's silence.

The soldiers froze, their cigarettes dropping to the snow-dusted floor. They'd set their rifles against the pillar, expecting Faraj's bluster to drag on. Now, they scrambled, cursing in Pashto. Li Jing, pinned under Faraj's twitching body, yanked his pistol from his holster. Her movements were frantic but practiced from years of training in hand-to-hand combat.

She fired twice, the shots deafening. The scarred soldier took a bullet to the chest, collapsing with a grunt. The younger one lunged for his rifle, but her third shot caught his throat. He fell, gurgling, hands clawing at the wound.

The scarred soldier, still alive, grabbed his rifle and fired wildly on full automatic. Ricocheting bullets and stone fragments flew in every direction. A bullet grazed Li Jing's arm, creasing her jacket and drawing blood. She didn't seem to notice, pain buried beneath her rage. Rolling out from under Faraj, blood slicking her hands, she fired again. The scarred soldier's head snapped back, and he went still. The younger one was already dead, his blood pooling on the stone, black in the dim light.

Li Jing stood, chest heaving, the pistol hot in her hand. The hall was silent save for the wind's wail, snow drifting through the broken roof. Her arm bled, a shallow wound she ignored. Limping to the soldiers' bodies, she embodied fury. "You let a boy do a man's job," she spat, firing a final shot into each corpse. "And Faraj was no man."

She stripped their warm coats, pulling a heavy woolen one over hers. The weight was a comfort against the cold that clung to her like a second skin. She took their rifles, slinging one over her shoulder and gripping the other. She tucked Faraj's pistol into her waistband. The blizzard roared outside, the monastery's walls trembling under its assault. Li Jing's eyes burned with purpose. Smith was out there, thinking he'd escaped her. He was wrong.

Stepping into the storm, she vanished into the swirling white, her footprints swallowed instantly. The mountains stretched vast and unforgiving, their slopes buried in snow. Each step was a vow, each breath a promise.

"You betrayed me, Smith," she whispered, her voice lost in the howling wind. "I will find you, and you will learn what your betrayal has forged—a woman unbroken and deadlier than you can imagine."

***

The blizzard howled through the jagged peaks of the Afghan mountains, a relentless wall of snow and wind that seemed intent on swallowing her.

Li Jing staggered forward, her boots crunching into the deepening drifts. The bullet graze on her left arm throbbed, leaking small drops of blood that stained the snow before the storm erased her trail. Her gloved hand, numb and slick with blood, pressed against the wound as she squinted into the white abyss. Her world was reduced to this frozen hell.

Her mind churned, torn between speed and cunning. She could push forward, chase the fading tracks of Doctor Smith and his Taliban escorts, but haste would betray her. They would hear her coming, and she was too outnumbered to survive a direct assault. Stealth was her only option now.

She slowed her pace, her breath steaming in the frigid air. The storm would kill her if they didn't, but vengeance burned hotter than the cold. Smith had betrayed her, left her to die in that abandoned monastery with Faraj and his guards. She had killed them all—Faraj's heart pierced, the soldiers slaughtered without any hesitation. Now, Smith was her quarry. Anger and bitterness coiled in her chest, sharpening her senses. She was a predator, and vengeance was her only reason to endure.

Through the swirling snow, shapes emerged. Seven figures were trudging single file along the narrow mountain path. Smith's silhouette was unmistakable, flanked by six Taliban bodyguards bundled in scarves and thick coats. Li Jing crouched low, her rifle heavy in her hands. She caught the low murmur of voices, the clatter of metal against rock, before the wind snatched the sounds away. They hadn't seen her. She set her rifles down in the snow, her movements deliberate despite the pain in her arm. Her blade gleamed faintly in the dull afternoon light as she crept forward, silent as a moving shadow.

Two soldiers lagged, their heads bowed against the wind. Li Jing stepped close, her bloody glove clamping over the first man's mouth as her knife sliced his throat. He collapsed into a drift without a sound. The second turned, eyes widening, but her blade was faster, silencing him before he could cry out. She let them lie where they fell, their blood soaking into the snow. There was no need to hide the bodies; the blizzard would bury them soon enough. She retrieved her rifles, her gaze fixed on the remaining four soldiers and Smith, her primary target.

She stalked them, waiting for the narrow trail to turn in her favor. The path narrowed, twisting along a treacherous cliffside where loose rocks and ice demanded focus. The group slowed, moving single file, focusing on the ground beneath their feet. Perfect.

Li Jing looked for a sharp bend in the trail, a spot where the wind screamed and visibility dropped to nothing. She propped her rifles against a boulder, her wounded arm trembling as she steadied her aim. One man walked point, then Smith, followed by three soldiers. She targeted the three behind Smith, making certain no stray bullet would rob her of her revenge.

Her first burst, three shots, tore through the man directly behind Smith. He crumpled, blocking the path. The crack of gunfire pierced the storm's roar, and Smith and the point man spun around, seeing the body fall. They bolted forward, scrambling erratically over the uneven ground.

The two remaining soldiers in the rear turned, fumbling with their rifles. Li Jing fired again, another three-shot burst dropping one man as he screamed, his voice swallowed by the wind. The last soldier sprayed automatic fire, wild and inaccurate, bullets chewing into the rocky hillside above her. She took her time, aimed, and killed him with a single burst. His body slumped beside the others.

Smith was rushing now, but the point man was faster, too reckless. His foot slipped on the icy rocks, and with a shout, he plummeted over the cliff, vanishing into the void. Smith froze, alone on the path. He sank to his knees, hands raised, shouting something Li Jing couldn't make out over the storm's fury. She gathered her rifles and carefully advanced, her boots crunching methodically as she closed the distance. Her scarf did not entirely cover her wide grin.

Doctor Smith's voice became clearer as she advanced. "I'm unarmed! Thank God you came! These men were holding me hostage!"

Smith's voice was desperate, his face half-hidden by his scarf. Li Jing realized he thought she was an American soldier, her lips curling in disgust. He was already spinning lies, playing the victim. As she stepped closer, his eyes widened, recognition dawning. His expression shifted from relief to confusion then to a strained enthusiasm.

"It's you, my love!" he cried, his voice trembling with false sincerity.

Li Jing stopped a few yards away, her rifle trained on him. Snow clung to her dark hair, her face pale and fierce, the blood on her glove dark against the storm's white.

"Now I am your love?" she spat, her voice raw with betrayal.

"You left me to die, Smith. You abandoned me to Faraj and his dogs."

"No, no!" Smith shook his head, hands held out as if to embrace her. "It was a test for Faraj. The soldiers were there to protect you, to kill him if he tried to hurt you. I swear it!"

"You lying bastard!" she shouted, her voice cracking with fury. "Even now, you try to manipulate me! You think I'm still the fool who trusted you?"

Smith's face crumpled, tears mixing with the snow on his cheeks. "I didn't want to hurt you," he sobbed. "The Others forced me. They said they'd kill me if I didn't do what they wanted. I had no choice, Li Jing. Please, you have to believe me."

"All lies!" she howled, stepping closer, her rifle unwavering. Her voice dropped, trembling with pain. "I loved you, Smith. I trusted you with everything. I gave you my heart, my loyalty, and you used me. You're evil, worse than I ever was. I'm no saint, but at least I tried to love you, even when it was rotting my soul. All you've done is betray me, twist me into your tool. You're a coward who hides behind excuses."

Smith's sobs grew louder, but his eyes flickered with calculation. "I'm sorry," he whispered. "I never meant to hurt you. Please, Li Jing, forgive me."

She lowered her rifle slightly, her expression softening, though her eyes burned with intent. "Come to me, my darling," she said, her voice suddenly tender, beckoning him closer.

Smith hesitated before scrambling to his feet, hope flickering across his face. He stumbled toward her with arms outstretched, as if expecting an embrace. Li Jing's hand moved like a striking snake when he was close enough. She drove her blade into his chest, twisting it as she pulled him close. Smith gasped, his eyes wide with shock, blood bubbling at his lips. "I know you loved me, I just didn't know how to love you in return," he whispered.

She held him tightly, feeling his warmth fade as his breaths grew shallow, then stopped. His body sagged in her arms, and she let him slide to the ground, his blood staining the snow.

Li Jing stood over him, her face a mask of grief and rage. She rifled through his backpack, finding the cube-shaped communication device he'd guarded so closely. She hurled it over the cliff with a sneer, watching it disappear into the storm. The wind howled, the world indifferent to her victory, her loss.

She stepped to the path's edge, staring into the swirling white emptiness: the alien device, Faraj, the soldiers, and Smith —all gone. Vengeance had sustained her, but now it was spent, leaving only emptiness. She had nothing left to live for. Betrayed by everyone she'd ever loved, she was beyond redemption. The cold seeped into her bones, and she remembered what she said to Smith back at the cave. She'd rather die than live without him. The storm beckoned, a fitting grave.

"This is a good day to die," she whispered, her voice buried in the wind. She stood motionless, a solitary figure against the blizzard, her silhouette fading into the snow.

22

BUMP IN THE NIGHT

The air in Senator Jane Traficant's Georgetown home office hung heavy with the pungent mix of spilled merlot and burning paper.

Her silk blouse, once immaculate, clung to her body, blotched with crimson stains that mirrored the wine-soaked carpet beneath her desk. Her gray hair, usually sculpted into a politician's sophisticated hairstyle, was now twisted in wild tangles, framing a face pale with dread and the remnants of a drunken haze. She swayed slightly, one hand gripping the edge of her mahogany desk as the other fed classified documents into a shredder's hungry jaws. The machine's buzz filled the room, evidence of her unraveling empire.

Jane's eyes were bloodshot, but she was focusing more soberly. She glanced at the sleek, obsidian communication device on her desk—a gift from *those* who called themselves Thunderbird. For decades, it had been her lifeline to power, to promises of dominion over a world remade in her image.

Tonight, she had caressed its sleek surface constantly, her fingers trembling as she whispered pleas into the void. "Answer me, damn you. I've done everything you asked." Silence. For the first time, Thunderbird had not responded. The deliberate quiet, sharp as a blade. It wasn't the silence but all the things they used to say hanging in the air like forgotten promises.

Colonel Hanssen, her reluctant ally, had left hours ago, muttering something about "fixing this mess." Fixing how? She didn't know. She thought they had done everything possible. His arrogant, cryptic departure gnawed at her, but she couldn't focus enough to connect the dots. The safe behind her desk was empty now, its secrets reduced to confetti. She planned to finish burning the remains in the fireplace as an extra precaution. She knew the bastards would soon be snooping through every inch of her home.

She couldn't run—her face was too recognizable, plastered across every newsstand and television screen. Surrender was unthinkable. She'd rather choke on her pride than face a courtroom's judgment. And suicide? Her hand trembled at the thought, knocking over an empty wine bottle. No, she was too weak for that. All she could do was wait, a cornered animal in a gilded cage, waiting for the inevitable knock on her door.

The device pulsed suddenly, a low hum that vibrated through her bones. Jane froze, her breath catching as a sensation like cold fire surged through her skull. This was no gentle summons, no familiar whisper of Thunderbird's calculated allure. It was an invasion, a forceful intrusion that clawed into her mind, pinning her thoughts like a moth under glass. Her knees buckled, and she gripped the desk to keep from collapsing.

"No," she gasped, her voice a ragged thread. "Not like this."

"Human," the voice boomed inside her head, not one but many, layered and dissonant, like a chorus of gods pronouncing judgment. "Your time is finished." The words were not spoken but carved, each syllable a blade slicing through her wine-addled conscience. She clutched her temples, tears streaming down her cheeks as the overwhelming presence consumed her.

There was no escaping it. No corner of her mind was left unviolated.

"Please," she whispered, her voice breaking. "I can still deliver. The virus, the Others... I need more time."

Devoid of mercy, Thunderbird intoned, "You have already failed us. Your incompetence has led to chaos while we sought a solution. We grant no further grace."

Jane's heart pounded, her vision blurring as she staggered back, knocking over a chair. "But I've given you everything! My career, my soul, everything!"

"You are replaceable." The words landed like a guillotine. "We have recalculated. The Others can still be infected. Colonel Hanssen will execute our will directly. You are severed from our purpose."

"Hanssen?" Jane's voice rose, shrill with panic. "That snake? He's nothing without me!"

"He is pliable. You are not." A pause, heavy with finality. "Should he fail, Earth will be reset. You will not know the hour, nor the manner. Your use to us ends here."

"Reset?" Her mind reeled, conjuring images of cities crumbling, skies burning. "You can't... Will you send someone for me? To...finish it?"

Silence. The presence withdrew as abruptly as it had invaded, leaving her mind raw and hollow. She blinked, gasping, and realized no time had passed. The shredder still hummed, the clock on the wall still ticked. The device on her desk was inert, its once shimmering surface now lackluster. She was alone.

Jane stumbled out of the office, her bare feet sinking into the plush living room carpet. A single lamp dimly lit the room, casting long shadows across the opulent furniture. Her gaze fell on the fireplace, where a peculiar timepiece hung over the mantle—another gift from Thunderbird. Its face was etched with alien symbols that had once pulsed with life. Now, its hands were frozen, the cosmic time stilled. Her stomach churned. It was over.

She fumbled for her secure phone, her fingers clumsy as she dialed Hanssen. The line rang twice before his gruff voice answered. "What do you want, Jane?"

"Hanssen, listen to me," she gushed in a desperate rush. "We can still fix this. I have contacts and leverage. We can get the virus to the Others and make Thunderbird understand why. Work with me."

A low chuckle rumbled through the phone, sly and mocking. "You have nothing to bargain with, Senator. Nothing." His tone dripped with contempt. "I've always known you'd fail. You were too weak, too drunk on your self-image. I'm picking up the pieces now, and I don't need you."

"Hanssen, you bastard—" Her voice cracked, but he cut her off.

"Goodbye, Jane." The line went dead, his hollow laughter echoing in her ears.

She dropped the phone, her hands shaking as she sank onto the couch. Her gaze drifted to the coffee table, where the communication device sat beside her half-empty wine glass. No, not a device—a cube, its edges glinting faintly in the lamplight. She reached for her glass, her fingers brushing the air where the cube had been. It was gone, vanished as if it had never existed. Her breath hitched, a sob clawing its way up her throat.

A noise outside, a faint crunch of gravel, snapped her head toward the window. Her heart raced. Was it paranoia, or were they here? Had the government's enforcers come to erase her? She rose, swaying, and peered through the curtains. The street was dark, empty, but the shadows seemed to twist with malevolence. She backed away from the window, her pulse thundering in her ears.

She had once envisioned herself as a future queen—a

global leader. Now Jane Traficant realized she had become a pawn, stripped of power. The house creaked around her, a crypt of her own making. She poured the last of the wine into her glass, her hands trembling so violently that it splashed onto the carpet. She didn't care. Raising the glass to her lips, she whispered, "I'll see you all in hell."

Outside, the noises grew louder.

***

In the dim, foul tunnels beneath the Afghan mountains, Barth Anderson sprawled in a heap of Quds corpses.

His breath was shallow, his body smeared with blood and gore. The previous day had carved its cruelty into his flesh, but not as deeply as he'd let the Americans believe. His wounds—a gash across his forehead, a broken rib or two—stung fiercely but wouldn't kill him. Not yet.

His muscular body, lean from years of survival in the CIA field operations, trembled under the weight of an Iranian soldier's corpse, its warmth fading against his chest. Barth's face, gaunt and unshaven, bore the grime of battle. His deep-brown eyes, sharp and unyielding, flickered with a manic glint. His thick, dark hair, matted with sweat and blood, clung to his scalp like a second skin. He was alive. "Lucky," he muttered, the word a bitter prayer.

The American Green Berets and that overgrown Boy Scout, Maxx, who he despised with a venom that burned hotter than his wounds, had left him for dead. Their boots had echoed down the tunnels, fading into the dark. Barth shoved the corpse off him, wincing as pain lanced through his chest. He scavenged quickly, his movements methodical despite the chaos. From the remains of the Quds, he gathered a tattered jacket, a pair of gloves, and a battered AK-47 rifle with three spare magazines. His pistol stayed holstered at his hip. He grabbed the

Qud satellite radio, its casing cracked but functional, and slung it over his shoulder. The weapons felt inadequate, laughably so, against whatever *the things* were.

He hadn't seen them clearly—only flashes of movement, sleek and wrong, as they tore through the Iranians. Pinned beneath the dying soldier, he'd caught glimpses: limbs too long, motions too fluid. Shadows that ripped and tore through the soldiers with ease. Aliens, he was certain, though the why of it baffled him. Why attack the Iranians? Had the plan shifted? Were they hunting anyone who wasn't Smith? The thought tightened his grip on the rifle. He was still in danger.

Barth scanned the tunnel. From the sounds of it, the Americans had chased the main Quds force deeper into the labyrinth, their tracks scuffed into the dirt. He chose another exit from the cavern, where a faint breeze brushed his face—an exit, maybe. Anything to avoid the Americans and the shadows. His boots crunched over stone as he moved, the air growing colder, fresher. An hour later, the tunnel branched, and he spotted signs of passage: a discarded Taliban scarf, a smear of blood, and tracks leading upward—Smith's people. The tunnel opened into the mountains, and he exhaled, his breath clouding in the frigid air.

"Hallelujah, lucky again. Finally."

The blizzard roared outside, snow swirling in vicious gusts. Barth squinted against the whiteout, his stolen jacket flapping as he followed the tracks left by Smith's group. Or at least what he hoped was Smith's group. It didn't matter. He was committed now.

The trail was faint, dissolving under fresh snow, but the path was clear: a narrow ledge winding through the mountains, flanked by jagged peaks and sheer drops. The wind howled, biting through his gloves, and the cold numbed his gashed face. The route snaked upward, treacherous with ice and loose shale. To his left, a ravine yawned, its depths lost in the storm. To his right, cliffs loomed, their faces scarred by centuries of wind. The tracks held steady, a single file of fading bootprints, and Barth pressed on, his rifle slung across his chest. Losing them wasn't a concern. There was nowhere else to go.

The trail leveled onto a plateau, and Barth spotted the monastery—a crumbling stone structure perched like a forgotten fortress. Its walls, weathered and eroded, leaned into the storm. He entered the building cautiously, his rifle raised, and searched room by room for signs that Smith had been here recently. It appeared they had gathered around a fire in one of the main rooms with a small group traveling deeper into the covered hallways.

Barth trudged through the monastery's shadowy hallway, his boots crunching softly on the thin, powdery layer of snow. Several sets of boot prints marred the frozen snow. He froze at the threshold of a cavernous room, its stone walls pitted with age. Three bodies sprawled across the floor, their forms twisted in the dim light. The scene was eerily still, with the only sound being the faint whistle of wind through the broken roof above.

Faraj, an Iranian scientist he recognized, was face down, his throat slit. Two others, Taliban by their garb, were nearby, clearly shot. Blood stained the snow crimson, already freezing at the edges. Barth crouched, his eyes narrowing. "What happened here?" he muttered. The wounds were typical of close-quarters combat—human work, not the chaotic savagery of *those things*. He exhaled, relieved. Whatever stalked the tunnels hadn't followed them out.

Tracks led away from the monastery, faint but visible, heading down a single path toward the west. Barth didn't rush. The storm would cover the trail soon, but there was only one way forward. He adjusted the radio on his shoulder and trudged on, the monastery fading into the blizzard behind him.

The path descended into a rocky pass, where the wind screamed through gaps in the cliffs. Barth's boots slipped on ice, but he kept his balance, his eyes locked on the fading tracks. An hour later, he reached a dirt track barely wide enough for two men to travel side by side that cut through the snow. And there, in the middle of it, was another body. Doctor Smith.

Barth stopped, his breath catching. Smith's corpse was mainly untouched, except for the bloody hole over his heart, and his eyes stared blankly at the sky. Barth knelt, his gloved fingers brushing the wounds. "Humans," he said, his voice low. The confusion gnawed at him. Smith was supposed to be untouchable, the linchpin of their operation. If he was dead, what did that mean? Barth's gaze swept the road, landing on another body below, half-buried in the rocks. Li Jing, he assumed, though he couldn't be sure from this distance. "Good riddance," he spat, his lip curling. She'd been a thorn in his side for too long.

He stood, the wind whipping at his face, and considered his options. The tunnels were a death sentence. Whatever creatures lurked in the shadows, they'd claimed that maze. He wasn't going back. The storm showed no signs of easing, and navigating the mountain pass alone was a fool's errand. The monastery, bleak as it was, offered some shelter. He could wait out the blizzard there, maybe get a signal on the radio once the skies cleared. He doubted it, but he was still feeling lucky.

Then there was Smith. Barth's eyes lingered on the corpse, a plan forming. If he survived this, if he was caught, he needed leverage. He knelt again, pulling a knife from his boot. With quick, practiced cuts, he carved a shallow wound into Smith's arm, then smeared his blood onto the blade. He tucked the knife into his jacket, carefully keeping it separate from his other gear. If anyone found Smith's body, they'd think Barth had killed him. "My 'get out of jail free' card," he said, a grim smile forming on his lips. No one was left to contradict his story.

Faraj, Li Jing, the Taliban—all dead. The Americans were miles away, chasing ghosts in the tunnels.

Barth turned back toward the monastery, the AK-47 heavy in his hands. The storm swallowed the road behind him, erasing Smith's body from view. He moved slowly, his broken ribs making it difficult to get a deep breath, but his mind was sharp. The mountains didn't care about his plans or the things in the tunnels. But Barth Anderson was a survivor, always one step ahead. He'd wait out the storm, and when the snow cleared, he'd find a way out.

The monastery loomed ahead, its silhouette faint through the blizzard. Barth pushed open the heavy wooden door, the hinges groaning in protest. Inside, the air was still, heavy with the smell of damp stone and decay. He set the radio on a cracked stone table. The bodies outside could freeze for all he cared; he wasn't here to bury them. He sank onto the stone floor, his rifle across his lap, and stared at the radio. "Come on," he muttered, twisting the dials. Nothing but white noise answered.

He leaned back, his eyes drifting to the narrow window where snow piled against the plastic sheeting. The storm would pass. It always did. And when it did, Barth would be ready. He'd survived the tunnels, the Americans, and those *things*. He'd survive this too. "Lucky," he said again, his voice echoing in the empty room. For now, it was enough.

23

STEP INTO MY WEB

Grey's skin tingled. "Why aren't they coming?" she muttered, her voice low, swallowed by the tunnel's oppressive quiet.

The weight of unseen eyes bore into her, a sensation that had dogged her since the firefight at the Qud camp in the tunnel cavern. Nothing attacked though. No lightning-quick shadows, no skittering claws. Only nervous silence, heavy and wrong.

The air in the tunnel was thick with the stench of blood and cordite, the walls slick with moisture and something darker. Miss Grey's boots scraped against the uneven stone as she slowly followed the remnants of the Green Beret team toward the faint glow ahead. Her breath fogged in the chill, and her gloved hand rested on the grip of her M4.

Behind her, Sergeant Zeller's heavy steps echoed, punctuated by the occasional grunt from Corporal Diaz and the quiet, measured tread of Private Hicks. The four of them were all that remained after the Quds Force ambush at the cave's exit, where the Iranian operatives had either been torn apart by the "things" lurking in the shadows or gunned down in their desperate last stand.

Zeller, his bearded face streaked with dust, glanced back, his eyes scanning the darkness. "Maybe they know you're trying to stop the virus. Maybe they're...waiting."

"For what?" Diaz asked, his voice tight, his weapon cradled like a protective charm.

Hicks, ever the optimist, snorted. "Don't start with that mystical crap, Sarge. They're probably full after lunching on those Quds bastards."

Grey ignored them, her focus on the light ahead. The tunnel opened into a jagged vista, revealing a snow-dusted mountainside under the cloudy March sky. It was late afternoon in the Hindu Kush, and the storm that had battered the mountain pass for days was finally relenting. Flurries drifted lazily, the wind reduced to a low groan. Visibility was poor, but Grey spotted the faint tracks in the snow—boot prints, chaotic and overlapping, leading west toward Iran. The Taliban had fled this way, abandoning their dead.

"Looks like they got out," Zeller said, crouching to inspect the tracks. "Sloppy. They're moving slowly. Must have been caught in the storm."

Grey nodded, her jaw tight. "We follow. Smith's out there. And he's got answers."

The trail was treacherous, a narrow ledge slick with ice and snow. The team moved silently, weapons ready, the mountain's vastness pressing against them. After an hour, the tracks led to a crumbling stone structure nestled against the cliff—an abandoned monastery, its walls ruined by time and war. A faint glow flickered from within.

"Got a light source," Hicks whispered, gesturing with his rifle. "Someone's home."

"Or was," Diaz added, his voice barely audible.

Zeller signaled for them to stack up. They breached the

heavy wooden door, boots crunching on frost-covered stone. The air inside was stale, heavy with the scent of decay. In the main chamber, a dying fire cast shadows across three bodies sprawled on the floor—frozen, their faces locked in rictus screams. Two wore Taliban garb. The third, a slight man in civilian clothes, had a neatly trimmed beard with his throat open from ear to ear.

"Faraj," Grey said, recognizing the Iranian scientist from the intelligence dossier.

A rustle came from the shadows. Zeller spun, his rifle trained on a figure stepping into the light—Barth Anderson, his muscular frame draped in a bloodstained parka, hands raised. His dark eyes flicked over the team, lingering on Grey.

"Well, damn," Anderson said, his voice smooth despite the situation. "Miss Grey, didn't expect you to make it this far."

Grey's finger tightened on the trigger, her heart pounding with a fury she'd buried for months. "You son of a bitch," she hissed. "You sold us out. You sold me out."

Zeller stepped between Anderson and Grey, his voice calm but firm. "You're about the last person I expected to find here, Anderson. We were certain you were dead when we left you in the pile of corpses back in the tunnel."

"Lucky, I guess," Anderson scoffed.

"Easy, Miss Grey. We take him back to Bagram. Alive," Zeller said.

"Why?" she snapped, her eyes never leaving Anderson. "After what he did to me? The virus, shooting Maxx, the Quds, all of it—"

"Because we're not him," Zeller said. "And we need what he knows."

Anderson smirked, lowering his hands slightly. "Listen to the sergeant. As I told you, I was trying to stop Smith. I finally caught up to him on the road west of here. I took him out, but

Smith... He came at me with a knife. Had to put him down. Li Jing, too. She tried to run, fell off a cliff."

Grey's eyes narrowed. "You're a lying pendejo. You never told me anything about stopping Smith, and I don't believe a word you're saying now."

"Am I lying?" Anderson gestured toward the door. "Go see for yourself. Smith's body is up the road. Killed him with my knife. Jing's at the bottom of the ravine."

They followed Anderson up the snowy trail, the monastery fading into the mist behind them. At a bend in the path, they found Smith's body, half-buried in snow, with a neat hole in his chest. Grey knelt, checking the wound, her face a mask of cold rage. "You didn't have to kill him," she said, standing. "You wanted him dead."

Anderson shrugged. "He was a traitor. Tell me you wouldn't have done the same thing after what he did on 9/11."

Grey stepped closer, her voice low and venomous. "You're lucky it's me and not Maxx who found you. He'd have tossed you off this cliff without a second thought."

Anderson's smirk faltered, but he said nothing. They returned to the monastery, the team tense, the air thick with unspoken accusations. Inside, Torres found a cracked Quds radio on a table. Its signal was weak but functioning. Grey dialed in Maxx's frequency.

Her voice clipped as she spoke into the hiss of the background signal. "Maxx, it's Grey. If you get this, you made the right call. Your white whale's dead. Smith's gone."

No response. She tried again, but the signal faded. "Damn it," she muttered. "No way to reach him."

Zeller rubbed his jaw, his eyes on Anderson. "Smith's confirmed dead. That's enough for now. We need to get back to Bagram. Call for a ride. If the weather is clear enough, they can land a bird on a wide spot on the road. We sure as hell are not going back through those tunnels."

Grey nodded, pulling out a secure satellite phone to contact Senator Traficant, her sponsor in Washington. Before she could dial, Anderson stepped forward, his voice urgent. "Hold off, Grey. You'll want to hear me out first."

She froze, her thumb hovering over the keypad. "What?"

"I know things," Anderson said, his eyes glinting. "About the virus, Thunderbird, the whole damn operation. I'll trade it for a deal. Immunity, or at least a head start."

The room went silent. Diaz and Hicks exchanged glances, their hands tightening on their weapons. Zeller's face was placid, but Grey's was a storm of barely restrained fury. Slowly, she set the phone down and drew her pistol, leveling it at Anderson's chest.

"Here's the only deal you're getting," she said, her voice like ice. "Talk or I kill you right here."

Anderson's hands twitched, his smirk gone. The firelight danced across his face, casting long shadows on the frozen bodies behind him. For a moment, no one moved.

"Alright," Anderson said finally, his voice quieter now. "I'll talk, but you will not like what you're going to hear."

Grey's finger stayed on the trigger, her eyes boring into his. "Try me."

Everyone seemed to hold their breath. The faint crackle of the dying fire was the only sound as Anderson began to speak. He described a web of betrayal and blood that would haunt them long after they left this cursed place. Outside, the wind in the tunnel whispered secrets that no one could decipher.

***

Gabby Fisher's voice carried a faint tremor as she leaned toward Janet. "Did you catch the Mariners' spring training news?" she asked, forcing a casual tone. "They're looking strong this year."

Janet's auburn ponytail swayed in the frenetic bustle of Code Brew. She paused, wiping her hands on her apron, a smile breaking through her early-morning hustle. "Oh yeah, Gabby. Saw the highlights. Those new pitchers are on fire. Are you and Maxx betting on another playoff run?"

The First Hill coffee shop pulsed with morning chaos. Nurses in mismatched scrubs traded stories over steaming lattes, their laughter mingling with the clink of mugs and the espresso machine's sharp hiss. Gabby's eyes, shadowed from a sleepless night in a seedy motel near the Space Needle, its walls reeking of mildew, betrayed her exhaustion. Her fingers, rough from gripping bus poles, clutched her coffee cup.

Gabby's smile faltered, her thoughts snagging on Maxx, whom she hadn't heard from since she'd left two days ago. "Maxx would love it," she said, voice softening. "He's probably got stats memorized already."

She'd checked her voicemails—nothing from Maxx, only worried messages from Andres, friends, and work, all wondering why she'd "disappeared." The silent calls chilled her—she was sure it was the man she'd glimpsed at Salish Lodge.

Janet chuckled, oblivious to Gabby's tension. "You two had better grab tickets for opening day. Edgar's Cantina won't be the same without you."

"We'll be there," Gabby murmured, her gaze snapping to the entrance as Torashi stepped inside. His gray hoodie and jeans were casual, but his eyes swept the room with predatory focus. She'd been evading him since yesterday morning, riding buses in aimless loops, paying cash for a new backpack, clothes, and a can of mace from a drugstore. She'd left clues, a receipt at a bus stop and a note at a diner, to lure him into a trap.

Now, her pulse thundered. Her plan had worked too well, and she wasn't ready to spring the trap yet. The mace in her backpack felt flimsy. She wished for one of Maxx's pistols, but their condo was too risky. How had Torashi found her so quickly?

She leaned closer to Janet, voice dropping to a whisper. "Janet, that guy in the hoodie... He's stalking me. I need to get out without him seeing. Can you distract him so I can slip out the back?"

Janet's eyes widened, flicking to Torashi then back. "I've got you covered, girl. I'll make a scene. Get to the back door. My car's in the alley—a baby-blue 1998 Toyota Corolla. Keys are under the mat."

Gabby's throat tightened with gratitude. "Thank you, Janet."

"Go now," Janet said, moving toward Torashi with purpose.

Gabby slid from the booth, her backpack slung over her shoulder, and she pulled her ball cap down low over her eyes. Janet's voice rang out, sharp and staged, as she "tripped," sending a tray of mugs crashing in a shatter of ceramic. Heads turned, Torashi's among them, his gaze snared by the chaos. Gabby darted through the kitchen, the air filled with pastries and steam, and burst into the alley. The morning chill bit her skin as she found the Corolla, grabbed the keys, and peeled out, tires screeching on wet pavement.

Minutes later, she dialed Janet's number using the cheap phone she'd gotten at the drug store. Her hands were trembling on the steering wheel. "Janet, you okay?"

Janet's voice was edged with worry. "The Asian guy flipped when he realized you were gone. Smashed a chair, scared everyone. We called the cops, but he bolted before they showed. Watch yourself."

"Thanks, Janet," Gabby said, voice fraying. "I owe you big."

She hung up, the weight of her solitude crushing her chest. Torashi was a badger, relentless and unyielding. She couldn't keep running alone. She dialed Maxx, her heart twisting as it went to voicemail again. "Maxx, where are you? I need you," she whispered, ending the call. Next, she tried Andres's cell, but Glen's gruff voice answered instead.

"Gabby? Where in the world have you been?" Glen's urgency crackled through the line.

"It doesn't matter, Glen. I'm back now."

"Just in time. Andres is in jail. Torashi stabbed him last night, and the cops arrested him yesterday afternoon. Things are getting wild!"

"Stabbed? Jail?" Gabby's voice broke, exhaustion amplifying her panic. "What's going on, Glen?"

"Torashi's a maniac," Glen said. "Andres was trying to protect you, and we wanted to trap him. Cops showed up, but it was the wrong place and time. Maxx is on his way back to Seattle now. Where are you?"

"I'm driving," Gabby said, gripping the wheel. "I'm going to get Andres out. Is he at King County?"

"Yep," Glen said with a snicker. "I'm sure the other prisoners in the holding cell aren't sure what to make of Professor Sandoval. I'll meet you there."

The King County Correctional Facility loomed in Downtown Seattle, a squat fortress of weathered concrete. Its thick, beveled windows glinted like cold, unblinking eyes. The morning air was damp, carrying the faint odor of seawater and exhaust.

Inside, the air stung with the sharp bite of bleach, the linoleum floors scarred and slick under yellowed fluorescent lights. Gabby's sneakers squeaked in the sterile halls as she navigated to the bail office, her body drooping with fatigue. Glen was already there, his broad shoulders tense, his flannel shirt rumpled from a sleepless night.

"You're okay," Glen said, pulling her into a brief, fierce hug.

"Barely," Gabby muttered, her voice frayed. They pooled $5,000 in cash, their voices hushed as they handed it to a bored clerk behind bulletproof glass. The wait was agonizing, the lobby's plastic chairs creaking under Glen's immense weight, the air thick with the stale scent of cigarettes.

Finally, Andres emerged, escorted by a stone-faced guard. Usually impeccably groomed, his tailored chinos and tweed blazer were a hallmark of his professor image, and Andres now looked like a ghost of himself. His shirt was torn, stained with dried blood from the stab wound on his side, now leaking through a sloppy bandage. His dark hair, normally combed back, fell in dirty strands over a bruised forehead, and his sharp cheekbones were shadowed with stubble. His eyes burned with the same fierce intelligence, even after a night in a cell.

"Gabby, you're safe," Andres said, his voice rough but warm, like gravel under silk.

"Andres, I'm so sorry," Gabby said, tears spilling down her cheeks, her exhaustion cracking her resolve. "I vanished to get my head straight, thought I could avoid being tracked, but Torashi found me anyway."

Andres shook his head, wincing as he adjusted his injured arm. "Not your fault, Gabby. Torashi's a damn lunatic. He must be stopped, and I've failed twice."

Glen clapped Andres on his good shoulder, careful but firm. "You look like you've been through a wrestling match, brother. But you're out. Now what's the move?"

Gabby's hands steadied, her voice finding strength despite her fatigue. "I have a plan to bring Torashi to us. Somewhere we control, where he thinks he's got the upper hand. It's risky, but he won't stop unless we make him."

"Risky how?" Andres asked, his jaw tightening, eyes glinting with vengeance. "What kind of setup are we talking about?"

Gabby hesitated, her lips pressing into a thin line. "It's better if I don't lay it all out yet. But it's a trap, and we'll need to move fast. Can you handle it?"

"Hell yeah," Glen said, his knuckles white as he cracked them, his face set with grim determination. "Torashi's got it coming. I'm in."

Andres nodded, a shadow of his usual confident smile flickering. "Torashi put a knife in me. I owe him. Count me in."

Gabby exhaled, a spark of hope piercing her weariness. "Together then. We do this."

Outside the correctional facility, Gabby, Glen, and Andres stood on the cracked sidewalk, the morning sky heavy with threatening rain clouds. Gabby's legs felt leaden, her body screaming for rest, yet her mind was sharp, fueled by the promise of an end to this nightmare. Her gaze was locked on the Olympic Mountains on the horizon.

"Andres, you sure you're up for this?" Gabby asked, her voice tender, almost lost in the city's hum. "You've already been through hell."

He turned to her, his bruised face softening for a moment. "Gabby, you and Maxx are family. Torashi crossed a line. No way I'm sitting this out."

Glen clapped Andres's good shoulder again, his grip steady. "We've got your back, man. And Gabby's. This ends today."

Gabby nodded, her chest tight with gratitude. Torashi had hunted her, but now she was turning the tables. With Andres and Glen by her side, the odds felt less crushing.

"Let's get moving," she said, her voice steady now, cutting through the morning chill. "We set the trap. We finish this before Maxx gets home."

Andres's lips twitched, a faint grin breaking through. "Damn right, we do."

Glen's eyes gleamed with grim determination. "Time to put this dude down."

As they walked toward Glen's beat-up pickup truck parked haphazardly across the street, Gabby felt Seattle's morning pulse around them—its gray sprawl, its relentless rhythm. Torashi had followed her breadcrumbs, but he didn't know what awaited him. For the first time in days, Gabby felt a spark of control, a sense that she wasn't the prey.

24

CREEPING DEATH

"We've done it, Dr. Xi," Mr. Green said, triumphant. "The backdoor program... It's ready to deploy. We can block every one of their devices, not only the one sitting in our lab." He gestured toward a sleek, obsidian device in a containment chamber, its surface pulsing faintly with an otherworldly green light.

Green, slouched in a chair, tapped a pen against a notepad, his eyes fixed on the flickering screen displaying lines of code. The XINXI lab, a concrete bunker deep below Beijing, lined with blinking servers and reinforced steel, looked like an electronic tomb.

Dr. Xi stopped pacing before the humming console. His thick glasses reflected the screen's glow as he studied the data. "Permanently block the Others' communication? All of them?" His tone was cautious, probing. "We're safe here, Green, but the retaliation would be catastrophic. Cities will burn. The death toll would be in the millions, maybe the billions."

Green leaned forward, his eyes narrowing. "And if we don't act? They'll tighten their grip. You've seen their transmissions. They're planning something big. We have the upper hand for now. I think we have to take the risk, while we have the element of surprise."

Xi's jaw tightened. He glanced at the containment chamber, where the device—an alien artifact recovered from a Tangshan crash site—loomed like a silent predator. "Let's test it first. One last time."

They initiated the backdoor program. Lines of code streamed across the screen, infiltrating the device's network. The chamber's sensors came alive, and the device's pulsing slowed, then stopped. Green grinned. "It's as good as it gets, Xi. We've got them by the throat."

Across the lab, Dr. Fang, a petite woman with dark hair pulled into a tight bun, hovered near a secondary console. Her fingers twitched over the controls. Behind her thick glasses, her eyes darted between Xi and Green.

"She's been off all night," Green muttered to Xi, keeping his voice low. "I don't trust her. Harry!" He waved over Harry Cull, their burly pilot and armed friend. "Keep an eye on Dr. Fang. Something's not right with her."

Harry nodded, stroking his thick beard. He positioned himself near Fang, his hand resting on the gun tucked in his jacket pocket.

Oblivious to the tension, Xi opened a secure channel to the Others. The lab's speakers crackled, and a synthetic, resonant voice filled the room. "You summon us, humans. Have you made your decision?"

Xi's voice was steady but firm. "We know your plans. We've cracked your communication network. We're shutting you out. Permanently. You are no longer welcome on our planet."

The device in the isolation chamber flared, its light intensifying. The Others were trying to seize control. The computer consoles glowed with power spikes, and alarms blared. "They're fighting back!" Green shouted, slamming commands into the keyboard to reinforce the electronic back door.

Fang suddenly lunged for the main terminal, her fingers flying toward the override. “No! You can’t do this!” she screamed.

Despite his colossal size, Harry was faster. He grabbed her wrist, yanking her back as if she weighed nothing. “Sit down, Doctor!” he growled, pinning her against the wall. Her eyes blazed with defiance.

Xi spun around, stunned. “Fang, why?”

Fang’s lips curled into a sneer. “You fools. Liu was right. The Others offered power, control. Fu killed Liu, but I can still finish what he started. Doctor Smith and I... We were promised everything.”

Green’s face darkened. “Liu’s dead, and you’re still chasing his lies? You’d sell out humanity to taste the Others’ promises?”

Xi shook his head, refocusing on the console. The Others’ counterattack was weakening. With a final command, the backdoor was sealed into place. The device’s light dimmed to a faint glow, and the alarms grew silent.

“Blocked,” Green whispered, exhaling. “We did it.”

Xi opened the communication channel again. His voice was cold, furious. “Leave Earth. Do not return. We have no place for you here. If you try, we’ll deploy the virus without hesitation. Your civilization will be erased.”

Green leaned into the microphone, his voice dripping with menace. “I hold the code to the virus given to us by Thunderbird. Test us, and you’ll see how serious we are.”

The alien voice returned, devoid of emotion. “We will go and leave you to our enemies.”

The communication abruptly ended. The lab was silent, save for the hum of servers and Dr. Fang’s heavy breathing. Xi slumped into a chair, his face pale. “Thunderbird,” he murmured.

Green’s expression hardened. “We’re not done, Xi. The Others are leaving, but Thunderbird’s devices are still out there.

We've only delayed the inevitable if we don't block them too. They'll reset Earth, like they've threatened."

Xi shook his head, his voice rising. "The backdoor wasn't designed for Thunderbird's tech. It's similar but different, too volatile. We need time to test it properly."

"Time?" Green snapped. "If they figure out we can disrupt their communications, they'll unleash chaos. Earthquakes, tsunamis. Maybe worse. We act now or lose everything."

Xi rubbed his temples, his resolve wavering. "Fine, but we must test it first. The Thunderbird device at the Tacoma facility in Seattle. If it works there, then we can consider a global rollout."

Green nodded, grabbing a secure phone. "Gene Heckman, head of security at Team Tacoma. We can trust him. He'll watch the device for us." He dialed. "Gene, it's Green."

Heckman chuckled. "I was wondering if you'd show up again. The last I heard, you were on your way to China, and Torashi was hot on your tail."

"Dr. Xi and I made it to China. We think we've found a way to defuse the threat. Can you get to the lab? We're running a test on the Thunderbird device, but I need your eyes on it."

In the underground Tacoma facility, Gene Heckman, a grizzled veteran with a buzz cut, jogged to the brightly lit lab. The Thunderbird device, a large metallic cube, sat in a reinforced glass vault. Its smooth, dark surface seemed to absorb all the light in the room. Gene punched a button on the phone and put them on the overhead speaker.

"Green, I'm in position. Ready when you are."

Back in Beijing, the lab was a pressure cooker. Xi's fingers shook as he input the final test parameters. Green stood over his shoulder, his breath shallow. "This is it, Xi. Everything we've worked for."

Xi launched the test. The Thunderbird device flared deep blue in the underground vault. Its light seared the lab walls.

Gene's voice came through, tense. "It's reacting to whatever you're doing. I've never seen this kind of effect before. The vault's holding, but the device is unstable."

The Beijing console sparked, error messages flashing. Xi cursed under his breath. "It's adapting. The backdoor may not be enough."

Green's hands flew across the keyboard, tweaking the code on the fly. "Come on, you son of a bitch" he muttered. "Stay down."

In the Tacoma lab, the device's light pulsed erratically and then dimmed. Gene's voice crackled through the line. "Green, it's... It's stopped responding. It's looking like a block of inert metal. You did it."

Xi collapsed back in his chair, sweat beading on his forehead. Green let out a shaky laugh. "Whew. We got it."

The lab fell quiet, the weight of their victory settling over them, leaving them exhausted. Fang, still restrained by Harry, glared but said nothing. Xi looked at Green, his voice soft but resolute. "We've bought ourselves time, but Thunderbird... We need time to understand if we've won the battle or the war."

Green nodded, his eyes distant. "The Others are gone. I don't see them risking a return while we have the virus. With Thunderbird, we may have only changed the battlefield."

Harry loosened his grip on Fang, who slumped against the wall, defeated. The lab's servers hummed, a reminder of the fragile line they'd walked. Outside, Beijing slept, unaware of the war waged beneath its streets—a war that had for now been won, but at a cost yet to be revealed.

***

Under the bruised night sky, Lt. Colonel Tom Williams stood outside the Operation Anaconda headquarters at Bagram Airbase, the tip of his cigarette glowing like a solitary beacon.

His hands trembled slightly as he exhaled a plume of smoke, watching it curl into the darkness. The weight of the day—so many lies—sat heavy in his chest, a heaviness he couldn't dislodge. He was nervous, more than he'd been in years, and the cigarette was poor relief for the storm brewing inside him.

His mind drifted back to the chaos of the past day, replaying the events that had led him to this moment. It started when Lt. Weih and the Ranger squad returned to Bagram, battered but alive, with news of the canisters that turned heads and raised questions. They claimed the canisters contained a mysterious virus, so they buried them in caves and headed back. They pulled them from the wreckage of an unidentified convoy ambushed by the Taliban. Williams had been there when they rolled in, escorted by that arrogant Homeland Security consultant, King. Their Humvees were shot to hell, and the men's faces were grim. He had seen the men escorted in, and he had known instantly that this was bigger than any of them.

The after-action briefing had been a crucible. Held in a stark room lit by overly bright fluorescents, it was presided over by Colonel McCray, a grizzled veteran with eyes that could cut through steel. McCray's decades of combat experience was its own presence, and Williams had been explicitly told to sit in the back and keep his mouth shut unless directly addressed. The general's staff filled the room, their uniforms crisp, their expressions skeptical. Still caked in grime, Lieutenant Weih and Sergeant Lacey stood at the front, recounting every decision from when Weih and the Two-Three stumbled on the convoy.

McCray had barked, "Explain it in excruciating detail from the second you saw that convoy, Lieutenant."

Drone and satellite footage flickered on a screen behind them, grainy images of the convoy under attack, of Weih's team engaging the Taliban, of the canisters being secured. At first, the staff's questions were sharp and dismissive, as if they thought Weih and his men were exaggerating to cover up some blunder. But as the Rangers laid out their story—what they'd seen outside the tunnels in the Hindu Kush—the room's mood shifted. The footage corroborated their account. Other units in the area reported similar sightings. The skepticism gave way to a tense realization. This threat was real.

Williams had felt the heat intensify when the questions turned to him. He'd been the one to green-light Weih's actions, to push for the canisters' recovery without waiting for higher approval. McCray's gaze had pinned him like a spider under glass. "You made a lot of calls out there, Williams," McCray said, deceptively calm. "Care to walk us through your reasoning?"

Williams had kept his answers vague, deflecting where he could. He didn't mention Colonel Hanssen or Senator Traficant. He'd thought he could skate through, but then an aide slid a stack of papers across the table—call logs from Washington, D.C., showing multiple inbound calls to Williams's secure line during the operation.

"Who was calling you from Washington, Lieutenant Colonel?" McCray asked, suspicious.

Williams's throat tightened. "Routine check-ins," he lied, forcing his voice to stay steady. "Logistics coordination."

The aide raised an eyebrow. "From DC? Starting at 0100 local time. Yesterday?"

The room went silent, the weight of their stares crushing the breath out of him. Williams doubled down, mumbling about time zones, but he saw McCray's jaw tighten. They knew he was lying. The logs didn't lie, and his flimsy excuse unraveled faster than he could think.

The briefing stretched on for two hours, a grueling dissection of every choice, every moment. When it finally ended, Weih and Lacey were dismissed with a nod from McCray. "You and your boys fought hard," he told them, his voice softening for the first time. "It didn't go unnoticed. Only mistake was dragging the civilian King into this mess."

Weih straightened, his eyes intense. "Sir, we'd be dead if Maxx King hadn't been there. Those canisters would be in Taliban hands." He stared directly at Williams. "He was the only person I could count on when things went to hell."

Lacey nodded. "He's a loose cannon, but he's why we made it back."

McCray grunted, unconvinced but unwilling to argue. "Get cleaned up. Back to your units. Dismissed."

After they left, the room's focus shifted. The CIA had gotten wind of the canister location and declared it a matter of national security, priority one. "There's a munition out there," a faceless voice on a secure line had said. "Recover it at any cost." A recovery force was assembled—engineers to dig out the canisters, armor, and air cover in case things went south, and CIA observers, including a man named Cavanaugh, to ensure the canisters' integrity. Failure, they were told, was not an option.

Williams snapped back to the present, the cigarette nearly burned to his fingers. He flicked the butt into the gravel and lit another, his hands still unsteady. The recovery force was out there now, scouring the site, and he was here waiting for the hammer to drop, his lies pointing to him like a loaded weapon. Should he come clean about Hanssen and Traficant? The truth might bury him, but the lies were already choking him. There was no good choice, only bad and worse.

He glanced up, distracted by a strange sight. The sky above the Hindu Kush was alive with streaks of light, like meteors but...wrong. They weren't falling but shooting upward, as if the mountains were firing stars into the heavens. "I've seen it all now," he muttered, a chill creeping up his spine. A few nights ago, back when this had all started, a meteor shower lit up the sky. "They must not have liked it here," he said with a hollow laugh. "Can't blame them. I don't like it here either." The lights felt ominous, a cosmic warning he couldn't shake.

The rumble of heavy engines broke his concentration. The recovery force was back, their convoy rolling through the gates. Williams crushed his cigarette under his boot and hurried toward the staging area. The vehicles looked battered but intact, and soldiers were already unloading crates that glinted under the floodlights, the canisters presumably. He scanned the scene, expecting a firefight's aftermath, but the men seemed calm, almost relaxed.

"Resistance was light," one of the engineers told an officer nearby. "A few Taliban snipers, nothing heavy. Not what we braced for."

Williams frowned. The Taliban didn't simply back off. Something wasn't right.

A man in battle gear, his face half-hidden by a scarf, approached the crates. "Cavanaugh," he said curtly, flashing CIA credentials. "I'm taking custody of these."

Williams watched as Cavanaugh and a handful of men with no unit markings inspected the canisters with clinical precision. They moved quickly, transferring the crates to unmarked trucks that idled nearby. No paperwork, no chain of custody, only efficiency that smelled like secrecy.

"Where are those going?" Williams asked, stepping forward.

Cavanaugh didn't look at him. "Airfield. Need to know, Colonel."

The trucks pulled away, their taillights fading into the night. Williams stood there, the dust settling around him, a hollow pit in his stomach. What the hell was going on? Those canisters, Hanssen, and Traficant were all slipping out of his control, and he was left with questions and feeling he was never going to see the payday they'd promised.

Before he could process it, two MPs appeared, their faces

blank. "Lieutenant Colonel Williams," one said, his voice flat, "you need to come with us."

Williams's heart sank. His mouth went dry, but he nodded, following them back inside headquarters. They led him to a vacant conference room, the door clicking shut behind him with a finality that echoed in his bones. He stood alone, his pulse hammering in his ears.

He was caught. The call logs, the lies, the half-truths—they'd unraveled, and now the truth was closing in. His mind raced, replaying McCray's piercing stare, the CIA's cryptic urgency, the strange lights in the sky. He felt exposed, like a man standing naked in a lightning storm. Hanssen and Traficant's names burned in his throat, begging to be spoken, but he knew that confessing now might only bring bigger trouble.

The door creaked open, and McCray stepped inside, emotionless. Behind him was Cavanaugh, his eyes intense. Williams straightened, forcing himself to meet their gazes, but inside he was crumbling. The room felt as if it was closing in, and as McCray began to speak, Williams knew there was no escaping what came next.

"Start talking, Tom," McCray said, his voice like a sledgehammer. "This time, don't leave anything out."

25

BRING YOUR FRIENDS

A fine mist dappled the window as she sat in the cafe at Alki Beach, the briny scent of Puget Sound mingling with the sweet steam of her hot tea. The Olympic Mountains loomed across the water, their peaks hazy in the rain-sodden clouds.

Gabby wore a faded denim jacket over a black turtleneck, clothes she'd picked up at a nearby thrift shop. Her fingers drummed on the table. She'd been waiting, first sipping coffee, then tea, her nerves tangled with anticipation and dread. Maxx was coming home.

The crunch of gravel snapped her attention to a beat-up Ford pickup pulling to the curb outside the coffee shop. Glen hopped out, his huge frame bundled in a raincoat, his thick black hair plastered to his head. Behind him, Andres idled in a sleek red sedan, his intense gaze scanning the beach like a hawk. As Gabby stepped onto the sidewalk, Glen tossed her the keys to his truck.

"Everything ready, Gabby?" Glen asked, his smile wide but his deep voice edged with concern.

She caught the keys midair, her lips twitching into a half-smile. "Yeah. Be prepared for anything."

Andres leaned out his window, his dark eyes glinting. "We always are, senorita."

Glen grinned, clapping Gabby's shoulder. "There are a couple of presents under the seat for Maxx. He'll know what to do with them."

Gabby nodded, her throat tight. Glen was happy for her, she could tell, but the weight of what was ahead pressed on them all. Andres revved the engine, and Glen climbed into the sedan. With a curt nod, they peeled away, leaving Gabby alone with the truck and the drizzle.

She slid into the driver's seat, the worn plastic bench seat creaking under her weight. The truck smelled of motor oil and Glen's cologne, which seemed oddly out of place this morning. When she turned the key, the engine sputtered to life, and she headed south toward McChord Air Force Base, her heart pounding. The radio crackled, landing on a Nirvana classic—Maxx's favorite. Gabby never got what "teen spirit" was meant to feel like, but the raw guitar riffs steadied her nerves.

Her mind churned as she drove. She was glad she'd stuck it out and fought for what she believed in. After Natalie tried to kill her, after she realized Torashi was hunting her, she had nearly broken down. She'd needed to recenter herself, to find her footing. Now, she wanted to finish this. Whatever "this" was. Torashi, the shadow trailing her for days, was closing in. She could feel it in her gut.

What about Maxx? Was he okay coming back early from Afghanistan? He'd been over there in the dust and chaos trying to save the world. Would he still trust her, after doubts and a sudden disappearance?

The rain thickened as she reached the civilian parking lot outside McChord's secured airfield. She parked, her breath fogging in the cold air, and waited. Her eyes scanned the lot, every shadow a potential threat. Then she saw him.

Maxx strode across the asphalt, his oversized backpack slung over one shoulder, his crew cut damp and tousled. He was tall, broad-shouldered, his desert-tan fatigues clinging to his body. A slight limp marred his walk, but a wide grin split his face when his hazel eyes found her. Gabby's heart lurched. She flung open the truck door and ran to him.

They collided in a fierce hug, her arms wrapping around his neck, his hands steadying her waist. "Missed you so much," she whispered, her voice cracking.

"Missed you more, Gabs," he murmured, his breath warm against her ear. They kissed, a hungry, desperate press of lips, as if they could erase the time apart.

They pulled back, foreheads touching. "How'd it go over there?" she asked softly.

Maxx's grin faded, his eyes darkening. He was silent for a long moment. "Got a message from Miss Grey. She's safe. They found Doctor Smith. Dead. Li Jing...presumed dead. We stopped them at least. But Thunderbird, the rest of it..." He shook his head. "I don't know. Gotta trust Green and Xi will sort it out."

They reeled at the news.

"Enough about my stuff. Are you okay, babe?" he said as he touched her cheek.

Gabby nodded, her stomach twisting. So much left unresolved. She forced a smile. "I'm doing better now. We'll talk about it when we're both ready. Glen left a present for you under the seat."

Maxx climbed into the truck, his movements stiff. He reached under the seat and pulled out a .45 caliber pistol, its metal gleaming dully. He checked the clip, confirming it was loaded, then tucked it into his waistband. Next, he retrieved a family-size package of Twizzlers, his grin returning. "Breakfast of champions."

"Ugh," Gabby groaned, rolling her eyes, "you two are disgusting."

He chuckled, tearing open the package and popping a red rope into his mouth. Gabby started the truck, pulling out of the lot, the rain pattering against the hood. They drove in comfortable silence for a few minutes, the Air Force base giving way to the gray sprawl of I-5 through Tacoma. Then Maxx stiffened, his eyes flicking to the side mirror.

"Gabby," he said, his voice low, "we're being followed."

Her grip tightened on the wheel, her pulse spiking. "Yeah. That's...Torashi. He's been on me for days."

Maxx's jaw clenched. "I know who Torashi is, but why now? What's going on?"

She swallowed, her mouth dry. "Give me a minute, Maxx. I need to concentrate. This truck is a handful."

He leaned back, his hand resting near the .45. "Couldn't we have him arrested?"

Gabby shook her head, her eyes darting to the rearview mirror. A black SUV trailed them, too close for comfort. "Torashi's got contacts in the Seattle PD. It's why Andres was locked up overnight. He's untouchable."

Maxx's brow furrowed, but he nodded. "Okay, so what's the play?"

She took a deep breath, her voice steady despite the fear clawing at her chest. "I have a plan. That's why Glen left you the gun."

He studied her, his gaze piercing. "You're asking me to trust you, Gabs."

"I know, and I need you to."

"I do," he said, his voice firm. "Always have. Except for the time you tricked me into eating kale."

Her heart swelled as she giggled. But the weight of what came next pressed down. The SUV was still there, a dark shadow in the rain. She glanced at Maxx, his face set, the Twizzlers forgotten in his lap. The pistol was a cold, brutal reminder at his side.

"Alright, my plan starts now," she said as she scanned the highway signage.

She flicked on the turn signal, easing the truck toward an exit ramp. The SUV followed, its headlights cutting through the mist. Gabby's hands trembled, but her resolve was like iron. Torashi had hunted her long enough. It ended today. She didn't know if Maxx was ready, if she was ready, but they were out of time.

"Hold on," she said, her eyes narrowing. "This may get dicey."

The rusty pickup truck roared down the ramp near Boeing Field, its tires squealing against the wet asphalt. The black SUV loomed in the rearview mirror, closing in fast. Maxx braced himself in the passenger seat, his hand resting on the grip of Glen's Glock. Rain lashed the windshield, blurring the world outside, and the chase began in earnest.

Gabby's knuckles whitened on the steering wheel as she weaved through the heavy morning traffic. Behind them, Torashi's SUV hung back, its headlights cutting through the drizzle. She'd expected him to ram them, to try to force them off the road with the brute aggression he was known for. But he didn't. He trailed close enough to keep them in sight, not rushing, not reckless. It unnerved her more than a collision would have.

"What's the plan here?" Maxx asked, his voice strained but steady. He glanced over at her, searching her face for answers.

Gabby kept her gaze fixed on the road. "Keep him following us until we can get him to a place to box him in."

Maxx shifted in his seat, the old plastic creaking under his weight. "How long?"

"Twenty minutes, give or take."

"You have a place picked out?" he pressed.

She nodded, her jaw tight. "Yes, Glen and Andres will be there before us. Waiting. We trap him, and Andres and Miss Grey have arranged for the Department of Defense to take him into custody. That way, we bypass the Seattle Police Department and any potential leaks at the federal level. It's a national security issue. Miss Grey will ensure he's taken care of for a long time."

Maxx's brow furrowed. "Taken care of where? Does TSA have a black site?"

Gabby's lips twitched. "A new place the government opened in January. It's called Camp X-Ray at a military facility in Cuba. He'll be held as part of the detention system for terrorists. He'll be there a long, long time."

Maxx let out a low whistle. "You mean Guantanamo Naval Base?"

"Exactly. Miss Grey says his attempts to kill Green and Xi are enough to qualify him for detention, but first we have to catch him. TSA and the FBI haven't been able to."

The truck jolted over a pothole, and Gabby corrected the wheel with a firm grip. Ahead, the road curved toward the waterfront, the gray expanse of Puget Sound visible through the mist. Street signs for the ferry terminal loomed, and she flicked on her blinker.

Maxx's head snapped toward her. "Hell no!"

She grinned, a flash of defiance in her green eyes. "Don't worry. No swimming required."

He shook his head, a reluctant smirk tugging at the corners of his mouth.

"We get him on the ferry. There's nowhere for him to hide or run. He's trapped. The ferry to Bremerton won't be busy this early, so we'll get on, and he won't realize we're onto him. Andres and Glen are ahead of us. He'll follow you and me up to the top deck. Glen and Andres will be waiting, armed and ready. Between the three of you, he'll surrender. Plainclothes TSA agents are on board to arrest him once we've ID'd him and have him cornered in a safe location."

Maxx rubbed his jaw, his stubble rasping under his fingers. "What if he jumps off the ferry? I am not going in after him."

"If he takes a dive, the TSA will call the Coast Guard. He's not getting away."

He studied her for a moment, his expression darkening. "Are you sure he won't fight? This guy is a psycho."

Gabby's voice hardened, her eyes flicking to meet his. "Part of me hopes he'll try. But he's trying to kill you, Maxx, and I'll do anything to make sure he doesn't."

The ferry terminal came into view, its concrete ramps slick with rain. A short line of cars waited to board the 9:55 sailing to Bremerton. Gabby slowed the truck, her pulse steady despite the adrenaline humming through her veins. In the side mirror, she saw Torashi's SUV pull into the queue behind them, four cars back. Ahead, Andres's red sedan rolled onto the ferry's lower deck.

"Glen's with him?" Maxx asked, craning his neck to confirm.

"Yeah. They're set." Gabby eased the truck forward as the ferry worker waved them aboard. The ramp clanged under the tires, and the vehicle rocked slightly as they parked on the steel deck. Torashi's SUV followed, being directed to the elevated parking ramp.

They climbed out, the air sharp with salt and diesel. Gabby buttoned her jacket against the wind and led the way to the stairs, her sneakers echoing on the metal steps. Maxx stayed close, his hand hovering near the gun tucked inside his belt. They moved casually, like any other passengers heading for the upper deck, but Gabby's senses were on high alert. She caught Maxx's eye, and he gave a subtle nod.

"Like old times, huh, Maxx?" she said with a lopsided grin.

Maxx rolled his eyes and gave a noncommittal grunt.

Torashi was behind them—she'd seen his reflection in the ferry's oversized windows as they'd entered. Alone. That was good. He probably had a gun, though Andres had told her that he was known to favor a knife for close work. He'd try to catch them by surprise, maybe race up another staircase to cut them off.

Maxx's voice dropped low as they climbed. "Gabby, if this goes south, stay out of the line of attack."

She shot him a look, her chin lifting. "Not a chance, Mister. I'm in this with you."

"Damn it, Gabby—"

"No, Maxx. We're doing this together."

He muttered something under his breath but didn't argue further. They reached the top deck, stepping out into the open air. The wind whipped Gabby's dark hair across her face, and she brushed it back, squinting against the drizzle. The deck was nearly empty, except for a few commuters huddled near the railing with coffee cups. The ferry's horn blared, and the vessel shuddered as it pulled away from the dock.

Gabby scanned the deck, her heart ticking like a metronome. Andres and Glen were already in position, leaning against the far railing, their coats concealing their weapons. They looked like ordinary passengers, but Gabby caught the subtle tilt of Glen's head, signaling he'd spotted Torashi climbing the stairs.

"He's coming," Maxx murmured, his hand brushing her arm. "Stay sharp."

She nodded, her mouth dry. They moved toward the center of the deck, positioning themselves where Torashi would have to approach head-on. The rain stung her cheeks, and the ferry rocked gently beneath her feet. She could feel Torashi's presence now, a shadow at the edge of her awareness, closing in.

"Gabby," Glen called softly, his voice carrying enough to

reach her. He and Andres stepped away from the railing, their postures casual but locked in. "You alright?"

"Yeah," she replied, her voice steady. "He's here."

Maxx unzipped his windbreaker, his eyes on the stairwell door. "Any second now."

The metal stairwell door swung open, and Torashi stepped onto the deck. He was lean and unassuming, his dark coat blending with the gray morning. But his eyes, sharp, predatory, locked onto Gabby and Maxx instantly. He paused, assessing, his hand slipping into his pocket. Knife or gun, Gabby couldn't tell.

"Easy," Maxx whispered. "Let him come to us."

Torashi took a step forward, then another, his movements fluid, deliberate. Andres and Glen closed in from the sides, their steps silent on the wet deck. The TSA agents, stationed near the other stairwell, watched from a distance.

The wind howled, whipping rain across the ferry's top deck. Gabby's hair clung to her face, but her eyes stayed fixed on Torashi. Then the stairwell door banged open. Two men emerged behind Torashi, their pistols glinting in the dim light. One was stocky with a shaved head. The other was tall, his jacket flapping open to reveal a holster strapped tight to his chest.

"Shit," Maxx muttered under his breath.

The few commuters huddled near the railing, clutching coffee cups, froze for a heartbeat before scrambling away. Their footsteps slapped against the wet deck as they vanished down the nearest stairwell, leaving the rain and standoff behind.

Torashi's lips curled into a grin, his teeth flashing white against the gray. "You thought you were clever. I have friends too, as you can see."

Andres and Glen had their weapons out, barrels trained on Torashi's backup. The stocky man's pistol wavered slightly, but the tall one held steady, his eyes darting between targets.

Gabby's heart pounded, but she stayed still. Maxx hadn't moved either, his hands loose at his sides.

Torashi's grin widened, his voice slicing through the wind. "I would prefer to kill you close. I dream of watching you die, Maxx King. Then I will kill your girlfriend."

Maxx's jaw tightened, but his voice remained calm, sounding tired. "Tell your friends to stand down. You and me, Torashi. Only blades. We'll see how good you are. Andres told me you're more lucky than good."

Andres shifted, his gun still trained on the stocky man. "Maxx, don't. Let me."

Maxx shook his head, his eyes never leaving Torashi. "No, this is between me and him."

Torashi laughed menacingly. He raised a hand, and his men lowered their pistols, though their fingers stayed close to the triggers. "Blades it is," he said, pulling a sleek knife from his pocket. The blade caught the morning light, its edge honed to a razor's gleam.

Maxx shrugged off his windbreaker, the rain soaking his uniform instantly. He wrapped the jacket around his left forearm, the motion casual but deliberate. Gabby knew what came next. She'd seen this movie before. Maxx's enemies frequently underestimated him, thinking he was big and slow, but they always paid for their miscalculation.

Torashi lunged, his knife slashing toward Maxx's chest. Maxx sidestepped, his movements fluid, almost relaxed. In a blur, he snapped his left arm, and the hidden blade strapped to his forearm flicked into his hand. The windbreaker concealed the motion, and Torashi didn't see it coming. No one ever did. His enemies assumed his right hand was dominant, dodging to his left, straight into his trap.

The two circled, rain pelting their faces. Torashi's blade darted out, aiming for Maxx's throat, but Maxx parried with his wrapped arm, the fabric catching the strike. Gabby held her breath, her fingers gripping the railing. The deck was slick, the ferry swaying beneath them, but Maxx moved like he was born for this. And in a way, he had been...thanks to his father.

Torashi feinted left then slashed low, aiming for Maxx's thigh. Maxx spun, his left hand a blur, and drove his knife into Torashi's side. His right hand clamped onto Torashi's wrist, his thumb digging into the nerve. Torashi gasped, his grip faltering, and his knife clattered to the deck. Maxx didn't hesitate. He yanked his blade free and stabbed again, deeper this time. Blood sprayed, bright red against the gray morning, and Gabby knew he'd hit an artery.

Torashi staggered, clutching his side, but his grin didn't fade. "Finish it," he rasped, blood bubbling at his lips. "Or are you too weak? Let your girlfriend do it if you can't."

Gabby's stomach twisted, but she didn't move. Maxx's face was unreadable, his knife still dripping. Behind them, Torashi's men exchanged glances and then bolted for the stairwell. The TSA agents shouted, sprinting after them, their boots pounding down the metal steps.

Maxx stepped closer, his voice low. "I've done too much killing this week. You're not worth it."

Torashi laughed, a wet, choking sound. "I knew you weren't man enough to look me in the eye while I die."

"You're right about that," Maxx said, his tone flat. "I don't want to watch, but you don't deserve to live either. You've got a couple of minutes if you're lucky." He glanced at Gabby, a faint smirk forming on his lips. "Let's see if there are sharks in the water. I say yes. Gabby tells me I'm imagining it. You get the deciding vote."

Before Torashi could respond, Maxx grabbed him by the collar and belt. With a grunt, he hoisted the man over his head like he weighed nothing and hurled him over the railing. Torashi hit the dark waters of Puget Sound with a splash, bobbing on the surface for a moment.

Something pulled him under, fast and silent. The waves swallowed the ripples, leaving nothing behind.

Maxx stared at the water, wiping his hands on his pants. "Still undecided, I guess."

Gabby's breath caught, her hands trembling as she unclenched them from the railing. Maxx turned to Andres. "Give it a few minutes before you call the Coast Guard to recover his body. If there's anything left."

Andres lowered his radio. Glen and Andres approached the railing, their weapons holstered now. Glen shrugged. "Damn, I wanted to see some sharks," he said with a note of disappointment.

Andres glanced at the water, then back at Maxx. "You good, brother?"

Maxx didn't answer. He bent down, picked up Torashi's knife, and slipped it into his pocket. The rain had slowed to a drizzle, but the wind still cut through Gabby's jacket. She stepped forward, her boots slipping slightly on the wet deck, and reached for Maxx. He turned, and for a moment they stood there, the world narrowing to the space between them.

"You okay?" she asked, her voice barely audible over the wind.

Maxx's lips twitched, not quite a smile. "Been worse." He pulled her into a hug, his arms steady despite the blood and rain. "Guess I owe you a coffee. Sharks or no sharks, I'm calling that a win."

Gabby laughed, the sound shaky but real. She pressed her face against his chest, the damp fabric cold against her cheek. "You're an idiot," she muttered. "But yeah, you're buying."

Glen cleared his throat, breaking the moment. "We should move. Those TSA guys will have questions. Like, where's Torashi? I'd rather not be here when they start asking."

Maxx nodded, releasing Gabby but keeping one hand on

her waist. "Let's go. Those Twizzlers aren't going to eat themselves."

As they headed for the stairwell, Gabby glanced back at the water. The surface was calm now, with no trace of Torashi or whatever had taken him. She shivered, not only from the cold, and followed Maxx down the stairs. The ferry churned on, carrying them toward the shore, where the world waited.

DAY THREE

26

SETTLING DEBTS

Deputy Director Manuel Gutierrez stood on the stoop of Senator Jane Traficant's elegant townhome, his dark suit impeccably pressed despite the clinging humidity.

Tall and slightly balding, his Yale-striped tie—a muted blue and gold—was the sole spark of color on a frame otherwise designed to blend into Washington's bureaucratic swarm. His unremarkable features, the kind that could slip unnoticed through a crowd of government workers, were taut with purpose. His jaw clenched as he raised a fist and knocked, the sharp rap against the polished oak door echoing like a gavel in the quiet afternoon.

From within, a voice rasped, hoarse and brittle. "Go away. I'm ill. No visitors today."

Gutierrez's eyes narrowed, his posture rigid. "Senator, it's Gutierrez. Open the door." His tone was steely, laced with an urgency that cut through the damp, afternoon air. "You'll want to hear this now, not later. If you don't open it, I'll have someone do it for me. Don't test me."

A heavy silence followed, broken only by the faint hum of a passing car. Then the faint shuffle of footsteps stirred within. The door creaked open, revealing Jane Traficant, her once-impeccable facade crumbling like a neglected monument. Her pale-lavender silk blouse hung wrinkled and untucked, its collar stained faintly with lipstick and wine. Her gray hair, usually swept into a conservative arrangement, was a tangled halo, strands clinging to her forehead. Her bloodshot eyes, ringed with smudged mascara, burned with a volatile mix of defiance and exhaustion. The sour tang of stale wine wafted from her, mingling with the musty air of the townhome.

"Make it quick, Gutierrez," she snapped, her voice sharp despite its tremor. "I've got a dinner meeting with the Ways and Means Committee to prepare for, and I'm in no mood for your games." She stepped aside, her movements unsteady, and gestured him in with a flick of her wrist.

Gutierrez crossed the threshold, his polished loafers sinking into the plush cream carpet. The living room was a jarring departure from his last visit, when every surface had gleamed under the glow of crystal sconces, every object arranged with surgical precision. He recalled the plastic sheeting she'd draped over the armchair he'd sat in, as if his presence might contaminate her pristine world. Now, chaos reigned.

Papers were strewn across the mahogany coffee table, some crumpled, others stained with coffee rings. An overturned wine glass had left a crimson splotch on the rug, its edges creeping like spilled blood. Dust motes swirled in the slanted light filtering through heavy drapes, and the air carried a faint staleness, as if the room had been sealed too long.

His gaze settled on a peculiar clock on the mantel, its brass face etched with strange, angular markings that seemed to shimmer faintly, like runes from another world. Its hands were frozen at 5:17, the second hand frozen. "Odd," he remarked, his voice measured as he nodded toward it. "That's a very unusual timepiece. Alien markings, if I'm not mistaken. Do you mind if I take a closer look? Maybe see why it's not working?"

Traficant's face twisted, her lips curling into a sneer. "Don't touch it!" she barked, her voice spiking with sudden venom. "Nothing works like it's supposed to! The clocks, the phones, the people... Useless, every last one!" She began to pace, her bare feet scuffing against the carpet, her hands trembling as they raked through her disheveled hair. "This city, this country, it's a broken machine, Gutierrez! It grinds and grinds and spits out nothing but chaos and betrayal!" Her voice rose to a fevered pitch, her eyes wild. "Do you know how hard I've worked to hold it all together? To keep this nation from collapsing under its weight? And for what? To be harassed in my home by a mid-level bureaucrat who doesn't know his place?"

Gutierrez stood motionless, his hands clasped behind his back, his expression a mask of calm scrutiny. "I'm not here to harass you, Senator," he said evenly, though his eyes never left her. "But you're going to want to hear what I have to say. Shall we sit?"

Her laughter was sharp, bitter. "Sit? In this mess? You must think I'm a fool, Gutierrez. Say your piece and get out."

He watched her, his expression unreadable. "Senator, I'm here about Colonel Hansson. He's been arrested and is cutting a plea deal. Is there anything you'd like to say about him before he talks?"

"Why would I have anything to say about Colonel Hansson? He's been working for me as a liaison. You know I'm on the Armed Services Committee and the subcommittee chairperson, not that it's any of your concern."

"Yes, I'm aware of your senatorial responsibilities. I was referring more to what the Colonel told us about your extracurricular activities."

Her eyes flashed with fury. "Hansson? That lying snake? I wouldn't trust a word that man says! I hope they lock him up and throw away the key!" She stepped closer, her voice dropping to a venomous hiss. "And how dare you imply I have anything to do with whatever he's involved in? You think you can waltz in here and accuse me of something? Me?"

The living room, already suffocating under its disarray, seemed to contract as Deputy Director Gutierrez stood at its center. His dark, neatly pressed suit was a shocking contrast to the chaos of scattered papers and stained rugs. His hands were clasped behind his back, the faint glint of his Yale-striped tie catching the dim light. His face remained an unyielding mask of calm, but his eyes burned with purpose, pinning Senator Jane Traficant where she stood.

"That's not all," he said, his voice cutting through the stale air. "Director Anderson from the Central Intelligence Agency has come forward. He's made a formal statement. He claims you authorized him to eliminate Miss Grey, a Homeland Security agent, while they were deployed in Afghanistan."

The room fell into a deathly hush, the only sound the faint creak of the townhome settling under the March drizzle outside. Traficant's face drained of color, her skin taking on the pallor of wax, but her jaw clenched with a defiance that seemed to hold her upright. Her bloodshot eyes darted to the side then back to Gutierrez, glinting with a mix of fear and fury. "Anderson's lying," she hissed, her voice low and venomous. "He's scrambling to cover his incompetence. You think I'd stoop to murder? Me? A United States senator? That's the kind of filthy, immoral game your people play, Gutierrez, not mine. You CIA types thrive on blood and shadows."

Gutierrez tilted his head, a subtle gesture that bore the weight of skepticism. His voice remained steady, each word deliberate. "Anderson's testimony is detailed, Senator. Dates, communications, and even a recorded call. The charges, if substantiated, would be catastrophic. Tax evasion. Conspiracy.

Treason. You'd be etched into history as the most notorious criminal this nation has ever seen."

"Tax evasion? Treason?" Her scoff was sharp but cracked at the edges, her voice pitching into a shrill edge that betrayed her unraveling composure. "This is absurd! A witch hunt orchestrated by jealous men who can't stand a woman in power! You've got nothing but rumors and a disgraced director's word!" She stepped forward, her wrinkled silk blouse swaying, her hands trembling as they gestured wildly. "Do you know who I am, Gutierrez? I've served this country for decades! I've sat on committees that oversee your agency!"

He took a measured step closer, his eyes locking onto hers with an intensity that silenced her tirade. "I came here as a courtesy, Senator," he said, his tone low but sharp. "You're under suspicion. Nothing formal yet, but the wheels are turning. The National Security Advisor has already stripped you of your security clearance pending the investigation. That's effective immediately."

Her hands clenched into fists, the knuckles whitening. "My clearance?" she spat, her voice quivering with outrage. "On what grounds? What fabricated nonsense are you using to justify this?"

Gutierrez ignored her question, his gaze unwavering. "The IRS and FBI are involved now. They're digging deep. Bank accounts, offshore transactions, encrypted communications, and your connections to Thunderbird. Every thread, every trace. They're pulling it all apart."

Traficant's composure shattered, her face contorting with rage. "Why are you telling me this?" she demanded, her voice a raw, trembling snarl. "What's your angle? You think you can intimidate me? Blackmail me? What's your game, you smug little bureaucrat?"

He leaned forward slightly, his voice dropping to a chilling whisper that seemed to fill the room. "Because I'm certain you've been entangled in activities that don't merely endanger the United States—they threaten humanity. I know more than I'm saying, Senator. Far more. The easiest path for everyone is if you come clean now, while there's still a chance to resolve this quietly. Confess everything. Names, plans, motives. Wait too long, and it'll be too late. For you. For the world."

Traficant stared at him, her chest heaving, her eyes wide with a mixture of defiance and dread. The alien-marked clock on the mantel seemed to loom larger, its frozen hands a silent witness to the unraveling of her plans. "You're bluffing," she whispered without conviction. "You've got nothing."

Gutierrez's lips twitched, the faintest hint of a grim smile. "Keep telling yourself that, Senator, but the noose is tightening."

She glared at him, a bead of sweat forming on her brow. Silence stretched between them for a moment, taut as a harp string. Then, she straightened, her voice cold and measured. "I'm not admitting anything. But if I had done any of those things, it was because I had no choice. Because someone had to make the hard calls. You think I wanted power for power's sake? I did what I did to protect this nation and the world from threats you can't even comprehend."

Gutierrez raised an eyebrow. "Enlighten me."

She turned away, her gaze distant, as if seeing something beyond the room's walls. "The aliens. They've been here longer than we have, watching, waiting. Thunderbird came to me, not Doctor Smith, not the president—me. They chose Manhattan for their first contact. Do you know why?"

He shook his head, though his eyes narrowed.

"To force our hand," she said, almost reverent. "A remote site like Mount St. Helens didn't get our attention. They thought we'd be more compliant after they demonstrated their destructive capabilities in 1980. But Manhattan? The heart of global financial power? It was a threat we couldn't ignore.

Thunderbird and I...saw the opportunity. The US wouldn't act unless it felt the pressure. So we orchestrated it. Then we forced the conflict to the Middle East, where we could control it and fight the Others on our terms with no direct risk in the United States. I saved us, Gutierrez. I should be honored, not vilified."

He glanced at her, his face a mask of disbelief and disgust. "You manipulated a global crisis. Risked millions of lives. For what? To play hero?"

"To survive!" she shouted, whirling to face him. "You think I wanted this? I carried the burden so pissant people like you could sleep at night!"

Gutierrez shook his head slowly. "You carried nothing but ambition, and it's over, Senator."

He turned toward the door, but she followed, her voice desperate. "You can't prove any of this. Nothing I've said here can be used against me."

He paused, his hand on the doorknob, and glanced back. "True, but the FBI had your phones and office bugged for weeks. You hung yourself long before today."

Her eyes widened, but before she could respond, he opened the door. Two FBI agents stood on the stoop, their faces grim. One held up a pair of handcuffs.

"Jane Traficant," the agent said, "you're under arrest for fraud, conspiracy, and treason." He proceeded to read her Miranda rights.

She froze, her breath catching. When the agents finished, with a bitter laugh, she turned to Gutierrez. "You think this is justice? History will judge me, and it'll judge you too."

He met her gaze, unflinching. "History will judge you harshly, Senator. And humanity won't forgive."

As the agents cuffed her, Gutierrez stepped onto the street, the humid air cool against his skin. The townhome door closed behind him, muffling Traficant's protests. He adjusted his tie and walked toward his car, the moment's intensity settling over him.

For Gutierrez, the resolution was bittersweet. He had spent years navigating the CIA's labyrinth, always a step behind men like Anderson, always deferential to power like Traficant's. But this case had changed him. He had seen the price of unquestioning loyalty, of ambition unchecked. As he drove away, he felt not triumph but clarity.

27

BABY'S GOT A SECRET

The XINXI lab was a marvel of sterile precision. Its walls, clad in matte titanium, gleamed under harsh fluorescent lights. Rows of humming computers lined one side, their screens flickering with streams of code. Behind a triple-layered glass chamber was the alien device at the center—a cube three meters on each side, its surface a paradox of light and shadow. It seemed to drink in the room's illumination while casting back distorted reflections, like a black hole trapped in a mirror.

Dr. Xi Jianguo stood before the glass, his reflection warped across the cube's surface. His sharp eyes, framed by wire-rimmed glasses, traced its edges. At 8:30 a.m., after a long night, the air in the lab still crackled with tension. The alien communication device was silent now, its ability to receive input severed, but the consequences of that act were only beginning to unfold.

Xi's fingers danced across a keyboard, his screen displaying a cascade of encrypted signals. Hours earlier, he and Green had executed a plan days in the making. Using a backdoor Xi had embedded in the cube's communication network, they had severed its link to the Others. The cube, and every other device like it, scattered across Earth, was now mute. The Others' plan to manipulate Earth's governments through seismic threats was thwarted, at least for now.

But victory was fleeting. The lab's comms buzzed with urgent chatter. The Chinese Communist Party, unaware of Xi's gambit, had detected the cube's silence. To them, it smelled of sabotage. Whispers of treason swirled, with Xi's name at their center. The lab was now under lockdown, its exits sealed by armed guards.

Green glanced at Xi. "You sure about this, Jianguo? We painted a target on our backs."

Mr. Green—nobody used his first name—was an enigma. A portly American in his late fifties, his Hawaiian shirts and easy grin belied his role as an experienced intelligence agent with a knack for navigating complex, secretive technology. Brought to Beijing by Dr. Xi to collaborate on the communication device, Green's ability to strategize was a tool, and his trust was hard-earned. He leaned against a console, watching Xi with a mix of respect and wariness.

Xi's voice was steady. "The device is offline. The Others can't touch us. That was the plan."

Dr. Xi was the linchpin of XINXI. Thin and meticulous, his calm demeanor masked a mind that raced like the computers around him. An engineer turned physicist, Xi had spent years decoding the cube's signals, earning both the trust of the Chinese Communist Party and the suspicion of its hardliners. His loyalty was to knowledge, not ideology, a trait that made him dangerous in the eyes of some.

Harry snorted, cracking his knuckles. "Plan's great until the firing squad shows up." Harry Cull was the muscle. A former US Ranger turned private contractor, his huge frame and scarred knuckles spoke of a life spent in conflict zones.

Fang lingered near the control panel, her eyes darting

between Xi and the door. "We should report this to Chairman Zemin. Transparency might save us."

Dr. Fang, Xi's former colleague and supposed friend, hovered near the lab's control panel. Her delicate features and soft voice masked a calculating ambition. Xi had once trusted her, but her recent actions had sown suspicion.

Xi's gaze hardened. "Transparency, Dr. Fang? Or surrender?"

Before she could answer, the lab's steel doors hissed open, revealing General Secretary Jiang Zemin, flanked by his bodyguard, Mr. Fu. The room froze.

Chairman Zemin carried the weight of a nation in his measured steps. His tailored suit and thick glasses belied the storm behind his eyes. Mr. Fu, an athletic figure with a face like carved granite, scanned the room, his hand resting on a holstered pistol. The CCP's leader had come to XINXI himself, an omen of either salvation or doom.

Zemin's voice was soft but menacing. "Dr. Xi, explain why the communication device is offline."

Xi stepped forward, his heart pounding, but his face a mask of calm. "General Secretary, the device was an ever-present risk. The Others intended to use it to invade and destabilize Earth. We neutralized it to protect China...and the world."

Recovered from a crash site in Tangshan many years prior, the cube was no mere artifact. It was a conduit, a voice to the stars, capable of interstellar communication with the Others, the alien civilization that had sent it. But its power came with a chilling edge. At the Others' command, it could unleash seismic devastation, reshaping the Earth. It was both a carrot and a stick.

Fang interjected, her voice sharp. "Neutralized? You mean sabotaged! General Secretary, Dr. Xi has been collaborating with the Americans. He's betrayed the party!"

Green's jaw tightened, but he held his tongue. Harry's hand

twitched toward his weapon, his eyes locked on Fu. Xi raised a hand, his voice firm. "Harry, stand down. Let me handle this."

Zemin's gaze flicked to Fang then back to Xi. "Dr. Fang's accusations are serious. The party suspects foreign interference. If you've acted against China's interests, the consequences will be severe."

Xi met Zemin's eyes. "I serve China, General Secretary. But the Others serve no one. Their devices were a trap. You are aware that we had to act."

Fu stepped closer, his presence looming. "And who authorized this action? The Americans?"

Green spoke up, his tone light but edged. "Nobody authorized anything. We saw a threat and moved. Saved your country a lot of trouble, if you ask me."

Zemin's lips twitched, a shadow of a smile. "Bold words, Mr. Green, but boldness doesn't prove loyalty."

Fang pressed her advantage, her voice rising. "They've been communicating with foreign agents! I have evidence, logs of Xi's encrypted transmissions to the West!"

Xi's stomach sank. Fang's betrayal was no surprise, but its timing was lethal. The lab's lockdown, Zemin's presence, Fang's accusations...a noose tightening around them. Harry growled under his breath, ready to fight his way out. Green's hand hovered near a screwdriver, the only weapon at his disposal. Xi's mind raced. He had one card to play, but its success hinged on Zemin.

Xi took a breath, his voice steady. "General Secretary, before you judge, hear the truth. This was no betrayal. It was a plan... our plan."

Zemin's brow arched. "Our plan?"

Xi nodded. "Last month, after my trip to Hawaii to meet with the Americans, I spoke with you secretly. We discussed the Others' intentions. You agreed their offer of alliance was a ruse. They wanted Earth's submission, not partnership. We devised a countermeasure. I'd use the backdoor I had programmed into their network, and you'd play with their demands to buy time."

Green's eyes widened. "You and Zemin? Dr. Xi, you didn't—"

Xi cut him off. "I couldn't risk leaks. Not even you knew the full scope, Green, but you played your part. Through you, I passed intel to Miss Grey in Afghanistan. She located Dr. Smith and his device. The Others thought they had us divided. They were wrong."

Zemin's smile was faint but genuine. "Dr. Xi speaks the truth. I allowed the perception of his disloyalty to flush out the real traitor." His gaze settled on Fang. "Dr. Fang, your communications with Liu's faction were...illuminating."

Fang paled, her hands trembling. "I... I was protecting China! Mr. Liu and Doctor Smith promised—"

Fu stepped forward, his voice a low rumble. "Enough." He seized Fang's arm, his grip unyielding. She struggled briefly then sagged, her eyes wide with the realization of her fate. Death awaited her, not for espionage but for betraying the nation she claimed to serve.

Zemin turned to Xi. "You've done well, Jianguo. The Others' network is silent, and their Afghan device is neutralized, but the cost was high. Trust is fragile."

Xi nodded, his voice soft. "I know, General Secretary. We had no choice."

Harry relaxed slightly, though his eyes stayed on Fu. Green let out a low whistle. "Hell of a move, Xi. You're a better chess player than I ever imagined. You had me thinking we were done for."

The lab's tension eased, but the stress of what had transpired lingered. Zemin departed with Fu and Fang in custody, leaving Xi, Green, and Harry to chart the future. The cube sat dormant behind its glass, a silent testament to their victory and a reminder of the work ahead.

Xi stood before the device, his mind already turning to new challenges. "I'm staying in China," he said, his voice resolute. "The cube's technology is a puzzle we can't ignore. I saw what TechCom's doing with artificial intelligence in the United States. We can do better. Reverse engineer this technology, blend it with our systems... China could leap forward a generation or two."

Green raised an eyebrow. "Ambitious. You think the party will let you play with their shiny new toy?"

Xi's lips quirked. "They trust me now more than they did yesterday."

Harry grunted. "Trust's a funny thing. You played Zemin's game, but you played us too. Don't make a habit of it."

Xi met his gaze. "I've learned something, Harry. Trust isn't loyalty. It's sharing the burden. I kept you in the dark to protect you. I won't make that mistake again."

Green clapped Xi's shoulder. "Good enough for me. I'm headed back to Team Tacoma. Time to dismantle our little underground operation in Seattle. Harry's flying me home as soon as we can get to the airport."

Harry smirked. "Don't get used to the service, brother."

Green's tone grew serious. "We've got our own cube to crack, the Thunderbird device. DARPA had tried to replicate it, but we never successfully cracked the communication protocols. Understanding how the backdoor works gave me the missing pieces of the puzzle. I want to beat you at reverse engineering the underlying science, Xi. Friendly competition?"

Dr. Xi chuckled. "You're on. But never again call me 'Master of War.' That title has been buried. But you've got a problem. Those Thunderbird devices are likely scattered across the world, invisible to most tech."

Green nodded. "The Squamish tribe's helping us. They've got a knack for finding them. We'll start in the area around Seattle and expand out. Still, it's a needle in a haystack."

Harry crossed his arms. "We'll manage. Always do."

Xi watched them, a flicker of warmth cutting through his fatigue. "You've changed, Green. You used to see this as a game. Now it's a mission."

Green shrugged, a faint smile playing on his lips. "Guess I learned something too. The world and the universe are bigger than I realized. And scarier. We're in this together, whether we like it or not."

As they spoke, the lab hummed with quiet activity. Technicians resumed their work, oblivious to the drama that had unfolded. On Fang's desk, amid a clutter of papers and monitors, a tiny cube, barely the size of a die, sat unnoticed. Its surface was dull, unremarkable save for a faint green light pulsing at its core. In the lab's bright glare, it went unseen.

28

BLESS YOU

The medical facility at Bagram Air Base was a sterile cocoon, its white walls and fluorescent lights a vivid contrast to the chaos of the Afghan caves Miss Grey had escaped. The faint hum of generators and the distant roar of a C-130 taking off seeped through the window, reminding her of the war that never slept.

It was midmorning, and the dry, cool air outside pressed against the glass, carrying the scent of dust and jet fuel. Grey was in her single-occupancy room, a concession to her status as a Homeland Security agent and the sensitivity of her ordeal. Her dark hair was clean but matted, her olive skin bruised, and her dark-brown eyes darted restlessly, searching for answers no one seemed willing or able to give.

"When can I go home, Dr. Clark?" Grey's voice was hoarse, her throat still raw from dehydration.

Dr. Emily Clark, a major in the US Army, adjusted the IV drip. Her blonde hair was piled up into a loose bun, and her soft green eyes warmed her military bearing. "Soon, Agent Grey. Your vitals are stabilizing, and the wounds are healing.

Another day or two and you'll be cleared for transport to Germany and then to the States."

Grey shifted, wincing as pain flared in her bandaged ribs. "That's what you said last night when I arrived. I need to know what's happening out there. Is the world still standing, or are we waiting for the end?"

Clark's smile faltered. "You've been through hell. Focus on healing. The news can wait."

"It can't," Grey snapped then softened. "I'm sorry. It's... I don't know who to trust anymore. Not after the past week."

Clark nodded, her expression sympathetic but guarded. "I understand, but you're safe here. There are a couple of military police officers outside, and Colonel McCray is coming to brief you soon."

Grey's stomach tightened. Safe was a relative term when the man who'd kidnapped her—Director Anderson, a rogue CIA operative—had nearly buried her in those caves. She'd spent a day and a half in darkness, bound and battered, until an attack on the Qud forces gave her a chance to slip free. Maxx and his Green Beret team had found her, half-dead from dehydration and wounds, and pulled her to safety. Anderson was in custody now, but the bigger questions loomed. What was happening with Thunderbird? Where were the Others? And why did she feel like the world was teetering on the edge of oblivion?

The door opened, and Colonel McCray stepped in, his boots clicking on the linoleum. He was a towering figure, his gray hair cropped close and his face etched with lines from years of combat and command. His uniform was crisp, but his eyes carried the burden of too many secrets.

"Agent Grey," he said, his voice rough, "good to see you in one piece."

"Colonel," Grey replied, sitting up straighter despite the pain. "I'd feel better if I knew what was going on. Anderson, the caves, the...whatever those things were. You have some answers, don't you?"

McCray glanced at Dr. Clark, who took the hint and stepped out, gently closing the door behind her. He pulled a chair beside the bed, its metal legs scraping softly on the linoleum. "I've got some answers, Grey. Not all of them. Let's start with what you already know."

She recounted her ordeal. Anderson's betrayal, the caves, the Qud forces, and the strange, almost otherworldly presence she'd encountered in the tunnels. The Green Beret team had found Doctor Smith dead, caught Anderson after her escape, and a Black Hawk had whisked her back to Bagram. She'd been in recovery overnight, but the gaps in her knowledge gnawed at her. "What's the status with the Others' invasion, Colonel? And don't tell me it's above my pay grade."

McCray leaned back, his jaw tight. "The Others are a black project. Alien tech, or so I'm told. I don't have the full picture, only that it's tied to someone or something called Thunderbird. Anderson was running his own plays, and you got caught in the crossfire."

Grey's pulse quickened. "Alien tech? You know we're dealing with a possible extraterrestrial invasion and don't think that's worth clarification?"

"I'm saying I don't know enough to clarify any details," McCray said firmly. "But you're alive, and Anderson's in a holding cell. That's what matters."

"For now," Grey muttered, her mind racing. The world felt fragile, as if one wrong move could shatter it. And she wasn't sure McCray or anyone was telling her the whole truth.

McCray's briefing was a patchwork of half-truths and omissions, and it set Grey's nerves on edge. He confirmed Anderson was in CIA custody, but when she pressed for details, he deflected. "They're handling it, Grey. If you want justice, you'll have to trust the system."

"Trust the system?" She laughed bitterly. "Anderson was the damn system. He tried to kill me, Colonel. And you think the CIA's going to hold him accountable?"

McCray's eyes narrowed. "I don't like it any more than you do, but my hands are tied. Focus on getting well."

She shifted topics, her voice sharp. "What about Senator Traficant? She was pulling Anderson's strings, wasn't she?"

McCray hesitated and said, "Traficant's being dealt with at the highest levels in Washington. I've been assured she won't be a problem for you again."

"Assured by whom?" Grey pressed. "The same people who let Anderson run wild?"

McCray stood, his patience thinning. "I understand you've been through a lot the past few days. More than anyone should, but my advice is to tone down the criticism. You're fishing in waters too deep for me, Agent. I've told you what I can."

Her thoughts turned to the corpse at the bottom of the cliff outside the tunnels, the body Anderson had pointed out. Li Jing, he'd said, though she wasn't sure why. It was impossible to tell who was half-buried in the rock debris.

"What about the body of Smith's assistant? You're leaving it down there?"

"It's too risky to attempt a recovery," McCray said. "The CIA thinks it's Li Jing, but we can't spare the resources to confirm, not with Operation Anaconda still in full swing."

"That's a dangerous assumption," Grey said, her voice low. "If it's not Li Jing and she's still loose, we're flying blind."

McCray didn't respond, but his silence spoke volumes. She pressed him about the virus canisters Anderson had been obsessed with, tied to Thunderbird. "Where are they now?"

"CIA took them," McCray said. "Flew them out of my area of operations. If you want answers, you'll have to go through Homeland Security channels. Good luck getting a straight answer."

Grey's fists clenched under the blanket. The CIA, Traficant, Anderson—a web of deception, and she was caught in the middle. She didn't trust McCray to dig deeper, and she didn't trust herself to let it go. The world was on a knife's edge, and the answers she needed to help fix the mess were slipping further away.

As McCray prepared to leave, he paused at the door. "You did well out there, Grey. Not many would've survived those caves. Rest up. You've earned it."

She didn't reply, her mind already churning. Rest was a luxury she couldn't afford, not when the truth was still concealed in secrets and shadows.

The room felt smaller after McCray left, the walls closing in as Grey wrestled with her doubts. The MPs outside her door reminded her of her vulnerability, their presence both reassuring and stifling. She gazed at the ceiling, counting the cracks, when her phone buzzed on the bedside table. The caller ID read, "Green."

She answered, her voice cautious. "Mr. Green, I didn't expect to hear from you."

"Agent Grey, I wanted to thank you. The flight from Seattle to Anchorage then Beijing... You made it possible. Saved our lives."

She frowned. Two days ago felt like a distant memory. "Glad I could help. I hope you were able to make a difference. I'm having difficulty getting straight answers from anyone here."

Green's voice lowered. "I owe you an update. You're one of the few people I can tell, and you've done enough to deserve my trust."

Grey glanced at the door, ensuring it was shut. "I'm listening."

"Dr. Xi and I managed to block the Others' communications," Green said. "Their devices are under our control now. Thunderbird's dead in the water, too."

Her breath caught. "You're saying you stopped the invasion?"

"For now," Green said. "The Others didn't want to stick around. They abandoned Earth, but not for the reasons you might think."

"Explain," Grey demanded, her heart pounding.

"It's the virus," Green said. "The canisters Traficant and Anderson were after. The Others were terrified of it. They didn't want to risk infection."

Grey's mind reeled. "Infection? What kind of virus are we talking about?"

Green paused, and she could almost hear his hesitation. "Before the canisters shipped out, I had the Centers for Disease Control test the canisters. It's a modified coronavirus—nothing exotic but tweaked enough to spook the Others: low infection and fatality rates for humans. The National Institute of Health will store the canisters' contents in a joint program with China. If Thunderbird or the Others come back, we'll be ready."

She leaned back. "You're telling me the Others ran because of a cold virus?"

"Essentially," Green said, "but it's not that simple. The Others' biology is different. What's relatively mild for humans would be catastrophic for their entire civilization. Have you ever seen the movie *War of the Worlds*? That's why they left."

Grey's thoughts darkened. "And you're okay with the NIH and China holding onto this? What if someone decides to weaponize it?"

Green's tone hardened. "I don't trust governments any more than you do, Grey. You know that. But we didn't have a choice. It's out of my hands, but it's containment, not escalation. Our countries stopped the immediate threats and bought time, nothing more."

She rubbed her temples, the horror of it all pressing down. "Time for what? Another war? Another betrayal?"

"Time to prepare," Green said. "Humanity's not ready for what's out there, but we're learning."

The call stretched on, Green filling in details about their efforts to break into the Others' tech. Grey listened, but her mind kept circling back to the virus. A common coronavirus, tweaked enough to scare off an advanced species. It sounded too neat, too convenient. And the idea of it sitting in a foreign lab, under the control of bureaucrats and scientists, made her skin crawl.

When Green finally wound down, he said, "I've got a plane to catch back to Seattle. Stay safe, Grey. You've earned some peace."

"Peace," she echoed, her voice flat. "Sure."

The line went dead, and she glared at the phone, her thoughts a tangle of suspicion and dread. Green and Xi had saved the day, but for how long? And who else was watching, waiting to turn the virus into something far more dangerous?

The hospital room was quiet now, the buzz of Green's call fading into the hum of the base. Outside, the sun climbed higher, baking the dusty runways and casting harsh shadows. Grey settled back, her body aching but her mind racing. The world hadn't ended, not yet. The Others were gone, their invasion thwarted by a virus they feared. But the victory felt hollow, overshadowed by the chaos still unfolding in the Middle East.

She thought of what McCray said about the region heating up. "Kicking the hornet's nest," he'd called it. Anderson's actions and Traficant's schemes had stirred a conflict that wouldn't die down easily. Green said China would stay out of it, focusing instead on AI research—a different kind of race that could reshape the world as surely as any conflict.

Grey's thoughts turned inward. She'd always prided herself on her independence, her ability to navigate crises alone, but the caves had taught her otherwise. Without Maxx's relentless attempt to rescue her, she'd be dead, lost in the caves. His loyalty, his refusal to give up, it had saved her. And Green's partnership with Xi, bridging ideological divides, had stopped the Others and Thunderbird. Maybe trust wasn't a weakness after all.

Dr. Clark returned, checking her chart with a practiced eye. "You look like you've got the weight of the world on your shoulders, Agent Grey."

"Something like that," Grey said, managing a faint smile. "I'm trying to figure out what comes next."

"Home," Clark said firmly. "A hot shower, a real bed. The rest can wait."

Grey nodded, but her mind was elsewhere. Green's final words echoed. "Stay safe. You've earned some peace." She wanted to believe it, to let go of the suspicion that had kept her alive, but the virus nagged at her. Stored in a secret lab guarded by the US and China, a Pandora's box was waiting to be opened. What if someone, another Smith or Traficant, saw it as a weapon? What if the Others returned or, worse, something else came?

Grey stared out the window as Dr. Clark left, the desert and Hindu Kush stretching endlessly beyond. The world was balanced again, but it was a fragile equilibrium. And deep down, she knew the truth. Peace was an illusion, and the shadows she'd glimpsed in the caves were still out there, waiting for another chance.

29

CALL ME

The silence in the hospital room at Bagram was interrupted only by the remote hum of medical equipment and the occasional shuffle of nurses' footsteps. Propped up on a stiff hospital bed, Miss Grey stared at the tray of untouched food before her, a sorry excuse of a meal only marginally better than the MREs she'd choked down in the field. Her fingers traced the frayed edge of the thin blanket, her mind far from the sterile confines of the general care unit.

The Afghan sky beyond the narrow window deepened into a bruised purple, echoing the anxiety in her chest. She was alive, recovering from injuries sustained in a mission that had nearly ended the world. Still, her thoughts churned with worry for those she loved, especially Andres Sandoval, her boyfriend, who had texted hours ago promising to call soon.

"I need to go home," she said to the doctor, her voice low but firm, cutting through the quiet. "Then I'll be okay."

Standing at the foot of the bed, Dr. Emily Clark adjusted her clipboard with a practiced motion. Her blonde hair was still in a bun, although it looked messy, and her blue eyes were fixed on Miss Grey. "I can't do that, Agent. You're stable but not cleared yet. Another day or two, and we'll talk about getting you on a flight home."

Miss Grey's lips pressed into a thin line, her dark hair pulled back in a messy ponytail that framed her puffy face. The past week had left her raw, her resolve frayed by betrayal and sacrifice. She nodded, not because she agreed but because arguing felt futile. Her gaze drifted to the window, where the last sliver of daylight clung to the distant peaks. The world teetered on the brink of war, and she'd played a part in pulling it back, yet no one would ever know the cost. She didn't think she even knew the final score.

Dr. Clark's voice softened. "You need rest. Eat something, even if it's a bite." She gestured to the tray and then stepped toward the door. "I'll check on you later."

As the door shut, Miss Grey's phone buzzed on the bedside table—a clunky hospital-issued device, not her temporary cell phone. She ignored it, her thoughts spiraling. Andres's text had been brief, almost cryptic. "I'm okay. Calling soon." But what did "okay" mean after everything they'd been through? She'd sent him back to Seattle to protect Gabby Fisher, a friend and a key figure in their mission, and hadn't spoken to him in days. The silence gnawed at her, a reminder of the trust she'd placed in him and the fear that it might have cost him dearly.

The nurses' station had been fielding calls from Maxx King all day, his persistence bordering on obsession. Miss Grey learned this when a young nurse, harried and apologetic, poked her head into the room. "Ma'am, we've got a situation. Some guy named Maxx King keeps calling, demanding to speak with you. Security wouldn't let him through—protocol, you know—but Colonel McCray called and said to patch him in."

Miss Grey's brow furrowed, a faint smile tugging at her lips despite herself. "McCray said that?"

The nurse nodded, exasperated. "Said, 'He's a piece of work, but put him through before he calls the White House.'"

"Sounds like Maxx," Miss Grey murmured. She gestured to the phone. "Go ahead."

Moments later, the phone rang, and she picked it up, bracing herself. Maxx's voice crackled through, gravelly and laced with his signature sarcasm. "Damn, Grey, you're harder to reach than the president. Thought I'd have to fly back and storm Bagram."

"Maxx," she said, her voice warming despite the ache in her ribs, "you're back in Seattle. What's got you so worked up?"

"Checking on you. What else? You're the one laid up in a hospital. How's the food? Bet it's gourmet compared to those MREs."

She glanced at the congealed mashed potatoes on her tray and snorted. "Barely. You didn't call me to talk cuisine, did you?"

"Nah, but I figured I'd ease you into it." His tone shifted, serious now. "Got an update on the canisters. They're secured, thanks to us. Word is the brass is calling it a near miss. Understatement of the century."

Miss Grey's grip tightened on the phone, her mind flashing to the bioweapons they'd risked everything to neutralize. She hadn't told Maxx about the virus update she'd gotten from Green, a source she didn't fully trust. Maxx was loyal but impulsive. He might go rogue if he knew the full score. "Good to know," she said carefully. "Any word on Traficant?"

Maxx grunted. "All I know is what McCray told me, and he's tight-lipped. Probably the same information he gave you. Traficant won't be sniffing around you again, Smith's dead, and the CIA's got Anderson locked up. But I'm not holding my breath for justice with that guy. Those snakes always find a place to hide until it's dark."

She exhaled, her breath catching at Traficant's name. The

senator's betrayal had cut deep, her abuse of power nearly unleashing chaos. "You sound like you're done with it."

"Unless I see Traficant or Anderson in my sights, I'm finished with this rodeo. The rest is someone else's mess now." He paused. "You holding up, Grey? No bull."

The question hit harder than she expected. She leaned back against the pillows, the hospital's emptiness pressing in—the fluorescent lights, the faint beep of a monitor, the cold air seeping through the window. "I'm...processing. Trying to figure out what's next."

"Next is getting your ass back to Seattle. Speaking of asses, you talked to Andres yet?"

Her heart stuttered. "No, he texted that he'd call. Why? What's going on?"

Maxx's voice grew cagey, a rare hesitation. "He's recovering at home. He'll be ten out of ten soon. Let him fill you in."

"What?" Her voice sharpened, panic flaring. "Maxx, what happened?"

"Not my story to tell. You two sort it out." He deflected, but his tone softened. "He's tougher than a two-dollar steak, Grey. You know that."

She stared at the ceiling, her pulse racing. Andres was hurt? Recovering from what? Her mind spun through worst-case scenarios—gunshots, explosions, betrayal. She forced her voice to steady. "What about Gabby? Is she safe?"

"Yeah, Gabby's good. Torashi's out of the picture. Long story, but we handled it. I'm meeting her for coffee later, maybe a boat ride on Puget Sound. Spring's showing up early." His casualness grated against her anxiety, but it also grounded her, a reminder of the lives they'd saved. And the life ahead of her.

"Sounds nice," she said, her voice distant. "Tell her I'm glad she's okay."

"Will do. Look, I have to run, but if you need anything, you can call. Don't make me come and rescue you from that hospital." His laughter sounded partly serious.

She managed a weak laugh. "Deal. Thanks, Maxx."

As the line went dead, she set the phone down, her hands trembling. Maxx's loyalty was a lifeline, but his vagueness about Andres left her reeling. She glanced at the window, where the Afghan night had swallowed the last of the dusk. The world felt fragile, held together by the sacrifices of people like her, Andres, Maxx, Green Berets, DHS, FBI agents, and soldiers no one would ever thank. Trust had kept them alive, but betrayal had nearly destroyed them. She couldn't shake the fear that Andres had paid a price she didn't want to imagine.

The phone rang again minutes later, and the nurse's voice came through. "Ma'am, you've got another call. Andres Sandoval."

Miss Grey's heart leaped, a mix of relief and dread flooding her. She nodded, though the nurse couldn't see, and picked up the receiver. "Andres?"

"Hey, *mi reina*," Andres said, his voice warm but strained, like he was holding back pain. "God, it's good to hear your voice."

"Andres," she breathed, her eyes welling up. The hospital room seemed to disappear, the air thick with emotion. She clutched the phone, the cord twisting in her hand. "Maxx said you're recovering. What happened? He wouldn't tell me."

He chuckled, a soft, tired sound. "Maxx and his big mouth. It's not a big deal. Got stabbed, patched up at a vet's. Then I spent a night in jail before they sorted it out. I'm at the boathouse now and seeing a real doctor. I'm okay."

"Stabbed?" Her voice cracked, her free hand pressing against her chest. "Andres, that's not 'not a big deal.' Are you... How bad is it?"

"I'm healing. Stitches, antibiotics, the works. I'm watching the sunrise over the Cascades, wishing you were here." His tone softened, deliberate, like he chose each word with care. "I'll be fine, Grey. Promise."

She swallowed hard, tears spilling over. The hospital's white walls faded as she pictured him at the boathouse, the morning light glinting off the water, his dark eyes steady despite the pain. "You scared me," she whispered. "I sent you to protect Gabby, and...I worried I'd lost you."

"You didn't. I'm right here." He paused, his voice dropping. "When are you coming home? I can't wait to see you. And... maybe we should talk about something more serious."

Her breath caught. "Serious?"

"Yeah." He took an audible breath. "When I thought I might not make it, I kept thinking about you and what you mean to me. I don't want to waste more time, Grey. I want us to figure out what's next...together."

She wiped her eyes, a shaky smile breaking through. The monitor beeped softly in the background, a steady reminder of her injuries, but his voice anchored her.

"I'd like that," she said. "I've been thinking... Maybe it's time to leave DHS, do something less likely to get us killed."

He laughed, a genuine, warm sound that eased the knot in her chest. "You and me, living the quiet life? I'm in. But you mentioned you might talk to Maxx about the two of you working together. Are you still thinking about that? Guy's a handful. Remember what happened with his last partner?"

She snorted, the tension breaking. "Yeah, I know. But he's loyal and maybe a little smarter than he looks. I'm not deciding yet, but...I want something real. With you, with work, with life."

"Real sounds good," he said softly. "I love you, Grey. Always have."

"I love you too," she replied, the words familiar but different now, weighted with everything they'd survived. They lingered in silence, the connection stronger than the miles between them.

As she hung up, Miss Grey leaned back, the hospital's loneliness easing in her mind. She imagined Seattle's skyline, Puget Sound sparkling under a spring sun, Andres waiting for her at the boathouse on Lake Union. The world was still unsettled, teetering on the edge of chaos, but they'd pulled it back—her, Andres, Maxx, and others who'd never be named. Trust had been their shield, betrayal their enemy, and sacrifice the price they paid. No one would know what they'd given up, but she did. And it was enough.

She'd learned trust was fragile but vital, especially when challenging power. Maxx, for all his rough edges, was wiser than he let on, and she chuckled at the thought of working with him. Andres had taught her that every day was a gamble, a chance to seize what mattered. She wasn't ready to decide her future, but for the first time in weeks, she felt prepared to live it.

The Afghan night pressed against the window, but Miss Grey closed her eyes, picturing the Cascades at dawn. She was going home, not to Seattle but to Andres, to a life they could build together. The sacrifices they had made, the unseen heroism, would live on in the quiet moments they shared, in the love they fought for, and in the world they saved, even if it didn't know their names.

***

The air in Pike Place Market carried the sharp bite of early spring, laced with the faint sweetness of cherry blossoms beginning to unfurl.

Maxx limped through the narrow alley, his bandaged leg protesting each step, the damp chill of the cobblestones seeping through his sneakers. Ghost Alley Espresso's unassuming sign flickered in the soft morning light, dwarfed by the chaotic, bubblegum-splattered wall nearby. The alley felt alive, its shadowed walls whispering secrets of Seattle's underbelly, a history etched in the brick. Inside the quirky coffee shop—a former restroom attendant's room—aromas of roasted beans and steamed milk curled through the air, grounding Maxx in a moment of normalcy.

He pushed open the door, the bell jingling softly. Gabby was already there, her dark hair catching the glow of a vintage lamp, her fingers wrapped around a steaming mug. She looked up, her smile warm but edged with the stress of yesterday's chaos. Maxx's chest tightened—relief, protectiveness, something more profound. They'd met here last May, a chance discussion about the benefits of tea over coffee that sparked everything.

"Feels like a lifetime ago," Maxx said, easing into the chair across her, his bandaged arm stiff against the table.

"Ten months," Gabby replied, her voice light but her eyes searching his. "Where'd the time go?"

"Into hell and back, apparently." He managed a half-smile, the vivid memory of yesterday's ferry fight flashing in his mind. Torashi's knife, the glint of steel, the defining moment when Maxx threw him overboard. The FBI and DHS had questioned them for hours, but Miss Grey's boss at DHS had vouched for their story. Torashi, a murderer on the FBI's most-wanted list, was a messiness they wanted buried. Maxx and Gabby were free, but the scars—his and hers—lingered.

Gabby leaned forward, her gaze softening. "You okay? You're still limping like you fought a bear."

"More like a shark bit me." He rubbed his leg and winked at her. The wounds from Afghanistan beneath the bandages are throbbing. "You? After...everything?"

She shrugged, but her fingers tightened around her mug of tea. "Getting there. This place helps. Always has." She gestured at the cozy shop, its mismatched chairs, and faded photos of old Seattle. Maxx felt the same pull. Ghost Alley was their sanctuary, a quirky escape from the Starbucks sprawl, its history a quiet rebellion against the city's gloss.

They sipped their drinks, the silence comfortable but heavy with unspoken questions. Maxx's mind drifted to the call he'd had with Miss Grey last night, her voice distant across the ocean. He cleared his throat. "Talked to Grey. She's recovering, but she sounds rough. Depressed, maybe."

Gabby's brow furrowed. "She's been through it. Has she talked to Andres yet?"

"Nope. He's banged up too, as you know. Torashi did a number on him." Maxx hesitated, feeling the weight of their sacrifices pressing down on him. Andres had left Grey's side to protect Gabby, a choice that hadn't felt right to either of them. "I'm hoping they figure it out."

Gabby's lips quirked. "Grey's a lot, Maxx. You sure you want her in our orbit? She's like a hurricane with a badge."

He chuckled, the tension easing. "Maybe we need a storm to shake things up. Andres let slip that she's been considering working with me at the agency. Sworn to secrecy, of course."

"Of course," Gabby said, rolling her eyes. "I don't know, babe. She's a handful."

"Pot, meet kettle," Maxx teased, and Gabby swatted his arm, careful of the bandages. The banter felt like a lifeline, pulling them back from the edge of yesterday's violence.

She took a deep breath, her expression shifting to something brighter. "Okay, my turn. Big news." She paused, her eyes gleaming. "TechCom's promoting me. Dale Phi's old job managing the AI and Large Language Model development, but not limited to the Hermes project. DARPA's funding the cloud storage, so it's huge."

Maxx's stomach twisted, pride warring with unease. "Gabby, that's incredible. You deserve it." He meant it, but the words felt heavy. TechCom's race against China, the ethical minefield of artificial intelligence, was a world that could swallow her whole. It almost had.

She caught his hesitation. "You're worried. I can see it. Will you support me, Maxx? It's going to be stressful."

"Of course I will," he said quickly, but doubt lingered. He had seen what ambition did to Natalie, how it consumed everything they had. Gabby wasn't her, but the fear was a stubborn ghost. "Don't let it take over, okay?"

"I won't," she promised, her voice firm, "but I need you to trust me."

Trust. The word hung between them, brittle and deep. Maxx's military life had taught him that trust was a battlefield, won through blood and sacrifice. He'd trusted his Afghanistan team, Grey, to pull them through, and himself to stop Torashi. But trusting Gabby with his heart and a future was a different kind of courage.

The conversation deepened, the coffee shop fading as they peeled back layers of pain. Gabby leaned forward, her voice soft but steady. "When I took off, back when things got bad...I wasn't running from you. I left so you could do what you needed without worrying about me. I didn't want to be a burden."

Maxx's throat tightened. He'd hated her leaving, the emptiness her disappearance had carved in him. "I went to Afghanistan because I had to try, Gabby. To stop it all—war, chaos, everything. I didn't want to go, but if I'd stayed..." He shook his head, the consequences of his choice crushing. "What good would it have done if the world had ended?"

She reached for his hand, her touch warm against his calloused fingers. "We both screwed up, didn't we?"

He laughed, a rough sound that broke the tension. "Yeah, saving the world is a messy business."

"Next time, we talk first," she said, her smile teasing but her eyes serious. "Deal?"

"Deal." He squeezed her small hand, the promise grounding him. They'd faced betrayal—Torashi's knife and Traficant's shadowy powers pushing the world to the brink—but they'd chosen trust, action, and sacrifice. No one would ever know what they'd given up, what Grey, Andres, Glen, and countless others had lost to pull the world back from the edge. That was the heroism Maxx carried now, quiet and heavy.

Gabby's gaze softened, but her next question bit deep. "My promotion. Be honest, Maxx. How do you feel about it?"

He exhaled, the truth spilling out. "I'm proud of you, but I'm scared, Gabby. TechCom's world... It's DARPA, China, all that power. I've seen what it does to people. I don't want that for us."

Gabby's eyes held his, steady and fierce. "I'm not Natalie. I will not let this job swallow me. You can trust me, Maxx. I'm choosing us too."

He nodded, his voice rough. "Okay, I believe you."

She smiled, a sparkle of hope in her eyes. "Maybe it's time we think bigger. You know...a family. You and me, seeing where it goes."

Maxx's heart stuttered—a family. The idea felt like a dream he hadn't dared touch since his parents had divorced. "You mean that?"

"Yeah," she said, her voice soft but sure, "I do."

The coffee shop seemed to hum with possibility, the aroma of espresso mingling with the faint floral hint of spring drifting through the open door. Maxx imagined a life beyond the alley's shadows—a home, maybe a farm like the one he'd grown up on, fields stretching wide under a quiet sky. "What about TechCom?" he asked. "Could you work remotely?"

"I'd make it work," Gabby said, her grin infectious. "Picture me running AI projects from a barn, you chopping wood or whatever you farm guys do."

He laughed, the image absurd and perfect. "Deal, but I'm holding you to the barn part."

Their laughter faded into a comfortable silence, the weight of their choices settling into something hopeful. Gabby had learned to face problems head-on. Her brush with Torashi had taught her that evasion only sharpened the blade. Maxx too had grown. His military life had shown him that trust was a risk, but with Gabby, he was learning to open his heart, to let vulnerability be strength.

Gabby glanced at her watch. "We're meeting Andres and Glen soon, right? Boat ride?"

"Yeah," Maxx said, standing with a wince as his leg protested. "Not the houseboat, thank God. Andres's real boat. Glen has something to tell us apparently."

"Glen and his mysteries," Gabby said, rolling her eyes but smiling. She stood, slipping her small hand into his. "Ready?"

Maxx looked at her, the woman who'd faced fear, chosen him, and helped pull the world back from the brink without a single headline. His bandages itched, and his limp slowed him, but the alley didn't feel so shadowed with Gabby's hand in his.

"Do you think Glen's news is trouble?" Gabby asked playfully.

Maxx laughed and shrugged as they stepped into the Seattle morning, cherry blossoms popping, chatting like old friends who'd walked through fire and come out stronger.

30

OUR HEALING

The sailboat rocked gently against Pier 54, its hull nudging the weathered dock with a soft thud. Puget Sound stretched before it, a sheet of azure under the March sun, rippling with the promise of spring. Seagulls wheeled overhead, their cries sharp against the hum of the nearby ferries. The air carried salt and a faint tang of diesel, mingling with the warmth of the breeze that tugged at Maxx's jacket. He stood at the bow, one hand on the rail, his eyes tracing the horizon where the Olympic Mountains soared.

"Hey, Maxx, you planning to hug that rail all day?" Andres called from the helm, his grin wide as he adjusted the wheel. "Or are you going to pretend you love the water for once?"

Maxx shot him a mock glare, his grip tightening on the rail. "I'm here, aren't I? Doesn't mean I have to like it, Sandoval. This boat's one wave away from being a submarine."

Andres laughed, the sound carrying over the deck. "Relax, brother. I've kept her afloat this long. You're safer here than you were on that ferry."

"Low bar," Maxx muttered, smirking. "Keep this thing steady or I'll ask Glen to swim me back to shore."

"Swim?" Andres raised an eyebrow. "I'd pay to see that. You two would sink like bricks."

Gabby leaned against the mast, her dark hair catching the sunlight. She'd been Maxx's constant, her pragmatism a lifeline when vengeance threatened to consume him. At the helm, Andres adjusted the wheel, his face relaxed with the anticipation of taking his boat out for the first time this spring. Glen sat near the stern, his guarded eyes hinting at unspoken secrets.

Maxx's body ached, the scars from his battles—both physical and otherwise—still tender. Trust and survival had bound him to the people aboard this boat. Gabby Fisher, his anchor through the storm. Andres, fiercely loyal but missing Miss Grey. And Glen, his friend who had lost his son Scott, the boy murdered for stumbling onto TechCom's top-secret data.

The sailboat eased into Elliott Bay, the Seattle skyline shrinking behind them. A ferry churned past, its horn a low bellow. Maxx's jaw tightened as he waved, the gesture mirrored by Gabby and Andres. Glen remained still, his gaze fixed on the water. The ferry's wake rocked the boat, and Maxx's stomach lurched. The sight of the vessel stirred a mixture of relief and dread, a reminder of how close they'd come to losing everything. That near-death moment six months ago had reshaped their lives, forging bonds tested by blood.

Glen's voice broke the quiet, melancholy but steady. His fingers tracing the edge of a worn wallet. "Found something last night in Scott's room." He pulled a folded napkin from the wallet, its edges frayed. "He hid it in a secret flap. A note to me, in case... In case he didn't make it."

Maxx turned, his pulse quickening. Andres glanced over, his hands tightening on the wheel. Gabby's smile faded, sensing the shift in the air. Glen unfolded the napkin, revealing Scott's hurried scrawl. "Dad, if I'm gone, tell Maxx the president's the one pulling strings on the Omega device. His name is all over the hidden files. Thunderbird was his leverage. I'll let you know what's going on ~~when~~ (if, lol) I get home."

The words landed like dynamite in still water. Maxx's breath caught. Senator Traficant had been the face of the conspiracy, her ambition a global threat, but the president? It reframed everything. Scott's death, the war in the Middle East, their sacrifices. The police and FBI had missed this note, a small piece of paper tucked in a hidden compartment in Scott's wallet. It was likely true, but who would believe a dead boy's scribble? Maxx faced a choice. Act on this truth, risking everything they'd fought for, or let it lie buried in the past.

The sailboat cut through the water, its sails taut against the breeze. Blake Island loomed closer, a green smudge against the blue. Maxx gripped the rail, the napkin burning in his mind—trust versus betrayal—another twist of the blade. Exposing the president could topple a delicate world order, but letting Traficant walk free, likely pardoned for "political expediency," gnawed at him. Justice felt like an unpaid debt, yet peace was a brittle gift they had begun reimagining.

Gabby sat beside him, her voice soft but firm. "Maxx, we've lost enough. Scott and so many others. Chasing this...it could unravel everything. Not only for us but for the country. People need to heal, not tear open old wounds."

He met her eyes, seeing the weariness beneath her resolve. She'd held him together when rage had blinded him, when Haoyu had nearly ended him. "And if we let it go?" he asked. "Traficant gets a pass. The president stays untouchable. What's that say about us?"

"It says we're human," she replied. "We choose what we can live with."

Andres, steering from the helm, snorted. "Human? That's a cop-out. Scott died for this. Thousands of others too. We owe them action, not excuses." His voice carried the hard edge of a man torn between duty and loyalty. Miss Grey's absence weighed on him, a constant reminder of the life he and she had left behind to fight this war.

Glen remained silent, his gaze fixed on the napkin. His belief in being a man of action, once unshakeable, now wavered. "I raised Scott to believe in truth," he said finally. "But truth didn't save him. Maybe Gabby's right. Maybe it's time to let it go."

The boat rocked as a wave slapped the hull, spraying mist across the deck. Maxx tasted salt on his lips and felt the creak of wood beneath his feet. He thought of Scott, not even thirty, his life snuffed out for a secret he hadn't fully understood. Of Keith Hovis, gutted by Li Jing's knife, his sacrifice a footnote in their survival. Of Torashi, whose blade Maxx had pocketed on that ferry, a grim trophy of Gabby's near death.

"Glen," Maxx said, his voice steady despite his gut churning, "what do you want? This is your son's truth. Your call."

Glen's fingers tightened on the napkin. "I want him back," he whispered, "but I can't have that. So I want... I want this to mean something, but I don't know if it's worth losing you all."

The words hung heavy, unanswered. The sailboat pressed on, Vashon Island now visible in the distance, its shores a promise of refuge. But refuge from what? The conspiracy's shadow or their guilt? Maxx's mind raced, balancing the cost of action against the price of silence. Gabby's hand brushed his, a quiet tether to the moment. Andres adjusted the sails, his jaw set. Glen folded the napkin, tucking it back into the wallet. The choices simmered, unresolved, as the wind carried them forward.

An hour passed, the sun climbing higher. They spoke in fits and starts, memories surfacing like driftwood. Andres recounted diving into the sound to pull Maxx from the sinking car. Gabby admitted the terror of realizing that Torashi was hunting her. Glen spoke of Scott's laugh, his knack for puzzles, and the wallet he'd carried since his sixteenth birthday. Each story stitched them closer, mending frayed trust, but the napkin's truth weighed heavily.

The sailboat passed Blake Island, the water deepening to a rich indigo. Maxx stood at the bow, the napkin now in his hands. Glen had handed it over, his eyes weary but trusting. "You decide, Maxx. I can't."

The burden of it—Scott's final words, the conspiracy's last secret—pressed against Maxx's chest. He saw the path forward: expose the president, risk their lives, freedom, maybe the nation's stability. Traficant's likely pardon was bitter, but the president's shadow was overwhelming. Yet he saw another path: silence, safety, the chance to live for those they'd lost, not die for them.

Gabby joined him, her presence steadying. "What's it going to be, Maxx?" she asked into the wind.

He looked at her, then at Andres, who watched from the helm, and Glen, seated with the wallet in his lap. Their faces carried the scars of their choices. Andres's loyalty, Gabby's courage, and Glen's grief. Maxx thought of Scott, the Green Berets who had died in the Afghan tunnels, and the blood and betrayal that had brought them here. He thought of trust not as a weakness but as a choice.

"I'm done fighting shadows," he said, his voice firm. He held up the napkin, its edges fluttering. "This... It's not ours to carry anymore."

Before anyone could speak, he tore the napkin into pieces. The wind caught the fragments, scattering them across the sound like ash. They danced on the surface then sank, swallowed by the waves. Gabby's breath hitched, but she nodded. Andres's shoulders eased, a faint smile breaking through. Glen's eyes glistened, but he said nothing. Silence was a kind of absolution.

The act was a sacrifice, not of truth but of vengeance. Maxx felt the weight lift, replaced by something raw—hope. He turned to Gabby, taking her hand. "We're enough," he said. "You, me, us. We're enough."

She squeezed his hand, her eyes bright. "Yeah, we are."

Andres called from the helm, his voice lighter. "Let's dock at Vashon for lunch. I'm starving, and Miss Grey's not here to salvage my cooking."

Glen chuckled, a sound Maxx hadn't heard in days. "Your cooking's a crime, Sandoval. Let's hope the island's got better options."

The boat sailed on, the moment sealing their bond. Maxx felt the ache of his scars, the echo of Scott's loss, the sun's warmth, and the waves' rhythm. They'd chosen each other over the abyss.

The sailboat docked at the marina, the shore lined with pines swaying in the breeze. The sun was at its peak, casting bright sparkles across the water. Maxx helped tie the lines, his movements steady despite his wounds. The conspiracy's fallout would ripple—whispers of Traficant's pardon, the president's untouchable shadow—but here, now, it was distant. They'd contained the truth, not for cowardice but for survival, for the chance to rebuild.

They gathered on the deck, the boat creaking softly. Glen held Scott's wallet, his fingers tracing its worn leather. "Time to let my boy's memory rest," he said, his voice thick. He stood, walked to the rail, and tossed the wallet into the bay. It hit the water with a soft splash, sinking into the depths. They stood in silence, a moment of reverence for Scott.

Maxx reached into his pocket, pulling out Torashi's knife. Its blade gleamed, a relic of violence, a reminder of Keith Hovis's death at Li Jing's hands. "So many good people died," he said, his voice steady. "It's time to leave their memories alone." He threw the knife overboard, watching it vanish beneath the waves. The act felt final, a shedding of the past's sharp edges.

Gabby slipped her arm around Maxx's waist, her warmth grounding him. "You did right," she said. "For us. For them. I'm proud of you."

Andres clapped Maxx's shoulder, his grin wide. "You're still a pain in the ass, King, but I'd dive into that water for you again, even if there are sharks in there."

Maxx laughed, the sound surprising him. "Let's hope it doesn't come to that."

Glen joined them, his face lighter, as if the wallet's weight had carried his grief. "I'm proud of all of you," he said, looking at each of them. "Scott would be too."

They sat on the deck, sharing a meal of sandwiches and beer, the spring breeze soft against their skin. The conversation turned to small things. Andres's plans to see Miss Grey, Gabby's promotion, and Glen's plan to join Big Brothers. Maxx listened, his heart full. He'd spent so long guarding himself, expecting betrayal, but these people, he trusted.

They'd sail back to Seattle this evening, back to lives forever changed, but for now they were here, together, under the warm spring sun. The future was uncertain, but it was theirs to shape, and that was hope enough.

EPILOGUE

"Look at that sunset, Maxx. It's like the entire side of Mt. Si is glowing," Gabby called out, sitting on the front porch of their farmhouse.

The Carnation farm sprawled under the early-evening sun, its fields soaked in golden light that seemed to vibrate with life. Maxx paused, hammer in hand, and glanced at the horizon. He drove another nail into the barn's frame with a steady *thunk*, each swing proof of the future he was determined to build. Sweat glistened on his forehead, his dusty Mariners jersey clinging to his muscled arms as he worked, the wood's grain rough under his calloused hands.

"Those goats of yours are eating all my wildflowers again," Maxx teased, nodding toward Sage, Thyme, and Rosemary, who grazed contentedly nearby. The soft bleats of three miniature goats mingled with the rustle of wildflowers swaying and the whir of hummingbirds in the summer breeze.

Gabby laughed, brushing a strand of hair from her face. "They're adding their special character to the place." The air carried the sweet scent of hay, cut fresh that morning, and the faint smell from a pond where dragonflies glided, their wings glinting like tiny prisms. In the distance, the Snoqualmie River murmured, its current a constant rhythm, while Mt. Si loomed against the horizon, its rugged slopes a sentinel over the valley.

Gabby sat on the weathered stairs, her long, dark hair tied back, a pair of headphones looped around her neck. Three months pregnant, she radiated, her hand resting lightly on her belly as she spoke into her cell phone, her voice animated. "Yes, the algorithm's stable now. We're close to a breakthrough," she said, her smile wide, eyes catching the golden light. She worked remotely for TechCom, her mind still sharp with the puzzles that had once drawn her into a world of espionage and danger. Now, those skills built useful products, not conflicts, and the pride in her voice warmed Maxx's heart as he paused to watch her.

The farm was their shelter, a sanctuary built from the storms of their past. Two years ago, Maxx had nearly drowned in Puget Sound, trapped in a car shoved off a ferry, his life saved by Andres Sandoval's daring dive. The conspiracy that followed—TechCom's secrets, Scott's murder, Senator Traficant's betrayal—had nearly broken them. Yet here they were, rooted in this valley, the scars on Maxx's body and soul fading under the summer sun. The barn's skeleton rose before him, a symbol of permanence, but a faint unease lingered, like a cloud on the horizon. Bob Dylan's "Shelter from the Storm" played softly in his mind, its melody a reminder of how fragile peace could be.

Maxx drove the last nail into a beam, the barn's frame now sturdy, and wiped his forehead. He crossed the field to Gabby, who ended her call and stood, stretching. "You're going to have to speed up, Papa," she teased, nodding at the barn. "Our kid will need a place to hide from your terrible dad jokes."

He chortled, pulling her close, her warmth grounding him. "I'm building a legacy here, Fisher. Bad jokes included." His hand brushed her belly, leaving him in awe of the life growing there. "What do you think, Maxx Junior or Gabrielle the Second?"

She swatted his arm, laughing. "Neither. This kid's getting an original name, not your ego in lowercase."

Their chatter flowed easily, an easy rhythm enhanced by love. Rural life suited them. Maxx's carpentry filled his time outside work with his cybersecurity business with purpose, while Gabby's tech work kept her mind sharp. They'd traded Seattle's chaos for Carnation's quiet, their bond deepening as they planned for parenthood. Nights were spent on the porch, mapping dreams: a garden, a swing set, a life where their child would know safety, not shadows.

Euneva King's cottage stood a mile down the road, its porch lined with geraniums. Maxx's elderly mom had become their rock, her kitchen a haven of warmth. That afternoon, she'd stopped by, her silver hair pulled into a bun, her eyes twinkling as she surveyed the farm.

"This place is coming along, Maxx," she'd said, handing Gabby a jar of homemade blackberry jam. "But fair warning, I'm gonna spoil that grandbaby rotten. I hope they are smaller than Maxx was, though—twelve pounds! That boy nearly killed me."

Maxx grinned, hugging her. "You're going to be on diaper duty, Mom. So you know."

Euneva swatted him with a dish towel. "Bring it on. I've got years of practice." Her presence healed old wounds. Maxx's childhood had been rocky, his dad absent, but Euneva's love was a constant, coming to terms with the family expectations he grew up under. She'd promised to babysit, knitting tiny booties, her excitement a connection to the future.

Later, Maxx and Gabby walked down the road to the old cemetery, a quiet plot nestled in Carnation's hills. Maxx's grandma, Lois, had passed last winter, her stories of resilience a guiding light through their darkest days. They knelt at her grave, laying a bouquet of salvias, their purple and blue petals vibrant against the stone. Maxx traced her name, his throat tight.

"She would have loved this place," he said. "Told me once, 'Find a home where my heart can rest.' I think we did."

Gabby nodded, her eyes soft. "She'd say our kid's lucky to have you. And me, she'd probably say I'm the brains of the operation." Her smile was teasing, but her hand squeezed his, grounding him. "I want our baby to know her stories, to be strong like she was."

They sat in silence, the breeze carrying Dylan's lyrics. Lois's wisdom echoed in their determination, their shared hope for a child who'd grow up free of the battles that had threatened them. The moment sealed their purpose, a commitment to build not only a barn but a lasting heritage.

Back at the farm, Maxx thought of Andres and Miss Grey. A letter had arrived last week, scrawled in Andres's familiar hand. He and Miss Grey, now engaged, still lived on the houseboat in Seattle's Lake Union, its deck cluttered with plants and Andres's old university files. Andres still taught at the University of Washington, and his lectures on ancient archeology inspired a new generation.

"The kids keep me young," he'd written, "but I miss diving into trouble with you."

Miss Grey, a senior agent at DHS, hinted at trying her hand at something less risky. "Too many secrets, Maxx," she'd added in a postscript. "Maybe it's time for a quieter life." Their balance of love and duty mirrored Maxx and Gabby's own, a restless peace that left room for growth.

Glen Piper's update came through a phone call last month. He'd found purpose at a south-side community center, mentoring troubled teens. "Teaching 'em to box but mostly to believe in themselves," he'd said, his thick drawl voice lighter than Maxx had ever heard. The kids adored him, calling him

"Coach Tank," their laughter a balm for the grief over Scott, his murdered son. Glen's life had turned from loss to redemption, and his work was a quiet victory. Maxx smiled, remembering Scott's laugh, knowing Glen carried it forward.

These updates intertwined with flashbacks to some of their challenging times. Maxx recalled the sailboat, the napkin's truth scattered to the wind, a choice for life over vengeance. Gabby's courage in that moment—her hand steadying his—had cemented their trust. Andres's dive into the sound. Glen's tearful farewell to Scott's wallet. All surfaced in quiet moments, each memory a thread in their journey as a couple.

The sun dipped lower, painting the sky in hues of peach and lavender. Maxx and Gabby sat on the porch, sipping Earl Grey, the goats' bleats a soft counterpoint to the river's hum. The barn's silhouette stood against the nearby mountain, a promise half-fulfilled. They spoke of small things, names for the baby and plans for the large crop of tomatoes, when a low rumble broke the quiet. A sleek government SUV rolled up the dirt drive, its tinted windows catching the fading light.

Miss Grey stepped out, her dark hair pulled back, her DHS badge flashing at her hip. She wore a weary smile, her eyes scanning the farm with a hint of envy. "Nice setup, you two," she said, climbing the porch steps. "Makes me want to ditch the neon lights."

Gabby rose, offering a hug. "You're welcome anytime, Grey. Tea?"

"Always." Miss Grey settled into a chair, accepting a mug. Her presence stirred Maxx's instincts, a flicker of the old adrenaline. She'd been their ally through the Thunderbird conspiracy, her sharp aim and sharper mind a lifeline. Now, engaged to Andres, she carried a new gravity, her gaze distant.

"Where's Andres?" Maxx asked, leaning forward. "His letter said he's teaching, but you're here alone."

She sipped her tea, her smile tightening. "He's in Central

America. Research site, some tech project with UW. Off the grid mostly." She paused, setting the mug down. "But that's not why I'm here."

Gabby's hand stilled on her belly, her eyes meeting Maxx's. The air shifted, heavy with unspoken tension. "What's going on, Grey?" Gabby asked, wary.

Miss Grey leaned in, her voice low. "Something's stirring. An old intelligence network—I thought I'd buried it, but there's chatter. New players, same game. Andres stumbled onto it, and now he's digging deeper than he should." She pulled a folded paper from her pocket, sliding it across the table. "This was his last message. It's coded, but it's got some names you'll recognize on it."

Maxx unfolded the paper, his pulse rising. A string of numbers and letters, cryptic but familiar, hinted at a threat tied to their past. He saw the sailboat in his mind, the napkin's scraps sinking, and felt the storm creeping closer. "He's asking for us," Maxx said.

"He trusts you," Miss Grey replied. "So do I. But it's your call. You've got a lot more to lose now." Her eyes flicked to Gabby's belly then back to Maxx.

Gabby's hand found Maxx's, her grip firm. "We're not those people anymore," she said, but her voice held a question, a spark of the fire that had carried them through betrayal and bloodshed.

Maxx looked at the farm. The barn, the goats, the life they'd built. "If I could only turn back the clock," he whispered. But time moved forward, and so did they.

"We'll think it over," he said, his voice steady. "Tell Andres we're not saying no. I won't speak for Gabby, but I've tried to put all the violence behind me."

Miss Grey nodded, rising. "That's enough for now. I'll be in touch." She left the paper, her SUV's dust trail fading into the dusk.

Maxx and Gabby sat in silence, the coded message between them. The farm's peace held, but the pull of adventure tugged, a restless tide. They'd chosen shelter once, and if the storm blew in, they'd decide again—together this time. For now, they'd wait.

THE END

AFTERWORD

Dear reader, below is a list of songs fueled by my imagination as I envisioned the world and characters in the final days of this Maxx King story. I hope these songs add an extra dimension to your experience as you recall the world imagined in the book.

The complete playlist can be found on Spotify @ **Falling Angels.**

Prologue: "Coward of the County" — Kenny Rogers
Chapter 1: "I Want You Back" — Jackson 5
Chapter 2: "Everybody Hurts" — R.E.M.
Chapter 3: "Runaway Train" — Soul Asylum
Chapter 4: "Every Breath You Take" — The Police
Chapter 5: "Boulevard of Broken Dreams" — Green Day
Chapter 6: "Swim" — Madonna
Chapter 7: "Life Is a Highway" — Rascal Flatts
Chapter 8: "Should I Stay or Should I Go" — The Clash
Chapter 9: "Bittersweet Symphony" — The Verve
Chapter 10: "You Outta Know" — Alanis Morissette
Chapter 11: "Clocks" — Coldplay
Chapter 12: "The Way" — Fastball
Chapter 13: "Losing My Religion" — R.E.M.
Chapter 14: "One Headlight" — The Wallflowers
Chapter 15: "Lose Yourself" — Eminem [One Shot]
Chapter 16: "Smooth" — Santana (featuring Rob Thomas)
Chapter 17: "It's My Life" — Bon Jovi
Chapter 18: "Sunny Came Home" — Shawn Colvin
Chapter 19: "Somebody That I Used to Know" — Gotye ft. Kimbra
Chapter 20: "With or Without You" — U2
Chapter 21: "Bent" — Matchbox Twenty
Chapter 22: "Somebody's Watching Me" — Rockwell
Chapter 23: "Gangsta's Paradise" — Coolio, L.V.

Chapter 24: "Fever" — Madonna
Chapter 25: "Smells Like Teen Spirit" — Nirvana
Chapter 26: "Push" — Matchbox Twenty
Chapter 27: "Secret" — Madonna
Chapter 28: "Under Pressure" — Queen and David Bowie
Chapter 29: "Lean on Me" — Bill Withers
Chapter 30: "The Healing" — Gary Clark, Jr.
Epilogue: "Shelter from the Storm" — Bob Dylan

Three Bob Dylan songs inspired me to write the Maxx King trilogy:

- ❖ *Thunderbird Rising* — "All Along the Watchtower"
- ❖ *Masters of War* — "Masters of War"
- ❖ *Falling Angels* — "Shelter from the Storm"

A NOTE FROM JOHN H. THOMAS

Thank you for reading *Falling Angels*!

I have a request: Can you take a few minutes to review it? Reviews help others find my work. Without them, my books would be buried in the stacks of all the terrific books available. With millions of books online, a higher-rated book becomes more visible, and readers like you can enjoy this story too! So, please take a moment to share your thoughts with me and others. I'd greatly appreciate it. — John

Please take a moment to write a review on Amazon.

ABOUT THE AUTHOR

John lives in the Seattle area with his wife and the world's sweetest cat: Karmann. Raised in a nomadic military family, he is annoyingly curious, a consumer of whiskey, and a political junkie at heart, but his most significant interests are his family and their collective shenanigans. For the record, unlike Maxx, he enjoys swimming in Puget Sound.

OTHER WORKS BY JOHN H. THOMAS

BOOKS

Thunderbird Rising: Maxx King Series Book 1
Masters of War: Maxx King Series Book 2

AUDIOBOOKS

Thunderbird Rising
Masters of War

Printed in Dunstable, United Kingdom

64642549R00188